more...

...AND FOR

BLOOD MUD

• • •

"A master...Constantine excels."
　　—Marilyn Stasio, *New York Times Book Review*

"Conversations and interior monologues to cherish....
Constantine is at the top of his game."
　　—*Philadelphia Inquirer*

"Balzic is one of the great characters of contemporary fiction."
　　—*Boston Globe*

"Resonates with humanity...Constantine's dialogue is as
revealing as Elmore Leonard's."
　　—*Newark Star-Ledger*

K. C. CONSTANTINE

GRIEVANCE

Published by Warner Books

An AOL Time Warner Company

Copyright © 2000 by K. C. Constantine
All rights reserved.

 Mysterious Press books are published by Warner Books, Inc., 1271 Avenue of the Americas, New York, NY 10020.

Visit our Web site at www.twbookmark.com.

 An AOL Time Warner Company

The Mysterious Press name and logo are registered trademarks of Warner Books, Inc.

Printed in the United States of America

Originally published in hardcover by Warner Books, Inc.

First Trade Printing: August 2002

10 9 8 7 6 5 4 3 2 1

The Library of Congress has cataloged the hardcover edition as follows:

Constantine, K. C.
     Grievance / K. C. Constantine.
        p.   cm.
     ISBN 0-89296-648-3
     I. Title.
   PS3553.0524G75   2000
   813'.54—dc21   99-41380
                                                                                  CIP

ISBN 0-446-67849-X (pbk.)

Cover design by Rachel McClain
Cover photograph by Marc Yankus

ATTENTION: SCHOOLS AND CORPORATIONS
WARNER books are available at quantity discounts with bulk purchase for educational, business, or sales promotional use. For information, please write to: SPECIAL SALES DEPARTMENT, WARNER BOOKS, 1271 AVENUE OF THE AMERICAS, NEW YORK, NY 10020

GRIEVANCE

A short, thin man wearing a black tuxedo jacket and a black bow tie but otherwise naked was accepting a statuette on a pedestal. The foot-high statuette depicted a mother putting handcuffs on a child. On the pedestal were inscribed these words: "To Detective Sergeant Ruggiero Carlucci, for living with his mother continuously since birth—except for the army." After taking the statuette, the man bowed solemnly and deeply, thus enabling him to observe that the holster strapped to his right ankle was empty. A Model 34 Smith & Wesson .22-caliber revolver lay between his feet, the cylinder open, while six bullets scurried over his toes like ants. Looking up again, he saw many people laughing soundlessly at him, their faces wrinkled and red, their eyes teary. Then one voice among those faces suddenly came alive: "Hey! You dead or somethin'? Answer the goddamn phone!"

Carlucci lurched up with a gasp and nearly rolled off the bed. He had to clutch the sheets to hang on. His phone was ringing, and his mother was shouting from her bedroom on the other side of the wall, "You gonna answer that goddamn thing or what? Rung six times already—there goes num-ber se-ven! Hey!"

He lunged for the phone, shouting back, "Yeah yeah, right, sorry,

I got it, I got it." Before he spoke into the phone, he looked down at himself and saw with great relief that he was still wearing his shorts.

"Yes, what? Hello?"

"Detective Sergeant Carlucci?"

"Yeah yeah, me, right. What?"

"This is 911 dispatcher Shamika Corry? Sorry to disturb your sleep, Sergeant, but I was ordered to relay you this urgent message from State Trooper Milliron?"

"Yeah, yeah, right, Milliron. Claude. I know him. What?"

"Uh, he has a dead body? Uh, with gunshot wounds to the head? And he requests your assistance A-S-A-P? Says to tell you he has no one else available from the barracks, and the county crime scene truck is in New Kensington? They got a domestic multiple shooting there? And they won't be back for at least three, maybe four hours? He says for you to bring your cameras, and I'm s'posed to wait for a reply. Is there a reply?"

"Uh, yeah—wait wait, where is he?"

"He's on Club Road, uh, number one niner four."

"Oh man, that's in the township . . . he can't get nobody else for sure? Nobody else in the barracks?"

"That's what he said, Sergeant. Do you have a reply?"

Yeah, I have a reply, Carlucci thought. I got a great reply to all those fucking pols in Harrisburg, all they want to do is build more cells, don't wanna hire no cops, fuuuuuck no. Spent some money hirin' cops, I wouldn't be wakin' up to this kinda shit. None of which this poor woman needs to hear. "Uh, yes, tell him I'm on my way. One nine four Club Road, Westfield Township, correct?"

"That's correct, sir."

"Okay, okay, I'm on my way," he said, hanging up and rubbing his face with both hands. Then he stretched his hands upward while inhaling, then bent from the waist while exhaling until his palms touched the floor between his feet. He remained on the side of the bed, inhaling and exhaling while stretching his lower back, until he felt awake enough to stand.

His mother continued to complain from her bedroom about the

call and about how late he'd been out last night. "The hell were you doin' last night couldn't wait till today, huh? Wanna answer me that?"

"Told you," Rugs said on his way to the bathroom to empty his bladder and brush his teeth. "Wasn't work. Had a date."

"With that same girl? Huh? Same one?"

"Yes. The same one," he said between brushing and spitting.

"What kinda girl stays out that late, that's what I wanna know. You didn't get home till two o'clock. That cow—what's her name, that one's over here every night, like she thinks I don't know you pay her to pretend she's my friend, she's so stupid."

"Missus Viola."

"Yeah, her. All she did all night was bellyache about when was you comin' home. Kinda crap you call that, huh? And I guess you're gonna pay her overtime too."

Carlucci didn't respond to any of it. He was trying to clear his mind while getting dressed, while getting both his weapons out of his lockbox under the bed, strapping the S&W .22 to his ankle, then slipping the Beretta 9mm and holster over the waistband on his right hip. He made sure there were pens, notebooks, cameras, batteries, and film in his briefcase, then snapped it shut and tiptoed into the living room to get a time check from the ad channel on the TV.

Just as he was resetting his watch—either the battery or the watch was dying—his glance fell on an ad that stopped him in his tracks. It said, "Come on a bus trip to one of the greatest Marian apparition sites in the history of Catholicism, if not the greatest, in Bayside, N.Y. Monthly trips. Next one leaves June 18th. For more information call Mel at 751-5804 or call George at 931-0592."

Rugs felt his mouth dropping open. What the hell was "one of the greatest Marian apparition sites"? In Bayside, New York? Call Mel? Or George? Mel and George are pushing apparition sites? Fuck's an apparition site?

He tiptoed to the bookcase where his mother kept all her dictionaries for crossword puzzles. Just when he'd found *apparition* in *Webster's American College Dictionary,* his mother marched in, her flip-flops slapping the floor, looked at him and then at the TV and said, "Hell're you doin', watchin' TV? You actually watchin' that?"

"Just gettin' a time check, that's all."

"Then what're you doin' with that?"

"With what?"

"With that," she said, pointing with her nose at the dictionary.

"Uh, just lookin' up a word, that's all."

"What word?"

"Hey, I'll be outta here in a second, okay? I'm not watchin' TV, I promise you."

"Hell if you weren't, I could hear it. And I didn't hear you movin' around in here so you were standin' still. You didn't start movin' till I was almost in here. 'Cause the floor woulda squeaked, don't give me that. What were you watchin'? And don't lie to me now, I know you were watchin' somethin'."

"I'm not lyin' to you, okay? I'm gettin' a time check, that's all. They got the time to the second on that channel, and my watch's been losin' time, it's either the battery or the watch—"

"Is 'ere a clock in that dictionary? You seen somethin' on there, the TV—what're you lookin' up? C'mon, what?"

"Uh, apparition, okay?"

"Apparition? The hell you wanna know what that means for?"

"I just do, that's all, I saw somethin'."

"You *saw* somethin'? *You?* You're *seein'* things now?"

"No, I'm not *seein'* things. I saw an ad on the TV, okay? Just caught my eye. *Apparition* was in it, I wanted to make sure I knew what it meant, that's all."

"You were watchin' TV, don't try to weasel out of it. What were you watchin', c'mon, what?"

"It was an ad, Ma, okay? That's all it was. An ad, you know? Somebody advertisin' somethin'—"

"I know what an ad is. For what I'm askin'? What were they advertisin' for got *apparition* in it, c'mon—oh oh oh, I know what it was. I know what it wa-as, I know what it wa-as. It was that ad for that bus trip, huh? See the Virgin Mary someplace in New York, yeah,

yeah, greatest apparition site in the whole history of Catholicism, that's what you were lookin' at, don't lie to me, Ruggiero."

"I'm not lyin' to you, okay?"

"What, you turnin' Catholic on me now? Oh oh, it's that girl, ain't it? I knew it! I knew it! Goody little dago Catholic girl, got my Ruggiero's nose all twisted up, huh? What, you gonna start seein' the Virgin for this girl, is that what you're gonna do?"

"Ah, stop, please? This doesn't have nothin' to do with her, and anyway I told you she's only half dago. Other half's Polish—"

"Oh Christ that's worse! Only thing worse than a Catholic dago is a Catholic Polack. If she's half each that makes her twice as bad! I'm tellin' you right now, Ruggiero, you bring her around here, she better not start that Catholic crap with me, I'll throw her ass right outta here, I ain't gonna put up with that crap from nobody." She suddenly became almost coy. "Speakin' of which, when am I gonna meet her, huh? Am I ever gonna get to meet her? You ever gonna bring her around or what? What, you ashamed of me or somethin'?"

All he could do was try to deflect the questions. "You used to be Catholic yourself, Ma, remember?"

"I used to be young too," she snapped. "There's a whole lotta things I used to be I ain't anymore, Catholic's just one of 'em, stop tryin' to change the subject—you gonna bring her around, that's the subject. When you gonna do that? You been talkin' about this girl for months now, Jesus, maybe *she's* the apparition, huh? She better be for real, Ruggiero, you better not be seein' things on me—"

"First, she's not a girl, which I've told you before. She's thirty-five, she's a woman, she works—"

"Thirty-five? Well la-de-da, nobody can accuse you of robbin' the cradle, can they?"

"—she works nights, okay? Which I also already told you. So it's gonna be tough for her to ever make a time connection here, you know? Or with you?"

"Your tongue's slippin' all over the place, Ruggiero, better waaaaaatch it, I'm tellin' you, tough makin' a time connection here—*or with you.* Like I don't know what that means."

"I didn't mean anything by that, okay? Just meant she works at night and she works long hours, alright?"

"Good girls don't work at night."

"Okay, listen, I gotta go. So listen to me now, you're gonna be on your own here for a couple hours, okay? Missus Comito ain't gonna get here till seven, alright? You gonna be alright now? You want me to call her, I'll call her you want me to—"

"No I don't want you to call her! Bad enough she gets here when she gets here—"

"'Cause I can't wait, I have to go, okay? You gotta promise me you're not gonna go outside, okay? You hear me? I want you to promise me, you're not gonna try to go outside till she gets here, okay?"

"What's she do she works at night?"

"She don't work at night—"

"Your girlfriend—not that cow—your girlfriend—"

"Ma, Ma, I'm talkin' Missus Comito now, okay? I'm not talkin' anybody else, alright? And stop callin' names, okay?"

"She can't get a job in the daytime? Like regular people?"

"Ma, listen to me, listen to what I'm askin' you, okay? Forget about her—"

"How can I forget about her, that's all you got on your mind is this little dago Catholic girl, nobody wantsa hire her in the daytime—"

"Ma, Jesus," Rugs said, hanging his head, "I wish to God I knew why you don't wanna hear what I'm tellin' you, but the woman is a psychiatric social worker, okay? She works for the county. With people with substance abuse, okay? They're on probation. And most of them, *they* work in the daytime, so the only time she can see them is at night, it ain't about nobody hirin' her for a daytime job, okay, like there's somethin' wrong with her."

"That's the only kinda job she can get? She has to work with these people? What substances? You mean they smoke them cigarettes make you goofy? And smell glue? Stick themselves with needles?"

"Lotsa different things, yeah. But they're tryin' not to do that anymore, and it's her job to try to help 'em, okay? I gotta go, Ma, I can't talk about this now—"

"Oh what, you're gonna leave without givin' your mother a kiss now?" she said, sneering. "Don't you run out that door without givin' me a kiss, young man, I'm your mother, I mean it, get back here now!"

Carlucci cleared his throat, sighed, hurried forward, leaned in with just his upper body, brushed his lips quickly over her cheek, and bolted away before she could get a grip on his sleeves.

"My God, you act like I'm poison," she said. "I wanna meet this girl, Ruggiero, I mean it, it's time."

No it ain't, he thought, shaking his head as he went out, calling back from the porch, "Stay inside now, you hear?" He turned to look back at her, jabbing the air several times with his index finger. "I mean it now, okay? Stay inside."

"Oh get the hell outta here, you make me sick." She slammed the door.

He waited till he heard her walking away from the door, then he eased the two hooks into the eyes, one at the top, one at the bottom. He'd installed them a month ago when Mrs. Comito was helping his mother take a bath so she couldn't hear him on the porch working on the door and wouldn't ask what he was doing. Then, after the bath, when Mrs. Comito steered her into the living room to watch TV, he'd installed two more hooks and eyes on the back door.

Now, after going around to the back to hook those two, he trotted between the houses and down the steps to the city-owned Chevy. He unlocked it, slid his briefcase across the seat, and got in, thinking, please, please, don't let there be a fire, okay? And keep her in bed till Missus Comito gets here. Man, she gets it in her head to get out, she starts pullin' on those doors . . . oh fuck. Hey, if she does, she does, what am I gonna do about it? Better pissed off at me than lost.

Moments later, grumbling about Trooper Milliron, who had to call him because there was nobody else to call, and about politicians who thought the best way to get re-elected was to build more cells instead of hiring more cops, he was driving off Norwood Hill toward Westfield Township and 194 Club Road.

Carlucci started slowing down on Club Road when he saw the light bar from Milliron's cruiser flashing dimly through the dense stand of hardwoods on his right. The entrance road was unmarked except for the mailbox with 194 stenciled on its side, the trees being nearly a perfect screen between road and house, even with a full moon. Carlucci had to drive at least three-tenths of a mile through the trees before he even saw the house, three stories high and defined by spotlights at each corner of the roofs. In this light, Carlucci's first impression was that the house looked like houses he'd seen pictures of in books about England.

He pulled in behind Milliron's cruiser, parked at least forty yards from a three-car garage where a Jaguar sedan, either dark blue or maroon, sat in front of an open garage door. The garage was separate from the main house but connected to it by a covered walkway. The other two garage doors were still closed. The trunk of the Jaguar was open, and the legs and backside of a man stuck out of it, the toes of his shoes twisted toward each other on the macadam. Carlucci was immediately drawn to the body while looking around for Milliron.

The closer he got to the body, the more obvious it became to Carlucci that if the man had been shot more than once, the first one had to have killed him instantly to cause him to drop forward into the trunk while leaving no blood on the ground. And there was none, at least not that he could see with the light from his flash.

When Carlucci was a step away from the body, he leaned forward with his flashlight and shone it on the rest of the body and head of the man sprawled over a bag of golf clubs in the bottom of the trunk. There appeared to be a small round wound perhaps a quarter inch to the right of the midpoint of the spine at the base of the skull. Blood had spread over the man's neck, face, shoulders, and shirt, and over the leather golf bag and a white and green towel that seemed to be attached to the bag. Carlucci could see no other wounds, but he didn't linger to look more closely because he wanted to talk to Milliron first.

He went to the front door, found it locked, used the brass lion's head knocker, and continued to look around at the outside of the house until Milliron opened the door.

"Rugs, thanks for comin', man," Milliron said, standing back to allow Carlucci in. "Hated to ask you, but I didn't have any choice. Really appreciate it."

"What, this just happen? Where is everybody?" Rugs said. He caught a glimpse of a tall woman in a floor-length robe standing near a fireplace at the far end of a huge room off to his right.

"I got here, uh, lemme see, zero three fourteen hours," Milliron said. "It's, uh, zero three forty-one now. I spent the first five minutes with the wife, uh, then I started calling people, couldn't get anybody. Somethin' political goin' on? What's today, what was last night? Only people I could get were the 911 dispatcher and a deputy coroner, and I don't know where the hell he is, I called him before I called 911 and told them to call you. Sounded drunk, to tell you the truth, had to tell him three times where I was, kept askin' me to repeat the address."

"Uh, speakin' of which," Carlucci said, "where the hell are we? I just realized pullin' in here, this is the first time in my life I've ever been off the road back there. Christ, this is a different world, man. Never knew there were places like this here. Looks like somethin' out of a book I read once for history class."

Milliron nodded for Carlucci to follow and went outside, closing the front door behind them. He walked a good thirty yards from the house before he stopped, turned his back to the house, and said, "I know there are people like this, I mean, I've read about 'em and I've seen stories about 'em on TV, but I gotta tell you, man, this is about as far removed from where I come from as I've ever been. That woman in there? She is one cold woman, man. She might as well have been tellin' me how she wanted the lawn mowed. That's her husband there, and she's, uh, she's talkin' about him like, you know, 'he has his life and I have mine, and no, I wasn't at all alarmed that he wasn't home till after three o'clock, he often stays out that late, he plays golf everywhere, West Virginia, Maryland, Virginia, not just around here'—all in this, uh, really super controlled voice, man. You'll see what I mean. It's really weird talkin' to her."

"Yeah, well, exactly who are these people?"

"Oh. Uh, the deceased is J. for James Deford Lyon. And the cold fish is Missus Jessica Hale Bernhardt Lyon, of the Philadelphia Hale Bernhardts, and that's with no hyphen and don't you forget it—as though that was supposed to mean somethin' to me. Her name I mean. She took more time spellin' her names and tellin' me not to put a hyphen in there—like I was goin' to—she took more time tellin' me where she was from than she did tellin' me what made her get up and look outside at the car and see her husband hangin' outta the trunk."

"What time'd you get here again?"

"Three-fourteen. Got the call at three hundred zero one."

"Say why she didn't call Mutual Aid Ambulance?"

"Yeah. Get this. Said she knew he was dead as soon as she looked at him. Said her father was a surgeon, and he used to take her on rounds when he worked in these hospitals in Philly during the war. I had to ask her which war she was talkin' about. She said World War Two like I was some kinda idiot. Anyway, she said she'd seen lots of dead people, and soon as she saw the hole in the back of his head and she couldn't find a pulse in his neck, she said she just went back inside and called the barracks."

"Say she touched anything else?"

"I didn't get that far with her yet. Still tryin' to background 'em, and all she wantsa say is why do I wanna know this, why do I wanna know that."

"Well," Rugs said, "you may as well keep on with her, and I'll get my cameras and tape measure and work the body and the car as much as I can—when's daylight, you know? Got a guess?"

"No. I'd have to call. You're not plannin' to wait, are ya?"

"Nah, I was just tryin' to guess, that's all. We next up for the scene truck? They're not gonna go someplace else before they get to us, are they?"

"No, we're definitely next up, I got that promise from the chief of county detectives himself."

"Well, okay then, let's go to work. Oh. She ID the car as her husband's? So I don't waste time with DMV?"

Milliron nodded as he turned and headed back toward the house. "Yeah it's his. Really glad you're here, Rugs. I know you could've said screw it, and I wouldn't blame ya. I don't know what those people in Harrisburg are thinkin', man, I really don't. I'm workin' two watches 'cause I've been stakin' out this cabin on the Loyalhanna and when I came in tonight, damn if the watch commander doesn't ask me why I can't work traffic on 70 instead. Imagine that. Said he hasn't had anybody on that road for two days. Told him I've been tryin' to collar this guy for murder for three months and I got a tip he was comin' home to pick up some money he had buried behind his cabin. I tell the commander that, he just looks at me. I thought what is goin' on here, you know? When the hell are those guys gonna authorize a new class at the academy, you know? Man, we are so thin it's a joke. Ah, enough bitchin', let's do it."

Milliron went inside to continue his interview with Mrs. Lyon, and Carlucci returned to the Jaguar. He knelt on the macadam approximately twenty steps from the car, opened his briefcase, checked his compass to find north, then took out his sketch pad and made a quick boxy sketch of the Jag in relation to the house and garage and another of the body in the Jag. Then he made another of the three garage doors, noting the one that was open, and finally he made three of the Jag, from the left side, the rear, and then the right, careful to stay at least fifteen to twenty yards from the car as he changed positions. After he'd made the sketches, and noted the time and lighting, he put them into his case, got out his cotton booties and slipped them over his shoes, and, with his four-cell Mag-Lite, made four slow circuits of the Jag, starting from twenty yards out and getting progressively closer until he was satisfied that there was nothing on the macadam visible to his eye in this light that he'd be trampling while taking photos.

He got out his Nikon, loaded it with film, checked the batteries, and made a circuit of the Jag and the macadam, taking thirty-six exposures in all, making a note of exactly when he started and when he finished. His habit was to take two exposures a minute, his theory being that it would take him at least twenty seconds between exposures to note where he was moving to and where the last exposure would end and the next begin.

Then he went back to the briefcase, took out the sketches of the Jag he'd made earlier and marked on them as precisely as he could where he'd been standing when he took each of the pictures. Then he removed the film, put it in a drop canister, filled out the time and date on a sticker, affixed it to the canister, and then put that in his left front pants pocket. He always kept the film on him in the same pocket, and would feel it every so often to make sure it hadn't worked its way out while he was moving around.

Next he inspected the ground immediately around the feet of the victim and found two small clots of blood, which had apparently spurted backward when the bullet struck. He went back to his briefcase and got his yellow chalk and circled the blood for the scene techs. Then he went over the rear of the Jag, starting from under the back bumper and working his way around the man's legs, seeing nothing unusual until his eye fell on the license plate, JDL-1. Well, if he had enemies, he didn't do much to throw them off his trail, just ride around in a luxury car with vanity plates that said, this is me, and I'm number one. At least in his own mind. Who the hell is this guy? I know that name, why can't I make him?

Then Carlucci shone his Mag-Lite all over the interior of the trunk. Aside from the golf bag filled with clubs and the green and white towel, there were two pairs of shoes, one pair white and brown saddle shoes and the other pair all white. The white pair had metal spikes all over the soles and heels, but the bottoms of the saddle shoes were covered with round plastic grippers. A garment bag covered the bottom half of the golf bag. Aside from the spare tire and a vinyl kit for road emergencies, that was it. Having no idea what the man normally carried in his trunk, Carlucci wouldn't make assumptions about its contents, except to list in his notebook what he did see.

He then turned his attention to the interior of the car, shining his light in the backseat first and then up front. There was nothing on the floor or the seat in the back, and only a folded *USA Today* and a leather case containing three cigars on the front seat. The driver's door was open, and the smell of cigar smoke was still strong. Carlucci could see the wet end of a cigar in the ashtray. There was nothing on the floor in front of the driver's seat, and nothing that he could see leaning in while trying to avoid contact with any part of his body or clothing. The keys were still in the ignition, meaning the late Mr. Lyon had popped the trunk from a switch inside and probably opened the garage door with an electronic switch, which Carlucci found on the visor above the passenger side. In short, there was nothing to indicate that any kind of struggle had taken place in or around the car.

Carlucci went back to the body, and working from the soles of the shoes up, shone his light over every readily visible surface. The man's black loafers hadn't been worn much, the leather in the sole between the ball and heel was still shiny bright mahogany. The man's slacks were yellow, his polo shirt white, and his elastic cloth belt beige. Carlucci could see the outline of a very slim wallet showing in the left rear trousers pocket.

Just as Carlucci was removing the wallet, Milliron came out of the house, stopping about ten steps from the Jag, and said, "I'm ready to switch. You?"

"S'matter, she still hard-assin' ya?"

"Yeah. Can't figure out why either, I don't think she did it."

"And you're basin' that on what exactly?"

"I don't think wives kill husbands they don't give a damn about, and if she gives a damn about this guy she's a better actress than I've ever seen. It's like the only thing they had goin' was this house. Checked the wallet yet?"

"Just gettin' ready to now. What time you got? Either my battery's dyin' or I need a new watch, can't trust this thing," Carlucci said, taking his watch off and banging it against his thigh. It had stopped on zero four ten.

"Uh, four forty-two, goin' on forty-three, uh, right now. Find anything?"

"Not much," Carlucci said, resetting his watch and making sure the second hand was moving before he put it back on. "Whoever dusted this guy knew what he was doin'. Can't find another mark on him—course we haven't rolled him, but, uh, from what I can tell, that's all it took, uh, a .22 maybe, maybe a .25, certainly no bigger'n that. No burns on the hair that I can see, so whoever wasn't close. I didn't find anything on the ground, it's not the greatest light, but, uh, it's a long way from dark with all those spots on the house. I went at least six times around, first four just walkin' and lookin', next two were with my camera, but I didn't see anything within twenty yards around, on the ground I mean. Doesn't look like there's anything missin' from the trunk, but, uh, that'd be up to the missus, right? She have any guns?"

"Yeah, lots—or he did. She showed me the cabinet, in the trophy room. Get this, man, there were two pool tables in there. Two! I lifted the cover on one just to see what it looked like, but she gave me this look so I covered it back up. It didn't have any pockets. Didn't wanna act dumb so I didn't ask her, especially after that look—"

"That's billiards."

"Huh?"

"Billiards. There's pocket billiards and then there's billiards. No pockets, you just use three balls, two white, one red, and you gotta use the rails. I heard about it when I was in high school. I never knew anybody who played it, I didn't know anybody still did. Supposed to be real hard."

"And there's no pockets? I'll be damned."

"Yeah. The object, if I remember right, is, uh, you bounce the cue ball off the rails and hit the object ball, which is the red one. You score points when you hit it, but I don't remember any more'n that, it was so long ago. So what about the guns again?"

"Oh. Uh, four rifles, four shotguns, two handguns, all locked up. Stuffed heads all over the walls. Must be thirty of 'em. Animals I never saw, some of 'em. So I asked her if she had a key to the cabinet, you know, she said no, she wasn't interested, that was his hobby. Shooting, was how she put it. Not hunting, shooting. And then, you know, like it just popped into her mind, she said oh yes, she used to shoot skeet with him when they were first married, but she doesn't do that anymore, she has this arthritis in her shoulder, she hasn't done it for years."

"Yeah, but she did, so she's familiar with guns. Okay. You test her for trace metals?"

"Excuse me?" Milliron said, smiling. "That's what we have a lab for. What, you think I have one of those cans you spray—hell, you need an ultraviolet light for that, I don't have one of those. You?"

"Me? You kiddin'? We don't have shit like that. Thought you would."

Milliron snorted. "C'mon. Although you know what a guy told me worked one time?"

"What?"

"Said he bought a can of hair spray, then he typed up a whole lot of phony instructions and pasted 'em on the can? Told some shooter if he sprayed it on his hand it not only would show he fired a gun but when he fired it and what caliber. He didn't even have to push the button, just held it over the guy's hand while he was tellin' him that BS, and the guy confessed, you believe that?"

"Why not? Stupid as most shooters are, I'll believe anything. What time the techies show up in the lab, seven, don't they?"

"Yeah. Why, you gonna try to get her up there, or you gonna try to snow her?"

"Well, you know, whatever it takes. Either rule her out, or smoke her out, whatever. See which way she goes. Don't forget your booties."

"Huh?" Milliron looked down at his shoes, where Carlucci was pointing. "Oh. Yeah. Wait'll you see that trophy room, man, it's wild. This guy killed things, I'm tellin' ya, there's heads in there, I don't know what they are."

"Yeah, I'll bet," Carlucci said, opening the wallet finally. "Well, let's see who this guy is." The wallet was made of a kind of leather Carlucci didn't recognize. All he found were a driver's license, Master-Card and Visa, both platinum, a bank ATM card, and an AT&T credit card. "Man, when was the last time you opened a guy's wallet and this is all you found, huh? Most guys, they got their whole history in there."

"What's the license say?"

"Uh, J. Deford Lyon, issued six seven '96, date of birth five one '33, expires eight twenty 2000, sex male, height five eleven, eyes brown, must wear corrective lenses, same address. Makes him what, sixty-five?"

"Yeah. Sixty-five, right. Okay, Rugs—hey you got any bags?"

"Yeah, in my trunk. It's open. Here, you can bag the wallet."

"Yeah, okay. Good luck with her, man. Hope you can get her to open up more than I did."

Carlucci went in through the front door and into the room where he'd caught a glimpse of Mrs. Lyon when Milliron had first let him in, but she wasn't there. He stood there for a long moment, just gawking at the size of the room, filled with what looked to him like three complete sets of living room furniture and dozens more unmatched chairs and tables. There were lamps everywhere, but the light that immediately caught his attention was hanging from the center of the ceiling, looking like it belonged in a church. There were hundreds of glistening crystals in a pear shape four or five feet long, perhaps fifteen feet in circumference at its widest. Carlucci walked under it, and stood there gaping up at it until his neck started to hurt. Then he backed away, rubbing his neck, and, while stretching his neck forward, noticed that there were three rugs on the hardwood floor, each of them at least as big as his mother's entire living room.

He tried to estimate the dimensions of the room, then, with a quick glance to make sure Mrs. Lyon wasn't watching him, he paced it off. He couldn't believe it: thirty-some paces from the entrance to the stone fireplace on the opposite wall, thirty-*some* because he had to weave around furniture. Then he felt foolish because he couldn't remember how long his pace was so he still didn't know the size of the room. He didn't want to go outside and get his tape measure, so he just stood there thinking, God, my mother's whole house isn't thirty steps long. Hell, I bet it isn't even twenty steps long. My mother's whole first floor could fit in this one goddamn room.

For fully five seconds, he stood there awestruck, shaking his head, before he snapped back to the job at hand and went searching through the rest of the first floor for Mrs. Lyon. He returned to the entry hall and from there went into the dining room, which was just as long as the living room but only half as wide. From there he found the kitchen, which looked bigger than some restaurant kitchens he'd been in. The gas stove had six burners, a grill, two ovens, and two broiler drawers, and hanging from an oblong rack over an island workstation were dozens of pots and pans, most of them copper. Next he went through a room lined with shelves from floor to ceiling crammed with canned and bottled goods and cleaning supplies. Finally he arrived on the other side of the entry hall in what he surmised from Milliron's description was the trophy room, but still no Mrs. Lyon.

With every step, Carlucci felt himself gaping at the furniture, the rugs, the walls covered with paintings, drawings, and photographs, the tables, chairs, and lamps so ornate that the only place he'd ever seen anything like them was in magazines in doctors' offices. He didn't know the names for anything he was looking at; he just knew that it was all beyond anything he'd ever experienced—except for the pool table, the one with pockets.

He was more than familiar with that because he'd spent way more than his share of time in Maloney's Pool Room growing up. It was the only game he'd ever played. He'd been too small for football and too short for basketball; he was slow afoot, so track was out, and he didn't have the reflexes to hit a baseball. He did, however, have good hand-eye coordination and good vision so he'd played the only game that didn't require special clothes or equipment, the only game that if you got good enough at it, other people paid for your time on the table. By the time he'd graduated from high school, he'd made enough money off the regulars in Maloney's to buy a hundred-dollar cue and was being driven to other towns by a couple of "sponsors" who were continually scouting beatable opponents.

Fortunately for him, just when he thought he was getting good, he got into a game in McKeesport with an old man who limped around the table and played with a house cue off the wall rack, and lost a hundred and sixty-five dollars in less than an hour, every cent his sponsors had. To show their gratitude, they left him standing on the sidewalk. He had to hitchhike home, seventeen miles. While watching taillights dissolve into the night, he lost every illusion he'd ever had about his pool skill, and until he got to Vietnam a year and a half later, that was the longest, loneliest walk he'd ever taken.

Still, standing in this house now, in this room, he knew he was looking at great tables, the most expensive and well-built he'd ever seen. He lifted the dustcovers first on the pocket table, ran his fingers over the felt, over the gleaming dark wood beside the black rail. He rubbed the soft leather in the pockets, then replaced the cover with a faintly nostalgic sigh. He lifted a corner of the cover on the billiards table and tried to remember if he'd ever seen anybody play that game. He couldn't recall, which made him wonder if what he'd told Milli-ron a few minutes ago had anything to do with what actually happened on this kind of table. It was a waste of time to continue that kind of speculation, so he replaced the dustcover, smoothed it out, and again went looking for Mrs. Lyon.

He went up the widest stairs he'd ever seen outside of the old Bernanos Theater that had been torn down in Rocksburg in the sixties. At the top of the stairs he spotted her through a half-open door. He knocked, poked his head in, and found himself gaping once again at the size of the room. Mrs. Lyon was sitting very erect and writing something at an elaborately carved, ivory-colored desk.

He knocked louder, cleared his throat loudly, and said, "Missus Lyon?"

She turned slightly and peered at him over reading glasses.

"I'm Detective Sergeant Carlucci, ma'am, Rocksburg Police Department? I'm assisting Trooper Milliron? I need to speak to you, ma'am. So, uh, do you wanna do that here, or would downstairs be better for you?"

She continued to peer at him over her glasses. She was wearing a pale blue robe with a satin collar. When she stood to face him the robe touched the instep of her flat, golden slippers. She was very tall, even in her slippers. Her silvery-blond hair was pulled back from her face and held in place on either side by matching gold-colored combs. Hell, Carlucci thought, they might be the real thing, not just gold-colored. At the distance from the door to where she was standing, Carlucci couldn't tell her age. She could have been forty, she could have been sixty.

When she started walking toward him, he was struck by her posture, which was very erect, her chin up and shoulders back, like she had been taught to walk that way. Nobody walked that way normally, at least not anybody Carlucci had ever been around. It was too artificial. He thought that was the right word, but he wasn't sure if that was what he meant. Even though it looked like she'd been walking that way for a long time, it still looked somehow unnatural, somehow put-on. Maybe it wasn't her walk at all, maybe it was the way she was looking at him, like he was something she needed to call an exterminator for.

She stopped three steps away and said, "I called the state police. I did not call the local police. That was neither an accident nor a mistake." Then she swept past him and said, "I purposely did not call the local police because I do not talk to local police. So if you want to know what I've said, you'll have to ask the trooper because you and I are not going to talk, not here, not downstairs."

She stopped at the top of the stairs, turned, and glared at him, and without making a single other move, made clear that she expected Carlucci to get off this floor and out of her house immediately.

Carlucci shuffled past her and went down two steps before stopping and turning around. "Uh, I understand what you said, ma'am, I really do understand that. But see, the thing is, your husband, uh, he's, uh, well, you know where he is, and, uh, unless he was, uh, very flexible, he didn't shoot himself. Not where he was shot, and so, uh, that makes it a homicide, ma'am."

"I'm well aware of that."

"Yes, I know—I mean I'm sure you are. But what I'm tryin' to say, ma'am, is that, uh, in a homicide, any major crime really, see, it's standard procedure that two investigators work together, not side by side exactly, but I mean first he interviews you and I work the scene, now he's out there workin' the scene and I'm in here tryin' to interview you, and then afterwards we compare notes, that's, uh, that's how we do it, that's how it's done. Now I can understand if you don't wanna talk to me right now, it's late, you just had a terrible shock, but, uh, what I'm sayin', ma'am, is that you really don't have a choice about this. You could have an attorney present, if you wanted, but with or without an attorney, doesn't matter, you have to talk to me, I mean, because, uh, you were here. That's what it comes down to, you were here, and also you have other information we need. About your husband, where he was, who he was with, when he came home, things like that—"

"I told you, I've said everything I have to say to the trooper."

"Yes, ma'am, I know what you said. But see, that's, uh, that's not gonna work, I'm sorry. Missus Lyon, I'm gonna have to ask you, please, to get dressed now."

"Get dressed? Why? I will not."

"Oh. Wow. Okay. Uh, please, ma'am, don't make this harder than it is, okay? Please get dressed. Call your attorney if you want, I'm sure you have an attorney, probably two or three, but tell him to meet us at the state police Troop A crime lab. If he needs directions I'll be happy to give 'em—"

"The crime lab?! One second you want to interview me, the next second you want me to go to the crime lab?! Are you serious?"

Carlucci swallowed and sniffed. "Uh, see, Missus Lyon, listen, I'm tryin' real hard not to upset you here, okay? I know after what's happened here you're real upset—"

"You don't know any such thing."

"Oh. Okay. Well. Shouldn't've said that, I guess. I just thought you'd be upset, and I was tryin' to not make it worse, but see, the thing is, uh, look, there's no easy way to say this, I mean, the first thing I wanna do is eliminate you as a suspect, okay?"

"*Me?!* Eliminate *me* as a suspect? Do you know what you're implying, you little nematode?"

"Oh, whoa. Jeez, see, ma'am, no, that's not gonna make it, no. That's not—what'd you call me? Nema what? What is that?"

"I remind you that you're in my house, you impertinent little slug."

"I know what that is, ma'am, and you can't call me that either, but my presence was requested, see? Trooper Milliron asked me to come here, and now that I'm here, I mean, you have information we need in order to investigate this, uh, your husband's death, and you also, I mean, you told Trooper Milliron that you used to shoot skeet, so that tells me you're familiar with guns, so what I'm tryin' to do is to get you tested to find out whether you fired a gun, okay? That's why I'm askin' you to go with me—voluntarily—to the state police lab. And the negative test result I'm expectin' to get would eliminate you as a suspect, and then we can move on, see? We won't have to be worryin' about you, okay?"

"Worrying about me? Is that supposed to be funny?"

"No no no, no, that's not—listen, what I'm tryin' to do here is—oh man, all I'm tryin' to do, okay? You didn't wash your hands, did ya? Don't wash your hands, okay, please? And then afterwards, after the test eliminates you as a suspect—and that's all I'm tryin' to do, ma'am, okay? Then we're gonna sit down and talk, you and me, okay?"

She laughed contemptuously. "Who do you think you're talking to? My husband's J. D. Lyon, do you have the slightest idea who we are?"

"Well, uh, no, I guess I don't, but I have a real good idea who he is. He's the gentleman, uh, out there. You know? And when you found him, according to what Trooper Milliron told me, you didn't call an ambulance, you didn't attempt to get medical assistance, what you did was call the state police. And I'm havin' a problem with that—"

"For your information, little man, my father at various times during his career was chief of surgery at two of the largest public hospitals in Philadelphia, and he used to take me on rounds with him during the summers. I've seen more dead bodies by accident than you've seen on purpose, which means I know when a human being is no longer alive. So tonight, once I'd seen my husband and found no pulse, there was no logical reason for me to call for medical assistance."

"Uh, yes ma'am, that sounds logical and everything, but, you know, I still have to ask ya to get dressed, please? And also, please stop callin' me names, okay? Please don't do that anymore. Just get dressed, please?"

"I will not. And what *you* will do is get out of my house, now!"

Oh fuck, Carlucci thought, please don't make me have to throw her on the floor and cuff her, Jesus, please, that's the last fucking thing I wanna do.

He said softly, "Or what, ma'am? You gonna call the cops? Please do, I'm askin' ya, go 'head, call 'em. What you're gonna find out is, the only state cop in the vicinity is the one outside, who specifically asked for my assistance, which is why I'm here, okay? There's nobody else available at this time. If there was, I wouldn't be here—but you go 'head and call 'em, go 'head, find out for yourself, don't take my word for this. Don't take my word for anything. Call 'em. Please. Call your attorney too. Tell him I'm tryin' to eliminate you as a suspect, okay? Tell him I'm not *sayin'* you're a suspect, tell him I *have not said* you're a suspect, okay? Please call him and tell him that I have not *called* you a suspect, what I'm tryin' to do is *eliminate* you as a suspect, be sure and say that to him, okay? Exactly that way? But meantime please don't wash your hands, okay? 'Cause if you did happen to fire a gun recently I don't want you washin' away the trace metals."

Carlucci moved up two steps until he was on the same level with her. He pulled his upper lip back into his mouth and hung his head and looked up at her under his brows, bopping his head slowly. Then, continuing to speak as softly as he could, he said, "I'm not goin' away, ma'am. You need to call your attorney and tell him to meet us at the crime lab. You have information I can't get from anybody else, information we need to help us investigate your husband's death. Unless somebody's hidin' in this house somewhere—and I don't think anybody would be that dumb—uh, you're the only person aside from the shooter who was here at the time it happened—"

"Listen to me, little man. I didn't hear anything, I didn't see anything, I don't know anything. I went to sleep. I woke up. Something woke me up. I went to the window in his bedroom, I looked out, I saw him, I went outside to check on his condition, I found that he had no pulse, that's all I know. I can say this ten different ways, it's not going to come out any differently—"

"Excuse me, ma'am, *something* woke you up?"

"That's what I said, didn't I?"

"I know what you said, I'm askin' you to think about that now, and tell me what that something was—"

"*Some*thing is indefinite, that's what the word means. It's not *a* thing or *the* thing or *that* thing or *this* thing, it's *some*thing, that's the word I used because that's the word I wanted to use because that was the correct word—is any of this getting through to you?"

"How old was your husband, ma'am?"

"What?! For God's sake, what difference does that make?"

"The difference it makes is I'd like to get a profile of your husband. It doesn't look like this was a robbery, I mean, that's a real preliminary guess, but, uh, the more I know about your husband, the more things I can rule out, see? And nobody knows where this kinda information can go, people have information, they don't think it's important, it turns out it's real important, that's what I'm tryin' to tell ya. So how old was he?"

"Oh God. His age will help you rule out things? Are there people who make a specialty of killing men because they're sixty-five years old, is that what you're saying?"

"Sixty-five, huh? Carry cash on him, usually? Or did he do everything with plastic?"

"Of course he carried cash. You can't tip everybody with plastic. You can't tip doormen or parking valets with plastic."

"Uh-huh. How much, usually?"

"A hundred dollars, perhaps two, certainly no more than that."

"Uh-huh—"

"Wait wait," she said, shaking her head and covering her mouth with her right hand, mumbling, "How did this happen?"

"Excuse me? How'd what happen?"

"I'm talking to you."

"Uh, yeah. You are. A little bit." Carlucci waited. "And?"

"I have no idea why I'm talking to you," she said disgustedly. "I had no intention of talking to you, and now I'm talking to you."

"Oh. I see what you mean. Well, maybe you're findin' out it's not so hard. Or maybe you should call your attorney, if that would make you feel more comfortable—"

"Oh shut up!" She turned and walked briskly into her bedroom, Carlucci hurrying to stay close. She tried to shut the door on him, but he stiff-armed it with both hands. She turned on him, her lips tight, eyes and nostrils wide.

"Where do you think you're going?"

"Uh, sorry, ma'am, but I'm not gonna let you go in there by yourself, I don't know where your bathroom is—"

"I'm going to call my attorney, and I expect to do so privately, which means alone, which means I don't want you eavesdropping while I'm doing it, is that clear?"

"Oh yeah, real clear. But I'm not leavin'. You got a phone on your desk, I can see it from here—go 'head, call him, I won't listen. Promise. But I'm not leavin'."

She inhaled noisily through her nose, held her breath for a long moment while glaring at him, then wheeled around and strode back to her desk, where she picked up the phone, hit a speed-dial button, and said to an answering machine, "Ernest, this is Jessica Lyon, I know you're there, pick up, this is urgent. J.D.'s been shot. He's dead. I called the state police but there's a disheveled paramecium harassing me, claims to be a detective with the local police, wants me to go to the state police crime lab to be tested to find out whether I've fired a gun . . . Of course I know what time it is, don't be obtuse, Ernest, when have I ever called you in the middle of the night to chat? . . . Yes . . . Yes . . . No . . . No . . . Yes . . . Well get yourself together and meet me where I said—this, this person is standing right here, apparently to prevent my washing my hands . . . Yes . . . Yes. Immediately, I presume." She turned to Carlucci. "Am I correct in presuming you want to do this immediately?"

"Yes, ma'am."

She turned back away from him and said something Carlucci couldn't hear. Then she said, "Oh for God's sake of course I know where you're coming from, just get started will you please? I want you there." Then she hung up.

"Alright, little man, apparently you're going to get your wish. Now get out while I change."

"Uh, no, sorry, ma'am, can't do that. I still don't know where your bathroom is, and I can't let you alone—"

"You arrogant dog dropping," she said, looking around as though trying to find something to throw at him.

"Uh, hold it, ma'am, hold it, hold it, don't do anything stupid, you throw somethin' at me, that's assaulting a police officer, then I gotta arrest ya, which means I gotta put handcuffs on ya, and then you're gonna go just the way you are, so just cool out there, okay? I'm not gonna be lookin' at you while you change, I understand your privacy, but you gotta understand, I hear water runnin', that's trouble. I don't want ya goin' anywhere near a sink or soap, okay? So I'm not leavin'."

"You insufferable pile of excrement!"

"And I asked you about that too, okay? C'mon, don't do that, please. Just get dressed, okay? Please?"

"Would something less than human like you happen to have a card, a business card?"

"Yes, ma'am, I do."

"Does it have your shield number on it?"

"No it doesn't, ma'am. But I'll be happy to put it on there for ya, if that's what you want. If that'll make you happy, if that'll make you get dressed faster, then I'll be happy to make you happy." Carlucci took out one of his cards, wrote his shield number on the front under his name, and said, "There's all my phone numbers and my pager number too, you or your attorney can reach me at any time, anywhere. I answer all my calls soon as I can. Do you want this card, ma'am, or do you want me to give it to your attorney?"

"I'm going into this closet," she said, pointing behind her toward a door. "Do you want to inspect it to make sure there's no shower or tub, no sink, no faucet, no bucket, no fish tank, no hose, no whirlpool, no way I can possibly have access to water?"

Carlucci nodded and hurried across the room, veering off toward the desk to drop his card there, then continuing to the closet, where he leaned in while Mrs. Lyon held the door open. Once again, he was awestruck. It wasn't a closet—not what he thought of when he heard that word. This "closet" was as big as the bedroom his feet were still in. Four gleaming pipes running the length of the room were crammed with dresses, suits, blouses, sweaters, skirts, slacks, robes, coats, and jackets. The walls surrounding them were covered floor to ceiling with shelves, drawers, and shoe racks. Carlucci couldn't help himself. He closed his eyes, shook his head, and gawked at it all again.

"Well? Why are you hesitating? Go in, look, inspect away! God forbid there might be a molecule of water in there, and I might find it and you would spend the rest of your anal-retentive life with that on your conscience. Of course you think you don't have a conscience. You think what you have is a sense of duty. *Civic duty*. God, yessss!"

Carlucci sighed, cleared his throat, and made a quick walk-through among the hangers. Definitely no water. There wasn't room for water. The only space not taken up by clothing or shoes was barely enough space between the racks for one person to move around in.

He came back out, shrugged, and nodded for her to go in. Once she'd done that, banging the door shut behind her, he was left to try to analyze how he'd screwed up with her. Or whether he had. He went back over what he'd said to her, his attitude, his posture, his expressions, his tone of voice, his gestures, everything, but the one thing he kept coming back to was that she'd purposely called the state guys, she'd purposely not called the local guys. Then too, just a couple of moments ago, she'd asked for his *shield* number. Most civilians call them badges. Only people who call them shields are people connected with the law or people who've had problems with the law that got to the legal terminology stage. So it wasn't me, Carlucci thought. She had her skirt up over her head before I opened my mouth. This is about somebody else. Have to ask around, maybe Balzic'll know what the beef was. Probably got pulled over for a traffic thing, probably got pissed 'cause she wrinkled her blouse showin' her license. But why should I be assumin' it was even here? Could've been anywhere.

A couple of minutes later, Mrs. Lyon reappeared wearing a pair of tan slacks and a long-sleeved red tunic buttoned to the neck. She was carrying a pair of running shoes, which she put on over bare feet while seated at her desk. Then she stood up, put a long white wallet into a white leather bag, and, without a word, strode out of the room, down the stairs, and out the front door where she stopped, turned, and waited for Carlucci to catch up.

"I presume we're going in your vehicle," she said.

"Huh? Oh. Yeah. It's that one, over there."

Carlucci watched her stride to his Chevy in that walk of hers. He watched too to see if she looked at her husband as she passed his body. If she did, she did it with peripheral vision because she certainly didn't turn her head in his direction.

"Where you goin'? Crime lab?" Milliron said, on his haunches shining his flash on the ground near the Jag's right rear tire.

"Yeah. Hope somebody's there," Carlucci said.

"Probably not. Hey Rugs, wanna give the coroner another call, huh? Find out what happened to that DC. Shoulda been here an hour ago, this is ridiculous."

"Yeah, okay. Hey. The crime scene truck's here. I see the lights. Listen, I'm gonna tell 'em myself, but don't let these guys go home without collectin' all the small-caliber guns and ammo they can find inside, okay? Anything .25 or smaller, rimfire, centerfire, don't let 'em forget, you know?"

"I know. I won't," Milliron said. "Good luck."

"You too," Carlucci said, scooping his briefcase off the macadam as he trotted toward the Chevy, feeling to make sure the film can was still in his pocket.

"Okay, Missus Lyon, I think we're ready," he said. "First part of the test we can do right here, soon as that truck gets here, okay? All they're gonna do is swab your hands, okay?"

"Oh this is absurd," she said. "Utterly absurd! Ridiculous! Do you think if I'd shot my husband I would be so stupid that I wouldn't have thought to put on a pair of gloves?"

Carlucci got out and waved for the crime scene truck to pull over. He leaned back into the car and said, "I don't know, ma'am. Maybe you would, maybe you wouldn't, I didn't say you shot your husband. All I'm tryin' to do is prove you didn't, that's all. Now you wanna step out, please, and stand by me, okay?"

Jack Turner opened the passenger-side door of the scene truck and said, "Yo, Rugs, what's up?"

"Yo, Jack, wanna swab this lady's hands, huh? Before you do anything else? And then," he said, winking with the eye away from Mrs. Lyon, "be sure and send the spectrum up to the state police crime lab, okay? I wanna make sure they have the results soon as we get there, okay?"

Turner looked slightly dumbfounded for a moment. Carlucci winked at him again.

"Oh oh, yeah. Yeah, we can do that. I'm just so beat, man, my brain's tryin' to take five, I didn't know what you were tellin' me for a second there. Been on the road since six this mornin'. Some clown goes and shoots his wife, his sister-in-law, his mother-in-law, and himself." Turner went around the back of the truck, unlocked it, stepped up and into the van, rummaged around for a moment, then came back out with a bunch of cotton swabs, a bottle of nitric acid, and a plastic bag.

"Man, I'm tellin' you, Rugs, what a mess. This guy shoots his wife in the hand, her middle finger's hangin' there by a piece a skin, the sister-in-law, he nails her in the knee, the mother-in-law, he takes her earlobe off, and himself, get this, he shoots himself in the cheek, get it? Part of the bullet comes out his nose—swear to God—and everybody thinks that's all there is to it, I mean when we got there, this asshole was sittin' on the sidewalk playin' with this piece of bullet that come out his nose. Meanwhile, there's six or seven New Ken cops interviewin' everybody that isn't on the way to the ER, two of 'em are talkin' to this guy, and ten minutes after we get there, he keels over, man, deader'n dirt.

"Hold out your hands, ma'am," Turner said, and then he opened the bottle of nitric acid, dipped one swab in, and wiped Mrs. Lyon's left hand, put the swab in the plastic bag, and repeated the action with the right hand. Then he sealed the bag and marked it with a felt pen. "Got a case number yet, Rugs?"

"I don't. It's Milliron's case, not mine."

"What time you got, I got six oh eight, that what you got?"

"Ah crap," Carlucci said, "mine stopped again. Goddammit."

"Six oh eight's good enough. Six nineteen '98. Your name, ma'am?"

"Jessica . . . Hale . . . Bernhardt. . . . Deford. Missus. No hyphens."

"Okay," Turner said, printing Milliron's and Carlucci's names on the label. "CN pending. Okay. I'll send the results right up there." Turner winked at Carlucci. "You goin' there now? Huh? Should be there when you get there. So whatta we have here, huh? Man, look at this house." Turner whistled and shook his head.

Carlucci summarized what he knew, being careful to keep his report as free of prejudice as he could, adding, "Listen, man, just a couple things. One, there were no burns around the wound, least not that I could see in the light I had. So I'm figurin' it was a rifle. Almost a full moon, plus those spots on all the corners of the house, but I don't know when they came on, they might be motion lights, I don't know, maybe they're on a timer. But, to hit this guy where he hit him? I'm guessin' there was more than enough light for the shooter. What I'm sayin' is, try to figure the angle where the shot mighta come from, see if you can find anything in the woods on the other side of the driveway back there, see where I'm pointin'?"

"Yeah, I follow you."

"Okay. Then, two, it's a real small entry wound. Couldn't be bigger than a .25. Inside, there's a gun case, four rifles, some shotguns, two handguns, both semi-autos. I don't know where the ammo's stored—"

"Excuse me, Sherlock," Mrs. Lyon said, "but aren't you forgetting something?"

"Excuse me? You talkin' to me? What'd you say?"

"A little matter called a search warrant," she said. "You can't send these mice scurrying through my house without a proper warrant, even I know that much."

"Uh, no ma'am, that's not true. Until some judge says otherwise, this property, everything here, the house, all its contents, the cars, the garages, the grounds, everything, it's all a crime scene. A man's been shot and killed here, that's murder in my judgment—"

"That's not for you to say, that's for a coroner to say—"

"Yes ma'am, that's true, you're absolutely right. But until somebody from that office shows up and makes some kinda ruling, it's our judgment call about what happened here and what's a scene and what isn't. No judge is gonna say we had to wait around for some deputy coroner to show up, you know? Make a ruling before we could start investigatin'? There's no judge in this county gonna say anything that ridiculous. So I'm declarin' the whole place is a scene, and that means we can search anywhere around here. I mean if this isn't probable cause, ma'am, I don't know what probable cause is. Probable doesn't mean certainty, ma'am. Doesn't mean we have to find somethin' to prove we had a right to search. Probable means what it means. The man was shot, there are guns in the house, no judge is gonna say that's some illegal leap of logic for us to see if any of those guns might've been the one, you know? Wanna get back in the car, ma'am, please?"

Carlucci held the door for her. After she got in, he said, "Don't forget to buckle up, ma'am. And before I forget, I wanna thank you for cooperatin' with me here, about this test. I really appreciate it."

She eyed him stonily as he closed the door and walked around the front of the car. When he got in and started the engine, she said, "As my father used to say to officious civil servants like yourself, go urinate up a rope."

Carlucci drove to Troop A's crime lab and arrived there at zero six forty, but the only person there was a receiving clerk he'd never seen before. A wink and a shrug weren't going to work with this clerk as they'd worked with Jack Turner, so after finding out when the firearms techs showed up, he turned Mrs. Lyon around and took her back outside to the Chevy.

In the car, he said, "If you're wonderin' why we're back out here, I think your attorney would tell you that I don't want anybody to say I was tryin' to intimidate you into talkin' to me by keepin' you inside a place where you'd be surrounded by police officers and employees, a lot of 'em carryin' guns, and maybe you'd get the wrong idea." Which of course was exactly what he was trying to do. He'd just hoped there'd been an older, shrewder head working the receiving desk.

She didn't say anything. She just continued to look at him as though he were some kind of vermin. So he tried a different approach. "Uh, so what's the problem you have with the local police? I know it wasn't with me, 'cause I never saw you before."

"Are you trying to engage me in conversation again, is that what you're doing?"

He coughed and cleared his throat. "Uh, this stuff about you not talkin' to local police, I mean, you musta had a real problem with somebody once, I'm just tryin' to find out what it was, that's all. Maybe I could help."

She turned and fixed her gaze on him. Even though her stare made him squirm, he was starting to admire how long she could stare without blinking. "I gotta tell you, ma'am, I mean, you got a major-league stare goin' for ya, you know? I feel kinda like a rabbit and, uh, you're so far up in the sky I don't know you're there but you can see me, you know? Like a hawk or somethin'. Hungry one." He tried to laugh.

Her stare intensified. "You think maybe *you* could help? *You* could help *me?*"

"I don't know, maybe. Yeah. But I can't if I don't know what the problem is—or was. Is it an is, or is it a was?"

"Did the public schools teach you to talk like that? Or was it your mother?"

He leaned forward and banged his forehead once gently on the steering wheel. "Awwww, why you gotta do that, huh? You get somethin' outta puttin' people down? You like insultin' people, is that it? You get off on that or somethin'?"

"As a general rule, no, I don't insult people. But see, you're not people. You're local police. That's a far more primitive life-form than people. Far less well developed."

"Oh. Well. Listen, ma'am, I don't know what happened to you with some local cop somewhere, I'm just tryin' to find out, you know? So we can make a little more sense here—or try to. But one thing I do know. Whatever it was, whoever did it, it wasn't me. So I wish you'd stop actin' like it *was* me, okay? You're starin' at me, but you're not seein' me. I don't know who you're seein' but it isn't me. So why don't you stop starin' and start lookin', you know? At me? 'Cause I'm a person just like you."

She threw back her head and howled with laughter. There was nothing jovial about it. It was the meanest laugh he'd heard this month. "*You're a person? Just like me?* Listen to me, you officious amoeba, I myself pay the salary of the conductor of the Conemaugh Symphony, not my husband, mind you. Me. I pay that conductor eighty-five thousand dollars a year to give seven concerts a year. This is not a matching grant I'm talking about, this is not me saying I will pay such and such if it is matched by collections from the little people. This is a gift I make to the cultural life, such as it is, of this insufferable sinkhole. I pay half the salary of the director of the art museum. I gave two Singer Sargents to that museum last year, estimated at four hundred and fifty thousand, the pair. I did this. Not my husband. Me. Do you even know what a Singer Sargent is?"

"Uh, no ma'am, I don't."

"Would it help if I said his first name was John?"

"Uh, no."

"Have you ever once even set foot inside the museum?"

"Uh-uh, no ma'am, never been in there."

"Well if by some bizarre set of circumstances you should happen to find yourself there on any Saturday morning during the school year, you would see children studying art, more than a hundred of them from all over this wretched county, learning to draw, to sketch, to paint, to appreciate art. They're there because of me. I pay for those classes. My money buys the materials, my money pays the instructors, my money pays for the gasoline for the buses that go around collecting the children. My money. And my money pays the drivers of those buses. I do that, not my husband."

"Man, you're really mad at him, aren't ya? Your husband."

"Excuse me? Oh! I see. I'm telling you I've never had to depend on my husband's wealth or earnings to fulfill myself, and you, you unspeakable moron, you sit there psychoanalyzing me! My God, what arrogance!"

Carlucci got out of the Chevy, closed the door gently, walked to the back of the car, opened his left palm and punched it with his right fist. He was still standing there a minute later punching his left palm when a gray Mercedes drove up and parked in the handicapped slot. A portly man hurried inside the crime lab, only to return a moment later. He came huffing up to Carlucci and said, "Are you the one detaining Missus Lyon?"

Carlucci nodded. "You her attorney?"

"Yes. Ernest Lolley. I don't have a card, but I'll give you my numbers if you wish—after I speak with my client, of course."

"No, uh-uh, first we need to talk, okay?"

"Later if you insist, right now I want to speak with her."

Mrs. Lyon got out of the car then and said, "Ernest? God, finally— what, did you go by way of Maryland?"

"Please get back in the car, ma'am."

"Oh shut up!"

"Tell your client get back in the car or I'm gonna think she's tryin' to escape—"

"Oh for God's sake, there's no end to his idiocy. Ernest, will you tell this idiot who he's dealing with—"

"I mean it, ma'am, get back in the car. Tell your client, Counselor, I'm not foolin' around here—"

"Officer," the lawyer said, "I'll need to know your name and shield number."

"I already gave it to her, okay? It's on my card? Listen, Mister, uh, Holley, we have to talk—now, okay?"

"Lolley, not Holley—"

"Ernest, shut him up and drive me to a hotel. There are police swarming through and around my house. Now, Ernest! Not tomorrow." She started walking toward the Mercedes.

"Listen to me, Counselor, okay? She's not a suspect. Only reason she's here is I'm tryin' to eliminate her as a suspect, okay? But I need to talk to her, and you need to make her understand that, okay? And if she gets in your car and you try to drive away, I will take that as probable cause she's tryin' to escape—"

"Oh stop," Lolley said, laughing. "That sort of asinine double-talk may work with street thugs, but it's not working here and you know that as well as I do."

"Hey. You know fucking well told it ain't double-talk, you—"

"Steady, Officer, watch your mouth. Keep cool, or this conversation's over and my client and I leave."

"Okay I'll watch my mouth. And you know what? You can leave if you want. All of a sudden I'm too fucking tired to argue with you. I had somebody swab her hands already, we'll do the test, fuckit, we don't need her."

"What test? You aren't talking neutron activation analysis, are you? Be serious, nobody's going to do that test, not in this lab, and you know that as well as I do. Only reason anybody resorts to that test is their case is so weak that's all they have, so don't play games with me, I know you know that. And I know you brought my client up here to try to intimidate her, and it didn't work, and you're angry that she didn't tumble, but believe me, this woman tumbles for no man. So let's call it a day, shall we—or a night or a morning, whatever it is. Can't remember the last time I saw the sun rise. So what do you say, Officer? Can I take my client to breakfast now? And I say again my name's Lolley, not Holley."

"Hey, fine," Carlucci said. "Take her, what the fuck, go 'head. Just know this. I was there when she was talkin' to you on the phone. And I heard what she said to you. She said—and this is all she said—her husband was shot, he's dead, and I was gonna bring her up here, that's all you know. Yet when you get here, you don't ask me one fuckin' question about what happened to him or how or when or where, nothin', you don't have the slightest fuckin' curiosity about him, uh-uh, all you wanna do is get her away from me. Whatta you think this makes me think about, huh? You think this gets me all warm and fuzzy about her? Your ass, Counselor. Mister Lolley. 'Cause now I really wanna know why she don't wanna talk to us, huh? 'Cause not askin' about him, man, that really calmed me down, fucking-A, that really did, you helped her out a lot."

"Oh really, Officer—"

"Detective, okay? Detective Sergeant Carlucci, okay? Shield number four eight one."

"Then, Sergeant, presumably you've had enough training by now to know that this sort of interviewing technique, for want of a better phrase, is simply lost on people who know that nothing in our laws compels them to talk to the police. About anything. I know that annoys you, but you cannot make that go away."

"Well what's the fuckin' problem here? Why won't she talk to me? I didn't do anything to her. Never saw her before—"

"It's a long story, and this is not the time for it." Lolley started to walk away.

Carlucci darted forward to get around in front of him. "Listen to me, Counselor. Just listen a second. Try to put yourself in my place, okay? We got a body, bullet hole in the back of the head—"

"You're Rocksburg PD, aren't you?"

"Yeah, right, so what?"

"Well then it's not even your jurisdiction, I don't know what you're doing there—or here."

"State CID called me in—what, you think I'd be in this if I wasn't invited? I was asleep, man, dreamin', mindin' my own business when I got called, what the fuck. Listen, listen, okay? All we know about the man is what we found in his wallet. We don't know anything else about him, c'mon, man, why do you think I wanna talk to her?"

"You brought her up here to intimidate her—"

"Oh what—you don't think it's possible to have two reasons for doin' the same thing? I need to talk to this woman, Jesus Christ man, don't be dense—"

The passenger door on the Mercedes opened a crack, and there came that insistent voice again, "Ernest? How much am I paying you?"

"Oh yeah right, go 'head, Mister Lolley, don't stand here tryin' to give us any help, no, fuck no, we'll do all this background shit on our own, take us days, never mind you or her could give it to us in an hour, no, fuck no, go on, man, take her to wherever."

"At the first opportunity, Sergeant, I will give you a call."

"Ernest?"

Lolley turned without another word and trotted to the driver's side door of his Mercedes. It was out of the parking lot and disappearing into the grayish morning light before Carlucci could get to his Chevy.

Rugs went home to make sure Mrs. Comito had showed up to watch his mother, and to shower, change clothes, and get something to eat. He'd almost gotten away clean when his mother grabbed him by the back of the shirt as he was going out the door.

"Where do you think you're goin', huh? I wanna know what kinda crap you're pullin' with this woman."

"What woman? Missus Comito? What're you talkin' about?"

"She says you hired her to watch me. She says you pay her to watch me. That's a spy. Maybe you don't know that, maybe you think I'm so dumb I don't know that, but I know that. What I wanna know is why're you payin' her to spy on me? Your own mother, your own flesh and blood? What? I wanna know what the hell's goin' on here."

This was only about the two-thousandth time he'd heard these questions. He hung his head, took a deep breath, brought his lower teeth against his upper lip, and closed his eyes. Everything might've been okay if he just hadn't closed his eyes. He knew better than that. She hit him with her fist right on the point of his chin, driving his lower teeth into his upper lip. The pain shot from his lip to his nose and then to his eyes. He instinctively grabbed both her wrists before she could do it again.

"Ma, goddammit! What'd you do that for? Damn!"

"Let go of me!" she said, trying to pull her hands away.

"Back in the kitchen, c'mon, c'mon." He turned her around and backed her in, making sure to keep his legs as far away as possible because as soon as she thought she had her balance she'd start kicking.

"Back up, Ma, c'mon. Sit down, c'mon. Sit down I'm tellin' ya—and listen to me."

He backed her legs against a chair and pushed her forearms up and back so she had to sit. "You're hurting me," she said, and tried to kick him in the shin. She caught him with just the edge of her heel.

"Stop it, stop kickin', Ma, c'mon! And listen to me. I know you don't remember this, I know you only remember this every once in a while, but she's here to make sure you don't hurt yourself, that's all, okay? She is not a spy."

He shot a quick glance at Mrs. Comito, who was backed against the kitchen sink, wide-eyed, shaking her head, both hands over her mouth.

"I don't care what you say, she's a goddamn spy—and you're payin' her, so what's 'at make you, huh?" She tried to kick him again, but he juked away.

"Listen, Ma, I don't care whether you remember this or not, but you have to stop hittin', you hear me? That hurt, Ma, where you hit me." He stepped back and wiped his mouth with his fingers. "Aw Jesus, look at this, Ma. Jesus Christ. Man!"

He threw up his hands in Mrs. Comito's direction and motioned for her to come outside with him.

When they were on the porch, she handed him a wad of wet paper towels and said, "Rugsie, here, hold this over your mouth, you're bleedin' bad."

"Yeah, okay, thanks," he said, taking the towels and pressing on his lip for about half a minute. When he took them away to look at them, he was surprised to see how much blood there was.

"Uh, listen, Missus Comito, I can't stay, I gotta go, okay? I just came home to make sure you were here, get changed, you know?"

"I know, Rugsie, I know," she said, shaking her head. "Rugsie, don't get mad, okay?"

"At you? Why would I get mad at you?"

"What I'm gonna say, that's what I mean. Promise? Promise you won't get mad at me?"

"I won't get mad at you. Never, I'd never get mad at you. Jeez, Missus Comito, you save my life here every day."

"Well. Okay then. I'm just gonna say it. Rugsie, this can't go on. She's gettin' worse. I'm . . . I'm startin' to get scared, you know? I never turn my back on her, but I'm . . . it's gettin' harder for me to keep up with her all the time, you know? She scares me . . . and she's a lot stronger'n I am."

"Missus Comito, I've racked my brains about this. If I knew what to do I would, honest to God I would. I don't know what to do. I'm tryin' to find somebody to talk to about this who ain't gonna BS me, you know? I know she's gettin' worse. She never used to . . . you know, this, this hittin' crap, this kickin', man, she never used to do that, that just started."

He shook his head, looked off over her shoulder, took her arm, and squeezed gently. "Just hang in a little while longer, okay? I know I gotta make a move, I know it, I know it . . . I just don't know what kinda move I can make, you know? All I can tell ya is, do what you're doin', please. Don't turn your back on her, try to stay ahead of her, just keep talkin' to her the way you do, you know? Believe me, nobody knows better'n me she's gettin' worse. But I gotta go now."

He started down the steps, but she called him and came down three of the four steps herself. "Rugsie," she said, her lower lip trembling, "if she hits me, I don't know . . . nobody's ever hit me. In my whole life. I got so scared when she hit you, I got this terrible feeling in here, you know?" She pointed to her chest.

"Oh Jesus . . . listen . . . aw man. If she hits ya, here's what you do. First thing, you got the keys, right? To both doors, you got 'em?"

She took them out of her sweater pocket and showed him.

"Okay. When you go back in, make sure the back door's locked—"

"It's always locked, that's the first thing I do—"

"Okay, then here's what. If she does, you know, God forbid, I hope and I pray she never does that to you, but if she does, get outta there. Get out here and put the hooks on, that's what I put 'em there for, okay?"

She nodded glumly.

"Okay, good. So then, if you had to do that, the next thing, soon as you get home you call me, okay? The pager number. I'll call you right back, no matter what I'm doin'. Then stay home. Don't try to get back in, okay? And remember, she can still hurt ya with a spoon, we talked about that, remember? Long as she can still feed herself, don't take your eyes off her, 'cause she almost got me Sunday. I just did get my hand outta there or she woulda nailed me with the handle. You look on the table, you'll see the gouge she put in there. Man, she just missed me, so you watch your hands. Okay now, I really gotta go. I'll see ya. Thanks, Missus Comito, I couldn't do it without ya, honest to God, thank you. Just watch yourself now, okay? Bye."

He turned and trotted toward the Chevy, forcing himself to not look back.

At the station in City Hall, Carlucci went looking for Chief Nowicki and learned from civilian dispatcher Vic Stramsky that Nowicki was in the lockup downstairs with a locksmith. Carlucci found Nowicki inside the last of three cells holding up the door with a crowbar while the locksmith examined the bolt and latch. The door had been giving everybody fits for years because once it was locked it required at least two officers to lift the door to align the bolt and latch so a third officer could turn the key.

"Buildings shift and settle, what can I tell you," the locksmith said. "What, you think the bars are warpin' or somethin'?"

"Bars warpin', right, that's funny." Nowicki noticed Carlucci and said, "Yo, Rugs. Lookin' for me?"

"Yeah. Just wanted to make sure you were here. Need to talk to you, but I'll wait in your office, okay? Gonna be long, ya think?"

"I can go right now, right? Yo, locksmith, can I let go of this bar now, huh? My arms are on fire here."

"Why's nobody listen? Told ya let go two minutes ago. Also told ya, soon as I looked at it, you're gonna have to get this thing rebuilt, this building's gonna keep settlin', one day you're gonna come down here, you're gonna need a torch to get it open. You hear any of that?"

"Aw don't tell me that torch crap, huh?" Nowicki said. "One thing I know for sure, they don't build 'em like this anymore. Who makes cells like this now? Nobody. I doubt if anybody knows when this place was even built."

The locksmith, a wiry little guy with dense, tufted eyebrows that wriggled independently of each other, said, "You're the chief of police? And you don't know where to find plans for public buildings? Oh I feel real safe here."

"Aw okay, funny man, tell me where to start lookin', I'll look, okay? Just remember you're in Rocksburg, alright?"

"Like I could forget. This is still a third-class city, right? They didn't change that, did they? So even here you gotta have a code enforcement officer, a city planner, an engineer? And they gotta know a consulting architect, city probably even got one on retainer, and one of those people, guaranteed, gotta know where the plans are for public buildings, okay? Find the plans, you'll find out who contracted the work, who subbed the work out, who designed and installed these doors. Put a detective on it, you got one of those, don't ya?"

"Yo, Rugs, you would know, right? We got any of those?"

"Aw for cryin' out loud," the locksmith said. "Quit pullin' my chain. There are ordinances, statutes, laws for third-class cities, about how they're supposed to run—any of those words familiar to you? You got a cop's uniform on, you said you were the chief, I'm startin' to think one of these walls is a fake and you got the real chief bricked up behind there."

Nowicki looked at Carlucci. "This guy's been bustin' my balls since he got here—I'm leavin' now, funny man. Send your bill to council, attention the treasurer, you hear that? Don't send it to me. 'Cause you send it to me I'll lose it. On purpose."

Nowicki started up the stairs muttering, "Architect on retainer, Christ. Everybody's on retainer, everybody has to sue to get paid, only fuckin' people makin' any money around here are the shysters. So, Rugs, what's up, my man?"

Carlucci said nothing until they were in Nowicki's office and he closed the door. Nowicki poured himself a coffee, asked with a gesture if Carlucci wanted one, but before Carlucci could answer, he said, "Man, what happened to you? Your upper lip's all swollen, you got dried blood all over your chin. Downstairs, I thought what's he doin', is he growin' a beard or somethin'? A mustache? What'd you do, hit somebody—not with a city car I hope, Jesus Christ don't tell me that—"

"No, no, I didn't hit anybody—"

"Oh good. Christ, that's the last thing I need to hear—here, you want somethin' to wipe that off, here, use a paper towel. You can use that water in that carafe there, that's okay, wash yourself off. You think maybe you need to get stitched up, huh?"

"It's all over my chin? Really? Shit, I thought I got it stopped—"

"Well it is stopped, looks like. It's dried up—what happened?"

Carlucci sighed and looked at his lap after he wiped his chin, jaw, and mouth, the last very tenderly. "My mother, man. Closed my eyes like a stupid fuck and bam, she nailed me."

"Bam? She nailed you? *Hit* you? With what? You're shittin' me."

"Wish I was. Fist I guess, I don't know, had my eyes closed I told ya."

"Oh man, she ever do this before? She never did this, right?"

"Yeah she did. Just never nailed me this solid before. It was my own fault, I know better'n to close my eyes, musta had my head up my ass about this Lyon guy. Hear about him yet?"

"Yeah, soon as I came in Stramsky told me, said he picked it up on the state band. What, they so short again they had to call you?"

"Yeah."

"You got time to work it?"

"Yeah, I got nothin' hot. You tell me no, that'd just fuck Milliron up."

"What about the county? They don't have anybody free?"

"Oh I'm sure they're gonna be all over it, we had to use their scene techs, their truck, but, uh, they had somethin' in New Ken last night, I forget—one dead, two shot. Maybe three shot, I forget, I'm not thinkin' about that. I don't know what else they got cookin', I haven't talked to anybody in their office for a coupla weeks. I'm sure we'll be meetin' up there sometime today, but see, there's two things I have to talk to you about first."

"Yeah? So? Talk. Sure you don't wanna get that looked at?"

"Huh? Nah, I don't think. Later maybe. Uh, okay, you got any connections, you know, anybody at all in social services who ain't just some bullshit bureaucrat? I gotta do somethin' about my mother, man, I been puttin' it off, Christ, I don't know, for years I guess. Can't do that anymore. Obviously. Anyway, everybody I talked to in the last month—and that's when she started with the hittin' . . . kickin' too."

"Oh man, I'm sorry, Rugs. Jesus."

"Yeah I know. Thanks. Anyway, I mean, everybody I talk to, I get a different story, I don't know who the fuck to believe. And Missus Comito? You know? The lady watches her in the daytime? Jesus, the poor thing, man, I feel really bad for her, she's scared to death, and I don't blame her. And listen to this, God, this is how bad it's gettin'. I had to put hooks and eyes on the doors on the outside, man. You hear what I'm sayin'? The fucking outside?"

"Outside? *Outside* you put 'em? You shittin' me?"

"I know I know, but she started wanderin' off, man. Got lost twice, I didn't say anything about it, you know, it was handled, but fuck, I'm so scared she's gonna do somethin', you know, put a pan on the stove and forget about it—I mean, I was gone from there last night like, from three-thirty till almost seven. I can't leave her alone like that with those hooks on, I don't know what she's gonna do. She's gettin' really erratic, man, I mean really fuckin' erratic. One second she's chewin' my ass 'cause I haven't brought Franny home to meet her, next second she's chewin' my ass 'cause I'm leavin' the house without givin' her a kiss. Wanna know why she smacked me? Huh? 'Cause she thinks Missus Comito's a spy and I hired her to be a spy. Fuck you do with that, huh? I don't know. So, man, I'm askin' you, you know, as a friend, if you know anybody, you got any connections anywhere, you know? Please tell me."

"I know some people, yeah," Nowicki said. "Lemme give 'em a call, and I'll get back with ya. Meantime, you know, you wanna work that case with, uh, who is it—Milliron? Go 'head. Up to you. He's helped us out enough. I'll call ya soon as I know somethin', okay? What's the other thing? You said two."

"Oh. Him, this Lyon. Man, that's a different world out there. Ever been on Club Road? Not on it, I mean off it? Ever had any call to drive off it to look at any of those houses back there? That's a different world, man, I'm not shittin' ya."

"Matter of fact, yeah, I have."

"You have? Doin' what?"

"Some other time maybe, not now. So? What's the problem with him—that I could help you with?"

"Problem is the old lady won't talk to us, so I don't know anything about this guy. I thought maybe you might know somethin'."

"What's his name again?"

"J. for James Deford Lyon."

"Oh *that* Lyon? Oh Christ, I don't know who I was thinkin' of. You kiddin'? CEO of Conemaugh Steel, you don't remember him? J. D. Lyon? No shit, he's the one got shot? Oh man, J. D. Lyon, fuck yeah, I know him. So do you, c'mon. You tellin' me you don't remember all that shit, when was it, '84, '85? When he shut the whole fuckin' plant down? You gotta remember that. Christ, how many times did Balzic call out the whole department? What, you missed those parties, huh? Hung him in effigy a couple times, burned a guard shack down one night, another time they took a dozer in there, started tearin' up the railroad tracks, you don't remember that, or you weren't there, or what?"

"Yeah, I never went to any of that shit, I was always workin' a couple different things. But it's comin' back now, yeah. How'd I forget his name? Oh fuck."

"What?"

"That'll mean every guy he put on the street's a suspect. How many guys worked there? Three hundred?"

"Oh a lot more'n that—well it varied, you know, one time when it was really cookin', I think they probably had close to a thousand guys, all three shifts. But at the end there, there were probably no more than four hundred. Maybe not that many."

"Man, your mind, I'm tellin' ya—not yours, mine. Works in circles I swear. Last night I couldn't place this guy at all, name didn't mean a thing to me. I don't know, musta been too scared about my mother, lockin' her in like that. But yeah, it's comin' back now—oh man, I remember Balzic got into a big thing with him, right in this office, they were screamin' at each other, remember that? That fucker expected Balzic, oh man, remember? Yeah. He thought Balzic should put off-duty people out there round the clock, he was pitchin' a fit 'cause Balzic told him rent some cops, and, uh, oh he was pissed."

"Yeah he was," Nowicki said. "Asshole couldn't understand why just 'cause he lived in the township and they didn't have a department why we couldn't do that—just for him. He wound up hirin' Vanguard. And the reason I know that is 'cause I was moonlightin' with them then. Fact, coupla weekends there, I got stuck drivin' his old lady around. What a pain in the ass she was."

"No shit, you actually drove her? What's with her, man? She said some really nasty stuff to me. Said I wasn't people, I was a local cop, and, uh, what the fuck'd she say? Called me some names of things I never heard of. Said local cops are a more primitive life-form, not nearly as developed as everybody else, that's one thing she said."

"That's her alright. Oh yeah. Hated us. Hated me. And I never was anything but super polite to her, man, super nice. Didn't matter, she always looked at me like I was somethin' she didn't wanna step in. Yeah. She's the reason I almost quit that job. They finally let me drive for him for a while, but, oh man, I couldn't take her. Nastiest woman

I ever met, and I know it wasn't 'cause of anything I did. She'd get bubbles in the corners of her mouth, man, no shit, I'm not exaggeratin', she'd just look at me sometimes, and there'd be these little bubbles poppin' up, no shit," Nowicki said, laughing. "That woman's goin' into the bitch hall of fame, first ballot, unanimous, no abstentions."

"How about him, what was he like?"

"Mogambo, I called him—to myself, you know, not to him. The great white hunter. Yeah, I shot this, I shot that, I was over there in Kenya, I dropped this one from four hundred yards with one shot, that's all he talked about, just braggin' about everything he killed. Or how good he could play golf. Nothin' humble about him. Course when you got that much money from bein' the boss, humility don't make it. He's still the boss far as I know. Or was."

"Whatta you mean, still the boss?"

"Well they're still in business, just not here."

"You mean he was still runnin' the company? And the company's still runnin'?"

"Oh yeah, absolutely. He's the one moved 'em to South America, man. Brazil. But just 'cause he put everybody else outta work around here, that don't mean he put himself out of a job."

"Oh so somebody else is gonna move up. More suspects."

"Hey this shit's complicated, man. Way out of my league. All I remember is they merged, Conemaugh Steel, I think they merged with Knox Iron and Steel back in the mid-seventies—you know who would know a lot about this? Balzic's buddy. Valcanas. He did a lotta work for the local. Somehow, that local—I'm not sure about any of this, okay? But I think that local, even though it was part of the Steelworkers, you know, the big union, the national? For some reason, Conemaugh's local was never part of the whole bargaining thing, I don't know why. I think they were separate for some reason. But Valcanas is the guy you need to talk to. I had an uncle was shop steward one time, course he's dead now, so that's no help, but I remember him tellin' me what a no-bullshit guy Valcanas was. Call him. I'll bet he's got a ton of background on this guy—hell, everybody in the company—I mean from that time. You're bleedin' again."

"I am? Aw shit."

"You need to get up the ER, man, get that stitched. Grab some paper towels, keep some pressure on it. You don't, you're gonna ruin your clothes, man. Go on, get up there."

In the ER, Carlucci took seven sutures on the inside of his upper lip without anesthetic because the doctor convinced him a local would hurt just as much as the sutures. But after the third one, tears were spilling over his cheeks, his heart rate was going up, and he wanted to split the doctor's lip to see what he would say to himself about pain.

When a nurse helped Carlucci sit up, she asked him if he felt lightheaded. He tried to tell her he didn't, but he thought he sounded as though he had a mouth full of oatmeal. He asked her if he did. She looked at him impishly and said, "I can't understand you. You sound like you've got a mouth full of oatmeal."

The doc told him to hold his lip up when he was brushing his teeth and to stay away from solid food for at least a couple of days. Swell. Now not only couldn't he talk right, he was also going to be eating through a straw in the side of his mouth.

He was almost to the Chevy when his pager went off. He recognized the county DA's office number, but instead of going through the hassle of making himself understood by asking dispatcher Stramsky to patch him through from the car phone, he just drove to the courthouse, parked on a side street, and took the stairs to the third floor, his upper lip now feeling like a balloon full of cayenne pepper sauce.

Inside the DA's office, he learned from the receptionist the meeting about the Lyon case was being held in the detective bureau office. When he got there, he tried to deflect the needles he knew would be coming by pretending to read something in his notebook and heading for the back of the room. It didn't work.

"Yo, Rugs, what'd she claim, man, she lost the key to the cuffs?"

"Shit, he wasn't wearin' cuffs. He just stood there and took it like the punishment lover he is."

"Man, don't ever tell us you don't love kinky. Not after today."

"See there, boys and girls? That's what workin' for the Rocksburg PD'll get ya. Turn ya into a pig for pain and sufferin'."

"Oh baby, beat me, beat me, I love it when you spill my blood."

"Okay, gentlemen, we've got work to do here," said Les Harvey, first assistant DA, as he came striding in to preside over the meeting of county detectives, county crime scene technicians, State Trooper Milliron, and Carlucci. Half the staff from the DA's office followed him in, but to Carlucci's surprise, the DA himself, Howard Failan, was not with them.

The meeting lasted less than a half hour, and the only thing Carlucci heard new was that the scene techies had found a shell casing for a .22 Magnum cartridge in a weedy area at the edge of the woods between Club Road and the Lyons' house. They also found a couple of indentations in the ground that they were speculating had been left by a bipod. So they'd collected grass and soil samples to match against any suspect's clothing or rifle.

Harvey tried to make a joke by saying, "So we're thinking the shooter was definitely not your average small-game hunter," but nobody laughed. Then he said, "I don't think I'm overstating the case by saying this was a shooter with a mission."

He said some other things that Carlucci ignored because he was busy writing a note and handing it to Milliron.

Milliron read the note and then asked Harvey how far the shell casing and indentations in the ground were from Lyon.

One of the techies piped up, "Forty-two yards from the indentations to Lyon's feet, so with a scope, that's no stretch at all for a .22 Mag."

"Find one in the house? Gun or ammo?"

"Nope. Everything that wasn't a shotgun was centerfire, one rifle was a .243 Winchester, the other one was a .300 Weatherby Magnum. The handguns were both Brownings, a nine and a .380."

"Okay, so until we hear otherwise from the coroner," Harvey said, "what we're looking for is a .22 Magnum rifle. Which could've been bought anywhere, so I don't think we need at this time to waste manpower checkin' dealers. Later on, if we get desperate, we might try that, but not just yet.

"So," Harvey continued, "let's turn to the victim. What do we know? On the one hand not much. And on the other, way too much. We don't know where he was or who he was with, and his wife—who we're assuming is the only other person present when it went down, aside from the shooter of course—is, uh, to put it mildly, uncooperative.

"As to him, we do know that for a brief time back in the mid-eighties, he was certainly one of the most hated men in Rocksburg, if not the whole county, if not *the* most hated. In case you've forgotten, or were too young to remember, the fact is, he's the guy who ultimately decided to move Conemaugh Steel Corporation overseas, which put a lotta people around here outta work, and in doing so, he also made a tidy pile of money for himself. And that was very big news for a very long time.

"We also know, because of what he's done with a large part of that money, that some people regard him as just the opposite, one of the most generous men around. People in Conemaugh General Hospital, for example, think he walks on water because in the last ten years he's personally given more than two million bucks to the oncology department alone. This I know from my own experience with my volunteer work up there. One wing of that department is named after his mother. He raised the money for that wing and matched what he raised. So while there were many other contributors, he was the driving force behind its construction and its principal benefactor.

"So. While I think we can safely rule out that anybody killed him because he gave money to the hospital," Harvey said, "the man's history in the steel business, for those of you who don't know, is filled with scorched earth. He put at least three very large companies through bankruptcy reorganizations and pissed a lotta people off in the process—except the stockholders of course. Nonetheless, his stature, for both reasons, makes this anything but a routine homicide. And while I'm saying that, you all know that I know you have to work it exactly as if it were routine, keeping in mind of course—as if anybody's gonna let you forget—that Lyon's stature makes that impossible.

"In which regard, I call your attention to the fact that, in addition to the local papers, both here and in Pittsburgh, and every TV station there, we're also getting calls from New York, Washington, and Harrisburg, not only from the national media in those cities but also from people in government, elected and nonelected, everybody from the FBI to the SEC, you name it, we're hearin' from 'em.

"What I'm saying is this: the CEO of an international corporation takes one in the back of the head, a lotta noses get open real fast, so until we get a handle on this, everybody's gonna be watching us, and I can tell you right now, they already think we're a buncha rubes. My advice to you is keep your mouth shut and don't help 'em prove it. Anybody you don't know asks you anything about this case, your official response is, talk to the DA. Got that?"

It went on more or less in that vein for the rest of the meeting. Carlucci spent most of the time glancing around the room to see if he could read that anybody knew more than they were volunteering. When the meeting broke up, the only things he could say for sure were, one, this was the highest profile case he'd ever worked, and, two, the shooter had been practicing. Forty-two yards in a full moon, looking into the spotlights from the house, aiming at Lyon, who was probably upright for only a few seconds before bending over to retrieve whatever he'd opened the trunk to get—that was the result of real skill achieved through disciplined practice derived from genuine dedication. Plus there was the question of how the shooter knew to be there at that time. Nobody had even mentioned that. Had he known to be there at a specific time? Or had he been there on the hope that his target would just show up?

Carlucci caught up to Harvey in the hall and said, "You happen to hear from an attorney named Lolley?" He only had to repeat it twice before Harvey understood him.

"No. What about?"

"Her, the wife."

"Never heard the name," Harvey said. "What happened to your mouth?"

"Got punched. So, uh, you wanna try to see if this guy'll talk to you? Name's Ernest Lolley, I don't know where he's from, he's not in the local book."

Harvey said he'd check it out, then he excused himself, saying he was late for another meeting.

Carlucci went back inside looking for Milliron, who was hanging back in the corner opposite from the coffeepots, nodding for Carlucci to join him. When Carlucci got there, Milliron said, "Man, what happened to you? That looks painful."

"Some other time. I don't wanna think about it, okay? You're gonna have to do most of the talkin' for a while. I can't even understand myself."

"Okay," Milliron said. "Uh, so, uh you hear anything new here— aside from the caliber? I didn't. I was sorta disappointed with the coroner, man, I thought he would've done the post by now. Damn DC didn't show until about a half hour after you left with the wife. Grimes is usually right on top of things, wonder what happened." Milliron looked around nervously. "So what do you think, huh? Still our case?"

"Hell no, not if he's talkin' FBI and SEC." Carlucci only had to repeat that once.

"Yeah, it sure doesn't sound like it. And it sure doesn't look like it. Everybody from the county's havin' their own little meeting up there by the coffee. Well, hell," Milliron said, turning his back to the room, "that was the poorest excuse for an organizational meeting I ever saw. I mean, who the hell's in charge? Us or them? Walks outta here just tellin' us everybody's gonna be watchin' us and they already think we're a buncha rubes, then he doesn't say a word about who reports to who when, where, how, or why. I mean, do you know what we're doin'?"

"I don't know what anybody else is doin'. I was gonna go talk to an attorney named Valcanas. My chief told me he did a lotta work for the union local when Lyon was shuttin' down his place back in '83, '84, '85 or whenever. D'you know he was still CEO of the company? Conemaugh Steel? I didn't even know it was still a company."

Milliron shook his head. "All I know about this guy is what I heard today and what I surmised at his house. Otherwise, it's all new to me. I was waitin' to hear anybody say if he had any other heirs—did I miss somethin'? Huh? And who's supposed to work the wife? All I heard was she was extremely uncooperative—and I'm the one who told him that. Man, this was screwed up, you want my opinion. Don't you think?"

"Always is every time you get three or four departments pretendin' they're gonna cooperate. My old boss used to hate it when he had to work with the county. Course that was when they were just a buncha political hacks. Gotta give it to Failan. He's turned them into a real professional department. Still doesn't mean they like splittin' glory with anybody else. You know—don't ya?—I'm only talkin' for myself here. Right?"

Milliron nodded.

"Still, man," Carlucci said, "what surprised me most was Failan wasn't here himself. Can't figure why the hell he sent Harvey, that guy, man, I never did like him. Thinks he's funny. You know him? Harvey? Had any dealings with him?"

"You mean the guy that walked out without sayin' who was in charge, who was gonna report to who? Him?"

Carlucci nodded. "Watch it, here comes Failan now. Comin' straight for us."

District Attorney Howard Failan, cheerful as always, smiling warmly and waving to everyone with whom he made eye contact, walked directly to Milliron with his hand out. Milliron shook it and exchanged greetings while Failan patted him on the shoulder and looked intently into his eyes. Then Failan turned to Carlucci, again extending his hand, shaking it warmly, but stopping to say, "Rugs? Was gonna ask how you were, but wow, that must hurt. What happened?"

Carlucci shrugged, looked at his shoes, and mumbled something about being in the wrong place at the wrong time.

"Boy. How many stitches?"

Carlucci held up seven fingers chest-high.

"Woo boy, those things hurt, I don't care what anybody says," Failan said. "They always give you this line about the shot's gonna hurt worse than the stitches so you may as well take the lesser of two evils and get it over with faster, but personally, I just think those guys spread that propaganda 'cause they've never had to get sewn up themselves."

Carlucci started to mumble something else, but Failan was off in another direction.

"Listen," Failan said, lowering his voice and shuffling closer to both of them, "I've been on the phone with an attorney named Ernest Lolley. Missus Lyon's attorney? You know? Well, you fellows're off the hook with her, I'll take care of that myself. I'll work it out with Lolley, and if I still need to get with her, I'll do it with interrogatories, there's no reason for you fellows to have to take any more abuse from her. She and I go way back, I know she can be a real pain in the butt."

"Man, I was real polite to her," Carlucci said, "but she didn't wanna hear nothin'—"

"Forget about it, it wasn't you. She had a real nasty experience when she was gettin' ready to graduate from college. She and a bunch of her sorority sisters got buzzed up and started terrorizin' the local traffic in some little town in New Jersey. She was drivin' when a local cop pulled her over, and she was drunk enough to start crackin' wise with him, so he hauled 'em all in to teach the college girls a little humility, you know, made 'em stand around naked for a while, finished it off with an inspection of the brown round and so forth, and she just never got over it. Tried to sue 'em, got beat in the local court there, so, uh, she just can't get over the word local when it comes to cops, DAs, judges. You think you guys caught some flak? Trust me, she's burned my ears more times than I wanna remember. Real bad."

Carlucci looked at Milliron, Milliron looked back. Then they both shrugged.

Milliron spoke up first. "So, uh, who's in charge here? Is this our case, or'd, uh, you know, the county sorta take it over? The way it looks to me—"

"Just a second, Trooper, let's not get excited, I can see where you're goin', I understand your concerns, but let's not jump the fence before we find out where the dogs take their dumps, okay? I'm sure there's gonna be enough work to go around, and when this case comes to a successful resolution, which I'm sure with your work it will, there's gonna be enough glory to go around twice—"

"Yes sir, I'm sure you're right, but as of this moment, nobody knows who's in charge, who's reporting to who, who's doin' what work, I mean, right now, I don't know who's goin' where to do what—"

"That's why I'm here, Trooper. Just wanted to talk to you two fellows first, let you know what was what about Missus Lyon, okay? Now, I'm gonna go up front, and with a little luck, we're gonna get this thing organized, alright? That suit you better?"

"Fine. Yes sir," Milliron said.

"Rugs?"

Carlucci shrugged his approval.

"Alright then," Failan said, smiling, giving them both a pat on the shoulder. He turned and headed for the front of the room, asking for everybody's attention.

"I'm sure Les told you fellows the level of interest this case has already generated," Failan began, "so I'm not gonna belabor that point. We're all big boys here, and I like to think we're all professional enough to know to keep our eyes on the prize and not get bogged down in turf disputes about whose case this is and who's in charge, et cetera, et cetera. Just so there's no question about it, I'm in charge.

This one goes to the top of my list. And behind me comes Chief Detective George Sporcik—"

A rousing cheer went up from the cluster of county detectives and scene techs. Some of them were pummeling one of their companions, obviously Sporcik.

"Yeah yeah," Failan said, "I might as well announce that right now too. Was gonna save it for a nice little press conference—where nobody showed up except a couple hundred of George's closest relatives—"

"And both his friends," somebody shouted.

"His dogs," somebody else shouted.

"But then," Failan said, holding up his hands, "this other thing, uh, well, you know. So let me make it official. Tom Wurzel's decided the minor judiciary is where his career path lies, which everybody in the detective bureau and in my office knows, but for the rest of you, our former chief of detectives has decided to run for district magistrate and he's taken all the vacation time he's got coming to learn how to shake hands and kiss the committeewomen, so, uh, that left large shoes to fill. I looked around, and hell, it was no contest, George had his thirteens up on the desk, where he usually has them, so let me now introduce the new chief of county detectives, George Sporcik—"

Another boisterous cheer rose up, and Sporcik took more pummeling.

"—and offer my congratulations at the same time I advise you all that, after me on this case, George comes next. Then State Trooper Milliron and Rocksburg Detective Carlucci, the latter two the first officers on the scene. Everybody else reports to them, they report to me. And I'm very serious about this. I repeat, everybody else reports to them, they report to me—and the first time I hear somebody's backdoorin' somebody, undercuttin' somebody, trashin' somebody's technique, style, personality, character, whatever, you're gone, I won't tolerate it.

"Because, gentlemen, we don't take care of business here—and with due dispatch—I guarantee we're gonna have the FBI claimin' somebody said he, she, or it thinks the shooter crossed the Ohio line to get here and from that moment on we'll be trippin' over FBI every time we turn around. I don't know about you, but that's happened to me a coupla times in this life and I don't wanna even think about it happening again. So do your jobs and keep your turf problems to yourselves. First warning, last warning.

"Now. Here's the way I'm gonna divide the labor. Chief Sporcik, I want you and your men to find out who benefits from this death, personally and professionally. Real estate, joint tenancy, trusts, stocks, bonds, find out where it goes and how and when. Get the corporate organizational chart, the board of directors, corporate counsel, financial officer, and all the rest of the corporate officers. Any of those people tell you they don't have to talk, tell me, I'll take it from there.

"Now, as to our post. The coroner was givin' a paper in Cleveland to a bunch of his buddies yesterday, and since he won't drive at night anymore, he stayed over and left this morning, which means he should be back shortly. I've left word for him to expedite the post, which will be witnessed by Trooper Milliron and Detective Carlucci.

"Now, as I have already told those two gentlemen, I myself will deal with Missus Lyon through her attorney, one Ernest Lolley. I will tell you all, however, that the Lyons have two children, and to say that they're estranged from their parents would be putting it mildly. The son calls himself a troubadour, I think that's the word he uses. Mostly it's just an excuse to play his guitar, smoke a lotta dope, and lay all the impressionable young things. As for the daughter, well, let's just say she hasn't had a whole lotta luck with men. At least she's stopped havin' big weddings. As for her personal habits, she's never had much trouble convincing any number of doctors to write the kind of script she wants to have filled by her favorite pharmacists. Both of them have been to some of the more expensive rehab farms, uh, so while I'm presuming nothing about them, I do want to know that their alibis are unshakable, okay?

"Now. As I'm sure Les told you, J. D. Lyon was a hated man back in the mid-eighties. Some of you will remember, some of you are too young or were with other departments, but I recall the Rocksburg PD was called out more than once to disperse the, uh, for want of a better phrase, the loosely organized but very vehement opposition to Lyon's continued right to life. He was hung in effigy more than once, I do recall that, and I recall clearly that for two days we ran court well into the night for all the summary cases that grew out of one of those parties.

"What I'm sayin' is, a lot of people had their lives turned upside down by decisions that weren't reached in New York City or Chicago or Wilmington, Delaware. The wreckin' ball that started knockin' down the walls of their lives started right here, and J. D. Lyon was the man swingin' the ball. To make it short and ugly, a lotta people said it out loud, and they weren't shy about sayin' it. If they got the chance, they'd be proud to kill the SOB. Which means you've got an army of suspects out there. I leave it to you, George, how you want to break up the interview load, but while some of your people are working the top of the company, most of your people are gonna have to work the bottom. Start with the union hall, see what kind of membership lists they've got and how much they're willing to cooperate. Give you any crap, let me know, I've got some favors to call in.

"Questions? If not, we should meet back here at, say, fourteen hundred. By then with any luck we should have a little better map of where we are, okay? Oh. Very important, fellas. Anybody shows you a press badge, I don't care for what, local, national, print, broadcast, your only response is to give 'em my phone number. From this moment on, all information about this case comes from my office, period. Okay, if there are no questions, let's go to work."

After Carlucci informed Chief Detective Sporcik that he planned, on the advice of Rocksburg PD Chief Nowicki, to interview Attorney Panagios Valcanas, Carlucci called Valcanas's office to make an appointment while Milliron called the pathology lab in Conemaugh General to see if Coroner Wallace Grimes had returned.

"My guy can see us right now," Carlucci said. "How'd you do?"

"Grimes is in a garage in Youngstown. Whoever picked up said he had dirt in his carburetor, won't be back for at least two hours."

"C'mon, let's go talk to my guy while he's still sober."

"Drink a lot, does he?"

"Owns stock in a distillery is what I heard. Wantsa make sure it keeps operatin'."

"You kiddin' me?"

"It'd have to be a pretty small distillery, wouldn't it? One guy thinkin' he could make a difference?"

"Sometimes, Rugs, I don't know whether you're puttin' me on or not, you know?"

"If you don't know, I probably am. C'mon, man, look at me, I gotta have some fun. How'd *you* like your mother bustin' you one, huh? Surprised you even understand what I'm sayin'. You wanna drive or me?"

"Since you know where we're goin', why don't you?"

They walked out of the courthouse, turned north on Main, crossed at the light, walked to the middle of the next block, then Carlucci turned up the steps to a red brick building.

"What are we goin' in here for? Your car in back?"

"Uh-uh. This is it."

"This is it? This is where we're goin'? Why'd you ask me if I wanted to drive if we were only comin' here?"

"Well, I know how much you like to drive. I thought maybe you wanted to make the siren go, stop traffic in the middle of the inter-section or somethin'."

"You know, I'm not havin' any trouble understandin' you at all. I mean, I can understand what you're sayin'. It's just I don't understand *you* sometimes. I know you think I'm a good cop, why you pullin' my chain so much lately?"

"How tall are you?"

"Huh? How tall? Six one. Why?"

"How much you weigh?"

"How much do I weigh? What's this about?"

"Just tell me."

"Two ten, around there. What're you askin' me this stuff for?"

"Look at me, man," Carlucci said. "I'm five eight with my shoes on. Yesterday mornin' I weighed one fifty-two with all my clothes on—except my guns. I'm forty-six years old, I live with my mother, and she's startin' to punch me. I'm just clownin' with you, man, that's all, don't read nothin' else into it, okay?"

Milliron shook his head and shrugged, trying to figure out what Carlucci was telling him. Carlucci led the way back a hall the depth of the building to the office of Panagios Valcanas, Attorney-at-Law.

Milliron, pointing to the lettering on the door, said, "You know, I've never understood that, that attorney-at-law stuff. An attorney's a lawyer, right? So why's it gotta say attorney *at* law?"

"Not necessarily. Attorney's a person just actin' in someone else's turn. Like if somebody gives you power of attorney, that means they're sayin' you can act in their turn—whenever their turn comes. Doesn't mean you passed the bar exam."

"You puttin' me on again?"

"Look it up. Used to be spelled with a 'u' instead of an 'o.'"

"What did?"

"Attorney. Used to be spelled a-t-t-u-r-n-e-y. You can look it up." Carlucci went through that door and stopped in the cramped front office by the desk of a hulking, somber-looking woman who was typing so fast on an IBM Selectric typewriter it sounded like several people typing at once. He held his ID case out. She looked up at it and then at him while continuing to type without losing speed.

"I just called? To see Attorney Valcanas?"

She didn't interrupt her typing, just nodded toward a door behind her.

Carlucci led Milliron around her desk and knocked on the door she'd indicated and heard Valcanas say to come in.

They found Valcanas in his underwear washing his armpits with-paper towels in the sink in the john. "Have a seat," Valcanas said. "Be right with you. Gimme a minute."

They sat in two worn wooden chairs in front of a cluttered desk and exchanged smirks while Valcanas dressed. "I love garlic," he said, when he'd finally put his pants and shirt and tie on, "but sometimes my lady friend gets carried away. Keep telling her if she's gonna use four large cloves in two cups of marinara sauce, she has to sauté it first, otherwise the next day it just oozes out of every pore . . . but you know how women are. Some women. Italian women. Some Italian women. What happened to your mouth?"

"An Italian woman," Milliron chirped up.

"Hey, man, that's my mother, okay?"

"Just exchangin' information, that's all."

"Your mother did that?"

Carlucci nodded, then said, "Uh, Mister Valcanas, if you didn't hear, somebody shot this, uh, J. D. Lyon, and Chief Nowicki said—"

"Oh I heard alright, believe me, it's all over. News *that* delicious breaks the sound barrier gettin' around."

"Uh-huh. Well Chief Nowicki said you'd done a lot of work with the union back when he closed Conemaugh Steel down, and maybe you could help us out."

"Your mother did that? Really? Intentionally?"

"Yeah, well, sometimes with her it's not easy to tell. But this time, you know, I, uh, I'm pretty sure."

Valcanas gave a little whistle while shaking his head in commiseration. "That's rough. Ah, well, as to your other problem here, I don't know how much help I can be, what do you have in mind?"

"Well, you know, really, anything you can tell us. Anybody you think of, you know, who might have a real hard-on for this guy?"

"Oh God," Valcanas said, laughing. "Everybody except the stockholders. They would've made love to him in public if they could. Naturally. The man had just one interest here, and that was making money for the stockholders, and since his compensation was based on how the stock performed, it's no great stretch to imagine what his managerial style was. Slash and burn. So if you're lookin' for suspects, I don't envy you, you've got a lotta talkin' to do."

"Well could you sort of narrow it down?" Milliron said.

Valcanas shook his head. "Not possible. Look, that company was on the verge of collapse back in the middle seventies, and the board, as you can imagine, naturally got real antsy about the stockholders findin' out just how much they'd screwed up, so they went huntin' for a fixer. And they got one of the best. But fixers come on their terms, not yours. Lyon, hell, all the guys like him, first thing they do, they work out a real specific plan about what the directors expect, and they don't let anybody get mushy around the edges. They pin 'em down, they get it in writing, and they're either lawyers themselves—which Lyon was—or else they know some damn good lawyers.

"When he came in, I can't recall whether it was '76 or '77, I mean, comparatively speaking, he asked for peanuts, maybe a hundred thousand plus expenses the first year. But, if he turned the stock around, and I'm not gonna pretend I know the exact formula they worked out, but believe me, his contract called for huge bonuses, both cash and stock, based exclusively on the performance of the stock. And 'cause that's who they were worried about, you know, the stockholders, I mean who else would they be worried about? Hell, they didn't give a damn about anything else, equipment, plant, personnel. And when I say huge bonuses this is not barroom chatter. Don't quote me on the numbers, but the year he shut it down, he called in options that were worth twelve million plus.

"And every year since, even though he probably doesn't work—or didn't work more than five days a month on Conemaugh Steel business, he's still takin' home half a million a month—or he was. And I don't doubt that, not for a second. Course to be honest, I don't know that that was all comin' from Conemaugh Steel. Conemaugh, remember, was just the third company he'd shipped overseas since about the late sixties.

"But you have to give the bastard his due. I mean, when it came to steel, he saw probably before anybody else that the industry couldn't continue to function the same old way it had since Carnegie. Those days of integrated companies, you know, from ore to coal to coke to finished product and all the transportation necessary between fields and plants, hell, that kinda thing was history. The rest of those steel guys didn't want to believe what their own eyes were tellin' 'em. But Lyon, he believed it. He knew there was no way they could continue to make steel and all its raw products, wire and sheet and rods and tube the way they'd been doin' it, not with what they were payin' for labor. So in that sense, the man was a visionary. I mean, he looked, he saw, he analyzed, and he acted. Course when he was done, when he'd reorganized it through bankruptcy court, and then when he made the deal to merge with Knox Iron and Steel, and then, about six months later I think it was, he shut everything down and moved it all to Brazil, well, you know as well as I do what he left behind—not you, Trooper. But you, Detective, you know what I'm talkin' about. Hell, all you have to do is look around, see what you see. Empty, rusty buildings, a whole lotta people on welfare, and a whole lotta real estate generating no taxes for the city or the schools. That's the man's legacy. Plus all his charity dodges, of course."

"Yeah, but what about the union?" Milliron said. "The Steelworkers. I mean, I thought the union, you know, they wouldn't let anybody get away with that kinda stuff, just close it down without warning. There are laws about that stuff."

Carlucci shrugged at Valcanas and nodded toward Milliron. "He's a farmer. From Mercer. Believes all that crap about big, bad unions."

Valcanas smiled and shook his head. "First place, Conemaugh Steel was never part of national bargaining. They were what was called a me-too company. The big ones, U.S. Steel, National, Inland, Bethlehem, J&L, Armco, Republic, and, uh, oh God, what the hell's the other one . . . Christ, can't think of anything anymore—oh, Allegheny-Ludlum, yeah, that's it. They were the big boys, they were the ones who sent the negotiators. They picked 'em, they trained 'em, told 'em what to say and how and when. But Conemaugh was never part of that. They just went along with what the big eight did."

"Yeah, but I'm talkin' about the union, not the company—"

"I know what you're talkin' about," Valcanas said. "What I'm talkin' about is, the local here, in effect, was fightin' a man that wasn't there. Because the Steelworkers, hell, they're almost as hidebound as the companies."

"I'm not followin' you," Milliron said. "I thought there was just one big union."

"There was. Still is. But they weren't worried about companies like Conemaugh Steel. Hell, in its heyday, it never had more than a thousand employees. That was during Big Two and Korea. That's wars I'm talkin' about. Three, four years after Korea was over, they started cuttin' back, in the late fifties. By the time Lyon got here, they probably didn't have half that many employees. They weren't makin' coke anymore, they quit makin' steel by '58 or '59, they were just buyin' it and finishin' it. Next thing they shut down was the tube mill. And at the end, hell, all they had runnin' were the rail mill and the wire mill, and they were runnin' them with skeleton crews.

"But the Steelworkers, the national, hell, they weren't fussin' around with Conemaugh, they were too busy with the big dogs. What applied at Bethlehem in Maryland was supposed to apply to U.S. Steel in Homestead or Donora or wherever. But if the company wasn't involved in the bargaining on the national level, which Conemaugh wasn't, the national union didn't pay a whole lot of attention to the local either. They were dealin' with all the locals from the big eight—now they may've said they weren't, they may've put out the propaganda they were tryin' to deal with every local's problems but that was strictly for the tourists, 'cause believe me they weren't. I had that hammered into my head every day for three years. And anyway, the Steelworkers, of all the national unions, hell, they were about as democratic as the Teamsters. In fact, most of the time they were supposed to be adversaries? Huh? Steelworkers over here, big steel over there, and never the twain shall meet? That was bullshit."

"What?" Milliron shot a quizzical frown at Carlucci.

Carlucci said, "Just listen, okay? It ain't the way all these Republican-owned newspapers and TV stations say it is, okay?"

"Well I don't know about that," Milliron said testily. "I think big labor unions are exactly the way the Republicans say they are."

Valcanas reached down, opened a drawer, and brought up a bottle of gin and a small tumbler. He poured himself two fingers. "I know you fellows are on duty so I'm not gonna offer you any, but if I'm gonna have to explain all this, I'm gonna need some help." He tossed the gin back, poured two more fingers, and bared his clenched teeth while leaning back in his creaky swivel rocker.

"I'm only gonna say this once, so I hope you know shorthand or you've got a tape recorder, okay? You ready?"

"We're ready," Carlucci said, shooting his own frown back at Milliron.

"No matter what you think of big labor, so called, the facts in Conemaugh Steel's case are these as I know them, and I'm gonna leave out a ton of detail. Just gonna give you the overview.

"Number one, when Lyon came in to fix it, it was damn near broken. They'd been losin' money like crazy. And their accountants didn't have a clue what to do with the losses. First thing—I mean before he shut the coke plant and turned the furnaces off—first thing he told the board was they needed some accountants who were hip to the section of the IRS Code containing the net operating loss carry-forward—"

"The what?" Milliron said.

"The net operating loss carry-forward exemption. I forget the section number. The deal is, it was created at the end of World War One by Congress to give those companies a break that were retoolin' to go back to makin' peacetime goods. Supposed to last only until those companies got back on their feet, you know, but like a lotta things Congress does, once they pass it, they forget about it, which is what they did here. Forgot to repeal it after it did what it was supposed to do, which was, help those companies that had helped the government by stoppin' what they did in order to produce matériel for the war. So it just sat around in the tax code till the sharpies at Penn Central rediscovered it when they took that railroad through the Chapter 11 cha-cha back in the late sixties, early seventies, I forget exactly when. I'm not gonna explain the Penn Central thing now, but there's been plenty written about it so you can do your own research at your leisure.

"My point is, Lyon was very familiar with loss carry-forwards and the wonderful tax dodge they represented. As I've said, he'd already taken two other steel companies overseas and he'd put both of those through Chapter 11 reorganization first, so he wasn't doin' anything here he hadn't done before. The thing he did here that he hadn't done with the other two was, uh, part of his reorganization plan was to stop payin' the pensioners on the pretext that the pension fund was just another creditor, or vendor. And the state courts wouldn't even touch that, they said that was strictly federal stuff, so we took it through the federal courts, and I forget how far along we were exactly when the U.S. Supreme Court ruled against, uh, oh God, who was it now? Aw shit. Can't remember, was it Wheeling Steel? Or J&L? I'll be damned. Can't remember shit anymore. Anyway, it was one of those two, and the U.S. Supreme Court ruled against 'em, said they couldn't treat their pensioners like any other creditor or vendor, they had to pay 'em, so that made the local's suit against Conemaugh moot.

"But anyway, by that time U.S. District Court finally got around to docketing our suit that they open the pension fund books, and that's when we all discovered that there was some nefarious somebody, who to this day shall remain nameless 'cause the federal Labor Department or the Justice Department or the IRS could not—or would not—ever get enough investigators into the field to discover who that somebody was. This somebody had just taken the ol' pension piggy bank, turned it upside down, and everything that fell out, God only knows where he or they put it. Period. The fund's trustees were still there, the administrator was still there, there was just no money there.

"And all this stuff sorta came together at about the same time. Lyon arrived here in '76 or '77 I believe, then by '82 he had the company in Chapter 11, which of course enabled him to stop payin' everybody, which he thought also included the pensioners, then it was, uh, lemme see, '85 when they got outta Chapter 11, yeah, at about the same time as he was announcing the merger with Knox Iron and Steel, which is when we found out the pension money was gone. And then it wasn't too very long thereafter, six months or so, he was announcin' the move to Brazil."

"Wait wait wait," Milliron said. "If he was doin' all this, then how the hell could he—I mean you said his compensation was based on how the stock was doin', hell man, what you're describin' is a company goin' in the toilet."

"Exactly," Valcanas said. "But every time he shut down another department and laid off fifty or sixty more grunts, the stock went up. What, you're not familiar with that phenomenon?"

"Yeah, but how could that be, I mean, you said he had it in bankruptcy court. Stock can't be goin' up when it's in bankruptcy, c'mon."

"Look, I'm not gonna explain the tax advantages of loss carryforwards to you, I don't have time for that. Talk to an accountant. I'm givin' you the short course in how to bust out a company 'cause the detective here is a friend of a friend—and that's also why it's free, but I don't have all day to give you a seminar on all its aspects. You don't believe me, fine, do your own research. I will tell you, Trooper, that Chapter 11 means as long as your reorganization plan's been approved and is in effect, you don't pay your creditors. Loss carry-forwards mean you can write off your losses for as much and as long as the IRS says you can. You don't think those two things make it a whole lot easier for you to make money, then you need to study arithmetic—but I'm not gonna argue with you about your idea of Adam Smith's capitalism. Some companies make money by makin' a great product and marketing it efficiently, but a lotta companies—way too many in my opinion—a lot of 'em have discovered it's far easier to make money by manipulating the tax codes than it is by offerin' great products or services. Now you wanna debate that, some other time maybe, but not now."

"I don't get this," Milliron said, squirming around in his chair. "I mean, you're in bankruptcy court, you can't be makin' stockholders happy, that doesn't make sense."

"Talk to an accountant is what I said. Ask him to explain net operating loss carry-forwards to you. I assure you, it's not a fairy tale. A company with losses is permitted to carry those losses forward from year to year to write off against their profits. You can argue with me all you want, you're not gonna make that section of the IRC disappear."

Milliron suddenly stood up and started pacing. Valcanas shrugged at Carlucci; Carlucci shrugged back.

"Yo, Pinky, what's the problem?"

"My father, hey . . . this is crap. My father didn't do that. He had a loss, he took the loss, he didn't go . . . he didn't go . . . crap, I don't believe you."

"Uh, what did your father do?"

"He's a farmer. Still is."

"He do his taxes himself?"

"Yeah, course he did. We didn't have any accountant doin' 'em for us."

"Should've."

"But that's just nuts. That's not the way it's supposed to work! You run your farm right, you make money. You don't run it right, or the weather dumps on your head, you lose money. You don't get a tax break 'cause you lose money. Who ever heard of that?"

"Well, I can see this is very upsetting to you, Trooper, but yes you do—course now I don't know if operating losses apply to farmers, so I shouldn't be saying they do. But that would be all the more reason your father needs to get himself an accountant. No shame in needin' help doin' your taxes, son. Christ, I quit doin' mine twenty years ago. No way I could keep up every time Congress decided to reform the tax code, make it more equitable—God help us all."

Milliron swung around and glared at Valcanas. "You can bet your buns I'm gonna check this out, mister. And you better not be pumpin' mud up my rump."

Valcanas shrugged at Carlucci again. "Have I said anything here sounds like I'm tryin' to get in his wallet?"

"Not that I heard."

"Son, you're a state police trooper," Valcanas said. "So I'm assumin' you've been trained by the great commonwealth of Pennsylvania. Ask yourself what possible motive could I have for givin' you wrong information about the federal tax code? Seems to me you got a case of wantin' to shoot the messenger for bringin' you bad news. Uh, listen, fellas, I've got clients comin', and nature's callin' me, so, uh, if you don't mind, I think I've got to call a halt here."

"Oh. Sure, sure," Carlucci said. "Listen, if you can think of anybody specifically, you know, I mean, I heard what you said about how he screwed everybody around, this Lyon, but if you can think of anybody at all who mighta had a bigger grudge, you know—"

"Well, he wasn't the one who screwed the foremen around, that was done before he arrived, but he was the one givin' 'em the bad news, so they probably associate him with their particular problems. What I'm sayin' is, if I was in your place, I'd probably be talkin' to the foremen first."

"Why?"

"Well, 'cause those guys, they weren't blue-collar no matter what kinda clothes they wore, and the suits never really treated them as peers, and then they got really unhappy when they found out they were never part of any pension fund. Wouldn't've made any difference in the end of course, 'cause all the pension money disappeared, but I think it really bothered the hell outta some of those guys to find out that nobody, neither the company nor the union, had ever bothered to set up a fund for them. I know of at least two who died from gunshot wounds while hunting, officially accidents if you believe the coroner. God knows how many more drank themselves to death, drove their cars into concrete walls. But I'd sure start with who's left if I were you."

"Thanks, Mister Valcanas. Appreciate your takin' the time."

"Yeah. Thanks," Milliron grumbled.

"You're welcome. I think."

Outside, as they were walking back to their cars, Carlucci said, "Man, you really got pissed in there. I didn't know that about you. Always thought you were pretty cooled out."

Milliron let out a noisy sigh. "Hey. You don't know how many times I had to listen to how tight money was. First eighteen years of my life I never once put on new clothes. Which woulda been okay, lotta kids I knew had to do that. 'Cept I was bigger than my older brother. He got the new clothes, I was the one goin' everywhere with my socks and pockets showin'. Now I find out my father shoulda had an accountant? If that shyster's tellin' the truth—and I'm gonna check, believe me, I don't care if I gotta pay an accountant myself—I mean if that's true . . . damn, that's not . . . that's not gonna be real easy to live with."

"Yeah. Guess not. I mean, I can imagine," Carlucci said. "But look at you now. Long as your pants are, can't tell whether you're even wearin' socks."

"I don't wear pants, Detective. I wear trousers. Women wear pants. And guys that wanna look like women. Men wear trousers."

"Oh man, that sounds like some Marine Corps bullshit I used to hear in Nam—you weren't in the marines, were ya?"

"Yes sir. Aye, aye, sir. Four years."

"Oh you're shittin' me. You? A leatherhead? Christ."

"It's neck, not head, okay? Leatherneck."

"Oh, and I'll just bet you were a fuckin' MP."

"You'd win. Except for boot camp, did the whole hitch in Guard Company. That's what I went in for."

"And those dress blues too, don't shit me, Pinky, I can see the whole story now. Farm boy tired of wearin' hand-me-downs, wants those dress blues, with that pretty red stripe down the pants—"

"Trousers, okay? Not pants, trousers—"

"Okay okay, trousers. Red stripe down the trousers, pretty blue coat, white hat—"

"Cap, not hat, and it's not a coat, it's a blouse—"

"Aw man, what, you bought the whole bullshit?"

"It's not bullshit. It's as true to me as anything's ever been."

"Aw c'mon, man, don't get all semper fi on me, okay?"

Milliron stopped in the middle of the sidewalk and glared down at Carlucci. "Look. I don't know what you got against marines, but I'm really proud that I am one. I enlisted, I survived boot camp at Parris

Island, I survived advanced infantry training at Camp Lejeune, I served almost three and a half years in Guard Company in the Second Division and at Cherry Point. I got two meritorious promotions, I got a Good Conduct Medal, and I was recommended for re-enlistment. And four years, man, I won expert badges in rifle and three years expert in pistol. And damn right I put on the blues every November tenth, man, every Marine Corps birthday, better believe I suited up soon as I heard liberty call. And I wore my blues the rest of the day, and when I hung 'em up that night, there wasn't any puke on 'em either. Not mine or anybody else's."

Carlucci listened to all this with his chin in, his head drawn well back over his spine, looking up at Milliron.

"And I'm as proud of this uniform as I was of that one too, and don't you forget that either," Milliron said.

"Pinky," Carlucci croaked, "you can bet on that, man. I will never forget how you feel about your uniforms."

"Okay," Milliron said. "Okay. We're straight then."

"Woo boy," Carlucci said. "Never been straighter."

"Okay then. Let's go tell that DA where we are."

"Abso-fuckin'-lutely."

"Asbso what? You puttin' me on again?"

"No no. Hell no. Uh-uh. Abso-fuckin'-lutely is more absolute than absolutely, that's what I'm sayin'. That means I'm right here, right now, with you! All the way, yes sir, abso-fuckin'-lutely. You're goin' to the DA's office, report to the man, lead on, I'm with you, every step. Damn right, babe."

When they finally got in to see District Attorney Howard Failan, Carlucci tried to let Milliron do the talking. Failan listened, nodding occasionally, then said, "So Valcanas thinks you oughta start with the foremen, huh? Interesting. Well, the problem we're having right now is nobody seems to know what happened to their personnel records, Conemaugh's. Sporcik talked to somebody who said he thought their financial records were stashed in some cave in Fayette County. That turned out to be not true according to the firm that now holds title to that cave, but they gave us some more names. Apparently there are a couple companies in the business of cave-record storage and Sporcik's runnin' 'em down. So Valcanas was no help about this?"

"He helped," Carlucci said.

"He sued 'em enough times, he had to file in somebody's name."

"Anybody check the union?" Milliron said.

"That was the first place Sporcik tried. They claim they shipped all their records to Penn State like maybe twelve, thirteen years ago. Labor archives there, whatta they call it? Pennsylvania State University Labor Archives? Yeah. Harvey called them but they begged off searchin' for personnel rosters. Said they'd be happy to help if we sent somebody down to do the donkey work. I thought we oughta exhaust all the other possibilities first. Why don't you fellows go back to Valcanas, see if he'll turn his files loose, maybe you can get started there. Where's Grimes did you say? Youngstown? What the hell's he doin' in Youngstown?"

"Carburetor problems is what I was told," Milliron said.

Carlucci held up his index finger. "Uh, the feelin' I got from Valcanas was, uh, he thought the guys that might have the biggest bitch were the foremen 'cause apparently they weren't in the union, and also 'cause nobody set up a pension fund for 'em, so, you know, maybe Sporcik's wastin' his time with the Steelworkers, the rank and file."

Failan nodded several times. "Yeah, if that's true, he might be, but we don't know it's true, do we? So go pester Valcanas, scrounge some names out of him. Damn Grimes. He doesn't get back here soon, I'm gonna ship Lyon's body to Pittsburgh, get Wecht's guys to do the post. We can't keep screwin' around like this, we're gettin' calls from *Business Week, Barron's, Forbes,* the *Wall Street Journal*—I said all this already, didn't I? Yeah I know I did, don't answer that. Any of those people botherin' you?"

Carlucci and Milliron both shrugged and shook their heads no.

"You know," Failan said, scratching his nose and stretching, "the thing that's really botherin' me is we can't locate the kids—what the hell'd you do to her, Carlucci, huh?"

"Who?"

"Missus many names, no hyphens. Man, I could hear her grittin' her teeth just accepting my condolence. Tried to ease into some kinda empathetic rapport with her, but she was not forthcoming at all, wouldn't tell me where the kids are, gave me this crap about how they lead their own lives and they don't check in with her, and I know that's horsecrap 'cause I know at least two attorneys who sued her to collect bills from a couple different rehab clinics for both of those kids. I'm thinkin' that damn Carlucci, he must've really pissed her off. What'd you do to her?"

"Uh, Mister Failan, I think it was us told you she was not forthcoming, I told Pinky and he told you she had a real hard-on for local cops, you were who told us why she had the hard-on—"

"Pinky? Who the hell's that?"

Milliron cleared his throat and studied his shoes. Carlucci shrugged and pointed with his thumb at Milliron.

"You're Pinky? Why, 'cause your face—well I guess it is sort of on the pinkish side, now that I'm lookin' at you."

"Anyway, you said you'd talk to her, for us not to worry about it. Now you're askin' me what I did to her. I was super polite."

"You know," Failan said, "you better let, uh, Pinky here do the talkin', I'm havin' a helluva time understandin' you. Anyway, go on back to Valcanas, shake some names loose. And then, when Grimes gets back, and that better be soon, you two are up for the post, right?"

Carlucci and Milliron both nodded and left.

Out in the corridor, Milliron said, "Hey, d'you have to bring up my nickname?"

"Slipped out, that's all," Carlucci said. "Listen, we get in Valcanas's office, just ask him for the names, try not to start any shit about the union, okay?"

"Start what shit about the union?"

"The shit you wanna start every time you hear the word union. Just try to remember you're union yourself, you know?"

"Me?"

"Yeah, you. The letters FOP ring any bells for you? Whatta you think that stands for, funny organized police or somethin'? Fraternal Order of Police is a fuckin' union, case you forgot—"

"We're civil service, man—"

"Course you are, so am I, but who the fuck you think meets with the civil service guys, huh? You? Individually? Maybe you do, I sure as hell don't. FOP's who does my talkin', man. Fact, we're gettin' ready to sue the city right now for all the chief's pay I didn't get when I was actin' chief and for all the actin' sergeant's pay three other guys shoulda got. You think I'm gonna hire my own shyster for that? That's what I pay dues for. So you gonna act right now or what? 'Cause my lip's really hurtin' now, you got any aspirin, huh?"

"I got aspirin in my first-aid kit, don't you?"

"I don't wanna go back to my car. Don't you have any on ya?"

"Do you?"

"Just askin', man, you don't need to get testy."

"Don't need to get tethty," Milliron mimicked him.

"C'mon, man, it hurts. Let's go, Christ, maybe Valcanas'll have some. Many hangovers as he has, he gotta be buyin' big bottles."

O utside Valcanas's office, Carlucci stopped in front of the secretary who typed so fast she sounded like several persons typing. Unlike their previous encounter, this time she stopped typing while she glared up at him.

Milliron, talking over Carlucci's shoulder, said they were there on orders from the DA, and had to have Attorney Valcanas's cooperation, and was he available at that moment.

She turned her glare on Milliron. "Like that means something," she said, exhaling dismissively. She picked up the phone, pushed a button, then turned her back and said something neither of them could hear. Then she turned back, hung up, and nodded toward the door behind her. "Life's a party," she said. "Beware those who spit in the dip."

"Excuse me?" Milliron said, but Carlucci nudged him away from her toward the door to Valcanas's office. Inside, they found Valcanas standing by a floor-model stereo record player, humming and wiping a long-playing record with a blue cloth, looking over his shoulder at them as they came in.

"Forgotten but not gone . . . my favorite Dorothy Parker line," he said, then added, "Like you guys would know what I was talkin' about."

Milliron screwed up his face at Carlucci and said, "What are these people talkin' about, do you know? Spit in the dip? Dorothy who?"

"Just tell the man why we're here, okay?"

Milliron explained why DA Failan had sent them back, asking finally if Valcanas would be willing to help.

Valcanas listened while continuing to dust the record; then he put it on the turntable and carefully set the needle on it. In a moment there came a rhythmic scratching and then the sound of a piano, bass, guitar, and drums followed by the raspy, guttural voice of a woman singing something about a little red rooster.

Valcanas's face broke into a wistful smile at the sound of her voice and he eased into a sly dance across the room, snapping his fingers softly and mouthing the words as he headed toward his outer office. In a few minutes, he danced back in with a bulging accordion file, which he handed to Milliron as he slowly swirled past on his way to the stereo, where he restarted the record.

"Names in there are just the foremen who hired me, the ones naïve enough to believe the courts were gonna correct the, uh, oversight was the word they used. Yeah. Buncha people work for you for decades, see that your product gets made to your specifications and satisfaction, but when you think pension fund, somehow they don't quite make it up into your field of vision." While talking, Valcanas was rocking slowly in time with the woman singing about the little red rooster that just wouldn't stay home.

"And just because I'm full of public spirit," Valcanas went on, "I'm gonna save you fellas some time and tell you that at least two of the men named in there died from gunshot wounds when they were hunting. Coroner ruled 'em both accidents."

"You said that before," Milliron said.

"So I did, yes. Well, doesn't hurt to say things like that twice. Anyway, another one got dead, also officially accidentally, when he tried to move a bridge with his car. And yet still another used his car to try to chop down a tree, and the coroner also said that was an accident. And I also know that at least one was murdered by his wife, and I know that 'cause I defended her. Like to hear about that happy couple?"

Continuing to dance and without waiting for an answer, Valcanas said, "After J. D. Lyon moved everything to Brazil—except himself of course—this woman's husband started to believe his wife wasn't giving him her unquestioning loyalty, you know, when he couldn't find a job that paid anywhere near the one he'd lost and also when he found out he couldn't get welfare unless he allowed the state to put a lien on their house. So, he started blaming her for his bad luck. Started talkin' with his fists, in other words, so finally, to save herself, she did what any reasonable person would do. She got his deer rifle and shot him while he was snoozin'.

"Then, of course, the state felt obliged to prosecute her, spent many thousands of dollars doing that, and, despite my best efforts, she wound up doin' twenty-three months in Muncy for, uh, oh somewhere around forty-five, fifty bucks a day courtesy of the rest of us—all the while mind you, Mister Lyon continued to live like royalty on Club Road for nearly fifteen years—until recently of course. None of that little melodrama cost him more than a couple molecules of sweat 'cause see, he pays almost no taxes—paid—all his money being tied up in two charitable foundations, both of which he is of course the executive director of. And in that capacity he received a wonderful salary, plus expenses. But it certainly cost the rest of us a lot of money, don't you agree?

"Consider, for example, all the man-hours put in by various police officers to determine whether those fellas had indeed accidentally shot themselves while hunting. Or think of all the man-hours put in by the EMTs and the rescue people scrapin' those guys off the insides of their cars. You know, you can talk volunteerism all you want, but a lotta people doin' good works for their fellowman get paid actual Yankee dollars. And as the insurance boys love to say, every accident causes all our rates to go up.

"But I notice from your expression, Trooper, you think I'm exaggerating for effect. Well, maybe I am. But now, see, it seems somebody else has decided it was time for Lyon to share some of the social expense I've just been describing, and you sit there, Trooper, with my files in your lap, expecting me to be cheerful while you practically demand my cooperation."

"Excuse me? If I'm followin' you at all, it sounds like you're tryin' to say this Lyon deserved to get shot, is that what you're sayin'?"

Valcanas spun slowly to his left, then to his right in time with the scratchy rhythm on the record. "I think I've said everything I want to say—except for one thing. Before you start usin' my copying machine, be advised that I charge the state—which is to say *you*—the same as the post office charges the public, okay? Quarter a page."

Milliron shot a look at Carlucci. "Who said anything about usin' his copyin' machine?"

"Uh, Mister Valcanas," Carlucci quickly piped up, "okay with you if we use your conference room to copy these names?"

Valcanas nodded, eyes closed, still swaying in time with the troubles of the little red rooster, and Carlucci jumped up with a quick double tap on Milliron's sleeve to get him out before he said anything else to annoy Valcanas.

The secretary was inserting a fresh sheet of paper in her IBM Selectric when Milliron asked where the conference room was. She pointed with her thumb to a door on the other side of her desk. Then she started typing again, a rattling blur of sound that caused Milliron to give an admiring whistle at her speed.

Her hands flew up off the keys as though shocked. "This isn't a carnival, Smokey, and I'm not a sideshow," she growled, "so piss off."

"Uh, sorry. Jeez." Milliron bumped into Carlucci in his haste to move away from her.

Inside the conference room, Carlucci whispered, "Just curious. You thought it was a good idea to whistle at her?"

"Never saw anybody type that fast before, I was tryin' to pay her a compliment. Most people, you know, they like to be complimented."

"Uh, Pinky, my experience is, the last person you wanna piss off is the gatekeeper. 'Cause if you have to call her tomorrow, huh? You think she's gonna do anything but put you on hold forever?"

"Jeez, man, that whistle, that's a compliment where I come from."

"Well how 'bout where she comes from?"

"How am I supposed to know that? Okay, so maybe I shouldn't've whistled. Said I was sorry, Jesus. Man, what's with these people any- way—how's this guy survivin'? Middle of the day, he's half-looped, playin' records, dancin', got a secretary big as a bear, 'bout half as good-lookin', acts like her hind leg's caught in a trap—does he have any clients that pay him? You know, *actual* dollars?"

"Keep your voice down, man, she's right on the other side of the door. And how they survive ain't our problem, okay? He does alright, don't worry, c'mon, open that up, let's see what we got."

Twenty minutes later they'd copied the names and addresses of twenty-three foremen in Valcanas's two class actions, one against Conemaugh Steel Corporation, the other against the United Steel- workers of America.

"Okay, lemme just go ask him which ones are dead and then we'll find some phones and see how many of the rest of 'em are still around," Carlucci said. Then he lowered his voice and said, "And maybe you should be the one to give Supertypist this file back and, uh, you know, apologize again? Tell her you admired her skill and that's all that whistle was, you didn't think she was a dancin' bear or anything really stupid like that. Only Christ, hold it, don't even think the word bear, okay? 'Cause I already know you think she looks like one."

"Hey. I think I know how to apologize. I don't need any instruction from you. Gimme that thing, Jesus."

"Yeah yeah," Carlucci said, following Milliron out of the conference room and hurrying past Supertypist, knocking on Valcanas's door and quickly going in and asking Valcanas if he would please check off the names of the foremen he knew were deceased on the list Carlucci handed him.

Valcanas complained about his failing memory while reading over the list but finally put a check by five names and handed the list back. Carlucci thanked Valcanas again and hurried out, expressing his gratitude to Supertypist as he broke into a trot to catch up with Milliron, who was disappearing through the front door.

On the sidewalk, Carlucci said, "Well? She accept your apology?"

"I guess."

"You guess? Didn't she say anything?"

"Didn't bite my head off if that's what you mean. I think in her case that might mean she accepted it, but she didn't say *actual* words to that effect, no."

"C'mon, let's go down to my station, use the phones there. Think you're gonna have to do most of the talkin', I don't think anybody's gonna be able to understand me with this lip."

"I don't understand you, and your lip doesn't have anything to do with it. I don't understand anybody in this town. Never saw so many people so pissed off. It's like it's, uh, a communicable disease, like measles or somethin'. I mean it, man, I never had to deal with so many people so pissed off about somethin' I didn't know what it was."

"Ah, just Rocksburg, that's all. Most of the people livin' here, they know it's probably gonna get a lot worse before it gets better—if it ever does."

"Well they don't like it here, why don't they move? Go someplace else, what the hell's keepin' 'em here?"

"What, you think people can change their situation just because they want to?"

"If you really don't like your situation, yeah, of course."

"Where you from again? Mercer? Or Mars? What, 'cause you joined the marines, got away from Mercer, and now you're workin' for the state cops—I mean, where you livin'? Now I mean. You married, got kids?"

"No I'm not married—what's that have to do with anything?"

"Where do you live? House, apartment, duplex, what?"

"Apartment. Why, what's that got to do with anything?"

"Alone? Or you got roommates or what?"

"Yeah. Two other guys."

"Both troopers, right?"

"Right. So what?"

"So where you livin', where's your apartment?"

"In Westfield Township."

"Ohhhhh, out in the township, yeah, okay. Don't live in Rocksburg, no, you live in the country, yeah, so you look around here in Rocksburg, you think, man, why're all these people so pissed off, and if they are, why don't they do somethin' about it? If *I* was pissed off and *I* didn't like it here, *I* would do somethin' about it. I'd join the marines, I'd sign up for the state cops—I'd go to work for the government. Well you're here now, man. And you're gonna stay here till you get transferred. So if you wanted to get transferred now, and your bosses didn't wanna transfer you, what could you do about it?"

"Aw no, uh-uh, that doesn't have anything to do with what I'm talkin' about. These people—"

"Hey, easy now," Carlucci said. "*These people* are my people. You might not like 'em, and I sure as fuck don't like all of 'em, some of 'em are real assholes, but these are the people who pay me. Every two weeks, man, I get the check, straight outta their tax dollars, my livin', my mother's livin', it all comes from them. And I'm grateful for that. So don't start with these-people-this and these-people-that, okay? Wanna find out about these people, maybe you oughta get outta the township, you know? Move in here? Find out why most of 'em can't change their situation. You think they can just, what? Sell their house and move to Florida? Huh? Retire to the beach or somethin'?"

"No, not to the beach necessarily. But why not? Lots of people do, man. Lotsa people have."

"Oh shit, yeah, if somebody wantsa buy your house, yeah," Carlucci said, laughing. "Drive around, man. Take a look at all these houses with nobody livin' in 'em. What do you think, huh? The people got such a great price for 'em, that's why they're empty? That's why they fuckin' abandoned them? Last census, the city tax collector found out there were more than four hundred houses empty in town here. But you, man, shit, I don't believe you, man, really, people can just change their situation, Jesus. Look at my mouth. I got a situation I been tryin' to figure out how to change for years, I can't do it."

"You don't wanna do it."

"What? I don't *wanna* do it, is that what you said?"

"If you wanted to change it, you'd change it. People who say they want things to change, if nothin' changes, it's 'cause they like it the way it is, otherwise it wouldn't be that way, that's basic, man."

"You know what, Pinky? We better get back to doin' what we're supposed to be doin', 'cause I'm startin' to get a bad feelin' about you and I really don't want to."

"Fine with me. Let's do what the taxpayers pay us for. Which in my case means taxpayers all over the state, not just in this . . ."

"Not just in this what?"

"Nothin'. Never mind. Let's go."

Of the twenty-three foremen who'd hired Valcanas to sue Conemaugh Steel and the United Steelworkers, five were known dead, according to Valcanas. Back in the duty room of the Rocksburg station, Carlucci and Milliron learned over the phones that of the eighteen remaining, four others had died of natural causes, according to relatives, confirmed by either the Department of Health or the Registrar of Wills. The phone company said three others had terminated service more than ten years ago, and the post office had no forwarding address for any of those three. Another had moved to Florida; Milliron located him in a nursing home in Winter Park where he'd been for more than a year. That left eight still living in Rocksburg.

"So, see? Some people actually *do* try to change their situation. And you said these people couldn't change their situation."

"Okay," Carlucci said. "So some people moved. Wanna bet on what they got for their houses—if they even had 'em to sell?"

"How about instead you check whether the coroner's back yet."

"You check, I gotta check on my mother. Man, is it gettin' hot or what? When's summer start? Twenty-first or twenty-second, which?"

"When it starts doesn't have anything to do with how hot it is in here. Somebody needs to turn the AC on, you ask me."

Carlucci called home and talked with Mrs. Comito, who said that so far the only bump in the day came when Mrs. Carlucci got upset over the way Kathie Lee Gifford was talking to Regis Philbin. Before Mrs. Comito could stop her, Mrs. Carlucci had called Channel 4 WTAE in Pittsburgh and screamed at the operator that they fire Kathie Lee. "She said they needed to get somebody who knew when to shut up," Mrs. Comito said. "And somebody with more meat on her."

Carlucci shook his head and rolled his eyes listening to that story; there was nothing else to do. But when he was satisfied there were no other problems, he hung up, looked around, and saw that Milliron was gone. He found him by the door to the parking lot chatting with Chief Nowicki.

"We gotta go. Grimes is back," Milliron said.

"I'm still workin' on your problem," Nowicki said.

"Let's go, okay?" Milliron said, hurrying away.

"What problem?"

"She still owns the house, right, your mother? Still in her name?"

"Be right with ya," Carlucci called out to Milliron. To Nowicki, he said, "Yeah, it's still hers."

"So she's not indigent."

"Never said she was."

"I didn't say you did, that's not what I'm sayin'. I'm sayin' if you're thinkin' county home, that's gonna be a problem with them. Plus you bein' a cop here. All other things equal, if she gets on the list and gets moved in ahead of other people, you know there's gonna be somebody bitchin' you had an in."

"Well that's what the fuck I'm lookin' for, you know? An in? All the years I put in here, fuck, that oughta be worth somethin', right?"

"Hey, no argument from me, Rugs, but what I'm sayin' is if that's the way you have to go, first thing you gotta do is get the house in your name. 'Cause the first thing they're gonna do is check the title, check the assessment, find out whether it's in arrears, then they're gonna ask how come, if she's in such bad shape financially, she's still able to pay the taxes—you are current with the taxes, right?"

"Yeah. Course I am."

"Well then they start checkin' you out, find out you work for the city, what kinda insurance you got, what kinda savings, hey, that's the game, man, those are the rules, I'm not tellin' you anything. But if you can get past the gatekeepers, you know, I think it can be done. But you tried this once before with her, right? Wasn't that the time she went after Bellotti, uh, you know, in your kitchen? With a knife?"

"Yeah yeah," Carlucci said, hanging his head. "Oh man, every time I bring up sellin' me the house, she just freaks. How the fuck am I supposed to do that?"

Milliron blew the horn.

"Maybe you can get her declared."

Carlucci held up his left index finger in Milliron's direction. "Get her declared?! You shittin' me? How am I supposed to get her up there, huh? Soon as she saw where I was parkin', I'd have to put her in a jacket, you kiddin'? Get her declared?! You think I'm screwed up now? Right, I can picture it, man, me rasslin' my mother outta the parkin' lot into Mental Health. Christ, I'd be in therapy for the rest of my life. Like I shouldn't be now."

"Well you know better than me there's no way you're gonna get her into any private place. Even *you* don't make enough overtime for that. So what's left? Round-the-clock nurses? How much you payin' those two women now—minimum wage, right? And if I start crackin' down on your overtime, which Bellotti wants me to do by the way—"

Milliron blew the horn again, several times.

Carlucci held up his index finger again. "He does? Since when? You never said anything before—"

"I'm tellin' you now."

"Aw fuck, man, you cut my OT, I'm screwed, you kiddin'?"

"I didn't say I was goin' to, I said he wants me to—"

"Well what the fuck, how long you gonna put him off, you can't put him off forever. Aw man, see? Now I really gotta do somethin', whether I want to or not—like I know what the fuck to do!"

"Chill, Rugs, c'mon," Nowicki said. "I can keep him busy for a while, don't sweat it. All I have to do to shut him up is tell him the FOP shyster's gettin' tired of waitin' for the next meeting about where we stand about back pay for you, me, all the guys actin' as sergeants, you know. Every time I bring that up, man, Bellotti, hey, he can't disappear fast enough. So don't worry about it. Meanwhile, Milliron's about to dislocate his arm wavin' at you, you better get goin'."

"Huh? Oh. Yeah. Okay, Wick, I appreciate it, you know, everything you're doin' here? Wish I knew what the fuck I was doin'."

"Look," Nowicki said, pointing at Carlucci's mouth. "You got a head start on justification for an evaluation, man. All you gotta do is look in the mirror. The woman is now a danger to others as well as to herself—"

"She's not *the* woman, okay? She's my mother."

"Hey, you know what I'm sayin'. But listen to me, God forbid she punches one of those ladies you got watchin' her, huh? And that lady quits? Then what're you gonna do? How about she not only quits but how about she sues your ass, huh? Then some smart-ass with a grudge reads about the suit, calls the IRS? Huh? And they ask you where all the taxes are you were supposed to be payin' for those two ladies, huh? Then what? I'm tellin' you, man, you got no choice, you got to get her evaluated."

Carlucci nodded, then sighed, shook his head, patted Nowicki on the arm, and trotted out to the parking lot where Milliron was waiting.

"C'mon, man, let's go, Grimes is startin' without us."

"Aw fuckim, what's he gonna find? Lacerated brain, caused by gunshot, manner of death homicide—like we don't know that already? We gotta be standin' right next to him while he's slicin' and dicin'?"

"Hey, I'm just doin' my job for the taxpayers, that's all, same as you—man, you don't look good. You're not gonna throw up, are ya? Hey, not in here, okay? Not in this car, man."

"Nah, I'm not that kinda sick. Maybe I should take my own car."

"Well if you're not gonna hurl, stay here," Milliron said, squealing tires out of the parking lot. "Grimes said he was startin' without us."

"You already said that. But, hey, good! Hope he's done before we get there. Last thing I wanna listen to is that saw. Can't stand that, man, reminds me of a dentist drill. I could stand goin' to the dentist if it just wasn't for that fuckin' noise."

"Take a Walkman why don't ya, that's what I do."

"You take a Walkman to the dentist?"

"If I gotta get drilled, yeah. Turn it up so loud, he wants to talk to me he gotta tap me on the chest or somethin'. Only way to go, I'm tellin' you."

"Whatta you listen to?"

"Garth Brooks. He's good loud."

"The guy that wears that big hat? Black?"

"That's him."

"Then maybe you can tell me. I happened to see him on TV one night—believe me I don't watch much TV—but I was in this bar waitin' to interview this cook, and I just happened to catch his act, saw him do somethin' I still can't figure out. When he was done with this song, he wound up with his guitar like it was a baseball bat and another guy did the same thing and they swung 'em at one another, just smashed those guitars, man, just destroyed 'em. What the fuck's up with that?"

"What, you never saw that before?"

"Yeah, rock 'n' roll assholes, but I thought this Brooks guy was supposed to be some kinda all-American boy."

"He is."

"So why'd he do that then, bust those guitars like that? I don't think a guy like him, he's not playin' no twenty-dollar thing he picked up in a pawnshop, those things gotta cost money."

"Well, what I read once is, uh, some of those guys, when they think they sounded so good they'll never sound that good again? At least not with that guitar? They break it."

"You shittin' me?"

"Just tellin' ya what I read."

"Well fuck, that's stupid. That sounds like the guy that says, hey baby, you're not gonna fuck me anymore, you're not gonna fuck any-body, so he kills her."

"Not the same thing, c'mon. It's not a person."

"It's the same attitude. He was any kinda guy, he wouldn't bust it like that, he'd give it to some kid wanted to learn how to play. That'd make sense. Bustin' it don't make sense. How d'you think the guy feels that made those guitars, huh? If I made 'em and I heard about him doin' that, I'd tell him screw you, buy your guitars from some-body else from now on."

"Guys like him don't buy their guitars, you kiddin'? C'mon. Guys are beggin' him to play their guitars—beggin' 'em to smash 'em too. The more he smashes, the more they have to make. Somebody's payin' for 'em, you can bet on that. Just not him."

"Incidentally, where we goin'? What the hell we doin' on 119 South?"

"Huh? Whatta you mean?"

"I said what the hell we doin' on 119 South? Conemaugh General's in Rocksburg, back the other way."

"Oh Christ," Milliron said, flushing an even deeper pink than he normally was. "What the hell am I thinkin'?"

"Good question. I don't think I wanna know the answer."

"Man, I better move it, don't wanna keep Grimes waitin'."

"Kept us waitin' long enough, didn't he?"

"Not the same thing. He's the guy makin' the rulings, we're the ones takin' the notes."

Grimes had indeed started without them, and he barely looked up when Carlucci and Milliron hurried into the section of the pathology lab reserved for the coroner in the basement of Conemaugh General Hospital. Grimes was too busy examining internal organs and talking into his recorder to do more than nod at their tardy arrival.

When he'd finished, and with only one exception, Grimes's preliminary findings about the death of James Deford Lyon were exactly what Carlucci had predicted: homicide as a result of brain lacerations caused by a single small-caliber bullet fired from a weapon an undetermined distance away from the deceased. The bullet had fragmented into four pieces, which Grimes said made it an "insoluble problem for the ballistics boys. My guess is a .22," Grimes said. "Pieces are very similar in size. Haven't looked at it under a magnifier yet, but their similarity indicates there's a good chance it was altered."

"Found a .22 Magnum case at the scene," Milliron said.

"Well that would certainly explain the deep penetration. One of the fragments was lodged against the inside of the right frontal sinus, and another one was just above and slightly to the rear of the left canine root. Third one was in the right Eustachian tube. Fourth was in the base of his tongue. But somebody did him a favor."

"Excuse me?" Milliron said.

"Can I see the bullet, huh, the pieces?" Carlucci said, looking around for a box of rubber gloves.

"Weren't you fellas listening?"

Milliron shrugged at Carlucci and said, "Uh, when you're talking? It's, uh, it's all Latin to me. I'm listening, but once you start with the temporal lobes and the hypo this and the posterior that, I may as well be deaf."

"You don't know what carcinoma means? Let me put it more simply. The man was terminally ill with cancer. Right lung, liver, pancreas. Very advanced. Outwardly—and this is somewhat surprising—he still looks fairly robust, but this man didn't have three months left, four tops. Very little time left and a great deal of pain to come."

"So, uh, you sayin' whoever shot him did him a favor? That's what you're sayin'?" Milliron said.

"Trooper, I'm prejudiced of course, but sudden death has always had much greater appeal to me than the protracted, intense death this man was facing. I know I'm not you and I'm not presuming to tell you how to do your job, just offering an opinion, that's all, but I'd certainly be asking his personal physician if they were aware of his condition. I can't imagine that they were not. And it might give you a different direction to explore—I'm not saying it should be explored, or even that it can be explored, just saying it might be, that's all.

"I know Failan's anxious," Grimes continued. "Tell him he'll have my full report by tomorrow at the close of the day. Any questions? If not, let me get those fragments into an evidence bag for you, and you can be on your way."

"Wait a second, okay?" Carlucci said. After putting on a pair of gloves way too large for him, he took one of the fragments from Grimes.

"This was filed. Definitely. Look there," he said, holding it up for Milliron.

"Where? Your finger's in the way, what're you pointin' at?"

"Lemme see the rest," Carlucci said. "Oh yeah, look there, see?

First he went this way across, then he went the other way across. This is what they used to call a dum-dum bullet, right, Doc?"

"Let's have a look," Grimes said, taking the fragments back from Carlucci. He took them to a table where he had a circular light surrounding a magnifying glass. He turned the light on and held the fragments under the glass. "Oh yes, it's very clear, the striations are unmistakable. Can't imagine a saw blade this thin, but I'm sure there are files thin enough, something jewelers use, hobbyists, oh yes."

"Well hell," Milliron said, "all .22s are hollow points anyway. I never heard of a solid .22 bullet. Not sayin' there aren't some, but every box I ever bought said hollow points. So it was gonna mushroom. Why'd he do that?"

"Why do you think?" Grimes said, putting the fragments into an evidence bag, marking it, and handing it over to Carlucci and then raising his right index finger. "Don't forget to sign my sheet."

"Oh, right, Doc," Carlucci said, stripping off the gloves and signing Grimes's custody sheet, filling in all the particulars.

Carlucci didn't know what to think about what Grimes had just told them, but Milliron couldn't keep his thoughts to himself, all the way to the cruiser in the parking lot and then on the way back to the courthouse.

"I didn't get that, you know, Grimes talkin' about talkin' to the man's physician, did you? What's different because he had cancer?"

"Don't know," Carlucci mumbled. "I'm thinkin' about what it would take to doctor that bullet so it would frag. A .22's really small when you think about it. Same size as a pencil eraser, so to do that you'd have to have a really small vise and you'd have to be really careful not to put too much pressure on because if you got it out of round, it wouldn't fit in the chamber, so you'd have to file just deep enough to get to the hollow, but not so deep you ruin the bullet."

"My brain went into overdrive when he said cancer, but I don't even know why. What's that change? What, was he sayin' the guy paid somebody to kill him? You could use any size vise, just wrap some foam rubber around the bullet, just tighten it enough to hold it."

"What're you askin' *me* for? He said any questions, right? Go back and ask him, you wanna know what cancer means."

"Nah, uh-uh. He scares me."

"Who? Grimes? Grimes scares you? Why?"

"People that smart always scare me."

"People that smart? How do you know he's smart?"

"You kiddin'? First, he's a doctor, then he specializes in—"

"Doctor? Shit, that doesn't make him smart, that just means his head works a certain way—"

"—then he specializes in forensic medicine, you think you don't have to be smart to do that?"

"That means he knows his job, that doesn't make him smart. Lots of people know their job. Rest of their lives, they're as fucked up as everybody else. Like me. Forty-six, still livin' with my mother. Who's punchin' me out—and I'm as good at my job as Grimes is."

"Nah, sorry, uh-uh, Grimes is a whole lot smarter than you are."

"Why? 'Cause he knows the Latin for all the body parts? And he knows what causes people to stop livin'? I took biology from a nun knew the Latin for all the body parts. She wasn't smart. Besides, you don't know anything about his private life. Bet you a hundred bucks against a dime, we started nosin' around in his life, we'd find out he was as fucked up as everybody else. And as ignorant too. Bet he doesn't know tits from tomatoes about cookin'."

"Well hell, neither do I, what's that have to do with anything?"

"Proves my point exactly," Carlucci said, licking his upper lip tenderly and thinking about how careful you'd have to be to file a cross into a .22 bullet because if you got the least bit sloppy, you'd deform the bullet, which meant it wouldn't fit into the chamber, which would make it useless.

"Proves your point how? What point? By not knowin' how to cook, what, you think 'cause somebody doesn't, that means he's not smart? He's a guy, most guys don't know about cookin', c'mon."

"No. What I'm sayin' is, if he's like most people, he knows his job and he knows about maybe two other things, hobbies, or he keeps up with the news or sports or shit like that, but otherwise, he's just as ignorant about everything else as the rest of us. Hey, how 'bout you tellin' Failan, huh? What he said."

"What who said?"

"Grimes. I gotta take some more aspirin. Take me back to my car, okay? And then you go tell Failan and, uh, I'll probably meet you there. I gotta check on my mother too."

"You're *probably* gonna meet me there? What's that mean, probably? Failan sent us both up there, he's gonna wanna hear from both of us."

"C'mon, what am I gonna tell him you can't? And he'll have to ask me to repeat everything anyway. Tired of repeatin' everything. Makes me feel stupid."

"Couple minutes ago you were tellin' me how you're at least as smart as Grimes, now you're tellin' me you're stupid?"

"That ain't what I said, I didn't say I was smarter than Grimes. I said I'm—see how I gotta repeat everything? And it hurts, talkin'. Fuckin' stitches are pullin'."

"You don't have to repeat anything for me. I understand you fine. It's what you're sayin' I'm havin' trouble understandin'. And what you're doin'."

"Gimme a break, huh? Take me to my car, you go tell Failan, soon as I get some aspirin, check on my mother, I'll be up there, okay? No probablies, I'll be there, c'mon."

"Okay, okay," Milliron said. "But you should be there when I tell him about the cancer. I don't know what Grimes was tryin' to say. And you oughta start worryin' more about this case than, uh . . ."

"Don't worry what he was tryin' to say, just tell Failan, let him worry about it. I don't think it has a damn thing to do with anything anyway—not unless he had some kinda insurance that doubled up for anything other than natural causes. And the old lady made a really big deal of tellin' me she had her own money, she didn't need him for, uh, I forget what she said exactly, her self-esteem or self-worth or identity or somethin'. She didn't need his money, she made that plain as hell. And what was that you said about me? I oughta be worryin' more about this case than somethin' else? Huh? What was that? More than what?"

"Maybe she was lyin', his wife."

"If she was, so what? Guys like him, they don't have wills. Probably had a buncha trusts, in which case, she's probably the administrator for at least one of 'em, or her lawyer is, and she'll get it right away. Me worryin' more than what about what?"

"Maybe not. Maybe he left it to somebody else. Maybe there was a girlfriend. Maybe there were a coupla girlfriends."

"Hey, don't take this wrong, okay, but you watch a lotta old movies, huh? With those Hollywood plots and shit?"

"Oh I think I *am* gonna take that wrong. What're you sayin'?"

"I'm sayin' you don't know there's even one will yet. Or one girlfriend. The guy mighta had everything in a living trust, or two of 'em, mighta had everything tied up in those foundations, you know? Remember Valcanas talkin' about his foundations? We haven't backgrounded this guy for shit, man, and you're talkin' a coupla girlfriends maybe? You're not answerin' me—worryin' more about what?"

"And this is because I might be watchin' old movies, is that what you're sayin'?"

"You're not gonna answer me, are ya? Fuckit, never mind. My lip hurts, I'm constipated. This stuff you're thinkin'? Tell Failan, he might already have a handle on that, how the money's gonna go. Forget I said anything."

"But you think it's crap, don't ya?"

"Right now, doesn't matter what I think—hey, just let me out on the sidewalk here, you don't even have to pull into the lot. Five minutes, okay? I'll be there. Ten minutes tops. Just have to check on my mother."

"You want an answer, there it is."

"There what is?"

"The answer you're lookin' for. You need to start checkin' more on this case and, uh, less on your mother. Close the door."

After Carlucci closed the door but before he could think of an answer for that, Milliron had driven off. "Well kiss my ass," Carlucci said. "Since when's it your business who I'm worryin' about?" Milliron's cruiser was already out of sight so Carlucci was talking to himself. He took a deep breath, let it out, and then hurried into the duty room of Rocksburg's station in City Hall.

At his desk, he took a couple of aspirins, went downstairs and tried to move his bowels but couldn't, and came back up to his desk and called home. According to Mrs. Comito, everything was going smoothly there for once, so he hung up just as his mother jerked the phone out of Mrs. Comito's hands, which she did every time she figured out it was him calling. He knew he'd catch hell for hanging up when he got home tonight, but tonight was tonight. Right now, before the aspirins kicked in, was when he didn't want to hear anything about how he'd screwed up whatever his mother was aiming at today.

Then he went looking for Chief Nowicki, hoping to hear that Nowicki had something good to report about getting his mother into the county home, but Nowicki was on the phone with Mayor Bellotti. Nowicki kept shaking his head at the phone and finally wrote Carlucci a note saying that the mayor was bitching about the FOP's suit against the city for back wages while Carlucci had been acting chief. "Taking it personally again," was the last thing Nowicki wrote.

Carlucci shrugged and wrote another note back saying he'd catch Nowicki later. Then he gave Nowicki a wave and left, walking to the courthouse instead of taking his city car, stewing about what Milliron had said and also kicking around the idea of what it would take, both technically and psychologically, to file a cross into a .22 bullet deep enough to guarantee that it would fragment but not deep enough to ruin it. A light touch? Patience? Dedication? Definitely dedication. Who would have that? A machinist? A jeweler? A guy that made dentures? Nah. Wasn't the job. It was what was ailing him.

arlucci went into the courthouse through the parking lot in the basement. After clearing the metal detectors there, he went upstairs and found himself on the first floor pushing his way through TV crews from all three Pittsburgh stations and through clusters of other people who had that inquisitive expression and edgy, eager manner he'd long ago come to associate with reporters. He was very glad he'd thought to come in through the basement. If he'd come in through the main entrance, he knew they would have seen him handing over his weapons, cuffs, and shield in order to clear the metal detectors in the main lobby and they would have tried to squeeze him for as much information as they could, which, given the state of his upper lip, would have been difficult at best, embarrassing at worst.

Because he had come in through the basement and checked his weapons, shield, etc., with security there, he had no trouble getting past the reporters and up the stairs to Failan's office, where he arrived just in time to follow Milliron in.

"Just gettin' here now?"

"Took the bullet fragments up to the lab, remember? Part of the case? This case?"

"What's that mean?"

Before Milliron could answer, Failan was saying how he'd finally made some progress with Mrs. Lyon's lawyer and learned that J. D. Lyon had three living trusts, one for his wife and one for each of his children, that would make them all rich beyond their dreams. Also, there was no other financial instrument leaving anything to anybody else. Lyon's foundations would continue to avoid taxes by supporting his favorite charities with the directors obliged only to vote in new chairmen, or "chairperson," Failan said. "Probably her."

Failan then went on to say that county detectives had covered most of Lyon's movements the previous day beginning with golf in West Virginia and then dinner in Berkeley Springs at a B&B there, then a nap, then a fill-up across the street, then the drive home alone as far as anybody would or could tell, although Failan was quick to add that they were still canvassing. Then he wanted to know what Grimes had to say.

Milliron did the talking and told Failan about the fragmented bullet and then came to Grimes's opinion about Lyon's cancer, probable life expectancy, and asking his doctors about it.

"I'll be damned," Failan said. "His wife didn't say anything. Lawyer neither. Wonder if they knew. Ha. Imagine that. Maybe they didn't. Well what difference does it make anyway? I don't see that it's gonna make any difference at all. He sure as hell didn't pay somebody to kill him. You don't pay somebody to put one in the back of your head—not when guys like Kevorkian are around. Do you think? Rugs? Am I missin' something here, what do you think?"

Carlucci said nothing. Just shook his head no and shrugged.

"I'll get Sporcik to put somebody on it," Failan said. "You get anything from Valcanas?"

Milliron told what they'd learned there, and what they'd been working on when they got the call that Grimes was back.

"Well then I guess you oughta pick up where you left off," Failan said, stretching his arms back over his head. "Those reporters still trippin' over each other downstairs? Boy. We haven't had a circus like this since, oh God, when was it, when they moved that trial here for that gang from just west of Philly. Back in the early eighties, wasn't it? But it was nothin' like this. I've never seen this many cameras or microphones or tape recorders in this building, but hell, this is what happens when a man with money gets murdered. If he was makin' three hundred a week, the guy who covers the county commissioners for the *Gazette* would be doin' it."

Just then Chief Detective George Sporcik came huffing in without knocking. "Excuse me, Howard, this is important."

"Always love it when you don't knock and say something's important, George," Failan said with a tight little grin.

"Well then you're really gonna love this. Frankie Krull's brother-in-law just found him somewhere around his huntin' cabin. Apparently he took one in the back of the head."

"Frankie Krull?" Failan said, groaning. "You sure?"

"Well, we heard Troop A was sendin' out their CID and scene truck to some cabin on one of the streams feeds into the Cone-maugh, you know, dead male Caucasian, obvious gunshot wound in the head. I called 'em, and, uh, apparently his wife's been tryin' to re-port him missin' for, like, three days now. Apparently finally talked her brother into goin' out to their cabin today—don't ask me why she didn't go herself. Anyway, the brother found his truck, all his gear, apparently found him about an hour ago, about a quarter mile up-stream from his cabin."

Failan turned to Milliron. "You didn't get a page about this? Well obviously not, you would've mentioned a little detail like that."

Milliron shrugged. "Krull? Who's he?"

"President of the Steelworkers local," Failan said. "Or he was—till they disbanded, or maybe they haven't, maybe they're still active, I don't know. He's been in this building a few times, I can tell you that. Course that was before he got elected president of the local. Well, you know, George, there's no reason for us to be jumpin' to conclusions here, this could be an accident."

"It's summer, Howard. Don't need a gun for trout, or bass, or walleyes—well maybe *you* do."

"Just silverware and a napkin."

"But it was no accident. Nobody's said anything so far about findin' a gun."

"Could be domestic," Carlucci said. "Him and his wife had their battles. I had to testify once."

"Right, right. God knows they had their beefs," Sporcik said. "Or—and I don't want anybody to misinterpret what I'm gonna say—it could be extraterrestrials, you know? Alien assassins? But given that the CEO of Conemaugh Steel just recently took one in the back of the head? And a couple days later the president of Cone-maugh's Steelworkers local turns up with one in the same place?"

"Who said it was in the same place?" Failan said.

"No, not the same place. They just said head wound. I'm just sayin' I think we can safely rule out drive-bys here, you know, Crips, Bloods, general breakdown of the family in black neighborhoods 'cause of CIA introduction of crack? And the ETs, Howard, which you'd know if you'd keep up your subscription to *Alien Digest,* they generally do abductions, you know, probes of all the orifices? They don't do assassinations."

"What the hell is he talkin' about?" Milliron said.

"Oh it's just George doin' a little schtick, Trooper, nothing to get excited about. He's gonna do stand-up when he retires," Failan said. "But if this isn't an accident, or domestic, then I really do hope it's somebody from outer space 'cause if it isn't . . . well, it's somebody with a grudge, course that's assuming it has anything remotely to do with Lyon. So, Trooper, uh, whattaya say, huh? Your colleagues are already on the scene, how 'bout it, wanna check it out? I think they might be a little more open to sharing information with you than with George here. George, God knows, much as I love and respect him, he does tend to get on the nerves of, uh, fellows such as yourself—if you take my meaning."

"What, you don't want me goin' with him?" Carlucci said.

"Nah, I think—tell you what, Rugs, why don't you keep doing what you were doing?" Failan said. "Checkin' out the foremen, right? See what you come up with there. Better get goin', Trooper. George, go talk to Krull's wife. And don't forget to ask her for me why she didn't go to the cabin herself, okay? Don't leave, Rugs, I wanna talk to you a second."

Carlucci stood around while the others left, wondering what he'd done to rate a private audience with Failan.

"Somethin' the matter?"

"I hope not," Failan said, rocking in his swivel rocker, his fingers laced behind his head. "But that's what I wanna ask you."

Carlucci raised his hands, palms up. "So? What?"

"Got a call from Valcanas little while ago. Very upset about the trooper's attitude. Now wait, wait, before you say anything, I know Valcanas has a special hard-on for the state guys, I mean, as many times as they've nailed him for DUI, and as many hours as he's done community service, I mean, no surprise there, right? Still, you know, he, uh, well, he seemed to find this Milliron particularly objectionable, you know, attitude-wise? So much so that I'm wondering whether it might interfere with what he's doin'?"

Carlucci shrugged hard. "How you expect me to answer that? I don't know—I mean, he thinks everybody around here's got the attitude problem, not him."

"Everybody?"

"Well not you, he didn't say anything about you. But he really couldn't figure Valcanas. Or his secretary. And he got pretty uptight when, uh, Valcanas was tellin' him some stuff about taxes. Really shook him up, I think. It was about his father. Pissed him off."

"How so?"

"Hey, Mister Failan, is this, uh, is this important? 'Cause, you know, I'm gettin' real uncomfortable here, I mean, what's this gotta do with anything?"

Failan cleared his throat and gave Carlucci one of his better political smiles. "Big case, Rugs. Big, big case. Maybe the biggest one any of us is ever gonna work, you know? And I hear one of my investigators might have a personality problem, I get nervous."

"What kinda problem? Personality? What's that mean?"

"Personality, yeah. Valcanas told me he turned over a summary of his case files, named all the principals in a couple of suits, and this fellow Milliron, apparently, he didn't even say thanks. And Mo said when he was givin' you guys the short course in the company's demise, this trooper got loud with him, told him in so many words he didn't know what he was talkin' about."

"So you're askin' me what now, I'm not sure."

"What I'm asking, Rugs, is this guy's personality such that I should move him down the table of organization here, that's what I'm askin'. Looks to be about twenty-eight, twenty-nine. What's he done so wonderful he's practically Troop A CID's number two man, that's what I'm trying to understand. I mean, before I start callin' the barracks up there, I'm askin' you since apparently you've worked some cases with him, you know? I don't wanna do somethin' I don't really need to do, start pullin' rank up there in the barracks—but before you ask, Valcanas and I go way back—and this stays here, understand?"

Carlucci nodded.

"Good. A fact I don't broadcast is that every election Mo spends a ton of hours on the phone for me, and he doesn't make it a public thing. Puts it all on his phone bill, understand? I therefore owe him a respectful ear anytime he calls, not to mention that he's given me wise counsel more than once with some things that've been handled off the record. Juvenile things, you know? From certain addresses in certain parts of the county? Which if enough people heard about I would look like I was wearin' an omelet on my chin, take my meaning?"

"Yes."

"Well, what it comes down to is this. You have any influence with this Milliron, you remind him that a courteous public servant is a good public servant, and a good public servant is one who doesn't cop an attitude with people who're makin' his work easier for him, okay?"

"Uh, no disrespect, but, uh, why don't you tell him yourself?"

"Failan's eighth rule of political survival, Rugs. Never give anybody a whippin' if you can get somebody else to do it for you. He starts to act right because of what you say to him, next time I see him, I give him a big smile, pat on the back, and leave him fulla warm fuzzies about me and cold shrivels about you. Cruel world, Rugs, and very unfair, but anybody who can't handle it goes into gardening, not politics. Let me know what you turn up with the foremen, okay?"

"Yes sir, I will."

Carlucci walked back to his station, wanting to take his jacket off because of the heat, but keeping it on because he didn't want to upset people, especially older women, who seemed disturbed by the sight of him and his Beretta. Carlucci couldn't figure it out: people saw uniformed officers with their duty belts with sidearms, handcuffs, chemical sprays, batons, every weapon that could fit on their belts, and not think a thing about it. But let him take his jacket off and invariably some old woman would call the station about a man walking around town with a gun. Maybe it was just him. Maybe it was just him and old women.

So despite the midafternoon heat he kept his jacket on; by the time he reached the dispatcher's desk, his shirt was sticking to his back and chest. He shrugged out of his jacket and stopped to talk to Bill Rascoli, retired sergeant now working as a civilian at the same job he did the last ten years he was in the department.

"Whatta you pickin' up about Krull, anything?"

"Not much. How come you ain't out there?"

"Ah, Failan wanted me in here, alibin' some people out. Ever have anything with Krull?"

"Oh yeah, couple things. Both of them with that street crap he used to pull, you know, when he was still on the outs, tryin' to get in. Tell you the truth, I'm surprised he lasted this long, as many people as he pissed off."

"Yeah, he did do that."

"Think it's connected, huh? With, uh, Lyon?"

"I seriously hope not. But who knows?" Carlucci went to his desk, hung his jacket over the back of his chair, and got out his notebook with the list of foremen who were still alive and presumably living in Rocksburg or one of the surrounding townships.

Carlucci started his calls with Abramovic, Steven W., and learned from Abramovic's daughter that he'd been in Conemaugh General in the neurological ICU with a hairline fracture of his skull and brain swelling since the previous Saturday: he'd fallen off a ladder while repairing a downspout on his porch roof. A call to the hospital confirmed that.

Albert F. Bodnar's wife said he was on the road in his Kenworth tractor, as he was every week from Sunday night to Friday night. She said that at the time of Lyon's shooting her husband had been in Detroit picking up parts for GM dealerships in Philadelphia and Trenton, and she had phone records to prove it. She gave Carlucci the

Detroit numbers so he could confirm her husband's whereabouts, which he did.

John J. Czarowicz was either not at home or not picking up.

Regis A. Horvath answered the phone himself and said he'd been just outside of Buffalo attending his youngest son's wedding and would be happy to bring in a receipt from a Super 8 motel to prove it. Plus, he said, as soon as the pictures were developed he'd be happy to bring those in to show Carlucci as well—and they were all dated. He gave Carlucci his son's in-laws' number in New York so Carlucci could verify what he was saying and ended the call by saying, "I didn't shoot that sonofabitch, if that's what you really wanna know, but whoever did it, hey, I'd buy him a drink, 'cause that prick turned my life upside down, me and a lotta other people. Put me on welfare. Hada sign my house over to the goddamn state. Yeah. Fuckim. Hope he didn't die quick."

"Uh, thanks for your cooperation, Mister Horvath."

Edward T. Novotniak's wife told Carlucci he had Parkinson's disease and could barely feed himself, his hands shook so much. "You can come see for yourself, you want to. We don't go nowhere. Only place we go's to the doctor's or the drugstore."

Rudolph R. Shimkus said he had diabetes and was legally blind. "Just had to go through the whole thing with the income tax people 'bout when I lost my sight—officially they have to know, the pricks. What a mess. Wife hada get everything notarized, they don't believe nothin' you say. Or none of your doctors neither. All 'cause of that damn Reagan, he's the one kicked everybody off disability, make you have to go prove it. Well he's gettin' his now, ain't he, huh? Got that old-timers' disease, don't he? But he still won't know what it's like to talk to some goddamn bureaucrat 'bout whether you had your leg amputated or not like I did, from the knee down. I had to go down there, take the goddamn thing off, and shake it at 'em, said you think I could work with this? And I says, where am I 'posed to get a job anyway? Goddamn mill's closed, who cares whether I'm abled or disabled, ain't no jobs for me anyway—oh, I told 'em, I give 'em a piece of my mind, goddamn right. Finally give us back my disability, only took 'em 'bout two and a half years, that's all, the sonsabitches. But if I didn't go down the goddamn office and take my leg off for 'em, they wouldn'ta done that. And I ain't gonna tell you what we had to eat while they were makin' up their goddamn mind, I'm ashamed what my missus had to eat, I couldn't even look at her. Yeah, that's what them pricks did to me . . . me and my wife. Couldn't have dinner together no more. Couldn't look at her, couldn't face her, so goddamn ashamed what my money put on the table."

"Uh, I'm sorry about your problems, Mister Shimkus. Thanks for your help."

"Oh I'm gonna lose my other leg here pretty soon, yeah. But least now we got the Medicare, so that makes it a whole lot easier. Didn't have that, I don't know what the hell we'd do. Go stick up a bank and get caught, then they'd have to take care of me."

"Well, I'm glad you don't have to do that, sir. And I hope you're feelin' better."

Carlucci had the most trouble finding Paul J. Sroka, who was now not only working as a janitor in the First Pentecostal Church in Westfield Township but was also living in the church basement. He couldn't prove where he'd been every minute of the past week, but he was sure he'd been at the church every day because he'd been planting blue spruce trees around the parking lot, and he was sure his boss, the Reverend Whitman Whidby, would vouch for that. Sroka said he'd forgiven J. D. Lyon for the pain he'd caused him and felt sure God would forgive Lyon as well come Judgment Day. Carlucci called the Reverend Whidby and heard that Sroka "was always finding something to do. He's an excellent worker and we're just delighted to have him. Been planting trees and shrubbery since the ground's gotten hard enough to work after that rainy spell we had through May. We've had a lot of catching up to do on the grounds 'cause of all the rain."

"Ever miss work?"

"No. Course now that he's living here that would be pretty hard to do. Has a room in the basement. Fixed it up kinda nice. Couldn't stay in his house after his wife passed. Lost her the end of March. He couldn't stand sleepin' there without her, just bein' in that empty house. Well I can certainly understand that, so it's good all around, you know, that we have a place for him here."

Luke J. Stefanko had been painting his mother's apartment and sleeping there since Monday. He'd left there only long enough to get his mail and some fresh clothes—Carlucci just happened to catch him at home, otherwise, he said, he would've been at his mother's place. He gave Carlucci his mother's number, and she confirmed what her son had said, but neither of them could think of anybody else who could back them up, except of course the people at Conemaugh Paint and Paper on Estry Street who sold him the paint.

"You pay for the paint with a check, or with a credit card?"

"Oh no, cash. Strictly cash, yeah."

"Well that wouldn't prove you'd been there anytime recently, so why do you think they'd remember you?"

"Oh hell, everybody knows me in there. I deal there all the time, that's what I been doin' for the last ten years, paintin', yeah, insides, outsides, houses, garages, barns, yeah. Ain't real steady, but I get by, no, go ask 'em, they'll tell ya. Course they'll also probably tell ya I was just tickled as hell to hear that sonofabitch got his. Finally. Bastard. Many people as he put outta work? Hell, if I had any guts I'da done it myself, goddamn right. Oh I ain't sorry that prick's dead, not a bit, no sir. Bastard got rich on his stocks while we got poor. Jesus, hundreds of guys missed all that work all those years? Some of 'em still ain't workin', bet if you took a count, it'd be, hell, I don't know, couple hundred. More. But nobody ever counts 'em now, do they, huh?"

"But, uh, Mister Stefanko, can't you give me a name for anybody, other than your mother I mean, who could verify where you were the night he was killed?"

"Well, not if you put it that way, no, I guess not. So where do we go from here? Where's that leave us, huh?"

"I'll get back to you, Mister Stefanko. You keep thinkin' about it, okay? Not that I don't trust your mother, but, uh, see if you can think of anybody else can verify you were there, okay? And thanks for your cooperation, I appreciate it."

Carlucci tried Czarowicz again. Finally, on the tenth ring, just as Carlucci was getting ready to hang up, a gnarly voice said hello.

"John Czarowicz? Used to be a foreman in the shipping department at Conemaugh Steel?"

"Who wants to know?"

"Detective Sergeant Carlucci, Rocksburg PD. You John Czarowicz?"

"Maybe. Unless you want money. I ain't buyin' no tickets for no kids for no phony circus, I ain't fallin' for that crap again."

"Uh, that wasn't us, sir. That was a coupla grifters workin' a scam. If you mailed 'em money, I'm sorry, but next time anybody says they're callin' for money? And they say they're from the police department? You call us right away, alright? I can tell you right now, we don't do that, sir, we don't ever solicit money over the phone, for any reason. And if you'd've called us right away we might've saved you some money. But this isn't about that. I'd like you to tell me, if you can, where you were last night between, say, two and three o'clock?"

"Tell you if I can? Huh. If I can't, I don't know who can. Kinda question's that?"

"Well can you tell me, sir, where you were?"

"I was here. Watchin' TV probably. I don't sleep too good."

"Anybody else confirm that, sir?"

"How's anybody else gonna confirm that, I'm the only one here."

"Is that a house or an apartment, sir?"

"What difference does that make?"

"Well if it's an apartment and you had your TV on, maybe your neighbors heard it."

"This is a house, I don't live in no apartment. And my neighbors, they're all deafer than me."

"All of 'em? What, they never complain you make too much noise?"

"First place, I don't make noise. Ain't got any reason to. But if I did, which I don't, they wouldn't hear it, none of 'em."

"How come you're so sure of that?"

"'Cause every time I talk to 'em, I gotta repeat everything I say. Told ya, they're old, they can't hear nothin'. Best reason I know for livin' here, nobody pays me any attention."

"Uh-huh. Uh, you a hunter, Mister Czarowicz?"

"Oh, now I know what this is about. This is about that bastard Lyon gettin' shot, ain't it?"

"You heard about that, huh?"

"Hell, it's all over the news, don't matter what station you turn on, that's all they're talkin' about, J. D. Lyon this, J. D. Lyon that, shot in the head. CEO, president, Conemaugh Steel, dead."

"Bother you that he died that way?"

"Bother me?! Why the hell would it bother me? You wanna know when I got bothered, you should've talked to me when they laid me off. Or when I found out I didn't have no pension, when I found out all them years I put in there, all them years I thought I had a nice little nest egg buildin' up for me and my wife so we could sorta take it easy for a while? You know, come time for me to retire? Shoulda talked to me then, you wanna hear bothered, you'da heard it then, brother. There ain't any words for what kinda bothered I was then. Still ain't no words for what I was then."

"Uh-huh. But didn't you fellas get that settled with, uh, you know, with the help of Attorney Valcanas?"

"Settled? Shit. Compared to what we should've got, we didn't get nothin'."

"Uh, Mister Czarowicz, you mind comin' in, sir?"

"Comin' in? Comin' in where?"

"Here. Rocksburg PD station, City Hall. You know where it is?"

"I know where it is. What you want me to come in there for?"

"Just wanna talk, that's all."

"Thought that's what we were doin' now. Ain't we?"

"Well I really like talkin' to people face-to-face, I don't like telephones, I just use 'em to set up appointments really, if you know what I mean. So when you think you can come in, huh? How 'bout seven o'clock tonight, say? After dinner, can you get in here then?"

"I don't understand why you wanna talk to me there, when you're talkin' to me now. You accusin' me of somethin'?"

"No no, no, nothin' like that, no, c'mon, we're talkin' to everybody, tryin' to get a handle on this, uh, this shooting. You didn't answer me before. You hunt? Huh? You a hunter?"

"So what if I am?"

"Well, I mean, c'mon, Mister Czarowicz, you can understand why I'd be askin' that question, can't you? Sure you can, I'm not gonna insult your intelligence here. Just tell me, yes or no, you hunt?"

"So I hunt, so what? Been huntin' all my life. Every man in my family hunted. Taught my boys to hunt too. And not be no outlaw hunters neither. Never went on land I wasn't welcome on. Always asked permission and I always got it or I didn't put my boots on it. I knew what I was aimin' at and I hit where I aimed. Never shot an animal wasn't fair game, and everything I carried in, I carried out."

"Uh-huh, I'm sure you did. So I'll see you seven tonight? You're gonna make it in now, okay? I'm gonna be lookin' for you."

"Just to talk, huh?"

"Yes sir, just to talk."

"You got more questions to ask me, I don't see why you can't ask 'em now. What, you think you can tell when people are lyin' just 'cause you see their face? You can't. Bastards looked us right in the eyes, lied to us for years and years, never told us the truth once."

"No sir, I didn't mean to imply you were lyin'. What I mean is, lot of people, they don't know they know somethin' till they start talkin'. And one thing leads to another, and then sometimes it turns out they know a whole lot they didn't think they knew. Have to hear the right questions sometimes, that's all. Hear the right questions, one thing leads to another, be surprised what you might know."

"Uh-huh. Says you. What's your name again?"

"Carlucci." He spelled it. "Detective sergeant. There's public parkin' on the south side of City Hall. Come in that door, dispatcher's sittin' right there, just ask for me, he'll tell you where to go." He hung up before Czarowicz could protest again about coming in.

Then he called DA Failan to report that he'd alibied out seven of the foremen whose names had been supplied by Mo Valcanas and had made an appointment to interview the eighth face-to-face. When Failan asked why he was going to interview that one face-to-face, Carlucci said he wasn't sure, but he was sure the others had had nothing to do with Lyon's murder.

"What are you saying, Rugs? This one did?"

"No no, I'm not sayin' that. Just the way he talked. Could be just naturally defensive, or, I don't know, just somethin' about him. He wasn't any shyer about how much he disliked Lyon than any of the others, I just wanna look at his face when he talks, that's all. But he's not comin' in till seven tonight, so you got somethin' else you want me to do, uh, say the word."

"Well the only thing I can think of is why don't you go see what the state guys are up to with Frankie Krull, check that scene out, why don't you? But you'll have to call them to find out where it is, exactly. I just know it's somewhere out by the reservoir."

Carlucci followed the directions given him by the state police dispatcher. Fourteen miles from Rocksburg, at the end of the two-lane blacktop that ran along the eastern shore of the Conemaugh River Reservoir, the principal source of water for Rocksburg and surrounding townships, he found two state police cruisers and the Troop A crime scene truck. They were parked beside a square clapboard-sided cabin on a red-dog road about a hundred yards from where the blacktop ended and about thirty yards from a stream slipping quietly over rocks and boulders that about a mile or so back had fed into the reservoir. The last building he'd passed was a half mile back and belonged to the water authority; there wasn't another in sight.

Carlucci parked, got out, showed his ID, and asked a scene tech, who was bagging and tagging dirt by the back of the truck, where the scene was. The tech told him to head upstream for about a quarter mile. "Then it takes almost a ninety-degree turn east, and, uh, you'll see it. You didn't happen to pass a coroner's car on the way, did you? Called them, God, must've been two hours ago. What's with them?"

Carlucci shrugged and muttered something about how the coroner seemed to be running a little behind lately, then immediately set off upstream, struggling to keep his balance on the rocky ground and dry leaves and twigs. Within a minute he saw Milliron coming toward him, and Carlucci was struck at once by how different Milliron seemed here in the woods.

In town, Milliron was awkward, almost clumsy, though Carlucci knew it didn't have anything to do with his physical coordination. Milliron just never seemed at ease in Rocksburg. Carlucci had attributed that to Milliron's attitude about the people there, who he found to be generally gloomy, surly, and contrary. Strangely enough, he seemed to Carlucci to assume the very characteristics he didn't like about them, which somehow got transformed into the way he carried himself. But here he looked like he was in his element, clambering over fallen trees, dodging branches, never seeming to lose his footing. He appeared to be very much at home here, or at least not anywhere near as uncomfortable as Carlucci was. Carlucci asked him about it.

"I always liked bein' in the woods better than anyplace else," Milliron said, smiling. "I figured out when I was real young if anything messed with me there, it wasn't personal. If a rattler started shakin' his tail at me it wasn't 'cause I was dumb, or slow, or clumsy. It was 'cause he wanted me to know he was there and he didn't want me messin' with him, 'cause if I did he'd bite me, make me sick. Maybe even make me die."

"You had rattlesnakes where you lived? In Mercer?"

"Naw, not there, just black snakes, garter snakes. Well, maybe there were some rattlers, but I never saw any. I'm talkin' about up in the mountains, New York State. My one uncle, he had a cabin up in the Adirondacks. Lotta timber rattlers up there."

"And they could kill you?" Carlucci started looking more carefully where he was stepping.

"If you were a real small kid maybe. Had enough juice to kill a small dog. One of my uncle's beagles, he got bit, lived a couple days, leg swelled up about twice normal size before it died. Vet probably could've saved him, but my uncle was too much of a hardhead to go look for one. My aunt got really pissed at him."

"And, uh, got any of those around here, you think?"

"What, dogs?"

"Huh? No, rattlers, yeah, whatever kinda . . . timber."

"Probably. What, you never been called out on one of those?"

"One of what?"

"Suspicious death caused by double injection of pit viper venom, manner of death homicide as a result of aggravated assault by extremely short, limber, very defensive guy?"

"Oh, what's that, farm boy humor?"

"Look out! There's one!"

"Where where?" Carlucci said, instantly drawing his Beretta and sweeping the ground around him with it but not moving his feet. A wave of fear swept over him, but he moved nothing but the pistol, side to side while turning both ways as far as he could.

Laughing heartily, Milliron turned around and started heading back from where he'd come, saying over his shoulder, "Guess you wanna go check out the scene, huh, city boy? Follow me."

Carlucci felt the fear turning to anger and rushing outward from his chest, spreading up into his neck and down into his groin like electricity. Despite that, he tuned his ears as sharply as he could for a sound he'd never heard outside of a movie theater, while continuing to sweep the ground immediately around him with his Beretta, his eyes trying to focus on an unfamiliar thing even as he knew he'd just been jerked around. Then he looked up and saw Milliron pulling away from him and he hurried to catch up while continuing to scan the ground and sweep his Beretta belt-high, back and forth, in front of him.

Catching up to Milliron took a few moments, and Carlucci was still seething. He tried to cool out, tried to let it go, tried to tell himself that Milliron was just a hick with a hick's sense of humor, but no matter what he tried to tell himself, he couldn't let it pass. So he said to Milliron's back, "Stop, man, I wanna say somethin'."

Milliron kept walking and said over his shoulder, "What?"

"Don't do that, man. That wasn't funny."

"What?"

"Don't get stupid on me, you know what I'm talkin' about. That bullshit back there, that was not funny."

"Was from where I was lookin'," Milliron said. "Funnier than hell. Should've seen your face. Man, you turned white—"

"Stop walkin'!" Carlucci said.

Milliron gave a quick glance over his shoulder but kept moving forward.

"Stop walkin', goddammit! I said stop!"

Milliron stopped and turned around, his face pinched into a quizzical frown.

Carlucci lowered the Beretta to his side, by his right leg. "Listen to me, Pinky. Don't ever do that again. Never tell me there's somethin' there that could kill me when it isn't there, you hear me?"

"Jesus, man, you need to chill out, I was just—"

"Hey I don't care what you were just, okay? I was in Nam, remember? Maybe I didn't tell you but there were snakes there we called 'em two-steppers 'cause one of them bit you, man, all you were gonna take was two steps and you were dust, man. And nobody joked about that, you hear me? Nobody! Somebody said there was one near you it's 'cause there was one there and you'd better know how to spot it and you'd better know what you were gonna do next, you hear me?"

"I'm not deaf, Detective, and this is Pennsylvania," Milliron said somberly. "Conemaugh County. And no adult I ever heard of died from bein' bit by a timber rattler. And I really don't like you talkin' to me in that tone—especially holdin' what you're holdin'."

"Yeah? Well I don't care what you don't like 'cause you ever do anything that stupid again, I'll put one through your kneecap."

"You'll do what?"

"You heard me. And it won't matter what happens to me afterwards, you'll never walk right again, you understand that?"

"Oh I don't believe this—"

"Better believe it."

"Oh man, I don't believe it. I make a joke, you wanna shoot me in the knee? I don't fucking believe this, uh-uh."

"Believe it I said! My mind's too fucked up right now to have somebody's supposed to be my partner makin' that kinda joke—and not understandin' why it's not okay even after I explain it to you. And I don't care if you don't understand. Only thing you need to understand is never do that again. You hear me? Never!"

"Oh man . . . oh man, you got a problem, Detective."

"Right now only problem I got is you understandin' what I said. Just don't forget it, that's all. But we got to move on, so let's just move on, alright? Let's just go to work."

"Oh don't worry, I won't be forgettin' about this. But I'm not goin' to work. You wanna go to work, fine, go to work, you're the one needs to check out the scene, not me. I don't need to do anything else back there."

That said, Milliron brushed past Carlucci, bumping into his shoulder and knocking him back a half-step, heading back from where Carlucci had just come.

Flustered, trembling with anger and fear, Carlucci tried hard to compose himself. He knew he had to say something.

"Uh, gonna report to Failan? When you get back? Huh?"

"Whatta you care?"

"Still my partner. Still need to know what you're doin'."

"Want me to see Failan, fine, I'll report to him." Milliron continued to walk as he talked, but then he stopped and turned around. "Think I ought to report anything else while I'm doin' that?"

"Huh? Like what?"

"Like reportin' the fact that a police officer, while holding his weapon, made terroristic threats, huh? Threatened to put one through my kneecap, huh? Think I should report that? *Partner.*"

"Oh yeah right, go 'head and file the goddamn thing, why don't you? And I'll file one on you for givin' a false report to a police officer—"

"False report?! What false report?"

"For tellin' me there was a snake there when there wasn't. And I'm sure Failan'll really eat this up, us doin' this childish chickenshit while we're not doin' what we're supposed to be doin'. You wanna get transferred outta CID, huh? Maybe you'd rather inspect trucks, huh? Haul a portable scale around, weigh fucking trucks? Check their brake hoses, huh? That appeal to you? Or maybe gradin' the written part of drivin' tests—how 'bout that, you like the sound of that? I think maybe you oughta take some time, Trooper, go give yourself an attitude check."

"Hey, fine, fine with me, I'll do that. And maybe you oughta take some time, Detective, ask yourself how long you're gonna let your mommy interfere with your job."

"My mommy?! My *mommy!* Hey! Next time you got a body down? And you're lookin' around for somebody with a camera? And evidence bags? And it's three o'clock in the mornin'? Call your state rep, okay? Ask him run some bodies through the academy. 'Cause next time, pal, don't fucking call me, you hear?"

"Loud and clear," Milliron said, turning and stomping off, his shoulders settling into a rounded slouch, like he was already back in Rocksburg.

Carlucci felt something heavy in his right hand. He knew what it was but he had to make himself look at it. The Beretta. He closed his eyes and felt a sigh burst from his mouth as he sobbed once. "What the fuck am I doin'," he said aloud, hurrying to holster the Beretta. "What the fuck am I doin', Jesus Christ Almighty, what the fuck am I doin'?"

He turned around and started walking upstream again. He walked for perhaps another two hundred yards, his eyes blurry with tears, stumbling, slipping, falling once and landing hard on his right knee because he tripped on a root. He wiped his eyes with the back of his hands and slapped himself on the thigh. "C'mon, man, get it together, what the fuck, huh?"

His vision a little less blurry now, he saw that the stream made almost a ninety-degree turn east into a small hollow between two low rises of ground covered with towering trees that nearly blotted out the sun. It shone in spots on the ground and made Carlucci feel as though he was walking under a screen. As soon as he turned to follow the stream, he could hear voices and saw the other scene techs, two of them, each shuffling in a squat and looking intently at the ground while gently making sweeping motions with their hands. A state police corporal was fiddling with a camera near the body of a man spread-eagled facedown on the ground, his fingers in the water, his feet above him on the bank. A fishing rod lay beside him, but well beyond arm's reach.

Carlucci held up his ID and shield with his left hand and tried to introduce himself by extending his right hand to the corporal but the corporal ignored him and continued to inspect and polish the lens of his camera with a square blue cloth. Carlucci shrugged and turned his attention to the body and asked where it was okay to step.

"Anywhere. We haven't found anything yet, and those guy's've been lookin' since before I got here. They're sweepin' back in a circle see if they can find anything." The they he referred to were the two techs who were, Carlucci could now tell, making a systematic search of the ground away from the body. "You wanna join in," the corporal said, nodding toward the techs, "feel free."

An hour later, his thighs burning and his back aching, Carlucci gave up. He'd found nothing. Neither had anybody else. Just a lot of footprints, but none that didn't match either the victim's shoes or their own.

"Hell'd he do, shoot him from a chopper?" the corporal groused after listening to one of the techs tally the dismal results of the ground search.

"Nah," the other scene tech said. "Told you before, Corp, we need a tracker. A pro."

"A what?" Carlucci said.

"Tracker. Guy knows what to look for. What, you don't think there are such people?'

"Oh I'm sure there are," Carlucci said. "I just never heard of any around here, that's all. Got enough in your budget to hire one?"

The corporal, a ruddy-faced man with wide shoulders and very thick through the chest, thought that was very funny. "Do we got enough in our budget to hire one," he said, chuckling. "That's a good one. Who is this guy Krull anyway? From your corner of the county, isn't he? Brother-in-law said he was some kinda union honcho, huh? What kinda union? I asked Milliron before, he didn't know. You know?"

"Steelworkers," Carlucci said. "He was president of the local at Conemaugh Steel when it shut down. Before that, before he got elected president I mean, he was sort of, uh, you know, a rebel. Always organizin' some kinda protest about how the union was sellin' out the grunts, how the local officers were just linin' their own pockets, stuff like that."

"Any of it true?" the corporal said.

"You mean about the officers linin' their pockets? I don't know, only thing I ever had to do with him was one time his wife called, and I responded. That was to his residence."

"Oh. Liked to box the wife, huh?"

"Apparently. But she didn't just stand there. She was bloodier, but he had his share of lumps. Wound up in Family Court, I testified maybe five minutes, mostly about what I saw when I arrived, what I found, that's about it. I never had anything else with him."

"So whatta you think, think this ties in with the other guy? The CEO? What's his name again, Lyon? Heard he was a real beauty."

"I don't know," Carlucci said. "What'd Milliron say, anything?"

"Nah. Just talked about the guy's house. And his old lady. I didn't get the feelin' from him you guys had much of a line on anybody, that right?"

"Well, I wouldn't go that far," Carlucci said. "The foremen, they all took a real screwin' on their pensions. Somebody skimmed the company pension, and the union, uh, I guess it was a case of them thinkin' the company was supposed to set up a pension for those guys, the foremen, and the company thinkin' that's for the union to do, but whatever, the windup is nobody did it. Which left a buncha guys with, uh, you know, some big-league motives. Anyway, we have those names. And I was narrowin' it down."

"What happened to your mouth?" the corporal said.

"Fell offa my past," Carlucci muttered, head down. Then he turned and started back alongside the stream toward where he'd parked. Carlucci didn't draw his Beretta, but he kept his right hand on it while he searched the ground before each step, looking for rattlers, pissed off at himself for looking for something he knew wasn't there but not able to stop looking for them. And pissed off worse about Milliron for that mommy business.

How long am I gonna let my mommy interfere with my job—is that what he said? What'd he say before? Back in town didn't he say people who say they wanna change something, they can talk about changing it all they want, but if they don't do anything about it, then they might as well be hooked to it—is that what he said? Hooked? Like some goddamn junkie? Is that what he said? Goddammit, why can't I remember what he said? My mommy. Said that clear enough, the prick. Did he say that stuff, or do I just think he said that? Why can't I remember what he said? Man, this is makin' me nuts, I got to talk to somebody about this. No, uh-uh, this isn't makin' me nuts, I'm lettin' it make me nuts . . . goddamn him. Milliron. . . .

Carlucci called Franny Perfetti at home and caught her on her way out the door to her job with Conemaugh County Substance Abuse Services. He wanted to see her so much he was afraid, especially with his lip, that he was going to sound like he was begging, but he calmed himself enough to get the words out. He asked if she had the time and if she wouldn't mind meeting him at Lenny's. "You know, that pizza joint you like? In South Rocksburg? Where they have that great veggie pizza?"

"I just ate," she said, and his heart sank. "But I could have a beer maybe. I'm starting a new group tonight, so they sit around all day trying to come up with some brilliant excuse for why they shouldn't have to go through this silly shit, and a couple'll get lost, so we never get started on time. I could be a little late."

"Well, I've got an interview at seven myself, so I can only stay for, uh, what time is it? My watch is screwin' up here, need a new battery or somethin'."

"Five to five," she said. "So, uh, see you in ten minutes?"

"Huh? Yeah yeah, ten minutes, good, I'll be there." Man, he thought, lucky I caught her before she left. Lucky too that tonight she was starting a new group and didn't care if she was a little late. He wanted to just see her—that would have been enough—but he also wanted to hear what she thought about what Milliron had implied about his not being able to break free from his mother. And that mommy crack was stuck sideways in his throat, and it hurt almost as much as his lip.

When he got to Lenny's, Franny was already there and sitting at a table in the corner, the table they'd sat at the first time she'd gone out with him. He couldn't believe how long ago that was.

"Really glad you could get away," Carlucci said, head down, sitting across from her and propping his elbows on the table and folding his hands in front of his mouth. "Order anything yet, or you just get here?"

"Just this minute walked in. What, you're not gonna sit in the corner? Something the matter?"

"Why?"

"Well you usually sit in the corner, you know, with your back to the wall. And you sounded funny on the phone. Sound funny now too."

"I sit with my back to the wall?"

"What, you don't know you do that?" she said, smiling.

He shrugged defensively. "Like to see everybody, that's all."

"Oh see everybody, yeah, right. Keep everybody in front of you you mean—why do you have your hands up like that? And why are you talking like that?"

He put his hands down on the table.

"Oh God, what happened to you? God, that looks painful."

Carlucci tried to be as brief as possible, but she kept asking for more details.

"Look," he said, trying to signal the barmaid with his left hand, "I can't tell you everything you wanna know."

"Why not?"

"'Cause for one thing it'd take forever, how this got started, me and my mother, I mean, what's the point? Point is, I don't know what to do about it. Been thinkin' about it for years, still got no answer."

"Oh there'll be an answer whether you want it or not," she said.

"What's that mean?"

"Well, maybe answer's not the right word. Maybe resolution is a better word."

"So? Answer, resolution—what's it mean?"

"Means there will be a resolution. There will. 'Cause nothing ever stays the same. So the question is, do you wanna resolve it, or do you wanna let somebody else resolve it for you?"

Carlucci ordered a Pepsi, and Franny ordered a draft Rolling Rock, which surprised him. Then he remembered that when he called she'd said she could drink a beer instead of eating. "You drink before you, uh, you know, work?"

"Before I work?" She laughed. "Well, I wouldn't want this to get around, you know? But whenever I'm starting a new group, I get pretty nervous. Pretty nervous, ha! Listen to me. I get jumpy as hell. Normally I leave the house at six-thirty for a seven-thirty group. But today I was ready to leave at four. Had to practically tie myself to the kitchen table to talk to my mother. Then you called."

"Well, uh, I mean, you know, aren't you supposed to be counselin' people, you know? To not use? Or drink? Or to not have to use?"

"And so here I am confessing I need a beer? To do *that* job?"

"Well, yeah."

"Listen. One beer's not gonna interfere with what I do. It's gonna help me do it better. I tried takin' different kinds of pills, you know? They didn't work. Alcohol's just a liquid pill for me, it works way better than any pill I ever tried. I never need more than one, one beer, one glass of wine, whatever taste I feel like I want in my mouth, but it gets the birds that're flyin' around in my gut, okay? It gets 'em to quit flyin' and fightin' each other so I can do my job, that's all there is to it."

When the barmaid brought his Pepsi and her draft and after he paid, Carlucci looked at the Pepsi and said, "Don't know what I ordered this for, I can't drink it. Need a straw." Then he sighed and said, "Hope you didn't think I was, you know, makin' you explain yourself to me, okay?"

"No, it's alright, it is, I can understand why you'd ask."

"You never get any flak for it?"

"Oh sure, you kidding? Of course. Anybody with half a nose is gonna give me grief if they get close enough to smell it on me. And they do. And they try to give me grief, believe me. But I tell them the same thing I just told you—plus, I tell 'em, I quit after one. If you could quit after one, you wouldn't be here, you'd be home—or you'd be sittin' where I am."

"Well, see, that's sorta what I wanted to see you about anyway. Okay if I ask you somethin'? About what you do?"

"Sure. I'm just surprised you think you have to ask first, you know?" she said, smiling that smile that lit up his mind.

Carlucci felt himself blushing. "I guess. I just—I don't know, I just can't start right in talkin', you know?"

"Good," she said, letting the tip of her tongue slip between her lips. "I'm glad I make you nervous."

Carlucci had to look away. If she only knew how nervous she made him. "Uh, listen, what I wanna talk to you about is, uh, this guy I'm partnered up with right now? He's a state cop. And he said somethin' today really rattled me. Couple things. I wanna know what you think."

"Well, my experience is, state cops, they're the worst usually. I wouldn't pay too much attention to him. But go 'head, tell me."

"Okay. Here goes. He said some people, they get in a bad situation? And they talk about wantin' out of it? If they don't do anything to get out of it? It doesn't matter how much they talk about wantin' out, if they don't do anything, they're like, he said—not in these words exactly—but they're like they're hooked on it. You know what I'm sayin'? Hooked like an addict?"

"And you think he might be right? About you?"

Carlucci blushed again. "Well, yeah. I mean otherwise, why would it be botherin' me?"

"And so you're askin' me? Because of what I do?"

"Well, yeah. I mean, that is what you do."

"And then I tell you I have to have a beer in order to do it, that must've made you feel good, huh? Given you a lotta confidence?"

If she only knew how good it made him feel just to sit across a table from her. He wished he could say that, but he knew if he tried, especially with his lip the way it was, he'd screw it up.

"Well," she said, "if by what I do you mean work with addicts, yes. But that's a real qualified yes. 'Cause it doesn't make me an expert on anything, least of all addiction. All it means is, I see the corners people paint themselves into a little bit sooner than maybe you would, that's all. Doesn't mean any more than that."

"C'mon, you know what you do, don't be modest."

"I'm not being modest. I've been doing what I do way too long to think I know why people are hooked. Or get hooked, or stay hooked, or get unhooked, or whatever."

"But that is what you do, right? I mean, isn't it?"

She sighed and slumped, canted her head, and her tongue slipped out between her lips again. "Um, no, uh-uh, what I do is lead groups. Anybody gets unhooked in there, it's 'cause of them, not 'cause of me or anything I do. My job's to keep 'em focused, that's all. When they start comin' off the wall and headin' for the ceiling, my job is to bring 'em back. Other than that, I'm not gonna tell you or anybody else I know why they got hooked or why they get un-hooked—if they do.

"Now I used to think I knew. When I first started I had all kinds of theories, I knew everything, I was cocky as hell. But it was all out of books. 'Cause, believe me, the longer I do this? The less I can honestly claim I know why anybody's hooked. On anything."

"Well, okay then," Carlucci said, "I can see you don't wanna get tied down to anything you say here, so let me go at it another way. I was talkin' to this CO one time, real smart guy, and he told me—"

"CO? Corrections officer?"

"Yeah? What, you don't think a CO can be smart? 'Cause of what they do?"

"I didn't say that, but go 'head, I didn't mean to interrupt."

"Yes you did," he said, hoping it didn't sound smart-assy and smiling until he had to stop because his lip hurt. "Never mind. Anyway, what he told me was—and this is a guy has to deal with a whole lotta addicts every day, you know?"

"Oh I'm sure he does. Unfortunately."

"Okay. So anyway, he told me—hope I get it right—he said an addict is anybody with an itch who's convinced the only way he can scratch it is by puttin' something into, or on, or around his body. And no matter how many times he finds out he can't scratch it that way, he still can't get through the day without puttin' somethin' into him. Food or alcohol or nicotine or caffeine or THC or speed or coke or crack or heroin, whatever—somehow, some way, makes no difference what it is, you know, uppers, downers, foods like Momma used to make, booze to go to sleep, coffee to wake up, clothes to look good in, shiny car to arrive in, state-of-the-art stereo to serenade his ears, this guy says an addict is forever huntin' for somethin' to scratch this itch that won't go away. 'Cause he's convinced that whatever ails him, you know, it can only be cured by some *thing* somebody else has. And also, he's convinced that if he just had enough of this, whatever it is, all the rough edges would round off, all the jolts in the middle of the night would just dissolve, you know, they'd just turn into sweet peace, love, harmony, satisfaction, whatever."

Franny gave a little shrug and said, "Yeah. Be hard to argue with that. I'm sure that would fit a lot of addicts."

"Well see, I used to think the guy was right. But then this trooper says this to me about, uh, my situation, you know?" He pointed vaguely to his mouth. "And he implied I was hooked to it. Or on it. Like some crackhead. And I got really pissed at him. I was smokin' inside. Still am. All day. Ever since he said it."

"I don't know," she said, shaking her head warily. "I usually get into trouble when I talk to cops about this, especially state cops."

"About what? Being hooked? Oh what, I'm just a cop now?"

"No, not you necessarily, and don't get defensive, okay? But yeah, you. I mean we are what we are." She smiled again, and his mind lit up again. "But my experience with state cops—and I've met a lot of them, believe me—I mean, most of them, they come from these little towns, God, a hundred miles from nowhere, you know? They might as well be from Alabama. All they know different from what they learned at home is what they were told in the state police academy. It's not their fault, I'm not puttin' them down for where they came from, it's just that the ones I talk to, really, they don't impress me as bein' too eager to learn anything different from what they grew up believing."

"Well," Carlucci said, "just for the sake of argument here, let's pretend I'm not a cop, okay? For sure I'm not a state cop. And I really wanna know what you think about this. We haven't talked about this much, and my mother's, uh, she's, uh, how do I wanna say this?"

"Just say it."

"It's not that simple. You don't know my mother."

"Try me. Tell me about her."

"Nah, I don't wanna do that," Rugs said, hanging his head. "It's way way too complicated, I don't wanna get into it, you know? My mother's my mother, she's, uh . . ."

"She's what?"

"Some other time, okay? Lemme get back to what this guy said today—or if you don't wanna do that, then, you know, tell me what you think an addict is, that's what I wanna hear. Then maybe I can apply it to what he said."

"Oh I doubt it. But if that's what you want, okay, I'll give you a definition. One anyway. My most abstract, most philosophical description of what I think an addict is. And this is so general it could fit almost anybody, okay?"

"Yeah, okay, go 'head."

"Okay," she said. "Here goes. Addicts are people who can't let go of an attachment to the way they think things ought to be."

"Come again? Can't let go of what?"

"An attachment to the way they think things ought to be. As opposed to the way they are."

"Well where's the whattaya call it, the chemical stuff? The biological stuff—doesn't that enter into it? What you said there sounds like you don't think there's any of that in it, and you don't believe that—do you?"

"Oh God no, no," she said, laughing. "No, there's way too much evidence about how molecules in certain substances attach themselves to receptors on certain cells and how they alter the neural-chemical pathways. God, I don't know enough to argue with the hard-science people. But the people I deal with every night, see, I'm not dealing with them in a chemical way, I'm dealing with them strictly with words. It's talking therapy, that's all. I'm not handin' them a pill, I mean, the last thing in the world they're gettin' from me is a different kind of high. Theoretically they've all kicked. The doctors say they're clean or the judges wouldn't let 'em into the program, simple as that. So what I'm doin'—or tryin' to do—is helping them figure out a way for *them* to keep *themselves* clean. 'Cause if they don't *stay* clean, they go right back in. And that's the last place they wanna be, especially the ones with the really hard jones, you know, crack and speed? 'Cause inside they're just candy for every predator in there. And I don't want that on my conscience."

"So to keep 'em off your conscience, you tell 'em what again? They got an attachment to the way things oughta be? That's what you talk about?"

"Yeah—no, not the way things oughta be, the way *they think* things ought to be. But I don't tell them that. I try to direct them to it. And if I'm lucky, they get to it by themselves."

"How? What the hell you say gets 'em to that?"

"Not me, please. The group. Well, we use that Robin Williams line a lot. You know? 'Reality, what a concept.'"

"You lost me again."

"Well what they're all runnin' from in one way or another is their reality—you don't know who Robin Williams is or what?"

"I know who he is. Don't tell me about him, tell me—"

"I'm trying to, Detective. Boy. He really messed with your mind today, your partner, huh?"

"Yeah. But only 'cause I let him. C'mon, just tell me."

"Okay. They're all runnin' from their reality, whatever it is. If they weren't, they wouldn't be puttin' all these crazy things into their bodies. Can you imagine thinkin' you're gonna get something good from sniffin' gasoline? Or paint thinner? Jesus, c'mon, that's desperation with a capital *D*—not when they start, no. A lot of 'em start 'cause it's fun, it's somethin' to do with their friends, or to be accepted, all that kid stuff that drove us nuts 'cause we thought we were so weird and nobody else was. But after they started, if they keep doin' it, I mean, real fast it turns into their whole life—everything else becomes second. And remember what the nuns used to tell us? Despair was the greatest sin because it was the one that denied hope."

"Oh-oh. Makin' me a little nervous here." Everything Carlucci's mother said about "good little Catholic girls" started bouncing off the walls of his mind.

"Why?"

"Guess 'cause I never heard you talk religion before."

"I'm not talking religion," she said, taking the last sip of her beer. "I'm talkin' reality. People I deal with, they just don't want to look at it sober, that's what it comes down to. They think dealin' with it buzzed up is gonna make it somehow easier to take, easier to relate to, easier to comprehend, to live with, or around, or beside. The operative word is easier. But the fact is, in the program, this great big reality has jumped up in front of them and said, hey, listen up, people, reality is exactly what you have to face—sober. 'Cause if you don't, you're goin' right back where you do not wanna be. So you pick. Clean and sober outside, drunk and dirty inside, up to you. And presumably, if they keep showin' up every time the group meets, sooner or later here it comes, you know—yo, brothers and sisters, what is it you're runnin' from? Why you always tryin' to go over the wall? Why you always tryin' to go AWOL from life?

"And you get every story plus all the variations: my mother hated me, my stepfather molested me, my father beat me, my mother starved me, they threw me outta the house when I was twelve, my uncle, my brothers, my sisters, my boyfriend, my girlfriend, my boss, my lawyer, my probation officer, whatever word comes after *my*, that's the reality they're runnin' from. And until they get over their attachment to the way they think whatever comes after the *my* should be, or oughta be, the sooner they can accept that reality. But acceptance, Jesus, that's the, uh, that's the toughie."

"Yeah, well, exactly what is that? Acceptance."

She shrugged again and held up her empty glass at the barmaid. "Best definition I ever heard—and I'm ashamed to say I can't remember who said it—but whoever it was, he said acceptance is not just acknowledging your reality—whatever it is. It's acknowledging it, and it's getting comfortable with it, so you can stop bein' angry about it. Because as long as you're angry about it, you're gonna make bad decisions. And because if you don't accept it, if you stay pissed off about it, then eventually you're gonna start tryin' to go over the wall again, start tryin' to escape again. So acceptance is the first step, that's the place I'm always tryin' to get them to—whatever it is. But I can't just tell 'em that—and I sure as hell can't drag 'em there. They've got to see it for themselves, they've gotta hear it, feel it, smell it, taste it— all by themselves. They have to put their arms around it, snuggle up to it, get comfortable with it, or else they'll get so lost nobody'll find them. Which happens way more times than anybody wants to admit."

"Wait wait," Carlucci said. "They have to get *comfortable* with *what?*

You mean, say like some young girl, she has to get *comfortable* with her stepfather molestin' her? She has to get *comfortable* with that? Man, I don't get that."

"No no, no, I didn't say they have to get *comfortable with bein' molested,* God no. What that girl has to do finally is face up to the fact that she has to get out of there, *she* has to do something with her life that takes her out of that reality. But the first step is acknowledging it. She's got to say to herself, that prick did that, and if I stay there, he's gonna do it again because that's the way he is and me wishin' he was different is not gonna change him. I'm not doin' that to me, he's doin' that to me, but if I don't get outta there, then I'm refusing to acknowledge that reality, and until I recognize that and admit that's the way it is there? If I go back there, then what I'm doin' is walkin' right into a trap I've set for myself, 'cause what I really want to do is find an excuse to use again, and I'm usin' *him* to give *me* that excuse.

"That's what groups wind up callin' the nutcracker. Or the ballbuster. Getting to the point where you accept your sobriety by saying that your reality's a bad situation, but it's your reality. Only you are no longer gonna stand around arguin' with God, or the cops, or the courts about how if life was really fair, that wouldn't be your reality. That prick wouldn't be your stepfather, your mother would've married this really great guy who took you to picnics and bought you ice cream and kept his hands to himself—except when you needed somebody to steer you through traffic. That's what I mean about bein' attached to an impression of the ways things are supposed to be instead of the way they are. You have to recognize the reality, that has to come first. Then you have to acknowledge it. And then you have to get comfortable with it. Soon as you get comfortable with it, soon as you can say yeah, that's it and it's not gonna change unless I change, and as soon as you accept *that,* then you can start to change yourself, which is the only thing you have any power to change anyway.

"So, far as I'm concerned, I don't care if they're clean chemically. They can pass all the urine and blood tests the judges lay on 'em. But if they're still pissed off that things are no different at home, or at work, or in school, or wherever, then as far as I'm concerned they're still addicted to the idea that they know how the world should work and they're still pissed off that it's not workin' that way. And as long as they're pissed off about it, they're eyebrow-deep into denial, and they're hair-deep into their addiction. They're what the AA'ers call dry drunks. The only thing they've changed is they don't consume the alcohol, but otherwise, they're still the same as when they were drinkin', and when they're in that stage, boy, believe me, there's no bigger pain in the butt anywhere. Everybody else is wrong or stupid or lazy or hateful, everybody but them."

"How long you been doin' this now?" Rugs said, as the barmaid returned with another round of drinks. Franny slid hers away.

"Fourteen years. Sometimes it feels like forever. Most of the time it doesn't."

"Hmm."

"Hmm what?"

"Where do they, uh, I mean, where do they get this idea about what their reality's s'posed to be like, you ever deal with that?"

Franny shook her head. "Uh-uh, I generally try not to go there. 'Cause I don't think they have to know that to believe it's trouble. But who knows where they get it? Other people's houses? TV? The movies. There was a guy in one of my first Pittsburgh groups—"

"Pittsburgh groups?"

"Yeah, that's where I got started in all this. I've only been back here, it's not even a year yet. This county didn't have any kind of program at all till I got here. They told me they had one, said it was up and runnin'—and fool that I am I believed them—then I got here, and I found out they wanted *me* to get it up and runnin'. First coupla months, I was ready to go back to the 'burgh."

"Why didn't you?"

"Oh just the thought of that parkway commute was too much. Plus my mother was, uh, you know, getting weaker, getting frailer. That commute was an extra hour and a half every day—and that's in good weather. And she just needed my help. It was a no-brainer really. So anyway, back to this guy. He was an only child, he said that all through his childhood he hung with a family that had three or four kids, and the parents, they were both sports nuts, and he wanted his family to be like them. But his parents, especially his father, said sports was a cultural shuck and jive, I forget how he said it exactly. Whatever, his parents didn't care about sports, so he saw this father in this other house in front of the TV all the time with his kids, they're all watching some game, and the old man's always got a beer in his hand. So the kid, the whole time he's growin' up, he had this warm, fuzzy image of all this TV togetherness mixed up with sports and beer.

"Then he goes to college. And same thing all over, he's hangin' with these guys, they're either playin' sports or watchin' sports and if they're watchin' 'em on TV, there's a keg in the room, and they all have glasses in their hands. By the time he graduates, twenty-one years old, he's drunk most of the time, and all because he equated beer with sports in this other house and in his fraternity house."

"So what'd you tell him?"

"I didn't tell him anything. The group told him the father he should be talkin' to wasn't the guy with the beer in his hands. The reality he needed to face was his own father. But he kept insisting he couldn't, his father was aloof, was cold, distant, hard to talk to. Group said, in so many words, bullshit. That's the fantasy you created about him because you liked what you saw in the other house and because your old man didn't behave the way you thought he should behave, so you'd rather get drunk than talk to him—as he is, not as you've been hopin' and wishin' he was. Group wouldn't let him slide. They can be brutal.

"This guy had a real hard time with that. Big, good-lookin' guy, otherwise, you know, tough, smart, but he just couldn't kick this idea of how his father was supposed to be in this fantasy family."

"So what happened to him?"

"Last I saw him, he was a classic dry drunk. Clean and sober, you know, according to the court. Drank soda water, but he was still soooo pissed off at his father for not bein' the kind of father he had a lotta fun with in the other house. What's sad was, right before he left the group, even he was admitting the other father was just a loud-mouthed asshole sports fan. But he just couldn't let go of the idea that his own father should've been better somehow. So even though he stayed out of legal trouble—far as I know he still has—and this is just my opinion of course—I don't think he's ever gonna be satisfied with himself till he works it out with his father. And he's not gonna do that until he starts seein' his parents for who they are, and not for who he wishes they were—and not until he gets comfortable with that."

Rugs shook his head and sighed. "Man. Gettin' comfortable with your, uh, parents. Whoa."

"What?"

"I mean, to think of that word, comfortable, it's so hard, you know? Gettin' comfortable with . . . man, I can't even say it."

"You can say anything you want. You can."

"Oh what, you gonna make me like I'm in a group here or somethin', huh? With you?"

"This is just us here, Rugs, that's all. And nobody can make you do anything you don't wanna do, least of all me."

"Hey, Franny, no disrespect, okay? But that's BS. People can make you do things—ha, man, I mean, the last thing in the world you think you're gonna do, you get with some other person? Bingo, you're doin' stuff you never thought about doin'."

"We're just talkin' now, Rugs, that's all."

"Woo boy, I don't know. You make me think about things I don't wanna think about. In ways I never thought about thinkin' about 'em. Gettin' comfortable with my . . . hey, why not, why can't I say it? Gettin' comfortable with my mother, wow, I mean that's a pipe dream, gettin' comfortable with her."

"No, uh-uh, excuse me, but a pipe dream is a dream that comes from smoking opium in a pipe, that's where that expression comes from. When you're dealin' with your mother on a daily basis, you're not smokin' anything. You couldn't be. Not and do what you do."

"Now how do you know that, huh? I mean I know you're smart and everything, but you've never been around me and my mother.

She walked in here right now, you wouldn't know her from the bar-maid."

"Course not. But it's not as though the subject hasn't come up. You know what you talk about every time you pick me up? When you first get there? All you do is apologize for bein' late—and you were late once—every other time you're early. But you invariably find some way to apologize 'cause you had to make sure the woman who watches her wouldn't mind stayin' for another couple hours. And tonight? No matter how many ways I asked you about what happened, all you kept doin' was explaining how you have to make sure somebody's with her all the time, how you have to make sure she doesn't hurt herself. And then, what do you ask me about? Whether you think you're addicted to your situation. 'Cause some state cop you're partnered up with, he said so.

"Now, knowing what I do, and knowing what you told me happened today, what else do you think I'd be doin' if I wasn't tryin' to understand what's goin' on with you and her, huh? First, that's just normal curiosity. Second, Jeez, I listen to people talk about their reality and their impression of their reality and their interpretation of it and their attachment to it or their detachment from it—I don't wanna brag, Detective, but sometimes I'm pretty good at what I do. I'm as good at what I do as you are. You good at what you do?"

"Huh? Yeah, I don't know, I guess. I mean if I make a good pinch, you know, if the people in the DA's office tell me I made the case, hey, then, I guess I'm good at it. But, uh, there's lots of other stuff I do that nobody sees, I mean if I don't do it, it doesn't get done, and if it doesn't get done, then no way makin' a good pinch makes up for it. But none of that has anything to do with whether I'm ever, you know . . . ever gonna get comfortable with my mother. I mean, hey, she's only gonna get worse. And what am I s'posed to do with her, huh? Shoot her? She tells me that all the time, just shoot me, she says. You got two guns, Ruggiero, just get one of 'em why don't ya, and put one right here. Then she starts jabbin' herself between the eyes with her thumb. Makes me crazy.

"Talk about somebody attached to a reality that doesn't exist. Man.

Hated my father for makin' me join the army—which he didn't do, I did that all on my own. Hated me for joinin' the army. Hated me for bein' in Vietnam, for puttin' her through all that anxiety, which she saw on TV every night the whole time I was there. Hated her husband for crashin' the car into a utility pole. Hated him for dyin', hated me 'cause if I hadn't joined the army and gone to Nam, she wouldn't've been fightin' with him in the car, so he wouldn't've crashed the car . . . it never stops, Christ. I mean I accept that, I recognize that. But what the hell do I do about it? All I been doin' is just keepin' on doin' it, that's all, one foot in front of the other. But it's goin' nowhere. And now, Jeez . . . now . . . now she's punchin' me."

"Yes, right, Rugs, but while you're puttin' one foot in front of the other, you don't get high, you don't drink till you pass out, you don't snort white powder up your nose or cook it and hype it between your toes, you just keep puttin' one foot in front of the other, Jeez, man, give yourself some credit for that."

"Yeah, okay, alright, I know what you're sayin'. But I sure as hell ain't comfortable doin' it. Not anymore. Been doin' it, for, God, I don't know, man, since '73. But it ain't gettin' any easier, that's for sure, especially . . . ah, man, I'm sick of talkin' about it."

"Give yourself some credit for doin' it, I'm telling you. Most people would've put her in a full-care facility years ago."

"Oh man, put her in one of those? You know what they cost, huh? Cheapest private one in this whole county is like twenty-eight hundred a month, and I wouldn't put a dog in that one. Most of 'em are three thousand a month, thirty-five hundred. And I'm talkin' to people about gettin' her in the county home—but that's a whole different problem. I mean, she's not goin' there, not as long as she's conscious."

"Ever talk to her about this?"

"Huh? I didn't tell you this before? Man, I thought sure I told you this, how the mayor was tryin' to get me in his pocket? How he said he could get my mother in there? I didn't tell you that?"

She shook her head no.

"Oh yeah, this was when he was pretendin' he wanted me to be chief, he comes up with this plan to move her up to the top of the list out there, and I told him, yeah, go 'head. Only *you* tell her, I'm not tellin' her, I wanna see *you* tell her. Which he did, I mean, I gotta give him that much."

"What happened? You mean he came to your house?"

"Oh yeah. Yeah, he walked in, sat down, talked for about five minutes, until, you know, she figured out what he was sayin', then, holy Christ, she jumped up, man, she went for a knife. Jesus, it got really hairy for about ten seconds. I mean, it's funny now, but it sure wasn't funny then. Thought Bellotti was gonna wet his pants. I almost wet mine. My mother's a lot stronger than I ever thought she was, I had a helluva time gettin' that knife away from her. I mean for somebody just sits around watchin' TV all day, she's stronger'n hell." He threw his head back and laughed but had to squelch it because of his lip.

"Well at least you can laugh about it."

"Hey. If I don't I'll cry, you know?"

"Yes but you don't cry. You laugh. And you don't run. You're a lot more comfortable with it than you know."

"Comfortable?! Shit, that's the last thing I am."

"Oh man, Rugs," she said, grabbing his arm and shaking it. "Stop puttin' yourself down, honest to God, give yourself a break, why don't you? Most people would've dumped her, believe me. I've known people who took their parents to the emergency room of the nearest hospital and left 'em in the parkin' lot—in a wheelchair."

"Get outta here."

"I'm serious. Two guys, in different groups, both admitted that."

"You're shittin' me. You're not? Hey, I didn't mean to say that the way it sounded, I gotta start watchin' my mouth."

"Stop saying that, will you? I've heard everything there is to hear. You know, there are only so many words in the language that people call profanity. And once you hear them on a regular basis as part of your job, I mean, they're just punctuation, that's all. Just pauses and punctuation, that's all they are. Just like people who can't get through a sentence without 'you know' or 'like'? Well there are people who

can't get through a sentence without 'fuckin'' this or 'motherfuckin''
that. You're lookin' at me funny, I'm tellin' you the truth.

"My first boss set me straight about that. My first group, I got all
hyper because they were almost all young, black guys, and they were
'motherfuckin'' everybody and everything, every time they opened
their mouths, and I went to him, practically hysterical, and he said,
hey, girlie, who'd you think you were gonna get in this kinda program? Sisters of Mercy, huh? Monks, ministers? Let me show you
something. And he sat me down and made me watch a bunch of
tapes he had of politicians during debates or press conferences, and he
said, here, listen to all these little ticks and tocks these guys throw
into their speeches to give themselves time to get their thoughts together. And the last one he showed me was a tape of one of the
Nixon-Kennedy debates? Every time John Kennedy opened his
mouth, he would say something like, Let me say this about that. And
my boss said, I'll never forget it, he said, that was John Kennedy's way
of sayin', Lemme tell you motherfuckers somethin'. He said, try imagining a black dude on the streets of Homewood sayin', Let me say this
about that. You can't. Any more than you can imagine Kennedy sayin',
Let me tell you motherfuckers somethin' right now, this the way this
shit goin' down.

"Believe me, my first boss, he saved me a lot of useless grief about
the way people talk."

Carlucci couldn't help himself: he felt his mouth hanging open.

"What?" she said. "What?"

Carlucci closed his mouth and shook his head. "For a second there,
I thought I was someplace else."

"Don't fudge," she said. "What you meant is for a second there you
thought you were *with* somebody else."

"I guess."

"You're still fudgin', Detective," she said, smiling large and leaning
away from him.

Carlucci continued to shake his head. "It's just hard, that's all. Hard
to look at you and hear that, you know, comin' out of your mouth.
You sayin' that. When you look like that. Like you do."

"Earth to Rugs, come in, Rugs. I'm as real as that chair you're sittin' on. Don't be puttin' me on any goddamn pedestal, I hate that. And just so you don't, I'm gonna tell you something else about me, okay?"

"Anything," Rugs said, and then blushed when he thought about how that sounded.

"Watch it, buddy," she said, pointing at him impishly. "Listen. Just listen. When I went to my first group, it was in East Liberty. I was so scared when I got there, and the whole time there, and the whole way back to my car and goin' home afterwards, I was so scared that the next day I signed up for every self-defense and weapons course I could take. Look." She opened her shoulder bag and pulled out a comb and a ballpoint pen. In its handle the comb concealed a conical plastic blade with a needlelike point. When she clicked the button atop the pen, a quarter-inch-long blade shot out.

She held up her right leg and pulled that leg of her slacks up. A small revolver was in a holster strapped above her ankle. "At five yards I can put all eight of 'em into a five-inch circle."

"Eight?" Rugs said. "That holds eight? What is it?"

"It's a Smith & Wesson Model 317. Know what else?" she said, smiling ever more brightly.

"Uh-uh, what?" His mouth immediately fell open again.

"I've been taking judo and karate lessons for fourteen years. And I've also taken lessons from some of the best self-defense instructors in the Pittsburgh PD and from the Allegheny County Police. Which doesn't mean I think I could whip a guy who knew as much as I do, and which doesn't mean I'm not scared in a lotta iffy situations, but anybody messes with me? They're gonna be in the fight of their life."

"Man, you sold me. You can bet I'll never mess with you, cross my shield and hope to die. But you know," he said, pointing to her right ankle, "you should never show that just to be showin' it, you know what I mean? Can never tell who's watchin'. And you don't ever wanna give up your edge. Ain't no skill to equal surprise, I'm tellin' ya."

"Nobody's payin' any attention to us in here, I'm just showing you," she said. Then she stretched her arms in front of her, crossing her wrists and lacing her fingers together, and then drew her hands back toward her chin so that her palms were together. She let her mouth rest on her fingers and she looked at him in a way that sent tremors through his mind and body.

"I wanna ask you something," she said behind her fingers. "And I want you to give me a straight answer, okay?"

"Huh? Yeah, sure. But wait, wait."

"What?"

"You still never told me whether you think this trooper, what he said, you know, about my situation, like was he right or what?"

"Rugs," she said, taking her hands apart and putting them atop his while leaning close. "Just 'cause you can't figure your way out of a problem doesn't mean the problem's an addiction. You know, for a while there, I couldn't turn on the TV 'cause every time I did, there was some yo-yo on some talk show sayin' everything in the world was an addiction. Dope, booze, sex, gamblin', food, work, play, everything, this, that, the other, exercise, everything was an addiction. And if it takes over your life, whatever it is, yes, you could call it an addiction. But so what? Just givin' it a name doesn't make it what the name implies. Any more than givin' it a name makes it go away. Just tell me one thing."

"What?"

"She ever hit you before?"

He shook his head glumly.

"So your situation has changed. It's not the same situation it was the day before she hit you, right?"

"Right."

"Do you think what this trooper says is gonna change it in any way? Make it any worse or any better?"

"No."

"You're wrong. You've already let him change it for the worse. 'Cause you let what he said get to you. Your situation is tough enough all by itself without lettin' some asshole put a bad name on it."

He hung his head and looked up at her under his brow. "I screwed up, huh? But I said that already. I already said I let him get to me."

"Oh will you stop! Jeez, Rugs, Jeez-oh-man, you're . . . you're, man, I don't know what you are. But cut it out! Stop doin' that to yourself—"

"Hey. What I am, you know? What I am is a guy, forty-six years old, still livin' with his mother. *His* mother. *My* mother, I don't even know what I'm talkin' about. And now she's punchin' me out—and I didn't even see it comin'. I mean, really, how's that sound to you, huh? If you didn't know it was me, if somebody just told you about me, I mean, what would you think? C'mon, I wanna hear what you would think of a guy like me. Would you even think about goin' out with him? Me. Him. Huh? Would you?"

"What are you talking about? Listen to yourself. Listen to how you sound when you talk about yourself, Rugs, honestly, I mean it, listen to how you put yourself down. If you were such a loser, do you think I would be here with you? I mean, do you really think that? If that's what you think, then what do you think of me for bein' here with you?" She slid her hands off his and grabbed his wrists and shook them. "Listen to me. You can't let some goddamn state cop, just 'cause he feels like runnin' his mouth, you can't let him mess with you this way. And you're lettin' him. Look around. Is he here? You know he isn't. But he's all over the inside of your head. And who is he that you're lettin' him, huh? Piss on him, he could get transferred tomorrow and you'd never see him again."

He blushed deeply again. And shrugged. And started to apologize for being a jerk, but caught himself, stopping the words in midthought.

She continued to shake his wrists. "Forget about this for a while, okay? Can you do that? 'Cause I wanna ask you something. Been tryin' to ask for the last ten minutes."

"Yeah. I'll try. Go 'head. Whatta you wanna ask me?"

"How many times have we been out?"

"Out? You mean like dates?"

"Yes. Out. Together. Like dates."

"I don't know. I haven't been countin'. Have you?"

"I haven't been counting either, that's not what I'm talking about. Here's what I'm talking about. Do you know that unless I touch you first you never so much as put your hand on me except accidentally, do you know that? I've had to practically trip and fall into you so you couldn't get around me without havin' to touch me. I wanna know if you're ever gonna do that without me havin' to trip and fall. You ever gonna do that, huh? Ever gonna touch me first?"

"Jesus," he said, barely above a whisper. "I dream about you. And I'm not even sleepin'."

"Well when you're dreamin' about me and you're not even sleepin', what do you dream about me?"

Carlucci didn't know what to say. His mind was bursting with words that somehow couldn't make it to his mouth, his heart was beating so loud he thought surely she must be able to hear it. But he didn't know what to say. He had been dreaming about her. He'd had a hundred conversations with her in those daydreams. He'd masturbated himself to sleep with her face in his mind's eye so many times he thought he was going crazy with desire. And here she was, inches away from him, their knees almost touching, her hands on his, and she was looking at him with those brilliant brown eyes as honestly, as clearly, as intensely as anyone had ever looked at him, and all he could think of was he had seven stitches in his upper lip and he must look like the king of the dorks. It was infuriating. She was practically begging him to touch her, and there he sat, nearly petrified with fear that whatever he did would turn out to be something unforgivably or unforgettably stupid, something that would cause her to run screaming away from him and never come back.

"I, uh . . . aw Jeez. Why can't I talk? What's wrong with me? Been sayin' a million words to you, can't think of one . . . shit." He hung his head.

He felt her pulling up his chin. "Just touch me, okay? You don't have to say anything right now."

He wanted to touch her with every molecule in his body, but reaching out to put his hand on hers was the most dangerous thing he'd ever done. When his fingers finally touched her fingers, a buzz of electricity went from his hand to his tear ducts and tears spilled over his lower lids, mortifying him. He blurted out, "I think about you all the time, I've talked to you a hundred times, I go to sleep thinkin' about you, I wake up thinkin' about you, if I'm not doin' my job, you're all I think about. I see your face . . . I see your face . . ." Oh God, was he gonna say that? No, please God, don't let me say that, don't let me say I jack off with her face in my mind, oh, God, if I say that, Jesus, *that* would be stupid, the stupidest thing I could ever say.

"What time is it?" he said, looking frantically at his watch, which had stopped at five-fifteen.

Her head pulled back reflexively. "You wanna know what time it is? Right now? At this moment that's what you wanna know?"

"No not at this moment—that's not the . . . that's not the thing I wanna know . . . but I have to know what time it is—I have to know that too! My watch is screwed up, and I got a guy comin' in—Jesus, Franny, you know . . . man, why can't I say what I wanna say here?"

"Just say it. Just say what you wanna say. Rugs, listen to me, okay? You have no trouble talking to me, you just think you do. God, talk, that's all we do. We go out, what do we do? We eat, we talk. We go home, we sit in the car and talk. I know you're a very shy person, I know you're not, uh, you know, very experienced with women— least I don't think you are—"

"Oh I'm not. No, hey, wow, that's the one thing I'm not, oh, believe me, Danny Date, you know, that's not me. I mean, whoa, I hate to tell you, you know, uh, when was the last time I was, uh, you know."

"Don't tell me. I don't care. I don't. I don't care if you were never with a woman, okay? I don't care if you were with dozens. Hundreds, okay? It doesn't matter. I don't like you 'cause I think you're gonna be good in bed. I mean if you are, fine. But I like you 'cause you talk to me. It's just that sometimes, you know, I would also like you to touch me, and I know you're scared to touch me. I'm not sure why you are. I think it's not because of me. I think it's because of what you think's gonna happen to you, or in you. I think you think you're gonna lose control—"

"Lose control? Huh? Like I'm gonna freak out or somethin'? What? Like turn into some gorilla groper or somethin'?"

"No no no, no, that's not the kind of control I'm talkin' about, no. God forbid, I don't think you're one of those guys lays his hands on me and then can't get 'em off, no, that's not what I mean. I just think you're so . . . I'm not sure—God I don't wanna say the wrong thing here, I know you, oh, wow. Let me say it this way. I know, because of my mother, because she doesn't have anybody else, because I'm it for her, you know? Like you are—"

"Yeah? Okay. So, uh, what?"

"Well sometimes I catch myself, I don't know, maybe it's because I'm getting older, I think, you know, if I let myself get attracted to someone, what's it gonna do to her? Now I don't think about this all the time. I never used to think about it at all, but here—here's what I'm tryin' to say. I think sometimes I just have this much love in me to give, and if I give it to somebody else, that'll mean I have that much less to give her, you know? And I'm just talkin' about time now, nothin' else, I'm not talkin' about love. Just time, that's all, you know, there are only so many hours in the day, and how much time can I devote to somebody else when, you know, I know she's at home? Alone. And she's stuck there. Nobody comes to see her, nobody calls her anymore. Her family's all gone, her last sister died a year ago last May, and she can't drive—you know what I'm sayin'. Any of this makin' sense to you, huh? Do you think like this? Ever?"

"Uh, Franny, don't get mad, please? I really gotta know what time it is."

"Well turn around and look, okay? There's a clock in every one of those beer signs. And there's another one on the Coke sign."

"Oh man, quarter to seven, I gotta get goin'. Listen, I hear what you're sayin', okay? I know what you're talkin' about. I think about that stuff all the time, who's gonna take care of her if I don't—"

"Well do you think thinkin' about that maybe might interfere with thinkin' about whether you wanna get close to me? Get closer? Huh?"

"I don't know . . . Jeez, there was never anybody else to consider before, you know? Aw what am I sayin'—course I think that. Hell yeah. Sure. I mean, I think about you so much, Jeez . . . I mean I get off thinkin' about you—"

She sucked in a breath, her jaw dropped, and her hand flew to cover her mouth. She looked around to see if anybody else heard. Nobody was paying attention. "Get off? *Get off?!* Like *that* get off, you mean?"

Carlucci felt his face heating up. He hung his head and wanted to disappear into the floor.

She got the giggles, then she threw back her head, both hands over her mouth, and laughed, joyfully, exuberantly.

Oh man, Carlucci thought, why don't you say something really fucking stupid? You think you could think of anything stupider? Huh? You fucking jagoff. Man. . . .

When he got the courage to raise his eyes to look at her, she was beaming, still laughing, but there was no ridicule in her eyes. She was shaking her head at him and beaming. And leaning toward him. And rubbing the back of his hand.

"What?" he said. "What?"

"God, Carlucci, you . . . you're so funny."

"Yeah, right, that's me. Carlucci the comedian—"

"No no no, that's not what I mean. I love it. I love it. The shyest man in Rocksburg . . . practices the safest sex anybody can do . . . and when he does it, he thinks of me. Oh God, I love it."

"Go 'head, go 'head, I deserve it."

"I'm serious, Carlucci. I love it. Only listen? You listening to me? I'm serious. Next time you do it, I want you to call me."

"Huh?"

"Call me. I mean it. I'm serious. When you're gettin' ready, you know, to, uh, you know—*think* of me? Call me."

"What, on the phone?"

"Yes! Of course on the phone, how else?"

"You want me to call you. On the phone. When I'm, uh—"

"Yes!"

He lurched up. "This is too weird. I mean it. Way too weird."

She grabbed his left hand because it was closer, and she pulled him back down to his chair. He was surprised by her strength.

"Listen, you, I know what you're thinkin'. You're thinkin' I'm puttin' you on, pullin' your chain, laughin' at you—but I'm not, okay? Look at me! C'mon! Look! Look at these eyes, Carlucci!"

He was caught in a cross fire of shame and anger. His own. But somehow he sensed—he couldn't have said how—that she was telling what she truly felt; so after a short but hard struggle with his shame and anger, he managed to get his eyes level with hers, and finally to meet her gaze.

"You have to believe me, Rugs, I know what I'm saying. This is a start for us. We both have these people who we think depend on us, and in some respects they depend on us way more than we know and in other respects they both wish we'd drop dead, and if we told the truth, you know? Sometimes, if we let ourselves, sometimes we'd be saying the same things about them. It's all mixed up, all this love and respect and responsibility, and right there on the other side of it, it's us sayin' who needs this? Life's tough enough, when's mine gonna start? And honest to God, Rugs, you don't know how sick I am of hearin' guys, you know, hey, there's Fran Perfetti, third-place Miss Pennsylvania, man, what a body, lemme get between her legs, hang her pussy scalp on my belt . . . I'm sick of all these lover boys, these guys think all I do every day is sit around waitin' for them to get a hard-on so they can stick it in me.

"And you come along, and all you can do, one way or another, is show me how scared you are, just to touch me. But the big thing you do, I mean, God, Rugs, you listen. When I talk, you listen to me. You're not lookin' at my tits, you're—God, you're lookin' at my eyes. You don't know what a turn-on that is for me. And then when you tell me what you just told me, I think whoa! This is great!" Her eyes were dancing; her smile was lighting up the darkest corners of his mind.

Carlucci was in love. For the first time in his life. But he still had to go. John Czarowicz was coming in at seven. Carlucci pulled his hands away from hers with an apologetic shrug and stood up again. But just as he was starting for the door, a clear clean thought burst through the fog and murk of his mind. Say it, he said to himself. Say it now, you fuckin' wuss, don't you fuckin' swallow this, get it out. So he did.

His voice cracking and quavering, he said, "I'll call you. I gotta go, but I promise. I'll call you. No matter what time, right?"

"No matter what time," she said. "Rugs?"

"What?" he said at the door.

"I can't wait."

Oh man, he thought, rushing out to his car. I musta died. And this must be heaven.

On his way back to the station, Carlucci distracted himself from thinking about that phone call to Franny Perfetti by trying to find Milliron. Aside from the obvious reason that he needed a partner to interview John Czarowicz, Carlucci didn't want to give Milliron another reason to think that anything going on in Carlucci's personal life was going to interfere with the work. He didn't want to give Milliron the satisfaction of learning otherwise. Then he thought, Christ, how long am I going to keep this chickenshit up?

Carlucci's calls didn't catch up to Milliron until he was back in the duty room of the Rocksburg PD. He caught Milliron just as he was leaving the pathology lab at Conemaugh General where he'd observed the post on Frank Krull.

"You been tryin' to call me?" Carlucci said, thinking as soon as the words came out, Oh that's sweet. Couple seconds ago I'm wondering how long I'm going to keep up this chickenshit and the first thing I do is ask him if he's been trying to call me. Like I would really like to have been interrupted when I was with Franny.

"What for?" Milliron said. "Meckler called me in to observe. The two of us was enough, we didn't need you."

"Meckler? Who's he?"

"He's the corporal in charge at the Krull scene. Thought I introduced you. You don't remember that?"

"No you didn't. You tried to introduce me to a snake, I would've remembered you tried to introduce me to a person."

"Whatever."

"No whatevers, if you'da introduced me to somebody out there I woulda remembered it. Never mind. What'd Grimes say?"

"Homicide, what do you think he said? Entry wound in the back of the head, just like Lyon. Same kinda bullet, .22. Four fragments."

"Tell Failan yet?"

"Meckler's doin' that now. I was gonna go get somethin' to eat, haven't eaten since this morning—why you callin' me?"

"I got a guy comin' in, one of those foremen. I alibied six of 'em out this afternoon, maybe seven—before I came out to the Krull scene—I told you that."

"No you didn't, you didn't say anything about that. I would've remembered that."

"Well I did—I mean I alibied 'em out, I'm not sayin' I told you I did. Anyway, this one guy, uh, name's Czarowicz, I don't know, he was too edgy, too somethin'. Thought he was worth an up-close-and-personal. You need to be here."

"When?"

"Seven."

"It's seven right now," Milliron said, then grunted something unintelligible. "I'll be there after I pick up a coupla burgers."

Milliron didn't arrive until a minute after Czarowicz did, and Czarowicz didn't arrive until ten after seven.

Czarowicz was a wiry man, five ten or so, with wide, bony shoulders, muscular, veiny arms, and hands that seemed too big for his body. His salt-and-pepper hair was wispy thin on top; his brows were black and gray tangles; his face was creased and lined; he didn't wear glasses. He had on a gray T-shirt, green chinos, white socks, and ankle-high black shoes that were polished to a high gloss.

Carlucci introduced himself to Czarowicz and shook hands with him and then introduced Milliron, who was juggling foil-wrapped burgers and a tall drink. Milliron held up the burgers and drink when Czarowicz offered his hand. Then Carlucci led them both back to the interrogation room in the rear of the Rocksburg station and held the door for them. Czarowicz went in, but again Milliron held up the burgers and drink and said he was going to stay out until he ate. Carlucci shrugged, went in, closed the door, and motioned for Czarowicz to have a seat on the other side of the rectangular metal table.

"Looks pretty official to me," Czarowicz said, pointing vaguely at the room and table. "Said all we was gonna do was talk. Sure that's all you wanna do?"

"That's all we're gonna be doin', Mister Czarowicz," Carlucci said. "Talkin'. If it was anything else, I'd have to tell you."

"Whattaya mean, if it was anything else? Anything else how?"

"This is an interview, okay? Nothin' more than that. Just wanna ask you about Conemaugh Steel, how things were when you worked there, and so forth, that's all. We've talked to some people used to work there, management, labor—"

"And the rest of us," Czarowicz said with a dismissive laugh.

"Excuse me?"

"You said you talked to people used to work there, management, labor, and I said, 'And the rest of us.'"

"Wait just one second here," Carlucci said, taking out his tape recorder and putting it in the middle of the table.

"What's that?" Czarowicz said, shifting around on his chair.

"Tape recorder. I have to record interviews because, fast as people talk, you know, I could never write fast enough to keep up with 'em, so I just get everything on tape, that's all, no big deal."

Before Czarowicz could say anything else, Carlucci ID'd himself for the tape as well as Milliron and Czarowicz, the date, day, and time. Because he'd never asked Milliron what case number he was using, he said the interview was in regard to the Lyon homicide, which was unprofessional as hell, he thought. Then he said, "Trooper Milliron is not in the room at the present time."

"Where's he, huh? That trooper. On the other side of that mirror there? I seen stuff like this on TV," Czarowicz said. Then he nodded at the recorder. "We ain't gonna just be talkin' here, uh-uh."

"Yes we are, Mister Czarowicz," Carlucci said. "That's all this is. Just us talkin', tryin' to get a handle on this thing, that's all. Would you, uh, state your full name and address, and occupation, if you have one?"

"Oh I know what's goin' on here, don't think I don't."

"Mister Czarowicz? Your name please? And address?"

"John Joseph Czarowicz, uh, 748 Frick Avenue, Rocksburg. Don't have an occupation, What I have is three jobs. I work for Panai's, whenever they need help makin' a pickup—"

"The funeral home?"

"Yeah, Panai's Funeral Home, right."

"Pickup? What's that mean?"

"Whattaya think it means? Pick up the body. Uh, I also work the funerals there, you know, movin' chairs around for the services, helpin' old people in and outta their cars, movin' flowers around, that kinda thing. Or takin' flowers up the hospital or to different nursin' homes, afterwards, you know, whatever the families want. I also work at the car wash. Good weather I get a lotta work there. He's related to Panai somehow, guy that owns it, I don't know how, cousins or somethin'. But whenever there's somebody laid out, I go to the funeral home."

"What's the third job? Said you had three."

"Chasin' carts. Shoppin' carts, you know? Giant Eagle, Foodland, Shop 'n Save. Whenever a kid don't show up, they gimme a call."

"So you're still workin', you're not retired, but you're old enough, aren't you? To be retired?"

Czarowicz put his hands between his knees and rubbed his palms together. "I'm sixty-six. But retired? That's a laugh."

"Well that's old enough for Social Security, isn't it?"

"If you wanna starve."

"How do you mean?"

"Know anybody on Social Security?"

"All I know about Social Security is I get taxed seven point three cents out of every dollar I make, that's all I know—well, that, plus my mother, she's, uh, she gets survivor benefits."

"Yeah, and I guess you think all us old farts, we're just usin' it up, huh? So there ain't gonna be none left. For youns young farts."

"I didn't say that."

"Yeah, but you're thinkin' it. Hear that crap all the time at the car wash, bustin' my stones about that all the time. They don't know nothin' neither, just like you don't. For instance, you know that at sixty-two, you try to collect—which I did so I know what I'm talkin' about—at sixty-two, for every two bucks you make, you lose a dollar in benefits? You know that, huh? They let you make so much—changes every year the amount, but after you make that much, whatever it is, for every two bucks you make over that, you lose a buck in benefits. So if you could be so lucky to, say, make twenty thousand a year you would have to give back every dollar they gave you. It's different for everybody, that formula, depends on how long you worked, how much you made, how much you paid in, and all that, but in my case, the year I made twenty thousand? I wound up havin' to give it all back. Every goddamn cent, huh? You know *that* about Social Security?"

"Like I said, I know what I pay and I know my mother gets survivor benefits, but I'm not gonna try to tell you I know the particulars of the law. I don't."

"Yeah. And when you get to be sixty-five," Czarowicz said, "the formula changes. They let you make a couple thousand more a year, but for every three bucks you make after that you lose a buck. And that goes on till you're seventy, or seventy-one, I forget. Then they let you make all you want. Like somebody's gonna hire you when you're seventy."

"But you are allowed to make so much, right?"

"Ain't that what I just said?" Czarowicz said. "But after you make that, whatever it is—it changes every year the amount—that's when they kick in that two-for-one and three-for-one crap. But if you think what you're allowed to make is enough to live on, you need to try livin' on it. 'Cause it ain't. Not with today's prices. And it sure ain't enough to pay your hospital bills, doctor bills, prescriptions—well you get a break on them from the state. 'Cause of the lotteries."

"Well if you're old enough to get Social Security, don't you automatically qualify for Medicare?"

"Yeah. I'm on Medicare now, yeah. Got on it last year. Finally. But when my wife got sick, uh, same year they shut the mill down, uh, yeah, that's when she found the first one, the first lump, uh, '85. So, that's when I find out I got no job, then I find out I got no pension, and then we find out we don't qualify for Medicaid. I was makin' way too much for them bastards, them and their goddamn charts."

"Excuse me? I was talkin' about Medicare, I didn't say Medicaid."

"I know what you said. I'm tellin' you what I said. Thirteen years ago, I wasn't sixty-six. I was fifty-three. You don't even think about Medicare till you're sixty-five. First year after the mill shut down, I got a job at Rosso's Construction, drivin' a truck. Made half what I made in the mill. My wife's hospital bills was twelve thousand. You still listenin'? Huh? Made twenty thousand, that's gross. After taxes, the ones they take outta your pay, I'm not talkin' about sales taxes, gasoline taxes, and all that other shit they stick ya for, I'm talkin' about what they deduct, you know? Lucky to clear fifteen. Try livin' on what's left after you pay twelve—you hear me? Twelve! That's what we paid to the hospital. I'm not talkin' about the doctors.

"First time we went up the hospital to get the X rays, get the results, I mean, talk to this radiology guy? I remember that day real good. It was colder'n hell. You could hear the bells from Mother of Sorrows all the way up there, real clear . . . and my wife, she went in there without me, I'll never know why she did that. Didn't say nothin', just left me standin' out there in the waitin' room like some goof. Then here she was, comin' back with this . . . with this look on her face. And she's breathin' funny, and her eyes're all fillin' up and I'm goin' what, what, and she says, 'I got it.' And I said got what, like some jagoff, like I forgot what we went there for. And she says what do you think? And I couldn't say nothin'. All I could do was, uh, was help her put her coat on. Remember that like it was this mornin'."

Czarowicz stared over Carlucci's shoulder for a long moment. "Anyway, that was the first time. Took that one off . . . then ten months, two weeks, three days later, they took the other one off. That was in '86, that time. Then both times there was the chemo, and then there was the radiation, and all that . . . all that goddamn torture, that's what that was. Shoulda never let 'em do it. Not the second time. First time we didn't know no better, second time, we were just, shit, she was just a . . . I don't know why they did it, they knew we didn't have no insurance, they knew we didn't qualify for Medicaid, they knew that, the bastards, they went ahead and did it anyway . . . put her through all that misery, that chemo, she got so sick with that. Where are ya now, Christ, huh? That's what I said. Where the fuck ya at now, huh, Jesus? When we really need ya, where the fuck are ya?

"Did all that misery to her, then the bastard turned us over to a collection agency. Then Rosso's goes el foldo, I lose the truckin' job, next thing I know I'm moppin' floors all night for three thirty-five an hour. That was minimum wage in '85, '86. Oh yeah. How'd you like that, huh? Doctors, they put you through all that misery, huh? Shoot her fulla all them chemicals, them poisons, then you can't pay, fucker sics a collection agency on ya. I'm workin' nights, my wife's answerin' the phone so I can get some sleep, what's she gotta listen to? Some cocksucker callin' her names, callin' her deadbeat, callin' her a bum, a parasite. She had to look that one up in the dictionary, didn't even know what that one meant. How'd you like that, huh? Knowin' you got cancer all through ya, and you pick up the phone and that's the kinda shit you gotta listen to, huh? 'Cause one of them prick doctors wants his money. The other ones, God bless 'em, they at least let me work out a deal, you know? Ten bucks a month. But not that one prick, uh-uh, no, that sonofabitch, he got to have his money right now. Cocksucker.

"Went to see him after she, uh, you know. She wouldn't let me while she was, uh, you know, still, uh . . . made me swear I wouldn't go see him. But afterwards, I got one of those calls, I threw the phone in the garbage, I went up that cocksucker's office, I sat there in his waitin' room till everybody left, and then I went in, and I said, you want your money, huh? You sonofabitch, how 'bout I tear up a twenty-dollar bill in little bitty pieces and how about I load it into a twelve-gauge shell and pump it into your fuckin' chest, huh? How'd you like that, you money-grubbin' cocksucker, you want your money so fuckin' bad, how'd you like it in front of a load of double-0 buck-shot, huh?"

"You know how to reload shotgun shells?" Carlucci said.

"You wanna hunt, and all you're makin' is minimum wage, you better know how to reload 'em. Or you better know somebody who does."

The door opened then and Milliron came in. "I don't understand something," he said. "Why couldn't you qualify for Medicare again?"

Czarowicz squinted up at Milliron. "I wasn't talkin' Medicare. I was talkin' Medicaid, 'bout makin' too much for Medicaid—"

"Medicare, Medicaid, I get 'em mixed up—"

"Oh is that right, can't keep 'em straight, huh? Well, Medicare's when you're old enough for Social Security. Medicaid's for people under the poverty line—if you're willin' to let the goddamn state put a lien on your house. And if you're willin' to drive a bucket of bolts. Told me I had to sell my car. You don't believe me, do you? You don't have to say nothin', I can see it in your eyes. Lemme tell you some-thin', Trooper, you went down the welfare office right now, today, hear what I'm sayin'? Today? You can't have a car payment more'n thirty bucks a month. Pricks that wrote that law think you can buy a car in 1998 for thirty bucks a month. And if you pay more than that and they find out about it, that disqualifies you for welfare, which means you don't qualify for Medicaid, and if you try—you hear me? If you try, they tell you all the penalties for welfare fraud, and then they arrest your ass."

Milliron sighed and looked at the ceiling.

"So you wouldn't let 'em put a lien on your house?" Carlucci said.

"Hell no! Damn right I wouldn't, that house is the only thing I got to show for all the sweat I give those pricks. Christ, we just paid it off. You just pay off a thirty-year mortgage, you think I'm gonna let the state put a lien on it? And to clear that lien you gotta pay back what they give ya? How you s'posed to do that, huh? When there's no way I'm gonna make the kinda money I made in the mill. Never again, huh? I'm no genius, but I ain't stupid, no way I'm makin' that kinda money again."

"Ever think about sellin' your house to pay these medical bills?" Milliron said.

"Excuse me?" Czarowicz said. "Who's gonna buy it? Who the hell's movin' to Rocksburg, huh? Maybe you wanna buy it. No? Think you'd give me anywhere near what I put into it, huh?"

"I'm sure you tried hard enough, you could sell it."

"Listen to this guy," Czarowicz said. "And meanwhile every week to this day those fuckers're still sendin' us letters—not us, me, listen to me, like she's still here. Us, shit. Me. They're sendin' letters to me, yeah, we gotta make some arrangement to pay these bills—like she's still alive. Yeah, here's the way they write, Dear Mister and Missus Czarowicz, you have to make some arrangement to blah blah blah. Jesus Christ Almighty, at one time we owed 'em thirty-seven thousand two hundred and twenty-eight dollars. We owed the doctors, the X-ray guys that give the radiation, the cancer guys that give the chemo, God knows what we owed them, I don't even know anymore. The doctors at least, you know, except for that one cocksucker, they all agreed to an installment plan, like ten, twelve bucks a month, those ones at least, they stopped sendin' us letters. Hospital too, they were real good about it."

"But you refused to think about sellin' your house? Never thought once you could've moved into an apartment?"

"Hey, you, c'mon, 748 Frick Avenue. C'mon, make me an appointment right now, I'll give ya a tour. And you can make me an offer."

"No thanks, I'm not in the market right now."

"Well neither's anybody else around here, okay? You don't understand that? Take a ride around. Whatta you think all them boarded-up windows mean, huh? You think it's to keep the insides all clean for the new buyers? City puts them boards up keep the kids and the dopeheads out."

Carlucci coughed, put his elbows on the table, and said, "Uh, Mister Czarowicz, which doctor was it? Turned you over to a collection agency? The one you threatened, what was his name?"

"Shit, that's his name. He don't have a name. Bastard. Called that collection agency, threatened us with all kindsa crap, made my wife sicker and sicker. Want my opinion that's what killed her. Cancer didn't kill her. It was the goddamn worryin' and bein' scared of what people would think of us. Gettin' those letters all the time, and the goddamn phone calls, that's what killed her. She used to worry what the *mailman* thought. She couldn't stand to look at the mail. Couldn't stand to even touch it.

"I tried to tell her—I don't know how many times I tried—I said what the hell do we care what the mailman thinks, huh? We should care what he thinks? Hell with him, we didn't do this to ourself, you didn't go out and get cancer by bein' stupid like some queer humpin' some other queer without no rubber on. Stop thinkin' like that, I says to her, cancer ain't your fault. It ain't nobody's fault, it just happened to ya'. But she kept blamin' herself, said she shoulda managed the money better, shouldn'ta spent so much money, shoulda been savin' it all the time . . . like she was some kinda frivolous doll baby or somethin'. Frivolous, Christ Almighty, she managed the money good. Helluva lot better'n I coulda, I'll tell ya that. Way better. I coulda never done it the way she done it. Good enough we put our second boy through college, that's how good she done it.

"Wanna hear some real crap, huh? Know what he took up in college, huh, our kid? This kid she busted her brain makin' sure he got this good education? Whattaya think he takes up in college, huh? Hospital administration, that's what he takes up. Hospital administration. And got himself a good job too, real good job. Out there in Arizona. Phoenix. But you know what? The ungrateful prick, huh? Never once asked us if we needed any help. Think of that, huh? Put him through college—my wife did all that talkin', talked to the counselors in high school, them recruiters that come around, whatever they call 'em, the people from the colleges, she was the one filled out all the forms for the loans, she was the one got all the figures together, all our tax forms, everything, she was the one did all that for that kid make sure he gets a good education . . . ha! Yeah. Right. Whole time she's sick, never once . . . never once comes around. Got this big-shot job in Arizona, runs some huge hospital out there, runs the whole goddamn place, the boss, you know? Never once showed up. Called once, huh? Imagine that. One goddamn time he picks up the phone. Yeah. After she told him in a letter she had it, he calls. Once. Never calls again.

"When I called him to tell him she was, uh," Czarowicz said, his voice cracking, his eyes flooding, "he, uh, he wanted to know if I wanted him to be there. *Be there,* he says, you want me to *be there.* I says she's your mother for Christ sake, do you have to ask that question, the hell's wrong with you? What the hell did we ever do to you was so terrible, huh? So terrible you have to ask a question like that. Woman never did anything in her whole life but look out for you, did everything she could to make your life good, and that's what you got to say? *You want me to be there?* Shit. Coulda killed him. Right at that moment, he'da been in arm's length of me, I woulda choked him, swear to God, I'da choked the goddamn life out of him . . . made me so mad, I threw the phone against the wall, broke that phone. Second time I hada buy a new one. Don't know what for. He never called again.

"Tried to call him once, found out he didn't only change his phone number, oh no, I call information, they tell me the person listed at that address, the one I had for him? That person was named Caro. Yeah. Not only changed his phone number, changed his whole last name. Now he's John Charles Caro. I wrote him a letter, this John Charles Caro, I didn't wanna talk to him. I was so mad, I said, I hope you're happy with your new name, you ungrateful prick. I hope you're happy with your new self. Your mother, she goes to her grave, her only survivin' son, where's he, huh? He's in Arizona. Ain't nowhere where I can see him.

" 'Bout three months later, here comes this letter from him. All he does for ten pages, ten goddamn pages, he tells me how bad we treated him. And how dumb we were. Everything but call us dumb hunkies, his own parents. And you know what it was about? Huh? Know what it come down to? Said we never paid no attention to him, all we did was walk around like zombies grievin' over our first son."

"Your first son?"

"Yeah. Our first son. He got, uh, he got killed in Vietnam . . . he was in the marines . . . like me. Told him, Jesus Christ, told him a hundred times, don't go, don't do that. Talked myself blue in the face, told him don't do that stupid shit, don't get in a fight you don't know what it's about, that's just askin' for trouble. He kept throwin' what I did back in my face, you did it he says, you enlisted, what'd you en-list for, what'd you go to Korea for? You know what Korea was about, huh? I said ya dumb shit, whattaya think I'm tellin' ya don't go for? Exactly 'cause of me, that's exactly why I'm tellin' ya not to join up, that's stupid. Least I had a reason, I says to him. Goddamn tax people, they took the house I was livin' in."

"Tax people took your house?"

"Yeah. Tried to tell him why I done it, he didn't wanna hear nothin'. Told him, I was just a kid when my mother died, think I was ten. And my old man, after she died, he just went to hell, he couldn't stand it, just drunk all the time. My last year in high school, come home one day, there he was. In the toilet, you know. Found him.

"So after I get that straightened out, and boy that was a mess too. So I'm livin' there for three months by myself, and one day, right after New Year's, here comes this fat fucker from City Hall, wantsa know why nobody's answerin' their letters. I didn't know what he was talkin' about, I didn't know nothin' about no letters. Turns out after my mother died my old man quit payin' real estate taxes. He just stopped payin' 'em, that's all. Eight years he didn't pay no taxes on the house. They sent him all these letters, registered or somethin', he

musta just threw 'em away, I never saw 'em. I didn't have 'em, I
didn't know what the guy was talkin' about. Tough shit you don't
know, he says, the owner of this house owes these back taxes, and he
tells me how much. Plus penalties, plus interest. And he's talkin' thousands of dollars. Thousands. I says where the hell am I gonna get that
kinda money, I'm still goin' to school. I was workin', sure, but I
couldn't pay how much they wanted, Christ. And I didn't know you
could work things out maybe, work out an installment plan or somethin'. I was a kid, what the hell'd I know?

"I worked second shift down Federal Enamel all the way through
high school, but it was just a flunky job, just minimum wage, I didn't
run no machine or nothin'. It was just enough dough to take care of
the old man and me, that's all. And the high school, they didn't give
me no diploma, they give me this, uh, this certificate of attendance,
that's all they gave me. I flunked everything, couldn't stay awake in
class. So every place I go for a job, all they got's the crummiest job in
the place, I was sick of that minimum wage shit, moppin' up, carryin'
garbage out. Federal Enamel didn't even wanna give me somethin'
better. They get this new shiny ass in the personnel office, he says he
wants smart workers, he don't want dumb workers, dumb workers
just cause trouble. I said Christ I worked here all through high
school, three years, ain't that good for somethin'? He didn't care, all he
knew was I wasn't smart enough to get a diploma, I wasn't smart
enough to work there, he didn't wanna hear nothin'.

"This is what I was tryin' to tell my kid, see? That was why I
joined up, I didn't have no place to live, I didn't have no parents, what
the hell was I supposed to do? Boys Club let me sleep there for about
a week, but they weren't gonna let me do that forever. Boys Club ain't
no YMCA. So some guy down the Boys Club, he says why don't you
join up, they'll give you a place to sleep, three squares. And anyway
when I joined up, I didn't even know about Korea, I didn't know what
the hell was goin' on over there, I didn't read the papers, I didn't know
nothin', I was a dumb shit. All I knew was, a couple stooges from the
sheriff's, they come in and said they're puttin' the house up for sale,
get the hell out, that's all, good-bye. Tacked some paper up on the

door, this fat-ass deputy sheriff, he takes me by the arm, he says see ya later. All he lets me do is go back inside, get a couple shoppin' bags, put my clothes in 'em.

"I needed a place to sleep, I'm tellin' my kid, a place to eat, and I'm a dumb shit. That's why the next week I'm down the recruitin' office, joinin' up. Why'd you join the marines, he says. 'Cause it was the first office I come to, I says. If the first office woulda been the army I woulda joined the army. Oh no, he says, I don't believe you joined 'em 'cause that was the first office you come to, I ain't buyin' that he says. Don't matter what I tell him, he don't wanna hear nothin'. Kids at a certain age, they don't believe nothin' you tell 'em.

"So he joins up, yeah. And seven months later, uh, here comes this lieutenant knockin' on our door, handin' me this official notice, tellin' me how sorry he is, or how sorry the president is, or somebody, somebody was sorry, I don't know who the hell it was. Private First Class William Edward Czarowicz killed in action in Khe Sanh. All I could think was Khe Sanh, huh? Where the fuck is that, huh? Ever hear of that, Khe Sanh?"

"Yeah," Carlucci said. "Lotta kids died there."

"You over there, huh? Vietnam? You look about the right age."

"Yeah. I was there."

"In Khe Sanh?"

"No no, army. I wasn't there, not Khe Sanh. Other places."

"Yeah. Me too. Other places. Korea, that's where I was. Winter there was, Jesus, so fuckin' cold. Everything kept freezin' up, fuckin' BARs, couldn't get the gas ports set right, fuckers'd quit all the time, specially when the temperature'd change real fast—"

"BARs?" Milliron said. "What's that?"

"Browning automatic rifles," Czarowicz said. "You never heard of them?"

"No."

"Yeah. Well, there was one in every fire team, three fire teams in every squad, all your basic infantry tactics in the marines, they were built around the BAR-man in each fire team. Which was okay if the goddamn thing worked the way it was s'posed to. We had so many

BAR-men get hit, killed, wounded, always somebody pickin' one of 'em up didn't know what he was doin' with it, you know? And the officers'd, you know, they'd keep hollerin' all the time, get the BAR, get the BAR. Then things'd quiet down, whoever picked it up, they'd try to clean it, even if they got everything else right, they'd screw up the gas port, set it wrong, then next time they'd have to use it, fuckin' thing wouldn't fire. Weighed almost twenty pounds, Christ. Each magazine, full, you know, they were so heavy, you could only carry four of 'em. Then the assistant BAR-man, he'd carry four more besides his own ammo for his M-1, that was heavier'n hell, all that ammo. Felt like every time you tried to move you were runnin' in mud.

"Wouldn't touch those fuckin' BARs myself, I stayed with my M-1, I knew how to make that full auto. Filed the sear off, that's all, I didn't need no BAR. I could fire eight rounds fast as any BAR-man could fire twenty. And you couldn't screw the gas port up. Didn't have no gas port to screw up, the M-1—I mean it had one, but you couldn't get at it just field-strippin' 'em."

Milliron looked at Carlucci. "You know what he's talkin' about?"

Carlucci shook his head no. "Not exactly. But I don't think the details are important. Do you, Mister Czarowicz?"

"Do I what?"

"Think the details are important."

"What details?"

"Whether anybody knows what you're talkin' about when you talk about these BARs or these M-1s, huh? Think that's gonna make any difference to anybody? That you knew how to make your rifle, what was it, the M-1?"

"Yeah."

"That you knew how to make it full automatic? Filed the sear off, is that what you said? What's that? I think I know, but tell me."

"The sear? That was this little hooklike hickey in the trigger housing, it's what caught the rear hammer hook, kept it semi-auto, you know, firin' one at a time, which was the way it was designed. So if you took that apart, the trigger housing, and you filed that little hook off, the sear, it'd fire full auto. Didn't take more'n a coupla minutes to file it off. Did it for every guy come in the platoon, we didn't need no BARs. Everybody come in my platoon had a full auto M-1 soon as I got my hands on it. Still wasn't no match for them burp guns them gooks had. But who cares about that now, right? All ancient history."

"Exactly," Milliron said. "That's my point."

"Well, see," Carlucci said, leaning forward and peering into Czarowicz's eyes, "they were still usin' M-14s when I first got over to Nam, but then the M-16s came in, but I remember hearin' the M-14s were just a different version of the M-1s. And I remember guys talkin' about filin' sears off those M-14s, turnin' them full auto. The manual said you weren't supposed to do that, but, uh, you know, just like you, I mean, you get in that situation, who cares about the manual, right? You sure didn't."

"Me?" Czarowicz said.

"Yeah, you."

"Fuck the manual. After boot camp, I never saw one of those. I was tryin' to stay alive."

"Yeah," Carlucci said. "That's what I thought. You're a funny kinda guy, Mister Czarowicz."

"Funny? Me? Whatta you mean funny? I ain't funny."

"I don't mean funny ha ha. I mean, I get the feelin' you don't speak up for yourself for a long time, you just watch what's goin' on, like with those BARs. But if somebody tries to make you pick one up, you don't make a fuss or get in an argument, you just go figure out what to do with your M-1. And then you go do it. Somebody orders you to pick up a BAR, you don't wanna pick it up, you don't pick it up, right? Huh? Hell with the order. That sound like what you did?"

"Yeah. Sorta. Why's that make me funny? I don't get that."

"Well, most guys, they wouldn't wanna go against an order. Most guys they'd almost be more scared of what would happen to 'em if they disobeyed an order—I mean more than they would be of the enemy, whatta you think? Ever think about that?"

"Oh I don't know about that. Never thought about it. I just never paid too much attention to the officers, that's all. I knew they weren't gonna be around too long anyway. First ones to get hit, usually. I mean I tried to tell the new ones, the lieutenants, you know, I'd tell 'em, lose 'em fuckin' gold bars, you might as well have a bull's-eye hangin' on ya. Most of 'em didn't listen, like if they didn't have their bars we wouldn't know who they were. But those ones, they ain't around anymore, snipers got 'em. Course lotta guys I went over there with, they ain't around anymore. There's only two of us made it through the whole time from my platoon. We got there September first, 1950, by the end of that month, ten of 'em was dead and there was fifteen more wounded good enough to go Stateside. Me and this kid from Jersey, both got hit three times, but none of 'em good enough to make it Stateside."

"That make you mad?" Milliron said.

"Make me mad? What?"

"Never gettin' hit good enough to go home."

"I didn't have no home to go to, why would that make me mad? Told ya, the sheriff put me out, what home was I s'posed to go home to?"

"Yes, but didn't it make you mad you had to stay there? While other guys were goin' home?"

"Listen, Trooper, Korea was for the duration, understand? You got there, that's where you stayed till you either got hit good enough to leave on a stretcher or in a box, otherwise you were there, so there was no reason for me to get mad about it. Just bein' there? Hey, I was just tryin' to stay in one piece, that's all. If I kept the gooks off my ass, off my buddies' ass, I was doin' good, that's all I was thinkin' about, believe me, I didn't have time to get mad at nobody else."

"Well you sounded pretty mad about Medicare."

"It ain't Medicare, I keep tellin' you it was Medicaid—"

"Okay, Medicaid."

"Don't say it like there ain't no difference, there's a helluva big difference. You just ain't run up against it yet, so you don't know. You think it's all one thing 'cause you don't need it yet, but you will.

You'll need it some day, then I'll bet you'll be able to keep 'em straight."

"Okay, Medicaid, alright? I got it now," Milliron said, glaring at Czarowicz.

"Then see if you can put yourself in my place. Try that. I know nobody can do that. I used to try to feel what my wife was feelin', you know? What she had? I knew it hurt like a sonofabitch, you'd have to be blind not to see that, specially at the end, Jesus Christ, I mean, I'd wake up in the middle of the night 'cause she was just bawlin' from the pain, and what the fuck was I s'posed to do, huh? Get her her drugs, that's all, get them painkillers didn't work for shit, that's all I could do. And then I'd lay there and try to feel it, like if I could feel it, maybe, I don't know, sounds stupid, but I thought if maybe I could feel some of it, she wouldn't have to feel it all herself or feel it as bad, or somethin'. But no matter how hard I tried I could never feel what she was feelin'. So I know you can't really know what it felt like when them fuckers at Medicaid, when they told us we didn't qualify, okay, I know that. But try. I mean, seriously, try it. Try to think how if you loved somebody—you married?"

"Me? No."

"Got somebody you love, huh? Anybody? A dog even, you got a dog? Ever have a dog that suffered and you hada watch him die, huh?"

"Yeah I had a dog that died. Yeah."

"Take him to the vet, huh? Have him put to sleep?"

"Yeah. We did that. My mother and me."

"Well, imagine if you got there and the vet said—I mean I know this ain't what I'm tryin' to say here—but imagine if you went to the vet and after he put your dog down, the sonofabitch kept sendin' ya bills, huh? And sicced a collection agency on ya, and those bastards, they called ya all kinda names—"

"They can't do that, those agencies aren't allowed to do that," Milliron said, shaking his head dismissively. "There're laws against that kind of harassment—"

"Laws?!" Czarowicz exploded. "You think laws stop people from doin' things they ain't s'posed to do?! Hell kinda cop are you? You gotta be the only deaf and blind cop I ever seen my whole life. Laws, Jesus Christ—"

"Listen, the hospital and the doctors, did they care for your wife or not? I mean they didn't put her out on the street, did they?"

"No—put her out—I didn't say that, don't be puttin' words in my mouth, I never said nobody put her out. Hospital took good care of her, the doctors, the nurses, none of 'em never held back—not that I could see. Did everything they could for her—I mean how the hell would I know whether they didn't, I ain't no expert. But nobody ever looked to me like they was holdin' back 'cause of the Medicaid thing, that's not what I'm sayin'. I'm askin' how you woulda felt if that's what the vet said after you and your mother took your dog to be put to sleep, huh? To be put outta its misery—how would you've felt? Can you think about that? Can you try?"

"He would've been pissed off if the vet kept harassin' him," Carlucci said. "Course he would, anybody would, in that situation. Isn't that right, Trooper?"

Milliron glared at Carlucci.

"Well that's all I'm talkin' about. But then imagine when this vet's sendin' you these bills, how 'bout you know there's no way you can pay 'em off, huh? And your dog's gone. And your job's gone. That job you thought was gonna last forever, it's in Brazil, somebody you never heard of, he got your job. He don't do it any better'n you did. He just does it a whole helluva lot cheaper. And all you got in life, your whole life, every day you wake up, all it is, once, twice a week, there's gonna be these letters in your mailbox that show up every week the rest of your goddamn life, they're gonna tell you what a deadbeat you are, and it's all 'cause some fuckin' cells went kaflooey in your . . . in your wife's body and she's . . . and nobody knew what to do about it, they couldn't fix it. How'd you like to spend the rest of your life knowin' that's the way it was gonna be, huh?"

"You sound really pissed off about it, mister, you do."

"I'm not talkin' about me, Trooper, I'm talkin' about you! I'm talkin' about if you can imagine it bein' like that."

"But we're talkin' about you, sir," Carlucci said.

"I know who you're talkin' about," Czarowicz said. "I never for a second *didn't* know who you were talkin' about. But right now I'm askin' him, okay? The trooper? I'm askin' him if he could try to think what that'd be like."

"Yeah but see," Milliron said, talking to Czarowicz but looking at Carlucci. "The issue here isn't whether I can imagine bein' in your shoes. The issue here is what you can tell us about the people you used to work with at Conemaugh Steel, that's what I thought we were doin' here, Detective. And tellin' us where he was last night. What do you think we're doin' here, Detective?"

"We'll get around to that, won't we, Mister Czarowicz, huh?"

"I guess we will. Since the trooper can't make his imaginator work."

"My imaginator?" Milliron thought that was funny. "Oh I think I could make my *imaginator* work all right, believe me, I know how to do that. I just don't think it's worth my time to be doin' that."

"Uh, let's go back to somethin' you said a while ago," Carlucci said.

"What?"

"You said when I said somethin' about labor and management, you said somethin' about all the rest of us, you remember that?"

"Yeah."

"What did you mean by that, all the rest of us?"

"All the rest of us that wasn't in labor or management, that's what I meant."

"Well you got to be one or the other," Milliron said.

"Ha. Right. Yeah, that's what I used to think. One day you're in the yard hookin' up, you're labor. Next day you're in the office. And next year, you're runnin' the shippin' office. And the local thinks you're management, but they never actually come right out and tell ya to your face that's what they think. And management, them pricks, they keep deductin' your dues, and the local keeps takin' 'em and shippin' off a cut to the national, but you're too dumb to know any of this."

"Oh man," Milliron said, stretching his arms overhead and walking in small circles in the room. "I'll tell you what, I'm havin' a real hard time swallowin' this. Guy doesn't know whether he's labor or management? I never met a union guy yet didn't know he was union, c'mon, what are we listenin' to here?"

Czarowicz leaned back in his chair and folded his arms across his chest. "Is 'at a fact? Met 'em all around here, huh?"

"I didn't say I met them all. But I've met more than one or two."

"Oh yeah? Well 'less you been hangin' around the union hall, you don't know any in this town, pal, 'cause there ain't been a steelworker cashin' a check in this town since 1985. They might be hangin' around the union hall, but they sure as shit ain't punchin' no clocks or cashin' no checks, 'cept welfare, the ones let 'em lien their house."

Milliron shook his head and shrugged at Carlucci. "How long we gonna let this guy keep makin' speeches? We ever gonna ask him anything? You know, that's pertinent?"

Carlucci shrugged back. "I don't know about you, but I've learned a lot that was pertinent. Far as I'm concerned, Mister Czarowicz, you can go."

Milliron tilted from the waist to peer into Carlucci's eyes. "What?"

"I can go?"

"Yep. If we need to talk to you again, we'll give you a call."

Czarowicz slapped his knees and stood up in the same motion, giving Milliron a strenuous nod as he walked around him to get out.

After Czarowicz shut the door behind him, Milliron put his hands on his hips and stared at Carlucci while Carlucci talked to his tape recorder, saying that the interview with John Czarowicz was over and giving the time it ended. Then he shut it off.

As soon as he did Milliron bent over from the waist, putting his face about a foot from Carlucci's. "Fuck's goin' on here? What'd you let him go for?"

"What, you want to ask him more stuff about the pensions? We already know about the pensions, Valcanas told us that. How much more you need?"

"How much more do I need? Christ! Everything. That guy has all the motive in the world, you never even let him answer when I asked him where he was last night!"

"That's right," Carlucci said, nodding slowly, then touching his upper lip tenderly with his tongue. "That's exactly right. Man has all the motive in the world. And that's all he gave us. Motive. Man lives alone. Who's gonna back up his story where he was last night? And if we'da sat here for another week and never let him sleep and. dripped water on his head, that's all he would've ever given us—more motive."

"Well if you believe that, then why didn't you stay on him till he gave it up?"

"Hey, you mighta been a marine, Pinky, but you weren't listenin' to that old marine."

"About what? What're you talkin' about now?"

"When you asked him if he was mad about bein' stuck in Korea and not gettin' hit good enough—or bad enough—to go home, didn't you hear what he said, huh? He said Korea, you were in for the duration and he didn't have any home to come home to anyway so what was there to get mad about, you heard him say that, I know you did."

"So?"

"The man that said that is a man can accept his situation when he knows he can't change it, so he doesn't waste time worryin' about it."

"So?"

"What'd he say next?"

"I don't know what you're talkin' about."

"He said all he cared about was keepin' the gooks off his ass, and off his buddies' ass, any way he could. If the BARs didn't work, he didn't waste time tryin' to make 'em work, he knew how to make his M-1 do the same job, man. And he did it. For every new guy that came into his platoon, he fixed all their weapons, you heard him say that."

"So what?"

"I knew guys like him in Nam. None of 'em knew what Nam was about any more than he knew what Korea was about. But once they got there, it was them and their buddies against everybody else, that's all it was, they didn't give a shit what else it was about. What else it was about didn't matter, it was cover your buddy's ass and he'll cover yours, that's all, whatever it took. Which is exactly what he did."

"If there's a message here, I'm not gettin' it. What're you tryin' to tell me?"

"This man has reduced his world to a very few people. You're either with him or you're against him. And if you fuck with him or any of the people who are with him, it's war, man. It's life or death. Nothin' in between."

"Oh man, Detective, you know what I'm hearin'? I'm hearin' you talkin' like you like this guy, like you admire this guy, like you respect him—"

"Likin' him or respectin' him or admirin' him has nothin' to do with it. I'm tryin' to tell you, guys like him will endure anything. They will put up with anybody's shit in this world, man, they will ask no questions, they don't care how you fuck with them, all they ask is half a chance, that's all. Just keep it even, that's all they want, and as long as they think it's even, they'll keep on puttin' one foot in front of the other, doin' whatever they have to. But you back one of these guys up and take away their half a chance? When they see one of their buddies go down, and people are still tryin' to fuck with 'em, man, it's war."

"I don't know what you're tryin' to tell me," Milliron said, stretching and walking in circles again. "All I know is, that man gave us one motive after another, that's all he was doin', all we had to do was stay on him, sooner or later he woulda given it up."

"You're not listenin' to me, Pinky. Only way you're gonna get a guy like him to give anything up is torture him, man. Then, yeah, he'd give it up, eventually. But I'm not gonna torture him. And I'm not gonna let anybody else torture him either."

"What? Where's that comin' from, what's that supposed to mean, you're not gonna let anybody else torture him, fuck's that about?"

"Never mind," Carlucci said. "Fact is, we just gotta get the admissible evidence, that's all. We could talk to him for a month, he's never gonna admit anything."

"Why're you so sure of that? Why're you damn sure of yourself about him, I don't get that."

"'Cause this man thinks that what he did was justice. This man doesn't think what he did is murder. This man doesn't think for one second there's one molecule wrong with what he did. He just sat there and gave us all his reasons, he was justifyin' himself. But there was not a flicker of remorse in that man's tone or expression or body language. That man saw his buddy go down, and in his mind there were people responsible for puttin' his buddy down, and he took them out—"

"Who's his buddy now? Where'd he come from?"

"His wife! Who do you think?"

"His wife's his buddy?"

"Hell yes, absolutely, who do you think he was talkin' about?"

Milliron gave a disbelieving whistle. "First time I ever heard this, guy's wife's his buddy. Where you gettin' this? From Oprah?"

"Aw I'm not gonna dignify that," Carlucci said. "I gotta go. Gotta check on my mother. Anything comes up, you got my numbers."

"You're not gonna dignify that? You better do more than that, Detective. You better explain it, in real clear terms. 'Cause you're startin' to sound like somebody owes this guy a free pass or somethin'."

"Nobody owes him anything. All I'm sayin' is, I know him. I look in his eyes, I'm lookin' in a mirror. In Nam? I *was* one of those guys, I was just like him. That's why nobody's even gonna think about torturin' him, no way. So see you tomorrow, 'less you need me for somethin'."

"Can't imagine what for—I got my *imaginator* in overdrive, but I still can't imagine why I'd need to see you before tomorrow."

"Well. Then good night."

Just after Carlucci had said good night to Rascoli and was reaching for the door to the parking lot, Rascoli said, "Yo, Rugs, hold it a second. Here, almost forgot." He handed Carlucci five phone messages.

"They're all your mother. First one was right after you closed the door back there. Even though she was, uh, pretty upset, I didn't think she was any more upset than usual, you know, so I figured you didn't want me interruptin' you for that, right?"

"Right, Bill, yeah, thanks," Carlucci said, flipping through the messages, each a request to call her immediately. Man, he thought, sighing, I got a lip full of stitches, I'm having an asshole contest with my partner, and my mother, what's she want, huh? Tell me she got a karate instructor coming to the house? So she can really learn how to do a job on me? Well why the fuck not . . .

He slouched back to his desk, dropped into his chair, and looked at the phone for a long moment. He reached for it once, then brought his hand back to rub his eyes. Finally, shaking his head with his eyes closed, he picked it up and pushed the buttons for his home phone.

He heard Mrs. Comito say hello, but then he heard scuffling and scraping and his mother saying, "Gimme that," as she struggled to get control of the phone from Mrs. Comito. "Ruggiero, goddammit, this better be you! Five times I called you, where you been? Five times!"

"Callin' you now, Ma, what's up?"

"What's up? What's up?! I'll tell you what's up. Some sonofabitch put hooks on the doors! On the outside—you hear me? You hear what I'm tellin' you! Some sonofabitch turned my house into a concentration camp! As if it wasn't already!"

Oh shit, Carlucci thought, hanging his head and rubbing his right eye with the heel of his hand.

His mother ranted on while he held the phone just far enough away to hear when she stopped. Finally she had to take a breath.

"Slow down, Ma, gonna hyperventilate, gonna pass out, you don't wanna do that, you hear?"

"Hell I care whether I pass out, I'm a prisoner in my own house!

You're the cops, Ruggiero, you get up here now, you hear me? Get up here right now and find the sonofabitch did this, I want him arrested, you hear? I want him in jail! Sonofabitch locks me in here, I want him to know what it feels like, you hear me? Jesus God!"

Here goes everything, Carlucci thought, sucking in a breath through clenched teeth. Now or never. He tried to interrupt her, but she was off again on another rant until she ran out of breath.

"Ma? Listen." He started to say it. He thought he could say it, thought he was prepared for the consequences, but he couldn't. The words were in there—That was me, I did that—they just wouldn't come out. Instead he heard this weenie voice saying, "I'll find out who did it, Ma. Just can't do it right now, okay?"

No answer. Just gasping.

"I'll find out, okay? Ma? Just try to take it easy, okay? Soon as I come home I'll take 'em off—"

"I don't need you to take 'em off, goddammit, I already did that! I need you to arrest the sonofabitch that put 'em on!"

Again, he heard the words in his head: That was me, Ma, you hear me? I'm who put them on. But still they wouldn't come out. Maybe Milliron was right. Maybe he was hooked on the way it was.

Her gasping was growing louder.

Then he saw those words and more on a chalkboard: You were starting to walk away, Ma. Starting to get lost, you know? I had to do something. But none of those words made it to his lips either.

Then he heard a scuffle and a shriek and then a noise Carlucci had no words to describe, a noise full of rage and regret, fury and fear, a noise so painful he recoiled from it like somebody was trying to stitch the inside of his ear, a noise so loud that Rascoli, seated more than fifteen feet away, turned and gaped at Carlucci.

"You bastard!" she screamed. "It was you! You're not my son, I don't know whose son you are, but you ain't mine! Lock me in my own house! You bastard! Anybody could do this to me was never my son! You hear what I said? You were never my son! Never!"

Carlucci was struck dumb. How'd she find out it was me? Oh God. Mrs. Comito. Then he heard Mrs. Comito pleading, sobbing, begging, calling his name and begging for help and then screaming with pain.

"Bill! Ho! Rascoli! Get a car up to my house now! My mother's flippin' out, get somebody up there now! Oh Jesus Christ," he said, dropping the phone and running out of the duty room, across the parking lot, and to his own car.

As soon as he had the car moving, he was on the radio, asking for assistance from anybody near Norwood Hill. "Carlucci asking anyone to respond to my home address, go inside immediately and do whatever you have to, I will meet you there, do not wait for me. Hey! Somebody wanna give me a roger?"

He got two rogers from both units on the streets, one from Patrolman Robert "Booboo" Canoza and the other from Patrolman Larry Fischetti.

Carlucci went through town with the portable roof light and siren on. When he turned the corner off McCoy Road past Mother of Sorrows Church onto Corliss Street, he saw that Canoza had parked at the curb and was already bounding up the steps to his house. As soon as Carlucci parked and opened his car door, he could hear both women screaming. He hit the street running, heard a siren, and glanced back and saw Fischetti turning onto Corliss Street.

Carlucci took the steps two at a time, bolted through the front door and into the kitchen, and saw Canoza and his mother caught in a wild circular dance, Canoza holding on to Mrs. Carlucci's left wrist while she swung round him while swinging something black and round around herself. Carlucci blundered right into it nose-first. The blow buckled his knees, blinded him with tears and jagged dots of red, orange, and white, and shot pain spiderwebbing across his face. He stumbled backward and collapsed on his tailbone, his head snapping back against the wall.

When he could focus again, his head was hanging and the first thing he saw was blood all over his shirt and lap and dripping in stringy clots from his nose. The next thing he saw was Canoza, six feet five and two hundred and eighty pounds, and Fischetti, six feet and two hundred pounds, struggling to subdue his mother, whose right hand was still free, still swinging a six-inch cast-iron frying pan wildly at Fischetti's head and face.

Blood poured from a gash over Fischetti's left eye, but he had his arms locked around Mrs. Carlucci's knees and lurched up and lifted her off the floor while she kept swinging at him. Canoza had her other arm behind her but for some reason couldn't keep his grip each time he caught hold of the arm swinging the pan. She screamed at Carlucci, "I didn't have you, you bastard, they just gave you to me in the hospital!"

Canoza let go of her left arm and grabbed her right with both hands, brought it around behind her, and did something to it until she screamed and dropped the pan. Then he caught her other arm and brought it around, and, after a seemingly interminable moment of her twisting and jerking her body first one way and then the other, finally got his cuffs on her.

"Got a belt? Yo, Rugs!" Fischetti said, still struggling to keep his hold on her jerking knees. "Get some belts, okay? Hey! Yo, Rugs? Belts, man, c'mon, need some help here."

Carlucci heard the words amid a buzzing whine, like a chain saw. He fell getting his feet under him, slipping on his own blood. He looked again at the blood all over his shirt, then he looked at Fischetti's eyebrow, open to the bone, a gash at least a quarter inch wide and an inch long. Carlucci was still seeing bright orange and red flashes, though less frequently now, but the chain saw in his ears made it hard to hear Fischetti.

"Yo, Rugs," Canoza said, "tell me where the belts are, I'll get 'em, just get over here and hold her, okay? Can you do that? You do that I'll get the belts, just tell me where they are."

"Don't you touch me," his mother said, trying to roll away from Canoza and kick her legs loose from Fischetti's grip.

"Missus Comito, you hear me?"

"Yes. I hear you. What?"

"You okay?"

"No."

"Show him, 'kay? Bedroom? Closet? On the hooks, back left." Before, when just his lip was stitched, he'd sounded like he had a mouth full of oatmeal. Now he sounded like the oatmeal was coming out his nose. He crawled on his hands and knees to his mother's side, his ears still buzzing with that high-pitched whine, eyes still filling with orange and white dots. He fumbled behind his mother's back until he touched metal. She twisted around and spit at him, hitting his forearm. He wanted to close his eyes and sleep, maybe never to wake up again, because waking up again would bring all this back.

"Raised you like you were mine," she growled. "But I knew you weren't. I always knew you weren't, I always knew you were a bastard . . . lock me in my own house . . . bring goddamn spies in . . . turn my own house into a jail . . . God'll get you for this, you just wait . . ."

"Don't have to wait," Carlucci said, trying to talk and breathe through his mouth. "You already got me. Twice. Think God can do worse, huh? Fuckim. Letim."

"You watch your mouth! You don't use that kinda language around me, I'm still your mother, you don't talk to me with them kinda words, not in my house, not as long as I'm your mother!"

"Yeah, 'at's great, Ma. Punch me . . . split my lip . . . bust my nose . . . but I have to watch my mouth . . . just fuckin' great . . ."

Canoza, with Mrs. Comito trailing, came back with three belts in his right hand. "Here you go, Fish." He dropped two of the belts on the floor, then knelt down and looped the third around Mrs. Carlucci's ankles, pulling it tight and knotting it as best he could.

"Ouch goddamn you, that's too tight! You're hurting me!"

"I know she's your mother, Rugs," Fischetti said, "but if she don't shut up pretty soon, I'm gonna stick a towel in her mouth, swear to God I am."

"Whatever," Carlucci said, holding on with his left hand to the links between the cuffs and trying to keep his balance with his other hand. "Quit movin', Ma. More you move, harder it's gonna get, I'm tellin' ya."

"Shut up, you! This is what I get. Get off me, you Nazi bastard, let go my knees, you're breakin' my legs! This is America, you bastards! I ain't no Jew! This ain't Germany!"

Fischetti glared at her, then shook his head at Carlucci.

"Fish, don't say it, 'kay?"

Canoza looped and knotted another belt around Mrs. Carlucci's knees, and then scooted around on his knees behind her and Carlucci and looped and knotted the third around her elbows. Then he stood up, blew out a sigh, pulled his radio out of his duty belt, and said into it, "Rocksburg PD Patrolman Canoza requests two ambulances and six EMTs—repeat six EMTS—to transport one—repeat—one very aggressive female to Conemaugh Hospital MHU, and to transport two injured police officers to Conemaugh ER." Then he gave the address and confirmed his requests for assistance.

Carlucci tried to stand up. He wanted to see how Mrs. Comito was. He was still too woozy. He got on his feet all right but had to bend over from the waist and put his hands on his knees to stop the room from spinning. His nose dripped blood in strings.

Canoza came around behind him and helped him to a chair. "Rugs, listen to me, put your head back." He turned to Mrs. Comito and said, "Can you get some ice, put it in a towel, Baggie maybe, huh? Oh Jeez."

"What?" Carlucci said. "What?"

"Her arm's busted. Here, c'mere, lady, sit down here, I'll get the ice, forget that, I'll do it, you sit down, okay?"

Carlucci looked at Mrs. Comito's left arm. She was holding it tenderly. Where it should have gone straight from the elbow, it bent away from her body about three or four inches from the wrist. She was also leaning forward and tilting from the waist as though something was wrong with her shoulder or maybe her chest. But what worried Carlucci more was her expression. She was showing no emotion, her eyes were vacant, and her skin was looking pasty. He tapped Canoza on the back and pointed first at his own face and then at hers.

Canoza took a close look at her and immediately got back on the radio to Mutual Aid Ambulance Service. "Hey, people, Patrolman

Canoza again, we got one woman, elderly Caucasian, broken arm, internal injuries very possible, possible shock, you wanna move it, please?"

Canoza hurried to the fridge, got three trays of ice cubes out of the freezer, and asked Carlucci where he kept the dish towels. Before Carlucci could answer, Canoza swiped a towel off the Formica counter beside the sink and wrapped a tray of cubes into it and handed it to Fischetti on his way out the door. In a minute Canoza was back with his first-aid kit.

Carlucci's head was clearing enough for him to get up and get to the drawer where the clean towels were. He filled another with cubes from a second tray and held it over Mrs. Comito's arm while Canoza rolled tape around it to secure it to her arm. She never made a sound, which worried Carlucci all the more.

"Sure, that's right," Mrs. Carlucci growled, "take care of the spy first, the hell with me. I'm just a prisoner here, that's all."

"You're the one did the damage here, Ma."

"Oh yeah? And what about the damage to me, huh? Don't see youns doin' nothin' for me! 'Cept getting ready to take me to another jail. Why you gotta do that I'll never know. What's wrong with this one right here, huh? All youns needa do is put some barb wire around it, be as good as anything youns got."

Canoza handed Carlucci a towel full of ice and said, "Listen, when the wagons get here, I'm gonna tell 'em put this woman—what's her name?"

"Comito."

"Okay, her and you and Fish are in one, and your mother's in the other one, okay? She goes to Mental Health, you guys go to the ER—hey, Missus, uh, Missus Comito, can you hear me? I'm gonna ask you to lay down on the floor now, don't be scared, I want you to lay down here, I'm gonna prop your feet up, okay, you hear? And then I want you to turn your face to the right, okay? That's it, take it easy, hold on to me, that's it. Just lay there, don't move, I'll be right back." He hurried away and returned in moments with two pillows and some blankets. He put her feet on the pillows and covered her with the blankets from the neck down.

"Ambulance'll be here in a couple minutes, don't worry 'bout nothin', you hear me? You're gonna be okay, just think you're over there in Italy someplace, lookin' at the Mediterranean, you know? You're at a nice table, huh? Havin' lunch? Good-lookin' young waiter, huh? It's all sunny and nice, waiter's flirtin' with you a little bit, brings you a real nice antipasto, you know? Some good Genoa salami, nice Asiago, good bread, some good olives, some wine. You like wine, huh?"

"Used to," she whispered.

"Used to? What're you talkin' about, *used to?* The heck kinda Italian are you, huh? Gotta start likin' it again, it's good for ya, good wine makes good blood, you know that, don't you? Huh? Sure you do, you know that—hey, don't go to sleep on me now, got to stay awake, you hear? What do you like to drink, huh? C'mon, missus, stay awake now, talk to me. Whatta you like to drink, huh, tell me."

Before she could answer, the sound of sirens carried into the kitchen.

Suddenly Carlucci was crying. At first he thought it was blood dripping onto his hands, but when he looked down, he saw wet spots on his arms. At first he thought it was from the pain, but then he knew it was from listening to Canoza. "Booboo." The gorilla. Being as tender with Mrs. Comito as a grandma with a sick baby. Carlucci could've kissed him. Instead he reached over and patted him on the back.

Canoza looked over his shoulder. "What? Somethin' wrong?"

Carlucci shook his head. He couldn't speak. He just nodded and patted Canoza again.

While the EMTs were putting Mrs. Comito on a gurney and taking her out to one of the ambulances, Canoza went to Fischetti, bent over, and put his arm around him.

"Man, Fish, I'm sorry," Canoza said. "She had somethin' on her arm, I couldn't get a grip on it, you know, I kept slippin' off. And she kept bangin' you, man, I thought, Jeez, I don't stop her she's gonna kill him. And she hit you three times, man, and I couldn't get a grip on her. I mean I had the one arm, you know? But the other one, Jeez, I'm sorry, man. You hear me? I'm really sorry, Fish, no shit."

"What happened?" Fischetti said, looking slowly around the kitchen. "All I remember is I tripped over somebody, soon as I come in. Then I see you with this woman, it's like you're dancin'. Next thing I know I got my arms around somethin'. I'm hangin' on to keep from fallin', I'm feelin' like, man, bombs're goin' off inside my head or somethin', I can't see for all the different colors in my eyes. Then I remember askin' somebody for belts, I'm thinkin', what, my pants fallin' down? The hell I need belts for? . . . Oh man, I think I'm gonna pass out." He started to slump forward but Canoza caught him and held him up. The towel he'd been holding over his left eyebrow opened and some ice cubes clattered to the floor but the rest were stuck to the cloth, which was stuck to his head.

"Whoa, Fish," Canoza said, "don't pass out, man, stay awake, c'mon, open your eyes, you hear? Yo, Fish, keep your eyes open! Hey, you guys!" he called out to the EMTs. "This one next, you hear? Head injuries here, three! Three blows to the head, here, c'mon, move it."

"Hey!" Mrs. Carlucci shouted. "What about me?" She kept shouting it the whole time as first Fischetti and then Carlucci were loaded into the second ambulance.

"What about her?" one of the EMTs said.

"Take them, go on, get goin', get outta here," Canoza said. "I'll stay here. Ain't nothin' wrong with her."

"Nothin' wrong with me?! You gorilla sonofabitch, my arms're breakin' here, it's too tight, I can't feel my hands no more!"

Canoza waited at the front door until the doors closed on the second ambulance and he watched it pull away. Then he went back into the kitchen, found a glass, filled it with water from the tap. He gulped it down, then filled it again and drank it more slowly as he looked down at Mrs. Carlucci, at the blood smeared on the floor, the overturned chairs, the broken dishes, the bloody towels, the melting ice cubes.

She continued to curse and complain that the belts were too tight. Canoza ignored her, thinking instead about all the rumors and gossip he'd heard for years about Carlucci and his mother. This was the first time Canoza had ever seen Carlucci's mother, or where Carlucci lived. And what he'd heard coming out of Mrs. Carlucci's mouth made him feel deep shame for Rugs. Canoza looked at her and tried to imagine how it was that this one woman could cause the damage she caused just a few minutes ago, to Fish, to that poor woman, and to her own son. And what she'd said to him? That he wasn't hers? Canoza had heard a lot of things said over his years responding to what he called dumb domestics but nothing matched what he'd heard here just minutes ago. And all she cares about are the belts are too tight, he thought. Man oh man, how'd Rugs put up with this crap all these years?

Canoza thought maybe he should say some of these things, lay some guilt on her for what she'd done. But every time he'd tried that with other people, it had always come out wrong. He'd always sounded like a schoolteacher instead of a cop. Those things always sounded better in his head than when he said them. So he said the one thing to Mrs. Carlucci that was really bothering him.

"Hey, missus, keep quiet a second and answer me somethin'. What'd you have on your arm? Every time I tried to grab your wrist there? Kept slippin' off. What'd you have on there, you had somethin' on there, what was it?"

"Untie these goddamn things, they're cuttin' my arms."

"Never mind about them, what'd you have on your arm?"

"If I tell you, will you unloosen these things?"

Canoza thought for a moment. "Maybe. I might."

"Jergens lotion. Happy now? Unloosen these things, c'mon."

"*Jergens lotion?* Is *that* what that was. Huh. Ain't nothin' in the handbook about that." He smelled his hands, shrugged, and said, "What, you keep it in a bucket? Dip your arm in it or somethin'?"

"Whatta you care? Unloosen me now, you said you would, c'mon."

"Uh-uh, I said maybe," Canoza said, looking around and thinking about what Fish had told Rugs he was going to do if she didn't shut up.

"You bastard, I knew you wouldn't." She started to howl again.

Canoza looked through the drawers until he found a clean dish towel. He balled one end of it up and stood over her until she took another breath and started to howl again and he jammed it into her mouth. Then he pulled up a chair near her head and sat down and watched to make sure she didn't choke.

"Breathe through your nose, missus. You breathe through your nose, you'll be alright," he said, shaking his head. "Jergens lotion. Jesus Christ."

After an LPN had cleaned the blood off his face, and after he'd been X-rayed, Carlucci, for the second time today, sat on the edge of a bed in Conemaugh General Hospital's ER holding an icy gel pack on a part of his face and waiting for medical professionals to repair damage caused by his mother. In less than twenty-four hours she'd inflicted more physical pain on him than he'd suffered in sixteen years as a patrolman and eleven years as a detective, more than he'd suffered in twelve months in the infantry during some of the most intense ground combat of the Vietnam War.

Unlike the first time he was in the ER today, however, his suffering was far worse this time because he was not alone. Others, in more pain than he was, were here because of his mother, and knowing that made his suffering so intense he wondered if he could die just by wishing for it. He wished not to die exactly, but maybe to slip into a long coma.

Then he remembered what Franny had said. The question, she said, was whether he was going to resolve his problem with his mother or whether he was going to let somebody else resolve it. Well,

he thought, that's not hypothetical anymore. I made sure of that—
which means somebody else is going to decide what comes next. Is
this what I wanted all along?

Then he thought of Franny's definition of addicts: people who
couldn't let go of an attachment to how they thought things ought to
be. Is that what I was attached to—the thought that somebody else
should make the decision? Was that the way I thought things ought
to be? That I would never have to make the really hard decisions
about her? *Her.* Yeah. Now it's just *her.* But is that what I was hoping? That I'd just make sure somebody was there to watch her every
day, make sure the utilities and the taxes were paid, the food was on
the table, the house was in good shape—all of which suddenly looked
a lot less like noble daily duties and more like procrastination.

I was never going to do anything, he thought. 'Cause I'm such a
goddamn weenie when it comes to her I didn't want to do anything
'cause if I did and it was wrong I didn't want it on my conscience,
that's why Mrs. Comito's here. Fischetti too, Jesus Christ . . .

No matter what else he tried to think about, it was the details of
the daymare in his mother's kitchen, some of which he recalled, some
he only imagined, that kept driving all other thoughts out: Canoza
spinning *her* around by the left wrist; that pan coming at his face;
Canoza and Fischetti wrestling with *her* after they'd heard everything
she had to say to me; *her* trussed up on the floor in my own belts
while she's screaming that nobody was doing anything for *her;* Fischetti cut to the bone above his left eye. . . .

And here he sat, the pain no longer a hot dull knife jammed into
the middle of his face; now it was an abscessed tooth from cheekbone
to cheekbone and from eyebrows to upper teeth. For one idiotic moment he consoled himself that this pain at least made him forget
about his lip.

He thought he could hear ER staffers working on Mrs. Comito
and then on Fischetti, thought he could hear their voices, but when
he peeked through the blue curtain surrounding his bed he didn't
recognize anybody.

Having to breathe through his mouth with his head back made his mouth dry and taste worse. He asked one of the nurses if she would bring him some water but when she did he couldn't drink it because he hadn't thought to ask for a straw, and he knew if he tried to drink it without one he'd spill it over himself. So he sat, holding the gel pack over the top of his nose with one hand and the gauze against his nostrils with the other, listening to the sounds of the ER, smelling his own blood, looking at the water, and thinking he didn't deserve a straw. He tried harder to wish himself into a coma.

When that didn't work, he tried to think of something hopeful or encouraging, anything remotely good that might come out of this. Every thought was ringed with guilt or shame. He didn't know how he'd ever face Fischetti again—and that was only if Fischetti's injuries were no worse than they'd looked back in the kitchen. Good God, Carlucci cringed, what if his skull's fractured? His brain damaged? And what about Mrs. Comito? What if she's in shock? What if her broken arm's just the least of it? What if, what if, what if? . . .

He tenderly lifted the gel pack so he could see, slid off the bed, pulled the blue curtain aside, and went asking everyone he saw if they knew how Mrs. Comito or Fischetti was.

No one did. Or they weren't telling. Finally after about five minutes of pestering people, he found himself facing a nursing supervisor who put her hands on his shoulders and said, "Listen, Detective, you can't be wandering around, you're just gonna get in somebody's way, and you don't want that, you know that."

"Know that lady, Missus Comito, huh? How's she doin', huh?"

"She's in radiology—"

"No shock? Man, looked like she was goin' into shock—"

"All I know is what I said—"

"Anything else wrong, huh? Besides her arm?"

"I don't know," she said, while turning him around and steering him back to his own cubicle.

"Hey hey, what about Fischetti, huh? The patrolman?"

"He's in radiology too, so just get back in bed, and keep your head back. Let me get you some fresh gauze. Keep that pack on too. Still cold? Let me feel it. I'll get you another one of these. Doctor Marino'll be with you in just a second—listen, you can't feel everybody's pain here, you've got enough of your own—"

"You don't understand," Carlucci said, suddenly sobbing, but stopping just as suddenly because crying hurt worse than anything. "It was my mother. These people . . . it's 'cause of her . . . 'cause I didn't have the guts to do somethin' . . . about her . . ."

"Your *mother* did this?" the supervisor said, her eyes going wide. "To that woman? And that cop? And you—she did this to you?"

Carlucci nodded. He couldn't talk. He wanted to cry but he knew he couldn't do that either.

"Oh God," she said, rubbing the back of his left hand and wrist. "Well. Listen. I know it's easy for me to say, but you've got to try to think about yourself right now, you can't be thinkin' about these other people. It was your mother, right? It wasn't you? You didn't do this, you didn't hurt them, she did that, right? So you have to try not to think about it."

"Can't think about anything else," he said, but his voice was so quavery she couldn't understand him and gave up after asking him twice to repeat it. She patted his hand again and then left.

After she was gone it came to him: the only good thing to come out of this mess. By now his mother had to have been admitted to the Mental Health Unit across the street; what she'd done today made it mandatory. Today she'd demonstrated clearly she was a danger to herself and others, so by statute the doctors in Mental Health were obliged to detain her for thirty days for a full psychiatric evaluation. Why hadn't he thought of this before?

For a few seconds after he thought of it, he felt his breathing slowing down. But when he tried to balance what would happen over the next thirty days against what had made it mandatory, he started to sob again. He couldn't help it; he started seeing Mrs. Comito's eyes going blank and her skin pasty gray and Fischetti's face covered with blood.

But once again he had to stop sobbing because once again that hurt more than anything. He got control finally by praying silently.

Please, God, I don't pray much, I never go to Mass, please don't let 'em suffer. Please. Especially her. She's a sweetheart, nicest lady you'd ever want to meet. Saved my behind for years. Took a ton of abuse from my mother. Please . . .

"Uh, Mister, uh, Carlucci, is it?"

"Huh?"

"I'm Doctor Marino," he said, while looking at X rays he'd brought with him in an envelope, which he then dropped on the bed. "Let's have a look. How'd this happen?"

"I remember you," Carlucci mumbled. "Last year. Brought my mother up here, three nights in a row. Three outta four. Uh, with chest pain, and we were both scared, uh, it was her heart, and you, uh, you told her it wasn't. You said anxiety attacks. 'Member that?"

"Um, no, sorry. Oh wait now." He glanced at the papers on the foot of the bed. "*Detective* Carlucci, right? Detective? I remember now, yes. So how's she doing, your mother? Ever get her to the psychologist I recommended? Didn't I write you a prescription for that? Something tells me I wrote you script for that, for the both of you to go. Ever go?"

Carlucci hung his head and shook it.

"Uh, you can't drop your head, Detective, I can't see what I'm doing here. C'mon, up, look at the ceiling."

Carlucci tried but he couldn't. He wrestled back another sob.

"Oh," the doctor said, whistling in a breath. "It was her. I'm sorry, I wasn't thinking. You don't have to say anything. But you do have to pick up your head, c'mon, up, look at the ceiling."

Carlucci got control of himself again and looked up, swallowing hard several times. "Whattaya think?"

"Well, the good thing is, no bones are broken, not in your nose or your cheeks. And it looks like the bleeding's stopped. How'd this happen, specifically? You remember?"

"No no, not me. The lady, Missus Comito? And the patrolman?"

"Uh, let's just concentrate on you for the moment, okay? How'd it happen? You know?"

"Uh-uh. She, uh, she was swingin' this pan, and I come around the corner, and I, uh, I don't know, I musta walked right into it."

"Uh-huh. Well, listen. The swelling makes it difficult to make anything better than an educated guess here. I am sure because of the pictures that no bones are broken, which I've already said, but because of the swelling I can't see any lacerations inside. There are none outside, I can see that, but something caused all this bleeding, and I'm going to assume there's at least one laceration inside, and the swelling may be obscuring that, so that's why we'll have to wait for the swelling to go down, three, four days, get a better idea, okay? Best we can do for now is just keep ice on it as much as you can stand, that'll keep the swelling down, then, uh, take extra-strength acetaminophen or aspirin every four hours, whichever you handle better, and try not to bump into anything, okay? Any questions? Pain gets too intense, uh, you might want Percodan, I'll give you script for that. Don't need it, don't take it, but you'll have it if you do, okay?"

"Yeah okay. But what about Missus Comito and Fischetti—"

"Last I heard they were both upstairs, that's all I know—do you understand what I said to you? About you?"

"Yeah. Three, four days, you want me to come back here—"

"No. Not here. I'm gonna refer you to a plastic surgeon."

"Huh? What for?"

"'Cause he knows a lot more about broken noses than I do—"

"You said nothin' was broken."

"No, what I said was no *bones* were broken. Your cartilage is a mess. And cartilage is a tricky thing everywhere, but in the nose, it's, uh, well, a plastic surgeon knows far better than I do how to deal with it. I mean, two, three months down the road you may discover you're still not breathing properly and it's 'cause the cartilage, as it healed, it distorted the shape of your nose and altered your breathing passages. That's not unusual at all. I'm not saying that will happen, just saying it's likely, and I think you need to get with somebody from the beginning who knows how to deal with it, should it happen, okay? And be sure and take photos of yourself along—when you see him? Full front, full profile. Least five-by-seven so he can see what your nose looked like before, that'll help him see what needs to be done. Or not done."

"That it?"

"For now, yes. That's all I can do. How's your vision?"

"Little blurry."

"Then you probably ought to call somebody to drive you home. Don't try driving yourself, okay?" The doctor then wrote the name of the plastic surgeon on the back of his own card and handed it over with the script for Percodan. He also asked a nurse to get Carlucci a couple of gel packs and told him to toss them in the freezer when he got home and to keep one on his nose for fifteen minutes every half hour for at least the next couple of hours.

Carlucci shrugged and said, "Can I stick around, see how they're doin', huh?"

"Fine with me, Detective. But in the waiting room, not here."

Carlucci stepped down off the bed and started walking toward the door to the waiting room.

The doctor called him back. "You might want to, uh, take that off and put your clothes on."

"Huh?" Carlucci looked down at himself and saw that he was wearing a hospital gown. When he started to take it off, he realized all he had on under it was his shorts and socks. He shrugged and headed back to the cubicle and started hunting for his shirt, pants, and shoes. He found them in a plastic bag on the floor beside the bed, along with his weapons, handcuffs, wallet, and ID case. When he tried to put his clothes on, he couldn't because they were practically glued together with his blood. "Jesus. The hell am I gonna wear?"

He pried his pants apart enough to get them on, but his shirt was like wet cardboard. He shrugged and kept the gown on. He had to hold on to the bed with one hand to get his shoes on. He left his shirt, weapons and holsters, wallet, and ID case in the plastic bag, and walked out to the waiting room without asking if it was okay to keep the gown.

Canoza was sitting with his back to the wall, reading a wrinkled *People* magazine, right on the other side of the ER door. As soon as he saw Carlucci, he tossed the magazine aside and jumped up, taking the bag out of Carlucci's hand.

"Rugs, whoa, gimme your arm, man. They lettin' you go? Huh? You ain't walkin' out, are ya?"

"Told me I could leave. I wanna stick around, see 'bout Missus Comito. And Fish."

"Oh they're keepin' 'em, man. Both of 'em, I checked already."

"You checked?"

"Yeah. Plus I just seen Fish upstairs."

"They tell you what's wrong with 'em?"

"No. But I heard. The lady, she got a busted wrist and a busted collarbone—"

"Aw shit."

"Yeah, they're operatin' on her right now. But Fish, all he got was a real bad cut and a concussion. He's stitched up already. They took a whole lotta pictures, did a brain scan on him, they're just keepin' him for observation, that's all. He's awake, he's okay, I was just up there talkin' to him. But he said you owe him big-time, paisan, the rest of your life, man, you're gonna pay, Rugs. You know Fish. He was nuts before, that fucker. Goin' be worse now, man, he ain't never gonna let you forget this.

"But from now on, he's Ironhead, that's what I'm callin' him. Your mother nailed him, Rugs. Wooo! I mean, she got him *good,* man, three times. But the second one, man, whoa, I'm tellin' you I never saw anybody get hit that hard—with anything. His head gotta be fucking iron. Know what's wild? Huh?"

"What?"

"He don't even remember gettin' hit that time. Or the third time neither. Just the first one, that's all he remembers. Ain't that a bitch, huh?"

"I guess. I don't know. How come you're still here?"

"Waitin' for you. See if they were gonna keep ya, and if they didn't, I figured you'd need a ride home."

"Oh. Thanks. Uh, listen, you over there, huh? 'Cross the street? Mental Health?"

"Yeah," Canoza said, sniffing and looking away. "Signed her in."

"Uh, you know, how'd it go? How was it? Bad?"

Canoza shook his head. "Ah, you don't wanna know that. Even if you do, I ain't gonna tell ya—c'mon, let's go, don't ask me nothin' else. But man, I gotta tell ya, your nose, whoa. Look like you got a yam growin' there, man. Sweet potato."

"Real funny."

"Oh man, I love yams. Sweet potatoes too. Know how I like 'em? Best way, huh? Just learned it, man. Ever use that Cajun seasoning, huh? I'm tellin' ya, Rugs, you cut 'em up like you were gonna make big steak fries, you know? Then you shake 'em up in a bag with that Cajun stuff? Spread 'em around on a cookie sheet, you know? Bake 'em in the oven? Man, last night I ate four all by myself, you know? Big ones.

"C'mon, Rugs, watch your step, man. You fall on that yam, you'll be needin' a transfusion. Wonder you got any blood left. Hey, you know you're wearin' one of their gowns? You do know that, don't ya?"

"C'mon, just take me home, 'kay? Don't ask me nothin' else."

O nce they arrived at his mother's house, Carlucci tried to say he didn't need help either getting out of the cruiser or getting inside, but Canoza ignored him. "Besides, there's somebody in there."

"Huh?"

"Lights are on. I was the last one out, I didn't leave any lights on. Stay here, I'll check it out."

Canoza got out, closed the door quietly, and tiptoed up the steps and inside. In a moment he was back. "It's okay, some lady's in there cleanin' up, says she knows you. Name's Viola. If you don't know her, you better introduce yourself, man, she got that place lookin' good."

Carlucci nodded. "Yeah, sure I know her."

"Well she's in there cleanin' her ass off, scrubbin' the floor."

"You're shittin' me."

"You'll see, c'mon." Canoza let him get out of the car by himself but steadied him up the steps and inside.

In the kitchen, on her hands and knees, Mrs. Viola was wringing out an old towel into a dishpan. There was a wooden scrub brush and a bar of yellow soap on another towel beside her knee.

"Missus Viola," Carlucci said, "what're you doin'? You don't have to do that, c'mon, Jeez oh man."

"Whatta you think? I'm cleanin' the floor, it was a mess."

"Hey, Boo. Robert, ho, man, help her get up—"

"Oh Rugsie, it's nothin', I do it every week anyway—oh Jesus God, look at your face. You alright? Oh no, you ain't, huh? Oh my God."

"Ah he's alright, he can take it, he's tough," Canoza said, reaching both hands down to pull Mrs. Viola up. "You just won't have to hate him 'cause he's beautiful no more—you 'member that commercial, huh? Remember that commercial where that chick says, don't hate me 'cause I'm beautiful? 'Member that one?"

Carlucci and Mrs. Viola both looked blank.

"Youns don't remember, huh? Well, obviously not. Always thought it was sorta stupid myself, but you know, I thought it'd make a good joke here. Never mind. C'mon, missus, get up, you're done here. Looks fantastic, you don't have to do nothin' else tonight, c'mon, grab my hands. Just tomorrow mornin', you know? You could maybe come over, check this bum's pulse, make sure he's still kickin', you know?"

"Wait wait, just let me wipe up this one spot here, then I can quit," she said, pulling her hands away from Canoza and sopping up some soapy water with the towel. "Honest to God, Rugsie, what happened, huh? God, does it hurt, huh? It looks awful."

All Carlucci could do was shrug and nod. "I'm real tired," he said. "Maybe tomorrow I'll tell ya what happened, okay? I don't feel like talkin' right now, okay?"

Carlucci went into his bedroom and got out of the hospital gown and his bloody pants and into some fresh underwear. Canoza hovered around making sure Carlucci didn't lose his balance, while Carlucci kept telling Canoza to walk Mrs. Viola home and not to take no for an answer. "But make sure she goes, okay? She don't go, she's gonna ask me a million questions, and I don't wanna do that right now, you know?"

Canoza nodded. "I'll take her, don't worry about it."

"Robert?" Carlucci said, plopping onto the edge of his bed. "Thanks. For everything. You didn't get here when you did? Today? Coulda been bad, man, coulda been real bad. It ain't real great now, but . . . coulda been really bad, you know?"

Canoza nodded. "Hey, you don't have to say nothin'. But you need anything? Anytime, you know? Gimme a call."

Carlucci nodded. His eyes spilled over and he turned away.

He waited till they both left, then he went back into the kitchen and looked around. Because of Mrs. Viola's cleaning, it looked like it did every day. Not every day. It didn't look like it had just a couple of hours ago. But otherwise, it looked more or less like it had looked for as long as he could remember. Except for one thing: his mother wasn't in it. For the first time in his life, he was in this house without his mother. For the first time in his memory, the TV sets weren't on, not the RCA color one in the living room, not the tiny Motorola black-and-white in her bedroom. For the first time, all he heard were the sounds of the house, the noises any building makes if no other noise blocks it. In this house there had always been noise to block those noises; his mother had made sure of that.

House noises to her were far worse than silence. She was always saying she could never understand how anybody could live without a TV or a radio on, because if you didn't have one of them on, then all you had was the house noises, and those things could make you crazy, all that creaking and cracking and scratching and groaning as the earth settled and the temperature changed. First thing she did when she awoke in the morning was turn on her seven-inch black-and-white Motorola. And the last thing she did every night in bed was turn it off. She left it on all day, even though she never watched it again except when she got into bed for the night.

Carlucci thought he wouldn't have any trouble falling asleep now—he was wrung-out, drop-dead tired—but he wondered how he was going to wake up tomorrow. He knew that not hearing the TV when he awoke would signal his mother's whereabouts in a way far louder than if she'd been there watching *Good Morning America.* He wasn't sure that would've made sense to anybody if he'd tried to explain it, but he knew where she was now, and he knew that no TV tomorrow morning would be a bullhorn in his mind about why she was there. And where Mrs. Comito was and why. And Fischetti.

He was still worrying about it when he reached out and dropped the last of the gel packs, long since warm, onto the floor beside his bed.

Just before he fell asleep, an ugly thought oozed through his mind: Milliron was right. Only reason I'm worrying about waking up in a quiet house is 'cause I *am* hooked to the way things were. If I wasn't, the last thing I'd be is worried. I'd be relieved. But I'm not. Mamma mia. . . .

Next morning Carlucci awoke, not to the sounds of an empty house but to the sound of the phone. It was Milliron. He identified himself but he didn't say hello and he didn't ask how Carlucci was.

"I'm informin' you that I'm bringin' Czarowicz in again," Milliron said. "And before you say anything, I cleared it with Failan. He approved it. And if you can't make it—'cause, uh, I heard you had more trouble with one of your relatives again—well that's okay too 'cause Failan's sending his new chief, Sporcik? He's gonna partner me."

"Oh yeah? Where?"

No answer.

"Where you gonna do this? And what time?"

"Say again?"

"Time, you know? What time you doin' this? And where?"

"Time am I what? Can't understand you. Sound worse today than you sounded yesterday."

"Fuck you. You understand that?"

"Oh *that* I understand, yeah, that was real clear."

"What time are you bring-ing him in? And where?"

"You're a detective. Figure it out," Milliron said, and hung up.

Carlucci looked at the phone as though that would explain everything. He used to be okay, he thought. Worked with him before, he was alright. Not just alright, he was good, he knew what he was doing. Competent, not too arrogant. The fuck happened to him, how'd he get to be this miserable prick? Ah, it's Lyon, gotta be. Lyon and Krull. He's not just seeing cases here. Nah. He's seeing career makers. And he thinks somebody's trying to take them away from him, he's been worried about that since the first meeting in Failan's office. Not somebody. Me. Or maybe he's still pissed about what Valcanas told him about his old man doing his own taxes. That could be. Nah, uh-uh, it's Lyon. Got his nose bent so far outta shape he's startin' to hear with it. He's twisted over this thing, that's what it is. Hey. Twisted or not, he's not going to dick me around, I'm not putting up with that.

Carlucci heaved his legs off the side of the bed and sat up. When he did, a swarm of invisible stinging insects attacked his face from cheek to cheek, brows to lips. He sucked in his breath and held it for a long moment until the stinging eased somewhat. "Oh God," he groaned. "What now?"

He was still holding the phone so all he had to do to get the Rocksburg station was depress the receiver button and touch the speed dialer. Civilian dispatcher Vic Stramsky answered, and Carlucci asked if a state cop had called to ask if it was all right for him to use Rocksburg's interrogation room.

"Oh he's here now," Stramsky said. "Wanna talk to him?"

"No. He's there? Since when?"

"Came in about ten minutes ago. Milliron—is that his name?

Yeah. Oh, and here comes, uh, oh what's his name? Oh . . . shit. Sporcik, that's it, yeah. With the county?"

"They're there now? Both of them?"

"That's what I just said, what's the matter with you?"

"Got anybody with 'em?"

"Yeah. Uh, Milliron, he brought a civilian in with him."

"That prick," Carlucci said.

"Huh? D'you say prick? Who, me?"

"No, not you. Never mind, I'll be right there." He hung up, and stood up, provoking the stinging sensation over his nose and cheeks again. The stinging was so intense he had to grab hold of his chest of drawers to steady himself until the pain passed.

Getting dressed challenged his pain threshold anew because every time he tilted his head to look for clothes or moved his body to put them on, the stinging began again. It was as though a nest of hornets had been turned loose on the underside of the skin of his face.

He knew better than to try to brush his teeth or wash his face or eat anything besides two extra-strength acetaminophens, which he managed to swallow without spilling water on himself.

Driving was worse than dressing because at every intersection he had to look in both directions, and the hornets inside his face went wild. Ten minutes and uncountable stings later he was in the Rocksburg station standing outside the two-way mirror on the back wall of the interrogation room, watching and listening to Milliron and Sporcik question John Czarowicz.

Carlucci debated with himself for a long moment whether to go in. He knew that wasn't a good idea; he was still far too angry that Milliron thought it was acceptable to use Rocksburg's facility, but not acceptable to invite him to sit in. The more Carlucci tried to control his anger, the more the hornets attacked. This puzzled him because, even though he'd already learned that movement provoked them, now he was learning that he didn't have to move to stir them up. Standing as still as he could, it became clear: today's anger turned yesterday's pain into real suffering. The more Carlucci looked at Milliron and listened to him, the angrier he became; the angrier he became, the more the hornets stung him. Obviously, he told himself, he had to lose his anger, and if he knew how he certainly would have. But he didn't. So the hornets kept marching, back and forth and up and down across his cheeks.

Sporcik was leaning, arms folded, against the wall. Milliron was doing almost all the talking. He was saying, "Look, we know you've been buying .22 Magnum ammo from Wal-Mart and Kmart. Clerks at both stores identified your photograph."

Identified his photograph? What photograph, Carlucci thought. We never took this guy's picture yesterday—I sure as hell didn't. And you didn't either, prick, not when I was around, uh-uh.

While thinking that over, Carlucci noticed something. Rather, he noticed that something wasn't right. He moved from one side of the window to the other, but Milliron's back obstructed his view of the whole tabletop separating Milliron from John Czarowicz. But on the parts of the table Carlucci could see, he didn't see a tape recorder. It was possible Milliron had it right in front of him. It was also possible that he didn't have one. Neither Milliron nor Sporcik was taking notes, and there was nobody else in the room. Jesus Christ, Carlucci thought, I'll bet that arrogant fuck thinks we got some kind of automatic taping system. Jesus, he's flipped out, he doesn't know what he's doing. . . .

Czarowicz was asking whether there was something wrong with him buying ammo.

"Not with buyin' it," Milliron said. "A whole lot wrong with shootin' somebody with it."

Czarowicz said nothing. He just returned Milliron's gaze.

"The clerks in Wal-Mart and Kmart," Milliron said, "they remember you comin' in practically every other day. Said every time you came in, you bought at least one box, most of the time two. Fifty rounds a box, that's a lotta ammo. What were you doin' with it?"

"Makin' halupkies. Whattaya think I was doin' with it, I was shootin' it."

"Shootin' it? At what?"

"Targets. Paper targets, you know?"

"Targets? People generally shoot at targets to practice for something. What were you practicin' for?"

"Who said practicin'? I wasn't practicin'. I was shootin' targets. Some guys bowl, you know? I shoot targets."

"You shoot targets fifty to a hundred rounds a day? Every day?"

"Yeah. I do. Told ya, it's like bowlin'. Only I don't bowl."

"But you aren't practicin' for anything. You're just shootin', right? You need to explain this to me. I mean, I've known some competition shooters, they shoot that much. More. But, uh, you shoot in matches or somethin', you on a team? I don't know too many people shoot that much if they're not on a team, not in some kinda competition."

"I ain't on any team. Hell I got to be on a team for? Just to shoot? That don't make sense."

"Well it doesn't make sense to me either, so explain it."

"Huh? Why? You want guys to explain why they bowl? I know a guy bowls six games every day by himself. He ain't on any team—I mean he is, he's on a couple teams at night. Different ones. But when he goes every day in the afternoon, he's not on any team, he's by himself. Now I guess if you saw him in the daytime, you'd think he was practicin' for when he bowls at night on those teams, but he ain't. When he goes every day it's 'cause he likes it."

"Pretty tough to kill somebody from forty-two yards with a bowling ball," Milliron said.

"Is 'at s'posed to be some kinda joke or somethin'?"

"No joke. You're not in here because you bowl, John. You're in here because you shoot fifty to a hundred rounds of .22 Magnum ammo every day, and because John Lyon was killed with a .22 Magnum bullet and so was Frank Krull. And also because we found an empty at Lyon's house. You forgot to police up your brass."

"I could shoot a thousand rounds a day long as I do it someplace there's a backstop, you know? A bullet trap? Which I do. I never shoot where there's no backstop. And long as I'm doin' it that way, there's no law against me doin' it."

"So you admit buyin' the ammo?" Milliron said.

Czarowicz laughed and shook his head. "So I *admit* it? What the hell would I be shootin' if I wasn't buyin' it? What, you think you can reload rimfire? Maybe where you come from. Where I come from I recycle my empties. Don't believe me, go down Conemaugh Valley Hardware, talk to the guy owns the place, Chuckie Jurista, he'll tell ya. Take my empties down there every week, ask him. Besides, when'd you take this picture of me you're showin' these clerks, huh? I didn't give you no picture. And you didn't take my picture when I was in here yesterday. I never saw no camera."

"We took it, don't worry about when," Milliron said.

"Didn't say I was worried. I asked you when you took it. I think you're makin' it up about this picture, that's what I think."

"Well the clerks at Wal-Mart and Kmart, they didn't think I was makin' it up. They picked you right out. Out of six photographs we showed them, you were their only choice, never any doubt."

"And this you did since I was in here last night, huh? I didn't get home till almost twenty after nine. I don't know when Wal-Mart opens, or Kmart neither, but it ain't even quarter after eight yet, and youns already been out there? Huh? Showin' this picture I don't remember you takin'? Must be magicians."

"Never mind what we are," Milliron said. "What do you have to say about those clerks identifyin' you?"

"What am I s'posed to say? You say you took my picture and you say you showed it to 'em and you say they say it's me—if I said it wasn't me, somebody'd be lyin'. One of us would."

"You sayin' they're lying?"

"Somebody has to be."

"Somebody *has* to be? Why's that?"

" 'Cause I don't buy ammo in either one of them stores. I buy all my ammo and all my reloadin' supplies from Chuckie Jurista. Have ever since he bought the hardware store. We was in Korea together—not in the same outfit, just the same time. Well I won't be dealin' with him anymore anyway, 'cause he's closin'. Wal-Mart, Home Depot, Lowe's, all of them places, they're puttin' him outta business. Can't compete with their prices."

"We'll be checkin' with him, this Jurista, you know that, don't you?"

Oh that's brilliant, Carlucci thought. Guy sets you up for a stone fool, and you tell him you're gonna check. Jesus.

"Check all you want. I'm tellin' the truth. And the truth is, I never bought a bullet in my life from Wal-Mart or Kmart neither. Not yet. And ain't goin' to 'less I can't find 'em someplace else."

Milliron was clearly flustered because for a long moment he didn't say anything. Then he said something totally illogical. "Sounds like double-talk. Why you tryin' to double-talk us today? You didn't do that yesterday. You were real straight with us yesterday."

"Us?" Czarowicz looked at Sporcik. "He wasn't here yesterday. And I'm bein' straight. Straighter'n you are about the picture."

"You're startin' to talk like a shyster, John. A lawyer."

"Well I'm not. Sometimes I wish I was a lawyer. Woulda saved me some money that's for sure. But I'm not. And I don't appreciate you callin' me by my first name neither. We're not friends."

"Alright, Mister Czarowicz," Milliron said. "Let's get back to how you talked when you were in here yesterday."

Great, Carlucci thought. Fuck what he says, just talk how he says it, that'll get him in front of a jury.

"How I talked? Whatta you mean?"

"Well yesterday you talked like a man. You talked about your problems, you didn't whine about 'em, you didn't split hairs, you just talked about 'em. You said what they were, you said how you tried to handle 'em, said what you did, you said what you didn't do. But today, you're tryin' to be real cagey about what you say, you're not bein' straight about anything."

"Oh, so that's what I'm doin', huh? Glad you told me. Uh, where's the other guy? What happened to him?"

"What other guy?"

"The other one was in here yesterday, that detective, uh, what's his name? Carlucci? What, he get fired or somethin', where's he at?"

"Why?"

Czarowicz shrugged. "He was, uh, I don't know, little easier to talk to."

"I don't know where he is, I called him, told him we were gonna be talkin' to you again today, but, uh, he hasn't shown up."

Carlucci knocked on the glass. "I'm here," he said, but his words were wasted. His knock wasn't—especially on the hornets.

"Sounds to me like he's out there," Czarowicz said. "Somebody's out there. Other side of that mirror there."

"Oh. Well apparently he did get here then," Milliron said, pointing vaguely with his thumb over his shoulder at the mirror. "He's had some problems, uh, with one of his relatives. He can't talk—not so you could understand him. But you don't need to worry about him, you need to start worryin' about yourself."

"Oh yeah? Why's 'at? You accusin' me of somethin'?"

"No," Sporcik said before Milliron could answer. "We're not accusing you of anything, Mister Czarowicz."

"Maybe you're not," Czarowicz said to Sporcik. Nodding toward Milliron, he said, "But he can't wait, huh? Can ya?"

"I'm not accusing you of anything either," Milliron said. "Right now all I wanna know is why you won't be straight with me. You're a man. Taxpayer, citizen, a veteran, a marine—just like me."

Czarowicz didn't respond to that.

"Yeah, a marine," Milliron said again. "Just like me."

"Uh-uh," Czarowicz said. "Other guy that was in here yesterday, he's been in deep shit, I could tell that. Might not've been in the marines, but he's been in deep shit. You . . . you picked up drunks."

Milliron cleared his throat and rolled his head as though he had a kink in his neck.

Well, that's it, Carlucci thought. Never had him, but he's gone now. When they start laughing at you, you're done.

But Milliron wasn't giving up. "What I'm sayin' is, uh, when your country asked you to put your life on the line, you did—"

"Hold it right there," Czarowicz said, hunching forward and holding up his right index finger. "My country didn't ask me nothin'. They didn't draft me, I enlisted. And all I was lookin' for was a place to sleep, and three squares, and clean clothes, so don't go puttin' no Veterans Day bullshit on it."

"Well yeah, you enlisted, that's right, you made that clear yesterday, and that's all I was sayin'. Doesn't matter what the circumstances were, you know, what your situation was back then, that, uh, that caused you to enlist, that's not what I'm talkin' about. Fact is, you enlisted. And you served. And you served with honor."

Czarowicz said nothing for a long moment. He just rubbed his palms together in front of his face. "How'd you know how I served? You weren't there. You don't know nothin'."

Milliron's shoulders rose, his head ducked forward, and he shifted around on his chair. "I'm just goin' by what you said yesterday."

"I didn't tell you nothin' yesterday 'bout how I served. All I said was what I did with the M-1s, that's all, when I was in Korea. Told ya how I looked out for my buddies and how they looked out for me, that's all I said, I didn't say nothing 'bout servin' with honor."

Carlucci could see Milliron taking a deep breath and trying to let it out slow, but when he spoke again his voice was tighter, higher. "Look, Mister Czarowicz, lemme just tell you something right now, okay? There's at least six detectives at your house searchin' it. Your car too. They're gonna find the rifle, they are. And when they do, they're gonna give it to the ballistics people at our lab, and they're gonna fire a couple rounds to compare with the ones the coroner took outta Lyon and Krull. And then they're gonna match up the firin'-pin mark on the empty we found at the house, Lyon's house, you know? They're gonna match that mark with the marks on the casings they shoot in the lab. That's gonna happen, mister, as sure as we're both sittin' here. And when it does, we won't need to talk to you anymore."

Carlucci knew Milliron had just lost his cool, otherwise he wouldn't have taken that clumsy a jump from trying to be Czarowicz's buddy to suddenly doing everything but Mirandizing him, which was what he'd done by boasting about the search—if there was even a search being made. Telling whoppers was perfectly acceptable, but to be effective, there had to be a center of truth to them. Milliron knew as well as Carlucci did that the bullets found inside the skulls of both men were too fragmented and the fragments too deformed to make any comparison of barrel markings stand up as admissible evidence. From the striations on the bullet fragments Coroner Grimes took out of both victims, it was obvious the shooter had filed an X into the bullets down to their cavities, guaranteeing that they would fragment on impact, and further guaranteeing that the fragments could not be used for comparison with bullets fired in a ballistics lab.

The firing-pin mark on the empty casing found at Lyon's house was a different matter, of course. That mark could be compared with casings taken from rounds fired in the lab, and those marks would stand up in court. But first somebody had to find a rifle to shoot. Until that happened, Milliron was just huffing and puffing.

Czarowicz said nothing for a long moment. Then he said, "Well if you won't need to talk to me once them detectives find this rifle you think they're gonna find at my place, how's come you're talkin' to me now?"

Yeah, Carlucci thought, talk your way out of that one. He knows the bullets fragmented because he made sure they'd fragment. So now, hot shit, where do you go from here? Only place you can go is try to humiliate him by telling him how he fucked up by forgetting to police up that empty. Because you're never going to think how to use the cancer angle. That's too subtle for you.

Milliron tried to control his voice, which was getting tighter and higher. "You're doin' it again, Mister Czarowicz."

"Doin' what?"

"Answerin' questions with questions. Talkin' like a shyster."

"That's what you say."

"That's right, that's what I say. But let me ask you something. Did I do anything to you yesterday, huh? I show you any disrespect?"

"Nope. You didn't show me any disrespect."

"Well we agree then, that's good, 'cause I know I didn't. But then I have to wonder, you know, why am I gettin' the feelin' you don't wanna be straight with me? What I'm thinkin' is, you know, if you're sure I didn't do anything to you, didn't say anything out of line, then, uh, I think you'd wanna be straight with me. And I think if you did somethin', what you should do now is be the man you were the last time you were in here."

Oh, man, Carlucci thought, he's beggin' now. That's pathetic.

"Be the man I was last time? The hell's that mean? I'm the same guy I was yesterday, same guy I always been."

"No, uh-uh, the last time you were in here, when I asked you a question, you answered me with an answer. If you did something, you said you did it, and if you thought something, you said that too, and if you felt somethin', you said you felt it."

"Uh-uh," Czarowicz said, "that other guy was doin' most the talkin', not you."

"Well that may be, but you said yourself I didn't do anything to you, so, uh, I don't understand. I think a man does somethin' and he's proud of it? You know, if he's proud of what he did, he should say so. And if he didn't do it, or if he wasn't proud of it, then he should say he didn't do it. Or he's not proud of it. But the worst thing I think a man can do is deny he's a man. And every time you deny what you do, you're denyin' you're a man."

God, Carlucci thought, this is a farce. What's with Sporcik, why isn't he saying anything? He doesn't jump in there pretty soon, this guy's never gonna talk to anybody.

"If I deny what I do," Czarowicz said, "I deny what I am—is that what you said? Never heard anybody say that before." He stopped rubbing his palms and brought his left hand to his mouth and started to rub that slowly, side to side, all the while returning Milliron's gaze.

"I'm a man," Czarowicz said. "There's some people think I ain't worth the space I take up. Or the time. Least that's how they treated me. Or how they thought they could treat me. But I'm a man."

"By how who treated you?" Milliron said.

"Who? Ha. Shit, you know who, everybody knows who. Just don't wanna talk about it anymore. Course the ones that're doin' it, they don't have to talk about it, they just keep on doin' it, 'cause there's nobody stoppin' 'em. And the ones gettin' it done to 'em, most of 'em, not all, but most of 'em, they're too scared to open their yaps. Course even if they do nobody pays 'em any attention."

"That's pretty vague," Milliron said. "What's it mean?"

"Don't understand it, huh? That's 'cause you're a kid. That's 'cause probably the only thing you got to lose is a car. Bet you ain't even thirty yet. Got a wife, huh? You married? Got kids?"

"No, but this isn't about me, this is about you."

God, Carlucci thought, who taught you interrogation? You want to be his buddy, but as soon as he tries to let you in you ridicule him, what the fuck?

Czarowicz laughed. "Think this isn't about you, huh? This is so much about you you don't know how much it's about you. You think you're just the cops, that's all you are. But when you put that badge on, you're the government. You're the whole goddamn state of Pennsylvania, buddy boy, you decide whether people live or die, you decide—"

"Oh give me a break," Milliron snapped. "I don't make the laws, all I do is arrest the people who break the laws, that doesn't make me the state, and that's all beside the point anyway—"

"You give *me* a break!" Czarowicz snapped back. "People like you, you wear the badges, the uniforms—don't give me that crap you ain't the government. Who do you think you're talkin' to, huh? Before you were born, kid, I had the uniform on, the badges, the globe and anchor. And I was the one carryin' the guns and I was the one shootin' at people. Only what I didn't know, huh? People I was shootin' at? They were just like me. Yeah. They're the people, people just like 'em, they're the ones got my job now. All them jobs used to be here, huh? Who ya think has 'em now? Who ya think's workin' my job down there in Brazil, huh? Some Chico guy, some Fernando jagoff just like me, believin' all the bullshit his bosses hand out. Just like I used to believe it.

" 'Cause when I come back from wearin' the badges? Come back here, 1954, I went to work for Conemaugh Steel, hookin' up in the yard. I joined the union, 'cause it was a closed shop, no way you work there you ain't in the union. Worked there till 1985, that's thirty-one years, Trooper. Thirty-one goddamn years. Know how many days I missed, huh? Thirty-one years? Ten days. Two weeks total, that's all the sick days I ever took. And once they made me foreman? Shippin' department, huh? Never missed a day, not a one!

"And then the bastards shut the place down, huh? Boom, bam, thank you ma'am, fuck you, you're history. And then's when I find out the pricks never set up a pension for me. Twenty years hookin' up in the yard, twenty years payin' union dues, and then when I get promoted to foreman, the union says fuck you, you're management. And what's management say, huh? Fuck you, you're nothin'! You're less than nothin'. All those years you thought you had this pension comin', you jagoff, ha ha ha! Joke's on you, we ain't gonna even pretend we set nothin' up for you, you jagoff. All those times you thought we said we did it and you believed us? You're a fuckin' moron! 'Cause we never said it. You *thought* we said it, you were *hopin'* we said it, but we never said it, not what you wanted to hear. Ya get it? Uh-uh, no, you don't get it, you're too fuckin' stupid, too fuckin' lazy to do any checkin' up for yourself. Thought the union was checkin' up on us. Well bullshit, buddy boy, your union wasn't doin' shit!

"And then—then I find out, when my wife gets cancer, even though I'm workin' like sixty, sixty-five hours a week minimum wage, which is barely enough to keep up the payments on the Chevy. Yeah. Bought it new in '84, but no, fuck no, I gotta sell it 'cause the fuckin' Welfare Department, they say my car payments is too high. Disqualifies me for Medicaid. Which was a laugh 'cause I was already makin' too much for them pricks down there at Medicaid.

"So, hey, Trooper, how'd you like to be in that fuckin' washin' machine, huh? You're so goddamn smart, how'd you like to wake up every day and go to work and know that even though you're workin' your ass off, two jobs you're workin', sometimes three, you still don't make enough to keep what you bought, huh? When you were only workin' forty hours, you had enough money to buy the new car, but two years later when you're workin' one and a half times the hours, you can just barely make the payments, but you're still makin' too much for Medicaid, huh? Pay the doctors and the hospital, huh? To take care of your wife—how'd you like that, huh? C'mon, Trooper, tell me! I wanna hear you say how'd you like that, c'mon, ya high and mighty sonofabitch, think you don't make the laws? Think ya just arrest the people that break 'em? Huh? Think you ain't the fuckin' government? Let's hear it, c'mon!"

Milliron shoved his chair back and said to Sporcik, "I need to take a piss call."

"Huh? Yeah, go 'head," Sporcik said.

"Piss call," Czarowicz grumbled. "Gotta take a piss call, listen to him, Jesus."

"Just tryin' to do his job," Sporcik said after Milliron left.

"Yeah? Is 'at right? You too I guess, huh? What *is* your job, huh? Put people like me in prison?"

"Only if you did somethin' wrong."

"And what would that be, huh? Think I shot Lyon?"

"Maybe."

"And Krull too I guess. And I guess you think I'm just gonna sit here and tell ya I did, huh? Confess, is that what you think?"

"Maybe."

"But it won't matter what I say 'cause your buddies, they're at my place searchin' it, right? And they're gonna find the rifle, huh? Ain't that what he said?"

"Somethin' like that, yeah."

"Well, buddy boy, they're not gonna find any rifle shot them two at my place. Not in my house, or not in my car, or not nowhere around there. They can tear the house down, they can dig the foundation up, they can dig the backyard up, they can do whatever they want, they ain't gonna find no rifle that shot them two there, I can promise you that."

"So you hid it someplace else."

"I said what I said, I didn't say nothin' about hidin' it someplace else. You said that. I said they ain't gonna find it there."

"So did you?"

"Did I what?"

"Hide it someplace else."

"You think I did?"

Sporcik nodded. "Yes I do. I think you probably buried it some-place nobody's ever gonna find it. Probably broke it down and buried the pieces, the stock here, barrel there, the bolt somewhere else, scope, bipod, magazines, scattered 'em. Whattaya say?"

"Couple minutes ago your pal here was real sure they were gonna find it at my place. Now you're not so sure, huh?"

"I'm not sure 'cause you are," Sporcik said, straightening up. He had been leaning on the table on his knuckles. "Excuse me for a sec-ond, I'll be right back." He went outside, found Carlucci on the other side of the two-way mirror, and did a double take.

"Whoa. Fuck happened to you? Jesus."

"Some other time," Carlucci said, pointing into the room. "Where's the tape recorder?"

"Huh?"

"Tape recorder? You want me to write it down? Can't you under-stand me?"

"What tape recorder?" Sporcik said. Then his face went slack. "Oh Christ. He said he had everything all set up. Oh shit."

"Yeah, oh shit," Carlucci said. "Just perfect."

"Okay," Sporcik said, rolling his tongue around the inside of his lips. "Listen, what do I gotta do to get an outside line? I'm gonna call his house, tell 'em to forget about it."

"You believe him?"

"What's not to believe? That's a confident man, only one reason he's that confident."

"Just dial nine, then the number."

"Okay, lemme go call 'em. Man, how'd I let Failan talk me into this shit?"

"Call who?" Milliron said, returning from the john.

"Guys searchin' his house."

"What for? Why you gonna call them?"

"To call it off, they're not gonna find any rifle there."

"Why, is that what he said? What'd you expect him to say? It's there? So they don't find the rifle, so what, so they might somethin' else, a diary maybe, letters, targets maybe."

"C'mon," Carlucci said. "This guy didn't write anything down. This guy's not lookin' for his day in court, he's not lookin' to tell his story."

"He told us, didn't he? Yesterday?"

"Not in any words Failan can use. And he just said a couple minutes ago, if anybody talks about what happened to guys like him, nobody pays any attention—"

"Oh God, here we go. This guy practically bragged about it, he had a grievance, he settled it. He looked us straight in the eye when he was givin' us all his motives."

"So he doesn't look away, so what?" Carlucci said. "So he told us his motives yesterday, again so what? That's all he needs to tell. Far as he knows, nobody gives a shit. For sure *you* don't give a shit—and for sure he knows you don't. And he knows you're typical."

"Oh so he didn't tell us now, is that it, he just told you?"

Carlucci shrugged.

"Why? 'Cause I don't understand him? I don't *feel his pain?*"

"Well since you put it that way, yeah, I don't think he told you. You just happened to be there when he told me. But we don't need to be talkin' about this now. Sporcik needs to tell those guys forget it, then somebody needs to go back in and start listenin' to this guy."

"Oh and that would be you, I guess, huh?" Milliron said. "Why? 'Cause you got all this, uh, what, empathy? That what you got? That I don't have?"

"Hey, man, all I been tryin' to tell you is you need to lower your fences and start listenin' to people, that's all. Specially this guy. But you need to do that for you, not just for him. But it wouldn't hurt if you also listened for his sake too."

"This guy's goin' to death row," Milliron said, raising his chest. "And you, you want me to go to sympathy school on him, Jesus."

"He's not goin' to death row on anything we have, and I'm not talkin' about anybody goin' to any kinda school. I'm talkin' about listenin' to the man, that's all. What he did in the last coupla days, that ain't what he was for the whole rest of his life. This guy was solid, man, John Q. Citizen. Went to work every day, raised his children— Christ, his son died in Vietnam! You were in there talkin' about him servin' with honor, he lost a son for crissake, you didn't say a fuckin' word about that! And he was in a war himself, just as ugly as Nam, everything I've heard about Korea—"

"Aw gimme a break," Milliron groaned. "Not another speech about the people's plight here, okay? This guy stalked these guys, you wanna remember that? He planned 'em, he carried them out, he doctored the bullets, he laid in wait, not once! Twice! These were as- sassinations, man. Two in three days—"

"We don't know the time sequence," Carlucci said.

"Okay, alright, we don't know the time sequence, forget I said that. But everything you think this guy was, everything you're tryin' to tell me I should listen to so I could get some kinda insight or some- thin'—I don't know what you want me to get. But whatever, he wiped that out in less than a second. Couple hundredths of a second. Two squeezes of the trigger. Boom boom, that fast—all he did was spread 'em out over a coupla days. I'm sorry, man—no. No, forget that, forget I used that word sorry. I'm not gonna say I'm sorry for not listenin' to some crap about how I need to listen to him for me, that's just bullshit. Fuck that."

"Okay. Don't. But somebody needs to call those guys at his place, they're wastin' their time and taxpayers' money—"

"And that's also your opinion. They should keep lookin' just 'cause nobody knows what they might find."

"Okay," Sporcik said, "I'm callin' 'em. And when you write it up, you can say you didn't agree with me, that's all. Got a problem with that?"

"No I got no problem with that. And you guys can write it up any way you want."

"Okay, then, I'm makin' the call," Sporcik said. "What're you gonna do, Rugs? Goin' in or stayin' out, what?"

"It's his case," he said, nodding toward Milliron.

"My case?" Milliron said. "That's a laugh. Hasn't been my case for, aw shit . . . forget it. But I'm not goin' back in there. No way. You got so much empathy, so much sympathy, you go. I'm stayin' right out here. Gladly."

Carlucci shrugged and said, "Fine. I'll do it." Then, without giving Milliron time to change his mind, he went inside, closed the door behind him, and sat opposite Czarowicz. Before he said anything, he took his tape recorder out of his briefcase and set it on the table between them. After he turned it on, he gave the particulars of the interview, time, day, date, participants, and so on.

"Mister Czarowicz, how ya doin' today? Remember me? We met yesterday."

Czarowicz nodded. "Sure. I remember. What happened to your face? Didn't look this bad yesterday. Did ya?"

"Ah, no, I'm sure I didn't, but if you don't mind, I don't wanna talk about that. It's private. Family stuff, you know, personal. Besides, the more I talk about it, the more it hurts. Uh, let's talk about Frank Krull, okay?"

Czarowicz shrugged. "Fine with me. 'Less you're gonna accuse me of shootin' him."

"No. No sir, just wanna talk about him. What was he?"

"To me you mean? Wasn't nothin' to me."

"No, I mean when you were in the union, when you were hookin' up, wasn't he your grievance man? Or was he, that's what I'm askin'."

"Oh you mean like that? Yeah. At first, that's what he was. Then later on he was shop steward. Then later on he got elected president. But when he got elected president I was already foreman."

"You mean president of the local, right?"

"Sure wasn't the national. Though he couldn't've been any worse than some of the jagoffs in the national then."

"So, uh, you have problems with him?"

"With Krull? Nah. Hardly ever talked to him."

"I don't mean personally. I mean union problems, job problems."

"Only problem I had with him was, uh, well, that wasn't when he was grievance man or shop steward. It was when I found out the union decided I was management. He was president then. So, yeah, that's when I went to him, and I also went to Jack Berk, who at that time was shop steward. What an asshole he was. Before he was steward he was Jack Berkowski. Gets elected he's Jack Berk. Asshole. I also went to see Bernie DeJulio, he was grievance man then, when I found out what the company was doin'."

"What were they doin'?"

"What were they doin'? Ha. Pricks were still deductin' my union dues. Four years after they bullshitted me I was management, they were still deductin' my dues. Four goddamn years payroll deducted 'em, mine and all the other foremen, and never said a word, not to me or none of the other foremen neither. And the pricks in the local, they took 'em, bet your ass they did, and they never said a word neither. When I finally figured it out, I said what the hell's this? And I called up all the other foremen, they all said the same thing. Local tells us we got no standin' with them, and the company's still collectin' our dues for the union, and the local's still takin' their cut and passin' the rest on to the national. Only fuckin' mill in America where this happened—that I know of. Maybe it happened someplace else too, like that, I don't know, but I never heard of it.

"Anyway. I said, hey, bullshit, I posted notices on all the bulletin boards, called a meetin', down the Polish Eagles, all the foremen. And the ones had somethin' between their legs, the ones weren't scared of their own shadow, they showed up. And we all agreed, you know, we finally said, hey, gotta hire a lawyer, sue their asses. What else could we do? Which we did. Both of 'em.

"Course, when we got to court, that's when we found out—in court, on the stand, their lawyer says, he's questionin' their, uh, personnel guy. Sued the company first. And he says it was company policy, the personnel guy. *Policy* he says, these guys ain't management. Meanin' us. They were never management, where'd anybody get that idea, ha ha ha, fucker laughed, yeah, right there on the witness stand he laughs. Course what else was he gonna say? That was the only way they could get away with sayin' that's why they kept deductin' our dues. Meanwhile, the local, those pricks, they told the rank and file, you know, don't talk to us. Yeah. Soon as they got served with the papers, that was it, wouldn't let nobody talk to us, the pricks."

"And this was when Frank Krull was president of the local?"

"Yeah. Nineteen seventy-five, that's when we sued 'em, the first time. Dumb bastards that we were, we were so happy just to get our dues back, four years' wortha dues, plus the judge made 'em pay our lawyer—'cause, shit, we couldn't pay him—plus a fine. That was the judgment. Wasn't any big deal, you know, five thousand bucks or somethin' like that the fine was from each of 'em, but we were so happy to get that little bit back, we didn't even think—none of us had the brains to ask at that time, whether one of them, which, the local or the company, whether either one of 'em was puttin' money into a pension fund for us—that's how dumb we were, we didn't even think of it. Jagoffs, that's all we were, just a buncha jagoffs. Shoulda known, I mean, Jesus Christ, pricks that took your dues like that for four years? They woulda done anything they thought they could get away with. And we shoulda known they would. But we didn't. And so they did it to us again. They stuck it in a different place, they twisted the handle, and then they broke it off."

"Did what exactly? I wanna be clear about this."

"They didn't set up a pension fund for us, all us foremen, that's what I'm talkin' about. Only time I was vested—whatever the hell that word means—and it don't mean much believe me—only time was when I was hookin' up. Eleven years I ran the shippin' department, none of those pricks put a dime into any pension fund for me. Or any of the other foremen neither. We didn't find that out till '85— we were the last ones outta the plant, you imagine that? Huh? We helped 'em shut the goddamn place down for Christ sake, you'd think they woulda give us a little consideration for all the fuckin' dirty work we did for 'em. Pricks screwed us, didn't even have the balls to tell us they screwed us. Hada call 'em, Christ, I don't know how many times I called 'em. Hundreds, hundreds a times. Just hope the sonofabitch invented the hold button is spendin' hell on hold, hope he can't get past the devil's secretary." Czarowicz jutted out his lower jaw and stared at the table, his eyes narrowing. He said nothing for a long moment.

Carlucci tried to wait him out, but saw that Czarowicz was drifting away, and finally said, "But I thought you guys sued 'em again. Isn't that when you hired Valcanas? Didn't you sue 'em over that? Both of 'em? And didn't you win?"

"Oh yeah, we won. So what? That's when we found out somebody stole everything, cleaned it out. Took every fuckin' dime, and nobody knows to this day who that thief is. So what were we gonna get? Can't get blood out of a stone."

Carlucci didn't know what to say next. He couldn't help himself; he was imagining how he would feel if he'd heard a court decide in his favor only to find out there was no money to pay the judgment. He sat for a long moment trying to read Czarowicz's eyes, gray eyes that never seemed to blink, or waver, or look away, eyes that said the man looking through them believed he was justified.

Carlucci stood up, walked in a wobbly circle while massaging the back of his neck with his first three fingers, trying not to irritate the hornets on the inside of his face that seemed to have gone into an acetaminophen doze. He was also trying not to berate himself for what he knew he couldn't postpone any longer. He knew the only way he was going to get to this man. But just thinking about doing it woke the hornets up again.

He took a deep breath, letting it out as slowly as he could to disturb the hornets as little as possible, turned, sat down, and said, "Lyon was a contemptible prick, wasn't he? You don't have to answer that, I know he was. Man, when I saw his house—ever see his house? On Club Road?"

Czarowicz didn't respond.

"You wouldn't believe it, I'm tellin' ya. I was there, I saw it, and I didn't believe it. His livin' room? You could set my whole house in it. My mother's house, not mine. His wife's closet? Man, I mean, lotsa people have walk-in closets now. But this lady's closet? His wife? Man, her walk-in closet, it was a room. A whole goddamn room. Bigger than my mother's whole second floor, that's how big her walk-in closet was—is. Four pipes, stainless steel, runnin' from one wall to the other. And hangin' on 'em was everything you can think of, man, it's like a clothing store in there. This woman—no shit, I started to count her raincoats, man, I quit after eight, you believe that? Eight!"

Czarowicz displayed not a flicker of curiosity, resentment, or envy. He just sat and matched Carlucci's gaze.

"And him! Hoo boy. Two pool tables he had. Imagine? Two! I know lotsa guys have a table in their game room, you know? But this guy, Jesus, two he has! And gorgeous tables too, you should see 'em. I know a little somethin' about pool tables. Used to shoot a pretty fair stick at one time, believe it or not. Yeah. Made some money, not much, you know, but the point is, I can recognize a good table when I see it. Never saw anything like this guy had. Has. They're still there. Just sittin' there. You know, dustcovers on 'em? Nobody usin' 'em. Goin' to waste."

Czarowicz edged forward on his chair. "Why you tellin' me this? You think I care what this guy had, huh?"

"Yeah. Yes sir, Mister Czarowicz, I think you do. I think you do care what this guy had. I think that's why you tried to take it away from him."

"Uh-uh. You're wrong there. I don't envy nobody nothin', that's the biggest waste of time there is."

"Mister Czarowicz, he had a wife. And she's still healthy. And she's gonna get a trust fund that's gonna make her rich beyond her dreams—least that's what the DA told us. Course what she told me, in no uncertain terms, believe me, she really let me know it, you know? She said she didn't need his money, she never needed his money, she had her own money. But right up till the second he died, Mister Czarowicz, he had her. Not like you."

"What're you tryin' to say?"

"Know what else he had, sir?"

"Told ya, I don't envy people, I don't care what he had. I'm not one of them guys thinks if somebody else got somethin', that means there's less for me, I don't think like 'at. Never thought like 'at."

"No, uh-uh, that's not what I'm talkin' about," Carlucci said, mulling over exactly how he wanted to say this. "What I'm tryin' to say is this. I think the person that shot those two? Lyon and Krull? Especially Lyon. I'm not sure about Krull. But I think the person that shot Lyon, I think that person thought he was handin' out justice. Not eye-for-eye, tooth-for-tooth justice, uh-uh. Not pain for pain. Or sufferin' for sufferin', uh, nothin' like that, this was, uh, this was more like, uh, indignity for indignity. Years and years of it."

"I don't know what you're talkin' about."

"Well, let me say it this way. I mean, for years and years somebody's good, you know? Somebody's worth somethin', somebody knows things, he's got skill, he's reliable, he's dependable, he shows up every day at work, you know. He does his job. And year after year, he does his job, and he does it right, and the people who're makin' the big money, hey, the reason they are, it's 'cause they're standin' tall up there on his shoulders. And on the shoulders of all the guys like him. Then, just like that," Carlucci said, snapping his fingers, "they're worthless. What they knew yesterday, that doesn't mean anything today. What they could do yesterday, which they could still do today, which they're still *willin'* to do today, hey, today, you know, it's not worth anything 'cause nobody wants it done anymore—not around here. So fuck 'em. They're worthless.

"But the guys who stood on their shoulders for all those years, hey, they're standin' taller than ever. What difference does it make to them that the guy you used to be, he's now Chico somebody, huh? And he talks Portuguese. And he's lucky if he makes in one day what you used to make in one hour, huh? What difference does that make to a prick like Lyon? Lyon's legs just had to get a little longer to stand on his back, that's all, Chico's."

Czarowicz started to fidget and squirm in his chair. He was rubbing his jaw, and his lips had parted, and he was nodding ever so slightly.

"Yeah. Longer legs, that's all Lyon needed," Carlucci said after a moment. Then he stood suddenly and said, "Excuse me, I gotta go get somethin'."

"Yeah, sure, go 'head," Czarowicz said.

Outside, Carlucci headed downstairs and in a minute came back up with a can of Diet Pepsi. Then he remembered that he didn't have a straw, so he couldn't drink it. God, I'm rattled, he thought.

"Startin' to get dry?" Milliron said. "Wonder you can talk at all, everything you're spreadin' around in there."

"Everything I'm *spreadin'*? Huh? You don't see the way he's movin'? Huh? Squirmin' around? His mouth startin' to open up a little bit, the way he's edgin' up on his chair—you're not noticin' that?"

"So what?"

"You don't see what's goin' on in there? He thinks he's found a buddy. A paisan, a soul brother. He thinks I understand him."

Milliron drew his head back and snorted a laugh at Sporcik. "Way you've been talkin' about this guy, I guess he has."

"See there? That's exactly what I've been meanin' about you. You got no feel for him. Or for guys like him. But when I go in there and break his heart—and that's exactly what I'm gonna do—you, you prick, you're gonna stand out here and smile. You're gonna smile 'cause I made your case for you, and that's all you give a shit about."

"Aw what're you talkin' about now, Jesus."

"Watch. Just watch," Carlucci said. He went back inside, sat down, opened the can of Pepsi, and pushed it across the table toward Czarowicz. "Help yourself."

Czarowicz shook his head no. "I don't drink that diet stuff."

"Okay, let it sit there then. So, uh, Mister Czarowicz, where were we? Oh yeah, right, I was talkin' about Lyon, talkin' about everything he had. And about you. And about everything you didn't have. Like his wife—man, she's tall, good-lookin'. Most of all, she's, uh, she's the picture of health, you know? And wealth? And happiness? And the person that shot him? Know what that person did?"

Czarowicz dropped his head slightly and shook it no slowly. "Don't know what you're talkin' about."

"I know you don't. I know you don't, sir. That's why I'm gonna tell ya. It's, uh, it's a ballbuster, Mister Czarowicz. And I hate to be the one to tell ya, honest to God I do. 'Cause it's gonna hurt. It really is.

It's a hall-of-fame ballbuster, sir. All the things that prick Lyon caused guys like you? Guys that had a decent life and then 'cause of him you lost damn near everything? All the work you did, the kinda life you had? Know what the guy did who shot him?

"I mean, what would be the worst possible justice a guy like you would hope you didn't get, huh? All the good things the man had, Mister Czarowicz? He also had one of the worst things you could have. And the man who shot him? That man saved him from all kinds of pain and suffering."

Czarowicz stiffened and squirmed forward on his chair. "What? Saved him? Saved him how? What're you tryin' to tell me?"

"He had cancer, Mister Czarowicz. All through him. Lungs, liver, pancreas. Coroner said he only had a couple months left. And the coroner said, uh, those last couple months, they were gonna be hell on earth. You know about cancer, sir. So what the shooter did—I mean, I wish I could say it some other way but I can't—but what the shooter did is he saved him from all that hell, all that pain. Instead of givin' him all the pain he deserved, that prick, turns out the shooter did him this huge favor. Did him this tremendous act of mercy."

Czarowicz sagged. His mouth dropped open. The color drained from his face. He said, "You tellin' me the truth?"

"Yes sir, Mister Czarowicz, I am. You can talk to the coroner yourself, you want to. I'll dial his number for you, tell him to tell you what he told us, he'll give you all the details. If that's what you want, sir, I'll call him right now. But what he said to us was, sudden death was way more appealing than what Lyon was lookin' at."

Czarowicz hunched forward, put his elbows on the table and his cheeks in his hands. He shook his head and glared at Carlucci. His breathing was getting shorter, noisier.

"Why you doin' this to me? Huh? I didn't think you was like that other one. Why you doin' this?"

"I'm sorry, Mister Czarowicz. There was no way I couldn't tell you this."

"Aw bullshit, don't tell me that. That other bastard, he'd say any goddamn thing. Told me he showed my picture around, he didn't do that, that was bullshit. But I expected that from him. But why you doin' this? You know what you're sayin' to me, huh?"

"Yes sir, I do."

"Oh I don't think you do, uh-uh, no, you don't. What you're doin', you're puttin' a knife in my heart tellin' me this. Why you doin' that? I never done nothin' to you, why you doin' this to me? This is torture, what you're doin' here, tellin' me this. Jesus Christ Almighty, tellin' me . . . tellin' me the person shot him, huh? Person shot him . . . did this man a favor, huh? Tellin' me . . . the person shot him, did him . . . did him an act of mercy? Goddammit, why you tellin' me this? I don't get that. Not from you."

Then his hands fell away and he began to pound the table with his forehead. And to sob. "Son of a bitch . . . lousy son of a bitch . . . did that greedy prick a favor . . . oh God, oh God Lydia, Lydia, God help me, what did I do? I missed . . . I missed . . . Oh God, I missed."

"You missed? You missed what? What did you miss?"

"I didn't wanna kill him! Jesus Christ, you think I wanted to kill him? Think I wanted him to die fast? I didn't wanna kill him, the sonofabitch, I wanted to paralyze him. But the sonofabitch moved! He bent over right when I fired . . . I was aimin' at his spine . . . I wanted to hit him . . . 'tween his backbones . . . 'tween seven and eight vertebras . . . I wanted that sonofabitch in a wheelchair . . . I wanted him stuck . . . I wanted him dependin' on other people for every goddamn thing, I wanted him to know what it was like to have everything and not have nothin' 'cause all the goddamn money couldn't get it for ya . . . oh God, Lydia, God, I couldn't even do that right, God help me . . . oh God help me . . ."

Carlucci jumped up, nearly tripped over his chair, and bolted out the room, his chest and throat tightening. He felt like he was choking, and the hornets were in a rage. Out of the corner of his eye as he scurried to get away from what he'd just done, he caught sight of Milliron rushing toward him.

Then Milliron was in his face. "Hell you doin' out here? You got him, Christ, you can't let him slip off now!"

"What're you, deaf? You didn't hear what he said? Oh man I gotta get outta here, I need a . . . I smell, I need a shower . . . oh man . . ."

"You need what?"

"A shower! I can smell myself, I stink!"

"Oh Jesus!" Milliron said, throwing up his hands. "You're really somethin', Carlucci, you really are. You know what we have here, you have any idea, huh?"

"I know what you *think* you have here. Only thing is, you're so goddamn greedy to get it, you don't know what you just heard. All you know is, if *you* have to go back in there and get the rest, he won't tell you anything! 'Cause you wanna hear it so bad you practically have a hard-on. And you know he's not gonna tell you!"

"Fuck's wrong with you? We don't have anything else, you know that, and he's ready to go! Get back in there, man, get the hell back in there and get the rest of it, c'mon!"

"Go, right, yeah, he's ready to go alright. Know what, Pinky? Ever since the first meeting up in Failan's office, what you been worried about? Huh? All you been worried about is who was in charge and whose case it was and who was reportin' to who, and we both know what that's about, don't we? You got this great case, huh? This career maker, that's what you got. Only you need me to get it for you. That guy inside there, he hates your guts. 'Cause you have no empathy. And you know it and you know more than anything else right now that he's not gonna tell you anything, just outta spite he ain't gonna tell you. 'Cause he knows what you want, man. It's been drippin' down your chin since last night."

Milliron advanced on Carlucci until they were only inches apart. "Oh you're not shittin' me, you want this for yourself—"

"Want it for myself?! You bastard, you got no idea how shitty I feel right now—"

"Oh like I care how you feel, right. What you forget is, it's my case, I'm who called you in on it. If it wasn't for me all you'd be doin' is readin' about it in the papers, watchin' it on TV."

"Which is exactly why he's not gonna tell you anything, you don't have a clue where he's comin' from, all you think this is is a case—"

"It *is* a case, you fuckin' jerk! And piss on where he's comin' from! Only thing that matters is where he's goin'! Listen to me, I've known guys made lieutenant in five years on cases weren't half this big. Half, shit! A tenth what this one is—".

"Tell ya what you do, Pinky. Call Failan. Tell him how close you are, what you got, what you don't got. He'll probably wanna wrap it up for ya, especially when he sees this guy got nothin' to say to you. But I'm goin' home, okay? I'm gonna take a shower, try to wash the shit off me. 'Cause I just did to him what I said I wasn't gonna let you do. I just tortured him. I just told him the one thing I knew was gonna break his heart. But fuckit, I'm done, I did it, but I'm not doin' it any more. You want him so bad, go get him! Go! Get to it, man!"

"You little momma's boy," Milliron said, glaring down at Carlucci.

"Right, that's what you think, huh? Well, I can't argue. I admit it. Sometimes, you're right, I'm so fucked up about my mother I don't know what's goin' on—but I know what I just did. That much I know, Pinky. I know somethin' else too. 'Less you had a tape recorder where I couldn't see it, you're fucked. 'Cause all you got is yours and Sporcik's word against his, neither one of you was even takin' notes that I could see. I'm the one got what he said on tape, and I'm takin' it home, so how you like that, huh? Momma's boy, huh? That's right. That's me. Busted nose, busted lip, and everything, man. This momma's boy is goin' home, yeah! And guess what else? He's takin' his tape recorder with him. And his tape! He got so many sick days comin', they're comin' outta his ass, and he's gonna take a whole bunch of 'em, whattaya think of that, huh? So you want this case, huh? Think I'm tryin' to steal it from ya? It's all yours now, Pinky. It's all yours, Trooper."

"You can't do that, you can't take sick days now, you nuts?" Milliron said.

"Oh yeah? Watch me." He hustled back into the interrogation room, collected his tape recorder and briefcase, and said, "Mister Czarowicz? Know that lawyer you guys used, huh? Valcanas? Call him. Don't say another word to anybody without talkin' to him first."

Czarowicz, raw-eyed, croaked, "Where you goin'?"

"Home. I need to take some time, my face is, uh, it's like there's these hornets in there? On the inside? And I got 'em all stirred up and they're just stingin' the hell outta me. Really hurts. But do what I said. Call Valcanas. Don't try to go this alone."

"If I wasn't alone, you think I'da done it?"

"You know what I'm sayin', sir. Good-bye and good luck."

The phone was ringing when Carlucci got home. He ignored it, set his briefcase on the kitchen table, and went to the freezer to get a gel pack. He took it to the living room, eased down onto the couch, put his head back, and laid the gel pack on his nose as lightly as he could. Within seconds it was burning, but at least the burning quieted the hornets down.

Two minutes later the phone rang again. Again he ignored it. He thought about the tape, about Czarowicz, about Milliron. He thought it would serve that prick right if he just erased the tape. Then he thought he should erase it, unspool it, cut it in pieces, and flush it. For a couple of minutes, the images of him erasing the tape, unspooling it, then snipping it over the toilet played on the screen of his mind and were wonderfully satisfying and comforting. But they were all coming from spite because of what Milliron had said about him and his mother. Momma's boy. God, that stung. Worse than the goddamn hornets.

Then he saw himself sneaking up behind Milliron and quickly wrapping the tape around his throat and pulling it tight with his knee in Milliron's back. As deeply satisfying as that image was, he had to give it up because the only way he could ever get his knee in Milliron's back—or the tape around his throat—was to hope there was a stepladder handy.

The phone didn't stop ringing this time. Whoever it was, probably

Failan, or maybe Nowicki, wasn't going to quit. He got up and disconnected it and went back to the couch, where he tenderly replaced the gel pack.

Then he got suddenly queasy thinking it was somebody from Mental Health calling about his mother. He didn't know what to do. He went into the bathroom to empty his bladder and, while he was washing his hands, took a long look at himself in the mirror. All the red was starting to turn a deeper shade, starting its run through the bruise rainbow.

How much do I care that call's about her? C'mon, Carlucci, be honest for once, how much do you care about that? "Oh I care," he said to the mirror, "'cause I'm the world's biggest weenie. Aw fuckit." He went back out to the kitchen and reconnected the phone, and it immediately resumed ringing.

After about ten more rings, he picked up.

"Rugs? Better be you, man, this is Nowicki. The fuck you at, huh? Been tryin' to call you for ten minutes—"

"Where am I? You're callin' my house number and I just answered, where the fuck you think I am?"

"Yeah yeah, alright, never mind, the point is I've been tryin' to call you ever since Stramsky said you took off. You sick, huh? If you're not feelin' good, man, you should go to the ER, but if you ain't sick, your bony ass belongs in here, you know? Those are your two choices, and I'm about five seconds away from makin' one of them a fucking order 'cause where you are is the last place you should be right now, understand?"

"What, Failan call you? He bustin' your balls about me or what?"

"Of course, man, what the fuck you think? You got the only piece of evidence they got to make a case, and almost the last word anybody hears from you is you telling the primary suspect he needs to get a lawyer? And you're askin' me if Failan's bustin' my balls about you? Two guys hear you tell the suspect to get a lawyer right before you tell one of them you're takin' the tape home—the tape with the primary's confession on it! So whose fuckin' side are you on, huh—that's what Failan wants to know. And I think you can appreciate why he might be askin' that question, right? So what I'm tellin' you is, you wanna cover your ass a little bit—for whatever reason I don't know, and I'm not sure I wanna know what reason you think you might have—I mean you wanna give yourself some time, huh? Fine. But don't do it at home is what I'm sayin'. You want some time to think maybe, I don't know for what—you need to get your ass in the ER, understand? That's the only place you can logically, safely be at this moment—am I makin' myself clear, Rugs, huh? 'Cause I guarantee you, right at this fucking moment Failan's huntin' down a judge to sign a warrant to search your house, your premises, your car, and your bony dago ass for that tape, so I sincerely fucking hope you have not done anything stupid with that tape, huh? Talk to me, Rugs, I don't hear nothin', man, say somethin', will you please?"

"When was I supposed to talk, you're goin' nonstop here—"

"You know what I'm sayin', Rugs, don't be fuckin' with me, I'm the best friend you got right now."

"That state cop's a prick. All he cares about is this case is gonna make his career, he doesn't give a shit about nothin' else, and on top of that he learned interrogation from the Three Stooges—"

"This is why you went home?! Are you shittin' me? Cause the state cop's a prick!"

"He said things he shouldn't've said, man. Chickenshit stuff about my mother—"

"About your mother?! A-bout your mo-ther?! And he don't what? He don't know how to interrogate?"

"Whatta you want me to say, huh? Did I tell the guy get a lawyer? Yes. I told him. Specifically Valcanas. 'Cause he needs one—"

"Rugs, whoa! Stop right there! Listen to me, huh? This guy you told get a lawyer? He is on the other side—the opposite side from the one you're on, you got that? From the one you and Failan and Smokey, you're all on the same side together, understand? And I don't care how he's pissin' you off or what he said about your mother, Failan wants that tape. Rugs, listen to me, don't fuck with that tape, you hear me? I don't give a fuck what your reasons are for walkin' outta there, okay? I don't care what's with you and Smokey, okay? Do not fuck with that tape, for your sake, do you understand me?"

"Yes."

"Yes what?"

"Yes sir."

"Nooo! What the fuck! Not yes sir, Jesus Christ! Yes I understand, yes I will not fuck with the tape, yes I will not do anything stupid, yes I got a whole career of smart moves, yes I got a whole fucking lifetime of good police decisions, and yes, I'm not gonna fuck up my entire career because some asshole said somethin' wise about my mother! That's what I wanna hear, I don't wanna hear yes sir, what the fuck—man, Rugs, this guy is really fuckin' with your mind, how'd you let that happen? Huh? I don't get that. The Rugs I know would not let this kinda shit happen, man, c'mon."

"What can I say? You're right. I let him fuck with my mind. But try to remember where my mother is right now, okay? And try to remember what I look like—oh fuck, last time you saw me the only thing wrong with me was my lip. And—oh shit! Try to remember where Fischetti is, okay? And Missus Comito too! I mean you know where they are? You hear what happened, huh? Last night at my house, you hear about that, huh?"

"Yeah, I heard," Nowicki said. "I'm sorry, man, you know? But that still doesn't change anything about that tape if you do somethin' stupid, you hear me?"

"Hey, wait a second, okay? I don't wanna sound like a crybaby here, man, but Jesus Christ, the last thing I need to hear is how I'm a momma's boy from some guy who's trippin' and fallin' all over himself tryin' to get a confession out of our primary, okay? I mean, I'm the one got the confession, not him, you know? And I hope Sporcik—I mean he was there, Sporcik—I hope he can find it in himself to remind everybody about which one of us got the confession, you know?"

"Rugs? Whoa, hold it, just answer me one thing, okay?"

"What?"

"You still got the tape, huh?"

"Yeah, course I got it, fuck you think? Think I'm gonna do something stupid, huh? Like erase it, or unspool it, huh? Or cut it up and flush it?"

"You sonofabitch you, you were thinkin' about it, weren't ya—you let that fucker get to you that much?! C'mon, man, he ain't worth that, huh? Hey, Rugs, you playin' with me here? Don't fuck with me now, I mean it, man, if you were to come in here now, you would have that tape with you, right?"

"Aw fuck you," Carlucci said, and started to hang up.

"Wait wait!" Nowicki shouted.

"What now?"

"You gotta go to Mental Health."

"Huh? Why? Somethin' happen?"

"No, nothin' happened. You just gotta go fill out some forms."

"What? Why do I have to fill 'em out? I didn't take her in there. Booboo signed her in, I wasn't there when he did that, but he told me he signed her in."

"Yeah but they can only keep her five days on that."

"Five days?! What're you talkin' about five days? Thirty days—"

"Thirty days? What are you talkin' about? No, uh-uh, listen, on the initial involuntary commitment, that's only good for five days, hundred and twenty hours, that's all. After that, I mean you want somethin' else to happen up there, you gotta have a hearing—"

"A hearing? What kinda hearing? You mean like Family Court?"

"Nah, it's up there. I think. I'm not sure. Been so long since I was involved with one of them I can't remember now—"

"Well I've never been involved with one."

"You never took anybody to MHU? Involuntary?"

"No. Never. I just thought thirty days was automatic."

"No no, what you're thinkin' is, it's thirty days before. When you sign somebody in, you're signin' 'em in on the testimony that they did something violent or dangerous in the previous thirty days, that's probably where you're gettin' that thirty days from. But there ain't nothin' automatic about involuntary treatment, man. And extended? C'mon, extended involuntary, you gotta petition the court, a judge gotta sign off on it, man, hey, it's complicated. That hearing, your mother, you know? She gotta have a lawyer sittin' there, man, makin' sure nobody violates her rights, it ain't some wam-bam crap."

"Oh Christ," Carlucci said, sighing. "I thought I was gonna have some time to think this over."

"Uh-uh, pardner. Listen, first you need to bring that tape in, and second, you need to get up there, MHU, and talk to those people, don't put that off now, I'm tellin' ya, that clock's runnin', you hear? Five days, that's it."

"I hear, I hear—oh fuck, somebody's knockin'—and the way they're bangin', gotta be Failan or Sporcik. Hey let me go see who it is." Rugs carried the receiver with him and peeked around the corner of the kitchen to see who was on the porch. It was Failan and Sporcik and four other county detectives.

"Gotta go, Chief. It's Failan. I'll talk to you—"

"Just hand it over, Rugs, okay? Don't fuck around, just hand it over, okay? Promise me, please?"

"I will, don't worry, I'm not gonna blow my job over this."

He hung up, went to his briefcase, took out his recorder, took out the tape, and ID'd the tape with indelible ink. Then he went to the front door, opened it, and before either of them could say a word, he handed it out. Then he drew it back just as quickly.

"You're signin' for this, both of ya. I'm not just handin' it over, understand? So c'mon in, have a seat, and soon as I find a receipt form in my briefcase here, you're gonna both sign it, understand?"

"Hi, Rugs, how are you, I'm fine," Failan said, leading Sporcik in and following Carlucci to the kitchen. "Though I must say you look not so fine. Sorry to say I heard about your troubles. If I can be of any help, just ask—I mean about your mother, or anything goin' on there with MHU. I know some of that stuff up there can get old real fast. And of course we'll both sign the receipt, wouldn't have it any other way. And before I forget, congratulations. George told me how you handled it. I'm proud of you. See, I had no idea what that business about the cancer would have to do with anything, and I have to tell you right now, Rugs, that was brilliant, using it that way, I don't think I would've thought of that. But, uh, just to mollify my persistently skeptical side—my wife calls it my darker side—uh, would you, uh, would you confirm that you weren't ever, how shall I say it, uh, you weren't ever really entertaining the idea that you were going to perhaps, uh, withhold this tape?"

Carlucci finished filling out the receipt for chain of custody for evidence and slid it around for Failan and Sporcik to sign. After they had, and after he'd turned over the tape, he shrugged at Failan and said, "When I think how much help I'm maybe gonna need about my mother, huh? You think I'd sit around fantasizin' about destroyin' evidence or somethin'? Just to spite that prick Milliron? You mean like, you know, erase it, and unspool it, and cut it up over the toilet? And flush it? You think I was here fantasizin' stupid shit like that?"

"That's what I'm asking," Failan said, smiling one of his better campaign smiles.

"Cannot tell a lie," Carlucci said. "I thought about it. But I would never've done it, man, that's not in me. I know you don't think, I mean ever since I told that lawyer for the guy that killed Bobby Blasco? Remember that? Ever since I told him to take a walk—"

"That's exactly what I was remembering," Failan said.

"Yeah, well that guy, I mean, Christ, he needed to take a walk, he was in over his head, and, alright, okay, I know you think 'cause of that I'm a little bit weird, but, uh, this? Nah." He held up the tape. "I mean, yeah, I did tell this guy today, Czarowicz, I mean, I'm not gonna say I didn't tell him to shut up and call Mo Valcanas, 'cause I did. And I'd do it again. I would. 'Cause I really feel for this guy. I mean if I was him and got screwed the way he did? Hey, I'd probably wanna dust somebody too. But screw with this tape? Nah. I couldn't do that. Not in a thousand years."

"Good, Rugs, glad to hear that," Failan said, standing and extending his hand. "And once again, good work, congratulations."

Carlucci handed over the tape and said, "But it ain't enough, right? I mean it isn't."

"Oh of course not, especially not if he takes your advice and calls Valcanas. Absolutely. Goes without saying. But, uh, who knows, you know? The three of us? Mo? You? Me? Maybe we can, uh, reach common ground with this fella."

Carlucci shook his head. "Nah, I don't think so. Who he killed? C'mon. Lyon's buddies out there? At the country club there? And down the Duquesne Club? In Pittsburgh? They're not gonna sit around waitin' for us to go reachin' any common ground with this guy. About anything. They're gonna want him on the gurney real fast, with the needle in. I'm not tellin' you anything you don't know."

"No, no you're not. Uh, George, wanna give us a minute here? Take the tape, make a couple copies, put one of 'em in my safe, put one of 'em wherever you put things, you know? I need a minute with Rugs."

Sporcik took the tape, nodded, and left. Failan waited until he could hear the cars starting and driving away.

"Rugs, I know you know how the world works. I know that because I'm the one who disbanded Eddie Sitko's commandos a few years back, remember? And I know how much work you did at that time finding out who really runs Rocksburg, and I know that because your old boss told me that. Balzic told me how much work you did finding out about the tax-exempt foundations, and what they do, and how they do it, and how they pay for exactly what they want to pay for, and how they don't pay for anything else, I know you know all this, I know you haven't forgotten it because I know you're not a stupid man. And I also know it doesn't take any genius to see where your sympathies lie with the primary here. I mean let's be honest, c'mon, you think I don't know that if there are no John Czarowiczes, there are no J. D. Lyons? C'mon, you know I know that. But the Lyons of this world, Rugs, c'mon, let's not kid ourselves here. They've got exactly the kind of government they want because it's exactly the kind they've paid for. They pay for the campaigns, including mine— I'm not leaving myself out of this—they pay for the campaigns to put people they want—like me, as I said—in positions of authority to make sure everything works the way it's supposed to work. Where do you think my campaign money comes from? From guys like Czarowicz? You know where it comes from. It comes from guys like

Lyon, precisely so they can continue to not have to pay for all the services they take for granted that will be done for them whenever they want them done for them by people like you and me. *And* by people like Czarowicz. I know you know this. Czarowicz is a good man. When the fellas down at the Duquesne Club wanted the commies stopped in Korea, it was the Czarowiczes they expected to drop what they were doing and get over there and stop them. And they did. And when they wanted the commies stopped in Vietnam, that's when you went. You guys fought that holding action until all the details could be worked out in Paris, you know? Took a while, but the world is running now exactly the way that Lyon and his pals in all the Duquesne Clubs all over the world want it run. Czarowicz, Rugs, c'mon, he screwed up, he turned his weapon the wrong way, he aimed the wrong direction, and you and I, like it or not, are supposed to make sure that all the Czarowiczes still out there see what happens to him. So they don't get any ideas. You followin' me here? Rugs? You're starting to look a little glassy-eyed, I'm not sure whether it's comin' from your nose problems or whether you're gettin' bored with my reality check. Which is it?"

"Why? I have to say, huh? Or what? Am I gonna have to take early retirement or somethin'?"

"C'mon, Rugs, you know what I'm saying here."

"Hey, I gave you the tape, whatta you want? I'm not gonna stand here and salute and give you the pledge of allegiance to the flag just so you can feel all warm and fuzzy about, uh, whether I'm gonna fuck up your case or not."

"Alright," Failan said, standing. "Then let me give it to you straight. The search at his house, no rifle, not on the grounds, not in his car. So all we have are his words on your tape because you and he are, according to Sporcik, walkin' in each other's shoes. Sporcik's told me—and I trust George more than almost any other detective I've ever worked with—George said it's clear to him that Czarowicz will talk to you and only to you. So, all we have are his words here to tie him to Lyon. And I know that if Valcanas takes his case, and knowing Mo, I know he will, 'cause it's the kinda case he lives and breathes for, then it's a simple matter. Somebody makes Czarowicz understand that the only way he stays off the gurney is to explain all the particulars and—and this is a very important *and*—and to show his most profound and sincere remorse. Both, understand? All the details? All the remorse? 'Cause the first without the second? He may as well be on the gurney right now. So you got any feel for him at all—which I know you do, you've made it very clear, you get him to give me the remorse, understand?"

"That's what I'm supposed to do, huh? Get his remorse?"

"For me, for you, for him, and—another very important *and* coming up now, Rugs, so listen carefully—and for all the J. D. Lyons in all the Duquesne Clubs all over the world. 'Cause, Rugs, you just don't turn the guns around on them, that's it."

"That's it? Shit, that's not it, that's everything—"

"No, see right there, Rugs, that's the attitude that will have you walkin' foot patrol in some mall someplace if you don't bury it right now, I don't care how, I don't care where. This is one duty you will perform like the exemplary public servant you are—and I emphasize the word *servant*, understand?"

"Oh yeah? So maybe I will do it, since I'm this what, this exemplary public servant, is that what I am? So just tell me one thing first. If he was over there in Korea stoppin' the commies, huh? Czarowicz? What was I doin' again when I was in Nam? Tell me again what I was doin' there, I forget. Doin' a holdin' action—is that what you said? Till they got all the details worked out in Paris? No shit. Holding action. I'll be damned, I never knew till just now that's what I was doin' there. Imagine that. Holding action. And, uh, just so I'm clear about this, if I don't? You're gonna make the case anyway, right? One way or another?"

"Oh of course. Hell, I know any number of guys willing to buy a .22 Mag rifle, and go bury it, and call in its location, anonymously of course, but if that's what we need, I guarantee we will have a rifle and we will have empty casings with matching firing-pin marks. So? Up to you, Rugs. Milliron said you told him, uh—how did you put it? You said, I believe, that when you were in Nam, you *were* Czarowicz. So how much does he look like you? Not now, of course, not with your, uh, not in your present condition I mean. But really. When you look in the mirror, how much do you look like him?"

Carlucci looked away, and then he said, "I gotta put a cold pack on my nose, you know? Hurts to keep on, uh, talkin'."

"Oh of course, I understand. Uh, once again, Rugs, before I go, congratulations. Using Lyon's cancer like that against Czarowicz, that really was outstanding. Brilliant. Really. I don't think I would've thought of that."

Nah, Carlucci thought, reaching into the freezer for a fresh gel pack, I don't think you would've thought of that either. When he turned around, Failan was going out the door.

Carlucci parked in the metered lot across the street from the boxy, red brick, unadorned building. It looked like any number of other buildings he'd seen and never paid much attention to. What distinguished this one was the rectangular white sign with blue lettering in the grass by the walkway leading to its front door, a sign identifying it as the Conemaugh General Hospital Mental Health Unit.

Carlucci sat in the city's Chevy staring at it for nearly a minute before he could pull himself together enough to get out and walk across the street. By the time he reached for the front door his knees were rubbery and his hand was shaking. Somehow he managed to get the door open and get inside, and then he heard himself asking in this mushy voice for information about his mother and who he had to talk to about signing some papers. Strangely enough, the receptionist had no trouble understanding him. She pressed a button on a keyboard in front of her and told him to have a seat, said she'd call him when a Dr. Moller or Mueller was free, but he wasn't sure if that was the name. She could have said Miller. There was nothing apparently wrong with her nose or lip, so now, he thought, in addition to everything else, his anxiety was affecting his hearing.

The waiting room was empty except for a woman in her midthirties who was rocking on the edge of her chair. She stopped rocking after about a minute, then broke into a wide grin, licked her lips loudly, then grinned some more, then grew very somber, and began to rock again. She gave no sign that she knew anybody else was in the room with her, and Carlucci started wondering if she was blind. But just when he did, she reached into a large canvas bag, took out a pen and notebook, and began to write furiously in it, bending far over from the waist.

The receptionist left her desk and motioned for Carlucci to follow her to the beginning of a narrow corridor where she stopped and pointed toward a door at the other end. "He's expecting you, just knock and go on in."

"Okay, thanks—uh, what's his name again?"

"Moller. It's on his door. He's real nice, don't worry."

Carlucci worried the length of the hall why the receptionist said that this Moller was "real nice, don't worry."

Carlucci knocked on the door under the sign Henry V. Moller, M.D., Director of Mental Health, Conemaugh General Hospital, and went in. Moller was just hanging up his phone.

"Detective Carlucci? Come in, come in, have a seat," Moller said, coming quickly from behind his desk, giving Carlucci's hand a quick shake, and pointing at a chair beside his desk.

"I, uh, I'm here to sign some papers about my mother?"

"Yes of course," Moller said, opening a folder and reading. "I'll have to have some information first, uh, whoever signed her in only knew her last name. I hope you have her Medicare card, we need her correct names, date of birth, et cetera."

Carlucci handed over his mother's Medicare and Social Security cards and waited while the doctor filled the blanks on several forms.

"Uh, you have to do this?"

"I'm sorry, do what? What do you mean?"

"I mean aren't you the director here?"

"Yes. Yes I am—oh you mean why am I doing this, why isn't some secretary doing it. Well, you'll have to talk to the administrator across the street and he'll give you a very long utterly uninformative answer, I'm sure. I'll give you the short one. We are woefully understaffed, and that's because we now serve, and have served, since the late eighties, all of us here in this building, at the pleasure of the insurance companies. Though it's gotten much worse lately. They, and by they I mean the insurance Nazis, they decide who gets what treatment, and when and where and how. So that's why I'm printing this information with a ballpoint pen instead of having it entered into a computer by a very competent woman whom we had to lay off more than a year ago.

"That answer your question? And while I'm complaining, I may as well tell you, Detective, that I'm on the immediate verge of becoming certified as a radiologist and the instant my certification arrives in the mail I will never set foot in any building having even the vaguest pretense of having something to do with human psychology. The insurance Nazis understand completely the necessity of radiographs and are quite willing to pay for them, no matter how many or for what purpose, but what they do *not* understand are those things which cannot be photographed except under the most rigorous experimentation using the most highly sophisticated technology, and even then the only part they're willing to pay for is that part which comes clearly under the heading of brain physiology. And now that I've forced you to listen to my lamentations, let's get back to you and your mother. This happened, uh, this latest incident with her, yesterday, is that correct?"

Carlucci nodded.

"And according to Patrolman Canoza, Missus Carlucci, your mother, assaulted three persons, including yourself, another police officer, and a Missus Comito, is it?"

"Yes sir."

"And it's Patrolman Fischetti?"

"Yes sir."

"And this happened in her residence?"

"Yes sir."

"And has this happened before, physical assaults?"

"Yes. But not like yesterday, I mean, nothin' this bad."

"How bad? And when?"

"Well, uh, long time ago, I'm not sure when exactly, have to think, uh—"

"Approximately."

"Right after I came home from Nam. Probably started early seventies."

"What happened?"

"First time you mean? Uh, she smacked me in the head when I wasn't lookin', I, uh, spilled boilin' water on me. On my hand. Uh, then, uh, another time, she whacked me with a rolled-up magazine, almost knocked me down."

"And, uh, you never thought she should see anybody?"

"Uh, no. Guess I shoulda . . . but I didn't."

"What about your family physician—you have one? She have one?"

"Yeah, oh yeah. Two doctors. Yeah, she has two she sees."

"Never discuss this with them—her aggressive behavior?"

"No. I, uh, I . . . no."

"Why two doctors?'

"She always wants a second opinion."

"Both family practitioners? Neither specializes?"

"No, both family guys."

"And you never discussed her behavior with them?"

"No sir I did not."

"Especially her aggressive behavior against you? Was it ever directed against anybody else?"

Carlucci shook his head no and shrugged.

"She on medication? If so, what kind—if you know?"

"Just for her blood pressure. Uh, and, uh, an ER doc gave her some tranquilizers last year."

"ER doc? What kind and what for?"

"She was havin', like, uh, well, she was thinkin' she was havin' heart attacks, but the ER people, they said it was, uh, anxiety. So he prescribed tranquilizers. And, uh, he also prescribed we should see a therapist."

"We? You mean you and her?"

"Yeah. But we never, uh, we never did that."

"Why not?"

Carlucci sighed. "No way she was goin' for that. I mean, you know, she thought I should go, but not her."

"And why did she think you should go?"

" 'Cause I wouldn't watch TV news with her . . . wouldn't watch anything on TV really, except if I needed to get a time check." Just saying that made him glance at his watch. It had stopped at ten after four. He shook it, but it didn't start the way it had been doing when he shook it.

Dr. Moller repeated what Carlucci said as though making sure he understood what he'd heard prior to making a note of it.

"Look," Carlucci said, "I might as well tell ya what's eatin' her, okay? Or at least what she says is eatin' her."

"Fine," Dr. Moller said, putting his pen down and leaning back in his chair.

Carlucci then explained his mother's problems as he saw them as briefly as he could while including all the pertinent details of his enlistment in the army, his service in Vietnam, the death of his father, and his mother's reaction to all that.

Moller listened, hands folded over his stomach, saying nothing until Carlucci finished. Then he said, "So there's no doubt in your mind that she's held you responsible for her situation since her husband's death. And for that as well, yes?"

Carlucci nodded. "Yeah. That's all I've been hearin' since I came home, since, uh, like '71."

"And you've been living with her all this time? Has she during this time been able to care for herself, does she dress herself, bathe herself, take care of her clothes, cook, et cetera?"

"Well there's two ladies I pay, I mean, they watch her when I'm not there, but otherwise, I do most of that stuff. I mean she eats, you know, she doesn't have to be fed, nobody has to sit there and feed her, she does that. And they clean the house, do most of the laundry, although I wash the heavy stuff, you know scatter rugs and things like that, blankets, plus my own clothes. And they cook, except on the weekends. Then I cook."

"Uh-huh." Moller was taking notes again. "And what brought this on, this latest incident?"

Carlucci told him that there were two incidents and described them both. "What do I think brought 'em on? Tell ya the truth I don't know why she punched me yesterday mornin'. But I know what brought last night's on, I mean she told me that."

"And what was that?"

Carlucci inhaled deeply and let it out. He looked away, sniffed, massaged his hands, and said, "She found the hooks. I, uh, put hooks and eyes on the outside. Of the doors. For when I have to leave, and, uh, when neither one of the ladies can be there. Like the other night I had to go, uh, help a state cop, it was three somethin', and I can't just leave her there, she'll take off. If she wakes up and I'm not there, she'll, uh, I don't know, I guess she goes lookin' for me. I'm not sure. But about a month ago, she was clear down in the Flats, you know, in her bare feet? It was colder'n hell. That's when I put 'em on. And, uh, yesterday she found 'em. Last night."

"I see," Moller said, sighing himself. "Uh-huh. Well. Do you understand the procedures here? You ever brought anyone in for an IEET?"

"A what?"

"Involuntary emergency exam and treatment."

"Uh, no."

"Well, we'll skip parts two, three, and four, and go to five."

"Excuse me? Skip what?"

"Parts of the admission procedure. This Patrolman Canoza took care of part one, part two is an authorization for transportation to an approved facility for exam without warrant and that was done, obviously. Part three is a warrant to be signed by a judge or a mental health review officer but since she's already here that's irrelevant. Part four is Doctor Wertz's affirmation that your mother's rights have been explained to her, and it's his opinion that she does not understand those rights."

"She doesn't?"

"That's the box he checked, and he signed it, so, uh, now what I need is to explain to you that, under part five, uh, your mother's health and safety needs are being met, and they are. And, uh, what you need to explain to me is that her personal property and the premises she occupies are secure."

"Uh, her health and what? Safety needs—is that what you said? They're being met?"

"Yes. Yes, she's calm, she's being cared for, being attended to."

"Can I see her?"

"No, that's not a good idea. I'm not going to permit that."

"Why not?"

"Look, Detective, I'm sure you're aware, probably better than most people who come in here, that occasionally people do things that place others or themselves in danger—I mean that's the whole point of IEET—and to keep them from doing further damage or harm, either to others or to themselves, they have to be restrained. So, uh, your mother is at this moment being restrained. I don't think it's a good idea for you to see that. And I also don't think it's a good idea for her to see you seeing her like that, and I think if you think about it for a moment you'll understand why it's not a good idea."

Carlucci swallowed and hung his head. "She in a jacket? Or she, uh, you know, just . . . to the bed?"

"I don't want to put a picture in your mind, Detective, so I'm not going to describe the particulars, do you understand?"

Carlucci nodded. "Okay. I guess."

"Fine. Now, can you verify for me that her personal property and the premises she occupies, can you verify that they're secure?"

"Yeah, they're okay, everything's all right."

"And you know this because you live there, correct?"

"Well, yeah."

"Okay. That satisfies part five. Now part six, that's the, uh, result of a physician's exam and his recommendation for treatment."

"So, uh, what's that?"

"Well it hasn't been made yet, to be perfectly frank."

"You mean nobody's had time."

"Yes."

"So, uh, what's next?"

"Well that's next. Whenever one of us gets around to it."

"And, uh, when you think that'll be?"

"Well, has to happen in the next four days or we have to release her."

"And if you don't get around to it?"

"We'll get around to it, don't worry."

"Yeah, well see, I mean, far as my mother's concerned, one of the things I do best is worry. And since she did this to me," Carlucci said, pointing with his thumb in the general direction of his mouth and nose, "and to the other two people she hurt, I mean, I'm a lot more worried than I used to be. So, uh, I mean before I leave here today, and by here I mean this office, I'm gonna know what my next step is, understand? And your next step. 'Cause I'm not leavin' here thinkin' you guys might not get around to examinin' her, you know, and four days from now I get home from work and there she is—"

"Well that won't happen. Because if for some reason, we haven't reached a decision about her, what we'll do simply is file a 303 application for extended involuntary emergency treatment, which, once it's approved, is good for another twenty days."

"Oh. Well. Good. 'Cause the last thing I wanna have happen is me, you know, come home in four days and be right back where I started, I don't mind tellin' you that, I mean, that is definitely not where I wanna be back at."

"Well there's not much chance of that."

"Good. I mean, you wanna know her property's secure, I wanna know what you're gonna do next—and I don't wanna throw any weight around here, but when I talked to the DA about this, he said I need any help here, just call him. And I just did a really big thing

for him. I got a confession in a case he doesn't have one other piece
of evidence to take to trial, understand? So I heard what you said before, about how the insurance companies are screwin' you around,
but that's still my mother, you know? And I know I got a ton of
problems with her, but I don't care, I mean, the last thing in the
world I'm gonna put up with is some fuckup 'cause you people don't
have enough people to do what needs to be done, okay?"

"I understand, Detective, I really do," Moller said, nodding many
times. "But sometimes, even with the best intentions from all concerned, some things just get out of our control. I'm not going to sit
here and promise you that your mother will be examined in the time
mandated by law. Things do not always work as prescribed. I will
promise you that I will personally make every effort to do right by
your mother according to the law."

"Yeah, but if you don't, you know—for some reason? Tell me again
what would happen."

"If we don't get her examined and evaluated, and work out a treatment program as required, then what we would do is file a petition
for extended involuntary treatment in the Court of Common Pleas
and get either the mental health review officer or a judge to sign it
and get a hearing scheduled. Which would be held here in this building, and an attorney would be appointed to represent her if she
doesn't have one, and if it's decided that she needs further treatment
after those twenty days expire, we would file another petition for an
extension under 304, and go through the same procedure again, only
the time periods for treatment are extended. Quite frankly, Detective,
uh, because of your work I'm surprised you're not more familiar with
the law here. Which, incidentally, if you want to research the law,
these numbers I've been using have a seven in front of them. It's not
302, it's Section 7302 and so forth of Chapter 15, Title 50, you know
what I'm saying?"

"Uh-huh. Well I just haven't had to bring anybody up here for so
long, I can't remember the details. Besides, I mean, look at me. I'm
as fucking stressed-out as I'm ever gonna get, 'cause hey, it's my
mother, you know? I mean bad enough she's here—but she's who did

this to me, you know? And two other people. Anyway, what you're sayin', if I understand you right, if you don't get around in the next four days to examine her, you're gonna file this petition and that means you can keep her for another twenty days, right? Unless a judge says otherwise?"

"Exactly."

"Oh. Okay."

"Feel better now?"

"No. Not much. I mean I guess. Yeah. Ah shit, I don't know what I mean. I mean I'm glad you're gonna, you know, you won't have to release her if you don't get around to, uh, evaluatin' her. But I mean it sounds to me like, you know, you guys are not gonna have a whole lotta time to spend with her. Or on her. Helpin' her."

"I'll be honest, Detective. If you had the right kind of coverage, it would've been much better, much much better, if you could've gotten her help on your own—course that's out of the question now, I mean now that she's committed these criminal acts."

"I just got the coverage the department has, that's all. But she would never've gone for anything like that anyway. Besides, waste of time talkin' about it now. So, uh, we done here?"

"I don't need anything else from you, and as soon as I know something worth knowing, I'll call you and let you know, fair enough?"

Carlucci nodded, shook Dr. Moller's hand, and started to leave, but then he said, "Uh, you think, uh, I mean, you know, when do you think I can see her?"

"I don't think now's the time to be deciding that, Detective, honestly I don't. I think the stresses here—on all concerned, I think it would be wise to give it some time, don't you? Give yourself some time, you've got some physical problems that need a little time to heal, eh? Think you should just, uh, give yourself a couple of days, say, then give me a call, and maybe then we'll be able to see a little more clearly where we are, hm?"

Carlucci shrugged, started to say something else but didn't know what to say, so he left, hurrying down the corridor past the waiting room, where the woman was still rocking, and outside into bright sunlight. On the sidewalk, he closed his eyes, tilted his head back, and let the sun warm his face for a long moment. When he opened his eyes and started across the street to the parking lot, he had to stop and step back up on the sidewalk to wait until his vision cleared; it was shimmery with tears. He dabbed his eyes dry with the hem of his shirtsleeves, being careful not to touch any part of his nose or cheeks. Ma mia, he thought. Ma mia. What the fuck. . . .

Carlucci drove back to the station and waited until Chief Nowicki was free and told him he was taking a sick day and maybe two, he still felt like hell physically, emotionally. "I don't know why I'm usin' this word," he told Nowicki, "'cause it ain't usually in my vocabulary, but honest to God, I think I'm sick, uh, spiritually."

"Huh? What, you mean like burned-out maybe?"

"No. Maybe. I don't know—I mean my spirit, it's like, I don't know, like somebody let all the air out of me and I'm like some cartoon balloon flyin' around every fuckin' which way, you know? Except those balloons, they land eventually—in the cartoons they do, anyway. But I'm just whizzin' around, all flabby, and it doesn't feel like I'm ever gonna land. What's worse, all the places I'm whizzin' over? Nothin' looks familiar."

"Well how many sick days you got comin'? I'll bet you got a ton of sick days—when was the last time you took off?"

"Can't remember."

"Wait a second, lemme check here." Nowicki rolled over to his computer and punched up some numbers on the screen. "Whoa, you're way over the limit, man. You got so many sick days—you know they're only gonna pay you for sixty days when you retire, you know that, don't ya? You got like, Christ, last time you took off? Guess, huh?"

"Just tell me, I don't wanna guess, c'mon."

"Jesus, the last time you took sick days was '93, you believe that, huh? You got five years of sick days here, man, hundred and fifty days, and they're only gonna pay you for sixty when you hang it up—"

"You already said that."

"So take a week, dummy, what's the problem? Don't fuck around takin' a day and sayin' maybe you might take another one, that's stupid, just take a week, what the fuck. You give the tape to Failan, right? Let them worry about that for a while, take the time, get yourself together—know what I'd do?"

"Oh this is gonna be good."

"No, see there? You're throwin' up fuckin' roadblocks before I even open my mouth. Just shut up and listen—at least wait till I'm finished before you say no. If I was you, see—which I ain't—"

"Oh, right, 'cause if you were me, you'da figured this shit out years ago and you wouldn't be in this fix now—"

"Exactly. But quit interruptin' me, close your mouth, open your mind for once, listen to what the Wickster got to say, huh?"

"Yeah, yeah, alright, go 'head."

"Call Franny, you hear?"

"Aw sweet. Call Franny. Right. And say what?"

"Shut up and I'll tell ya. Call her up, ask her to take off with you a couple days. Go to the beach. Jersey, Wildwood, Ocean City, someplace quiet, not Atlantic City—"

"Get outta here, fuck're you talkin' about, you nuts?"

"Why? Huh? C'mon, why, why am I nuts?"

"Because, man. Where'd I just come from? Jesus, you think I could go lay on a beach somewhere, whatta you think I'd be thinkin' about?"

"Not by yourself, jagoff—with her! With Franny! She'd keep you from thinkin' all that stupid shit you wanna think about—and don't even try to tell me you could be somewhere with her and be thinkin' about your mother, don't give me that bullshit, I don't wanna hear it. Listen to me now, I'm tellin' you what you need to do—"

"Ah will you stop, huh? I'm not gonna do that for a whole 'nother reason, man, c'mon. I never been anywhere with her. You kiddin'? We never even been on like an official date, you know?"

"Aw my ass, official date, gimme a break. It's time you went, that's what I'm tellin' you, fuck's wrong with you? How can you be so smart about other people and so fuckin' stupid about yourself? You don't have a clue what you need to do to take care of yourself, you know that? Honest to God, Rugs, I mean, remember me? Who told you, huh? Who told you get next to her, huh? Was that me? Or was that the fuckin' pope maybe. Maybe that's who told you, the pope. Honest to God, listen to me. Call her, tell her what I said. The two of you, at the beach, just tell her that way, that's all you gotta say, just tell her you got to get away, your head's fuckin' with your body as usual, nothin' new there, same old Rugs, everybody knows how you are, she knows how you are. Tell her you need to get the hot sand under your back and the sun in your face, and with her—that's the important part—with her, don't leave that out when you're talkin'. With her, right there beside you—and wait'll you see her in a bikini, I'm tellin' you, you're gonna shit yourself, that girl works out, that girl got a body. You know she's big in karate, judo, huh? Martial arts? She tell you that yet?"

"Yeah, she told me. Whatta you mean, my head's fuckin' with my body and everybody knows that and she knows how I am—you been talkin' to her again? About me?"

"Course I been talkin' to her about you, whatta you think? You think she ain't gonna talk to me about you? I work with you for what now? Fifteen years, huh? Course she's gonna talk to me about you, whatta you think?" Nowicki shook his head incredulously. "Smartest cop I ever met, no shit—when it comes to gettin' people to tell why they do the crimes they do, and he don't know diddly dick about himself. Some guy—listen to this, last week, no shit—this guy, he asks me do I read mysteries. I says to him what for? He says well ain't you interested in how people solve crimes? I says who do you think you're talkin' to, I'm a cop for crissake, remember? And he says well don't you ever get curious, you know, about a puzzle, a problem, a mystery? I told him—know what I said, huh? I said anytime I wanna be mystified, all I gotta do is look at this detective works for me, Car-lucci, that's all the mystery I can handle. And nobody I know is gonna solve that one. No shit, that's what I told the guy."

"I'm goin' home," Carlucci said.

"You're goin' home—call her, I'm tellin' ya. Say what I said."

"Aw stop. She can't go anywhere. She got groups every night, five nights solid, just started a new one. Besides, she got a mother at home too. What's she gonna do with her, smart guy, huh? You know every-thing I need to do to take care of myself—that what you said?"

"More fuckin' roadblocks he throws up. That's what I'm gonna call you from now on, no shit, Roadblock. No more Rugs. Roadblock Carlucci. Get outta here. Go home and call her, say we're goin' to the beach, you and me, that's a fuckin' order, how you like that, huh? I like the sound of that myself. I should give more orders. I like myself when I'm orderly. Does orderly mean that—givin' orders? Or does it just mean puttin' things in order? Do you know?"

"Like I said, I'm goin' home. And that's where I'm gonna be, you need me."

"Need you? Just told you get outta here, the fuck would I need you for? Go do what I said—why won't you believe me, go on, go!"

Carlucci shook his head and slouched out of the station. He drove home, thinking about what Nowicki had said, thinking about what Franny had said to do the next time he wanted to think about her. That really set his mind spinning. Picking up the phone and calling her when he wanted to masturbate? The phone in his left hand, her voice in his left ear—and in his right hand? He couldn't even think it—any more than he could stop thinking about it.

He parked, walked up the steps, and couldn't avoid seeing the hole in the door where he'd screwed the hook and the hole in the frame where he'd screwed the eye. Sour guilt rose in his throat.

He had to use a key to get in, the first time he'd used a key to open a door to his mother's house in the daylight in so long he couldn't re-member when he'd done it last—if he ever had. There had always been somebody there. Not now.

He went inside, dropped his keys and briefcase on the kitchen table, drank a glass of icy water from a carafe in the fridge, then went into the bathroom and tried to move his bowels. No go. Again. He tried to think of when he'd moved them last but couldn't remember. Was it the day before Milliron called him about Lyon? He wasn't sure. He went back into the kitchen and wrote himself a note on a tablet on the freezer door to buy a Fleet enema. If he didn't break something loose pretty soon, he thought, he was gonna hurt himself.

Then he went back into the bathroom and looked at himself in the medicine cabinet mirror, wondering how long it would be before he could quit breathing through his mouth. While studying his face and seeing that it was starting into the purple phase, his mind kept chewing on everything Nowicki said, especially the part about how everyone knew how he was, even Franny. Ah bullshit, he doesn't know what he's talking about, he's just talking. And how am I anyway—that everybody knows? Fuck him. And fuck them too, they don't know anything.

Suddenly he was talking out loud. "You gotta talk to somebody, man, you can't be listenin' to Nowicki, much as you want to. Be great if you could just pick up the phone, say, hey, Franny, it's me, you know, Danny Date? Wanna go to the beach? With me? Huh? Yeah, right. Every girl's dream, Danny the date dork, Danny with the busted face, you know me, you know how I am, Nowicki said so, everybody knows how I am, my body's at the mercy of my mind—well of course it is, Danny, can you shit, huh? Yo, Danny the doofus, can you eliminate your wastes? Like normal people? Aw stop it, man, who do you think they sell those enemas to? Anus pervs? They sell 'em to regular people. Regular people get stopped up too . . . occasionally. Oh yeah? Like when? Like right after their mother splits their lip? Or when she busts their nose with a cast-iron pan—where the fuck is that thing, that thing's goin' in the garbage right now, I'm never gonna look at that thing again."

He hurried into the kitchen and went through the cupboards where he kept the pans looking for the small cast-iron frypan his mother had smacked them with, him, Fischetti, and Mrs. Comito. He couldn't find it. "Where the fuck is it, gotta be here, that's evidence, that's a weapon in three assaults. Oh man, what am I thinkin', I can't throw that away. Oh right, I'm gonna have a moral debate here? Over something I can't even find? This is great, this is wonderful, Danny the dork detective can't find the weapon used in the assaults against him by the perpetrator, his mother. Holy fuck, I gotta talk to somebody, I'm crackin' up. Balzic. Right. Mario. He'll know what's up with me. When didn't he know? Always. Could always talk to him."

He straightened up, grabbed the phone, and hit the button beside Balzic's name on the speed dialer.

Balzic answered on the third ring.

"Mario, it's me, Rugs, can I come over, huh? Doin' anything, you free now? Need to talk to you, got fuckin' problems, big-time."

"Rugs, slow down, Christ, whoa. You sound like you're trippin' out on speed or somethin'. What's up?"

"I don't wanna talk on the phone—you doin' anything? Can I come over? Right now?"

"Yeah, sure, c'mon. All I'm doin' is watchin' my basil grow."

Carlucci hung up, snatched up his keys and briefcase, and drove to Balzic's house in eight minutes. A minute later he was on Balzic's deck, under the overhang, waiting for Balzic to come out of the kitchen with a plate of banana peppers and some provolone. Balzic had a carafe of jug chardonnay in his other hand and his little finger hooked around the stem of a glass when he came back out on the deck.

"Hey, Mario, I appreciate it, you know I do, man, but I can't eat that stuff, what you have there. Drink neither—not 'less you got a straw. But hot as it is, I don't know if I should be drinkin'. Especially with nothin' on my stomach, you know?"

"I got lotsa straws. Just gotta remember where I put 'em. They're in there someplace." He disappeared into the kitchen again.

Carlucci looked at the peppers and provolone, and his mouth filled with saliva but he knew he couldn't put either to his lip, especially not the peppers. He could smell the vinegar from three feet away.

"Knew I had some," Balzic said, waving a flexible straw around as he came back out. "Grabbed a bunch of these when I was in the hospital, you know? I'm the worst pack rat ever lived, always grabbin' somethin' I think I could use some day. Ruthie's gonna divorce me I don't clean the cellar pretty soon. All my stuff down there, honest to God, what a mess, you oughta see it.

"Here. Take this straw and suck it up, I never saw anybody looked like they needed some vino much as you do—what she hit you with again? Cast-iron frypan? Man, you're lucky she didn't fracture your skull."

"Fischetti's the lucky one, talk about luck. Hit him three times. That's what Booboo told me, I didn't see it. Opened his head up right to the bone, right here." He pointed above his left eye.

Balzic winced. "Oou, man. And she did this why now?"

Carlucci waited for Balzic to fill his glass with the wine, then put the straw in and sucked out three swallows. It was cold, it tasted good, and he thought, what the hell, maybe he ought to be drunk. Then he started talking. He told Balzic everything: the punch in the chin, the melee in the kitchen, the problems with Milliron over Lyon and Krull, his constipation, his yearnings for Franny, and what Nowicki had just suggested. He even told him what Franny had said about calling her the next time he wanted to "think" about her. He talked until his whole mouth hurt almost as much as his upper lip. He talked for two and a half glasses of wine, the most wine he'd ever drunk at one sitting, and strangely enough he felt more clearheaded when he stopped talking than when he first sat down. His body felt drunk but his mind felt clear. He even talked about that.

"Tried to tell ya, Rugs. Wine, sometimes, hey, best medicine there is. Maybe you need to just get shitface here."

"Nah. I hate bein' drunk, I don't like that feeling, I can't stand that." The numbness was already spreading across his face.

"You can't stand it, Rugs, if you don't mind my sayin' so, 'cause you're scared if you ever let yourself get drunk enough to fall down, you think you'd never be able to get back up. I think your problem is you don't understand what the Buddhists mean when they say you gotta learn how to let go, otherwise you'll never hold on to nothin'."

"Buddhists? What, you, uh, you ain't gettin' religion, are ya?"

"You don't have to get religion to read what they got to say. My kid's been buyin' me books, sendin' me tapes, you know, ever since I had my, uh, my second little polka with death."

"Your second?"

"Yeah. First one was on Iwo Jima, you know. Just a kid when I danced that time. But scared shitless—and I mean that just the way it sounds. Scared so bad I couldn't shit. I could sleep but I couldn't shit. Damnedest thing. Sound familiar, huh? You sleep good and you can't shit, right? Isn't that what you said?"

Carlucci nodded.

"You're scared, man, that's all. You got every reason to be scared, you're gettin' beat up by your own mother. There's nothin' worse. When my mother died, I was so pissed off at her, I mean I couldn't believe it. On the one hand I was just all chewed up with grief, you know? But at the same time I was mad at her. I was so pissed off, I couldn't talk about it, not even to Ruth. And she loved me, man, she didn't die to be mean to me, you know? I mean, my mother, Jesus, that woman, she was there, she was a goddamn house, bricks and mortar, you know? Kept the weather off me, kept me fed, kept me clothed, did it all herself too, she didn't have any help. But when she died, I mean—hey, look at me, Rugs. You know I'm tellin' you the truth, you know I wouldn't exaggerate this shit, right?"

"I know."

"Well I'm tellin' you, when she died, I felt betrayed, honest to God I did. Didn't last, that feeling. Only lasted a couple minutes, but I felt it, I'm tellin' you, I felt it clear down to my toes. Like electricity. And that was 'cause she had a stroke and died, you know? 'Cause it was her time. It wasn't 'cause she was beatin' me up.

"Now I'm sittin' here, lookin' at you, lookin' at your face, and what're you tellin' me? You can't move your bowels. Jesus, Rugs, it's a wonder you can still walk, never mind move your bowels. Whatta you expect, huh? Jesus Christ, man, I don't know what I woulda done if my mother ever beat me up like that. I can't imagine how you must be feelin', I mean, I feel for ya, man, I do, but I know I can't either. You know what I'm sayin'?"

Carlucci tried to answer but he couldn't. Tears were streaming down his cheeks and sobs were caught in his chest and throat because he knew he couldn't cry or his face would hurt more. He looked away for a long moment.

"Hey, I didn't mean to make you feel bad—or worse than you do, but I got the feelin' when you were tellin' me what was what here, you know, why you came, uh, that you didn't know this. That you didn't know how really crappy this thing with your mother was—am I right?"

"Guess not," Carlucci croaked, choking back more sobs.

"Well, listen. You stay here long as you want today, you hear me? Drink what you want, eat what you can, get sloppy drunk if you want—and don't worry 'bout it, don't worry about nothin', I'll take care of you, you hear? And this other thing you were talkin' about, you know, with this girl? You should talk to Ruth about that—"

"Oh man I couldn't, no, Mario, I couldn't do that, uh-uh, no—"

"Listen, listen to me. Ruthie's smart. Smartest woman I ever met, that's why I married her. And I don't know this Franny whatever, what's her name? Perfetti?"

Carlucci nodded, but he was leaning back, pulling away despite himself, afraid that Balzic was going to make him talk to Ruth.

"Rugs, at ease, man, you look like I'm sendin' you to hell, I'm not gonna make you say anything you don't wanna say to anybody, what the fuck? This is me here. I'm just tryin' to tell you, you got things you wanna talk over about this woman you're interested in, you oughta talk to Ruthie. No shit. She understands things about men and women that all I can do is read about, you know? And then I can't explain it even after I read it. Ruthie don't have to read it, she already knows it, trust me. But I'm not gonna make you talk to her, okay? Christ, you should see your face, man, you look like I'm gettin' ready to drop a grenade in your lap or somethin'. Relax. Have some more wine. Don't eat the cheese, that'll just bind you up worse. Hey, let's change the subject here, tell me about this shooter, what's his name?"

"Czarowicz. John Joseph."

"He did it, huh? No doubts?"

"Nah. But no evidence either. Just a shell casing, that's all. No good without the rifle."

"No prints on it?"

"Nah. He was careful."

"But you got him on tape? He said it and you taped it, right?"

"Yeah. But whatta you think Valcanas is gonna do with that, huh?"

"Mo? He hired Mo?"

"I don't know if he did or not. I told him to."

"You told him to? Is that what you said, you told him?"

"Yeah."

"Oh that musta thrilled the shit outta Failan, huh?"

"I guess, I don't know, I didn't talk to him about it. But when he hears, yeah, I'm sure he's gonna get all choked up. He's still pissed at me 'cause I told that guy's lawyer take a walk, remember? One killed Bobby Blasco?"

"Oh yeah, right, right," Balzic said, laughing. "I forgot about that. I remember now. But Failan's got the tape, right?"

"Yeah. But tell ya the truth, I don't know what's on it, I didn't listen to it. Could be garbled, maybe you can't hear him too clear, I don't know. Beside, Valcanas, I mean you know he's gonna ask for a suppression hearing. And all the shit he'll come up with durin' that? And to be honest with ya, I don't think anybody Mirandized him. I didn't, I know that. But I don't know what they said before I got there. All I know is they didn't get anything on tape."

"They didn't? Who's they?"

"Milliron and Sporcik."

"They weren't tapin'? They started without you, is that what you said? And they didn't tape?"

"Yeah. Sporcik thought Milliron had everything set up—that's what he told me. But I don't know what Milliron thought. Could be he thought we had some kinda automatic system, I don't know what the fuck he thought. Like maybe when your primary's ass hits the chair, it pushes the start button on a tape machine or somethin'. All he had to do was invite me in, that's all, I woulda let him use my recorder. But no, he thinks I'm tryin' to steal his case, so he uses our place, right? That's fuckin' fine with him—use our place, but shut me out. And then he winds up with nothin' on tape, the jagoff. How could you be that fuckin' arrogant, huh? And still be alive?"

"So you didn't Mirandize him, and even if they did, Milliron and Sporcik, it's not on tape, that's what you're sayin'?"

"Exactly. So what's Valcanas gonna do with that, huh? Two minutes into the suppression hearing, he'll have the judge laughin'. Shit, I could have a judge laughin'. And I can't tell jokes for shit. Can't even remember 'em. Man, Mario, I don't know whether it's the heat or what, or me not eatin', but I'm really gettin' blasted here."

The screen door opened, and Ruth stuck her head out. "Oh. Rugs, hi, I didn't know you were here. Mario, I'm goin' to the store, you want anything, what do we need?"

"C'mere. Forget about the store for a second."

"Oh don't, Mario, huh? Okay?"

"It'll be alright, don't worry. C'mere, Ruthie, sit down here a second, I wanna know what you think about somethin'."

"Mario? Huh? Don't, man, c'mon."

"Finish your wine there, c'mon, drink up, then you tell her what you told me, c'mon, it's okay, trust me, trust Ruthie, she would never screw you around, you can tell her. C'mon, finish your wine, I'll get you some more, and you tell her. Listen to me, it's okay."

Carlucci felt his face getting warmer. How could that be, when just minutes before he felt it getting numb?

"Mario, what're you doin'? Don't make him say somethin' he doesn't want to, look at him, he's blushing."

Carlucci sucked up the last of the wine in his glass, and, while Balzic was pouring more into it, to his own amazement he began to tell Ruth what Nowicki had told him to do about Franny Perfetti and about what Franny had said to him about phoning her the next time he felt the urge to think about her. He also told about Franny's situation with her mother at home and about the hours Franny worked and about how shy he was, things he'd thought just moments ago that he would never have been able to say. It had to be the wine; he knew

that sober he would never have revealed anything except the most su-
perficial details about Franny to anybody, least of all another woman.
Yet here he was, full of wine in the heat and pouring it out to Ruth
Balzic. Half of him couldn't believe he was doing it; the other half
couldn't wait to hear what Ruth was going to say back.

While he was talking he sneaked glances at her and saw her leaning toward him, her elbow on the table, her cheek on her knuckles,
looking at him without a sliver of amusement or condescension in
her gaze or expression. When he finished talking, he sucked up two
more swallows of wine and said he had to use the john.

"Yeah, you know where it is," Balzic said.

When he came back, they were talking and smiling and Ruth had
her hand over Mario's hand.

He cleared his throat and resumed his seat, picking up his glass and
sucking up two more swallows.

Ruth leaned closer to him. "I'm not sure I know what you were
telling me all this for. What's your problem? Do you think there's
something wrong with calling this girl? Like that?"

Carlucci blushed and hung his head. His face was very hot. "Well,
uh, I mean, I just . . . when I think about that, you know, the phone
in my hand and, uh . . ."

"And your johnson in your other one—"

"Yeah right, yeah, I mean, and, uh, her voice in my ear. I mean
that's like . . . it's way too weird, you know?"

"But it wasn't too weird for you to tell her that you think about
her, right? With your hand on your, uh, and so forth and so on—I
mean you did tell her that, that's what you said, right? She wasn't the
one who started talking about this, it was you, right?"

"Yeah, right. Me. I said it first, yeah."

"Well then what's the next step? Seems to me calling her is the
next step. And if you're nervous, or shy, well hell, Rugs, wouldn't you
be feeling that way if you were right there beside her? Right next to
her—shy, nervous, awkward? Right?"

"Well yeah. I mean, I guess. But . . . I don't know, I just . . ."

"Listen, you have not made love with her, right?"

"Right."

"And you want to. Right?"

"Oh God, c'mon, I'm really gettin' embarrassed here—"

"And up until the other night—I don't know when it was, I'm not clear about that, but that's beside the point anyway. Which is, she still has an obligation to her mother, right?"

"Yes. Right."

"And she has her job, and you have your job and until, uh, you know, you had your mother. So, I don't see what's the problem. I think you should take her at her word. She suggested it, right? You didn't. You just told her you've been thinking about her. A lot. And when you thought about her, when you saw her face, that's what you did, right?"

"Yeah."

"So no matter how shy you think you are, or how uncomfortable or awkward you think you're going to be, I mean, it's clear from what you said that she said she thought it was a great idea. Didn't you say she was smiling and laughing when she suggested it?"

"Yeah, right, she was."

"Then do it—what could happen? You call her up and you start talkin'. You both know what you're doin', you don't have to teach each other what makes you feel good, all you have to do is talk about it. Trust me, if she suggested it, you won't have to do too much talking to get things started. And then, hey, you both go to sleep with a smile on your face, and you both wake up and you don't have to pretend you like each other in the morning. Hell, I might try this myself. I think I'm gonna sleep in the girls' room tonight. Who knows, maybe you might wanna give me a call, big boy," Ruth said to Mario. Then she stood and said, "I still have to go to the store, it's my turn to cook, and I don't know what I want to eat. Any suggestions or requests? You are staying, Rugs, right?"

Carlucci couldn't answer. All he could do was nod. He was too busy noodling in the warmth of Ruth's practical attitude.

"Oh why am I asking you, look at you, you're both shitface. Grinnin' like a couple of idiots. I'm goin', I'll think of something—oh I know. Mar, get him Betty Dodson's book. *Sex for One?* You know? Know where it is?"

"Yeah, I'll get it for him, I know where it is. You gotta bring it back, Rugs, I'm not givin' it to ya, understand? This book's strictly a loan, got that?"

"Yeah, sure. *Sex for One.* Huh. What's it about?"

"Oh God, I'm leaving," Ruth said, and left.

"Uh, thanks, Ruth," Carlucci called out, but she was gone.

"Whatta we been talkin' about, huh? It's about makin' love alone. Christ, Rugs, sometimes you scare me, no shit. Don't go 'way, I'll be right back."

"'Bout makin' love alone? Huh? You two got a book about that? Somebody wrote a book about that? Man, where've I been? Oh man, am I drunk . . . ho-leeeee shit, I can't drink, fuck am I doin' here, drinkin' like this . . . I am shitface out of my skull . . . my lip is numb . . . my nose is numb . . . my nuts are numb . . . this is me here, Detective Numbnuts himself . . . mamma mia. . . ."

Carlucci woke up on the floor in dim and fading light in a room he didn't recognize. His lower back hurt, his face hurt, his mouth tasted like rusty iron, his temples were throbbing, and he had no idea where he was or how long he'd been there. He had to empty his bladder so badly he thought if he sat up the wrong way it would empty itself all over him, so he rolled over slowly onto his left side, pushed himself up with his left arm, and rammed the top of his head into something hard. He sat back down with a thump, grabbing his head and cursing.

Then Balzic was hovering over him, asking him if he was all right.

"Fuck was that, huh? I hit into somethin'. Or it hit me."

"Musta smacked the table here I guess."

"What table? Where? Whose?"

"This one right here," Balzic said, patting the table. "Whose do you think? Mine."

"Yours? Oh man, what'd I do, pass out here?"

"Yeah, you just got tired, that's all, had to lay down."

"Oh man, I gotta get outta here, I got this terrible feelin' like I did somethin' stupid, or said somethin', huh? I do anything? Say somethin' really stupid?"

"Nah, you were just talkin', that's all. Had a lotta things on your mind, c'mon, gimme your hand—watch your head there."

Carlucci held up his right hand and let Balzic help him up.

"God am I thirsty—you sure I didn't say anything really stupid, you know, insult Ruth or somethin', huh?"

"You were just talkin', that's all, you didn't do anything wrong. C'mon in the kitchen, I'll get ya a glass of ice water, some aspirin, you'll feel a little better. Think you can drive, huh?"

"What time is it?"

"'Bout eight-thirty, round there."

"How long I been sleepin' there?"

"'Bout four hours. Nice little nap. That's about how long it takes me to sleep it off I start drinkin' early as we did."

"Man, Mario, I don't know what got into me, I don't usually drink like 'at."

"Listen, paisan, you're in pain a couple different ways. You're confused about somethin', you came to see your friends, you talked a lot, you drank maybe more than you're used to, you took a little nap, that's all there is to it, don't worry about it, you got enough shit to worry about. Here, drink this." Balzic handed him a large glass full of water and ice cubes. "Wait, wait, here's a straw."

Carlucci sucked it down. He couldn't remember ever being this thirsty. He held out the glass to Mario. "Wine make you thirsty, huh? When you drink too much?"

"Alcohol makes you thirsty, it dehydrates you, you didn't know that?"

Carlucci shook his head and drank the refill Balzic handed him.

"Don't get pissed, Rugs, okay? But some ways, you're an old man. Some ways—I gotta say this, you know? Some ways you're a baby, you're barely able to walk."

"Why would I get pissed over that?" Carlucci said, handing the empty glass back to Balzic again. "It's true. I know it. Can I have more water, please? I'm dryer'n dirt here. Can tell ya this, I won't be doin' this again for a while. Man, I thought no way my head could hurt worse. I was wrong. But for a while there, it really felt better, ain't that somethin'? Life's nuts."

"That's why when they see somebody drunk, you know, people say he ain't feelin' no pain."

"Do they say, you know, afterwards is his head really gonna be poundin'—do they say that?"

"Not too much, now that you mention it. Don't think I ever heard that too much, no."

"Well if they're gonna say the thing about feelin' no pain, they oughta say the other thing too. Aw fuck, who cares? I'm goin' home. Thanks, Mario."

"For what?"

"For the wine—I think. For listenin' too—I think."

"You're welcome. Go on, go home, drink some more water, put some ice on your head, you got aspirins at home? Wanna take some now?"

"I got a big bottle at home, don't worry."

"You don't worry—and call that girl."

Carlucci hung his head and groaned. "Aw, see? The worst part about drinkin'—I never knew this, swear to God I didn't—you'll talk about anything. Man. I can't believe I came here and said all that stuff, Jesus, please don't say nothin' about this, okay? To nobody, promise, Mario."

"Will you get the fuck outta here, huh? Make me promise about that, I'll smack you one. Go home, get goin'."

Carlucci let himself be led to the front door and out to his car. He drove back to Norwood Hill in a smelly fog of conflicting and contrary thoughts and emotions. Inside his mother's house, he drank two

ice-tea-size glasses of water with ice cubes in them, standing with his
rump against the sink counter, trying to quench a thirst that now
seemed unquenchable. Then a new thought rambled through his
mind: What if she never gets out? What do I do about this house?
Long as she's in there, oh wow, I made a statement to that doctor, I
have to keep this property secure, I don't have any choice about that.
But then what happens? Oh shit, they let her out, Fish'll prosecute
her. Booboo won't, he'll let it slide, but not Fish, no fuckin' way
Fish'll ever let this slide. Fish is hard, man. He forgives nobody. Can
I blame him? Hey, I was him I wouldn't let it slide. Almost wanna
prosecute her myself—aw what the fuck am I thinkin' about, I'm
nuts. Life's nuts. Mamma mia. . . .

Carlucci spent the next two days at home watching his face progress
through the colors of the rainbow and stewing over every possible scenario involving his mother, her house, and the MHU. When
he wasn't thinking about her, he was thinking about Mrs. Comito
and Fischetti; when he wasn't thinking about them, it was Lyon,
Krull, and Czarowicz; and when it wasn't them, it was Failan, Milliron, Sporcik, and Valcanas. His mind was never at rest, never quiet,
never peaceful, and it wasn't because he was trying his damnedest not
to think about reaching for the phone with Franny Perfetti's face in
mind. Balzic's right, he thought: sometimes I'm an old man; other
times it's a wonder I'm old enough to walk.

But walk he did. From the kitchen to the bathroom to his mother's
bedroom to his own bedroom, and back to the kitchen where he
started the circuit again, stopping in the bathroom to check the
progress of the rainbow on his face or his beard. His face still hurt
too much to think about shaving or brushing his teeth. On the first
day, he stopped walking long enough to call the hospital to learn that

Fischetti had been released and that Mrs. Comito would be kept another night. Otherwise, he stopped walking only to make something
to eat, or to eat it, and to clean up afterward; or to go to the john to
shower or to pass water; or to his bedroom to sleep. The rest of the
time he walked.

Two days of walking and thinking led him to one conclusion: the
only thing he was sure of was that he had not moved his bowels in
four days. Or was it three? Suddenly he wasn't sure of even that. Then
he was sure he had to get to a drugstore to buy an enema, but when
his hand was on the front-door knob, he thought that Mrs. Comito
would be home by now and the least he should do was see if she
needed anything.

So he went out into bright sunlight and headed to her house, four
doors away. When he got there, she was standing in the doorway as
though waiting for somebody, the cast on her left forearm visible at
the opening at the end of a blue sling. She didn't react to him until
he knocked; she was just standing there, smiling weakly. She started
when she became aware of his presence.

"You scared me, Rugsie, I didn't see you coming," she said. But
when he walked in, she shuffled forward into his chest with her right
side and put her face against his neck. They stood like that for a moment, comforting each other, murmuring unintelligible things and
crying. Then he pulled back and asked if she was in any pain and told
her how sorry he was and she said almost the same things to him. He
asked her if she needed anything and when she said she didn't, he said
she should call him no matter what time of day or night it was if she
needed anything at all. He heard somebody behind Mrs. Comito and
looked up to see Mrs. Viola standing in the doorway to the kitchen.
He nodded at her and said, "Aw good, you're here. Thanks. Both of
you. For everything, you know? And I can't tell ya how sorry I am,
Missus Comito, you know?"

"How 'bout you, you need anything?" Mrs. Viola said.

He shook his head.

"Where is she?" Mrs. Viola said. "She, uh, she up there?"

Carlucci knew what she meant by "up there"; it was the same

place everybody in Rocksburg meant when they said it. Conemaugh General Hospital was sited on the highest hill in town, and the MHU was across the street from it. If you were going for some physical procedure, you were going "to the hospital" or "to Conemaugh"; if you were going to the Mental Health Unit, you were going "up there." So he nodded in answer to Mrs. Viola's question and left it at that.

"Rugsie, you eating, huh?" Mrs. Viola said. "You can eat here, you know."

He shook his head and said, "I'm fine. Made a big pot of soup, you know. And my old boss, he makes bread, you know? He gave me a big loaf. I put a slice in the bowl, put the soup on top, that's plenty. Don't feel like anything else, hurts too much to chew."

He asked again if they needed anything, saying he was going to the store and would be glad to get whatever they needed, but they said they were fine, so he gave them both another hug and left.

When he got home and got into the city-owned Chevy, he glanced up at the rearview mirror and saw George Sporcik pulling in and against his back bumper. They got out at the same time.

"What, you throw your phone in the garbage?" Sporcik said.

"Nah, uh-uh. Unplugged it."

"That would explain that then. Failan wants to see you."

"Yeah? What about?"

"Whatta you think? Valcanas won't let Czarowicz talk to anybody, but for some reason he wantsa talk to you. Failan thinks you should let him."

"So nobody found the rifle, huh?"

"Well, fuck, you knew nobody's gonna find that. Some archaeologist maybe. Two hundred years from now."

"You fuckers didn't lock him up, did ya?"

"On what? No. He's still walkin' around."

"Still shootin' targets?"

"As a matter of fact, yes he is. Only he's doin' it with a pistol. Got a .22 Mag. A Smith & Wesson. Stands there, squeezin' 'em off. One box every day."

"Where's he doin' that?"

"On some guy's farm he was in the marines with. Jurista. Fact, it's Jurista's pistol he's shootin'."

"Same Jurista owns the hardware store?"

"Yep. The same."

"That's where the rifle is then."

"You think?"

Carlucci shrugged. "Why not? What better place? How big is it?"

"'Bout fifty acres I think, more or less. Not too big."

"Well if I was him, what I would do—or what I would've done— I would've dug a deep hole, then I'd bury the rifle, or no, wait. I would've dug a lotta holes, deep, you know? Bury the parts. Then I'd cover them up with maybe a foot of dirt. Then I'd throw more metal in, you know? Stuff I took outta somebody's junkyard. Put that stuff right on top. Then I'd cover that up. And you could sweep that place with a battalion of guys with metal detectors and all they'd find is the junk."

"Got a devious mind, Rugs. Where'd you think that up?"

"Ah, somethin' I read about once, about how these drug pilots, you know? Guys fly in all that dope from South America? Pretty slick how they cheat the radar. Two planes come in, stacked up real close, like thirty, forty feet apart, one above the other, I don't know how far apart they are. But close. But on radar they're just one blip, they look like one plane. Then they get past where the radar is, one goes wherever he's logged to, the other one, the one with the dope, he goes to some private field somewhere. I don't know, maybe it was all bullshit. I just thought if I was buryin' metal to hide it, that's the way I'd do it. So, uh, Failan sent you up here, huh? To what, convince me it's a good idea to talk to Czarowicz, is that it??"

"Course he sent me. We don't have anything."

"Tape garbled or somethin'?"

"Nah. It's clear, your tape, real clear. But without anything else, so what? Valcanas is standin' around, practically darin' Failan to hold a probable cause hearing. But, uh, no, we're the ones fucked up—me especially. Milliron told me everything was set up, and asshole that I am, I believed him. So when we told him he was a suspect, and then we Mirandized him, you know, what the fuck, we were talkin' to the walls. Valcanas can't stop grinnin'."

"He already been in, huh?"

"Of course. Whatta you think? That's what you told Czarowicz, ain't it? Besides, he's Failan's buddy."

"I know. Failan told me."

"Well, it's all real cordial when they get together, real friendly, you know, please, sir, if you would be so kind, stop fuckin' harassin' my client, okay? And let's go to Muscotti's have a little Sambuca with our coffee."

"Ah fuck, man, tell Failan wait a couple years, this Supreme Court'll get him what he wants. They're chippin' away at it. Fuckin' exclusionary rule's practically worthless now. Give those fuckers enough time, they'll've figured out how to repeal the whole first ten."

"So, uh, not only are you devious, you little dago prick, you're cheerin' for the other side is what I'm hearin'. C'mon, what am I supposed to tell Failan? The lovely colors of your face, huh?"

"Tell him what you want, I don't care. And I've been lookin' at my face so I know how lovely it is—and fuck yeah. Right. Long as you wanna know, that's right, I am cheerin' for the other side. If I was Czarowicz, if I got fucked around like he did, I'da shot somebody myself. Maybe not Krull. I'm not sure why he shot him, But Lyon? Fuckin'-A. Many people as he fucked over?"

"Whoa, Rugs, easy. Watch how you talk, never know who might be listenin'."

Carlucci stiffened. "Never know what? Wait a second, you motherfucker, you wired? Huh? You wearin' a fuckin' wire on me?"

"At ease, Jesus Christ, chill out here, what're you, nuts? Fuck would I be wearin' a wire for? To get you bitchin' about rich pricks?"

"Take your clothes off then."

"Fuck you, take my clothes—this is me here. George Sporcik. My old man worked his whole fuckin' life in the labor gang at Knox Iron and Steel, that sound familiar? Merged with Conemaugh Steel, huh, remember that? Before Lyon took 'em to Brazil? You think I'd wear a fuckin' wire about this shit? For anybody? For any reason? Hey, this is Milliron's fuckup, not mine, his case, his fuckup, he can smother it with sliced jalapeños and eat the whole fuckin' thing for all I care. Any shit falls out on my back's gonna slide right off, partner, I don't care what Failan puts on my next fitness report."

"Oh yeah? So then what're you doin' here? Really."

"Told ya, dummy. What, you don't listen? Failan sent me up here to talk you into talkin' to Czarowicz, and if I can't do that, I'm supposed to bring you back to his office, so he can turn on the charm himself. Fuck you think? Think there's somethin' nefarious goin' on here? It's the DA beggin' and suckin' up, that's all. You think he wants the national press on him the way they're on those assholes out in Colorado? Over that little girl? You kiddin'? They haven't heard about our little snafu yet, the media types, you know? Milliron's snafu I mean. I gotta give Failan credit for keepin' it buttoned down long as he has, but he ain't gonna keep it quiet forever. And whose ass you think they're gonna burn over this, huh? It sure ain't gonna be yours. Not at first. You're the only one even looks halfway like you knew what you were doin'. How you think Failan thinks he's gonna look when those fuckers on *Dateline* get through with him? Or *60 Minutes*? Or *20/20,* huh? Think he ain't sweatin' it? Hey, Rugs, this ain't no little girl got dusted here. This was a big dog."

"So? For once it was one of them. 'Bout time, you ask me."

"Easy, Rugs, I'm tellin' ya, watch what you say, man, no shit."

"But you're not wearin' a wire, right?"

"I'm tellin' you like a brother, man, understand? And I really don't care whether you believe me or not. Just think before you talk, that's all I'm sayin'. And try to think, you know? When this shit hits this fan, just try, understand? Try to think how grateful Failan would be to anybody who could cover his ass a little bit, huh? Think how grateful you would be, you were Failan."

"Yeah? Well I'm not. And he's not me."

Sporcik sighed and looked at his shoes for a long moment. He stuck his tongue up under his upper lip and rolled it from side to side. When he looked at Carlucci again, he said, "This is from him, man. I'm just a messenger boy here, don't confuse things on me, alright? I wouldn't say this to you in a thousand years."

Carlucci folded his arms across his chest and took a step back. "Aw here it comes. Say what, go 'head, what's the screw, huh? It's my mother, ain't it? He's gonna fuck with her hearings, ain't he?"

Sporcik nodded and looked away.

"That motherfucker. Know what's wild? He told me, you know, when he first heard about Milliron givin' Valcanas some attitude? Valcanas called him right away, you know? And Failan told me to tell Milliron to watch how he talked to people, you know? Especially people who were doin' his work for him, and I said hey, why don't you tell him yourself? And he said, never beat somebody up yourself when you can get somebody else to do it for ya. Said it was his eighth rule of survival, or some shit. Seventh, I forget which. Fucker. Man."

"Yeah," Sporcik said, still looking away, over Carlucci's shoulder.

"Think he would? Huh? You know him better'n I do, think he'd actually do that?"

Sporcik shrugged. "What can I say, Rugs? Put yourself in his place for a while. It's rocks and hard places, you know? For everybody. How you think he got *me* up here? Just promoted me, you know? Man promotes you, he can sure as fuck unpromote you. He could have me in the Park Police tomorrow, you know? Cleanin' squirrel shit offa picnic tables."

"Aw fuck."

"C'mon, man, talk to him, that's all. Just come on in and talk to the guy, the man wantsa talk to you, that's all you gotta do."

"No, uh-uh, I talk to Failan, that gets you off the hook, but that puts me right back on it."

"Exactly. And with your mother there, you know, where she is? Plus, he got you for tellin' the primary to shut up, and also for recommendin' a lawyer. Plus you got a history with him of tellin' lawyers, you know, to get lost? Do I think he'll use it? Any of it? Fuck yeah, every bit. He used it on me to get me here. Why wouldn't he, you were him, huh? Wouldn't you?

"C'mon, Rugs, they're gonna get Czarowicz one way or another.

We don't get him, you know what the FBI's gonna do. They'll wait a year or so, then they'll nail him for violatin' Lyon's civil rights. He'll do ten years federal hard time, you know that. I keep tellin' you, this was a big dog, man. And the rest of the big dogs ain't gonna let this pissant get away with this, don't matter what happens with the rest of us pissants, c'mon, Rugs, you know what I'm sayin'."

"Ah fuck," Carlucci said. "This guy spent three fuckin' years in Korea. Got wounded three times. One of his sons is KIA in Nam. He gets fucked around by the government rules on Medicaid when his wife gets cancer, he gets fucked over by the company he spends most of his life workin' for, he finds out nobody sets up a pension fund for him, not the company or the union, his own union fucks him around, and of all the fuckin' people in this town he thinks he can talk to, he picks me. What the fuck. Picks me, the same week my mother picks to start beatin' the shit outta me. And I'm supposed to feel for Failan? Yeah, right. Know what else, huh? I can't shit. Not in four days. Or three, can't remember which. Feels like I got rocks in there. Man . . ."

"I know, I know," Sporcik said. "I feel for ya, man, I do."

"So, uh, what, I gotta see Failan today, is that it?"

Sporcik nodded.

"Well fuck this, huh? Hey. Tell Failan I was on my way to the drugstore, buy one of those, uh, Fleet enemas. Tell him soon as I do that, I'll be in—but not before. I'm on sick time here, and god-dammit I'm gonna take care of myself first before I start takin' care of him."

"I'll tell him," Sporcik said, holding out his right hand. Carlucci's hand disappeared in it. "Sorry, Rugs."

"For what?"

"I don't know," Sporcik said, shrugging. "I guess for us bein' little dogs."

"Speakin' of which," Carlucci said, canting his head, "I just re-membered somethin'. You been in our room lotsa times, I remember you workin' cases with Balzic. Fact, I remember you and him inter-rogatin' that Beecher, that guy made his wife disappear, you worked that guy for musta been two hours. You tellin' me you didn't know Milliron was fuckin' up? When he didn't produce a tape recorder? Huh? That's bullshit, man. You know better'n 'at, don't give me that story."

Sporcik got into his county car and looked up at Carlucci. "That's my story. And I'm stickin' with it. See Failan now, Rugs, don't fuck me around on this, I'm gonna tell him you're comin', okay?"

"Yeah, yeah. Call *me* devious, you sly fucker you."

"Call me irresistible, I don't give a fuck what you call me, just after you flush yourself out, you make nice with Failan, alright? Bye."

After Carlucci, to his great relief, used the Fleet enema to flush himself out, he took a shower, dried off, and then sloshed baking soda and water around his mouth several times to try to get rid of the foul taste. Then he put on a pair of chinos, a black T-shirt, and running shoes over his bare feet, and drove to the courthouse, trying to prepare himself for whatever Failan might have in mind. He was through the metal detectors in the basement garage before he realized he'd left both his pistols at home. I'm not too fucking preoccupied, he thought as he climbed the stairs to Failan's office on the third floor.

Failan wasn't in his office, but bent over Failan's desk with his nose in a book was First Assistant DA Les Harvey; he looked up and handed Carlucci a sealed envelope.

"What's this? Where's Failan?"

"Don't know. He said give that to you when you showed up, didn't tell me anything else," Harvey said, and stuck his nose back in the book. "Hope the other guy looks worse than you, Carlucci, 'cause you look about as bad as anybody I've ever seen who was still ambulatory."

Carlucci grunted, turned around, and started out, opening the envelope before he reached the door. There was a hand-printed note inside that said, "Go to Valcanas's office. He's been looking for you for two days. Don't disappoint him. S/Failan."

Carlucci left the courthouse and walked the half-block to Valcanas's office. It was hot and the only breezes were coming from passing traffic. Carlucci's T-shirt was clinging to his chest and back by the time he reached the surly woman who typed so fast it sounded like two people typing. Without lifting her fingers from the IBM Selectric, she raised her eyes and stared openly at him for a long moment before saying, "If you're Detective Carlucci, his Mo-ness is expecting you. And if that's a disguise, it's working."

"Huh?"

"That response could have come only from one of Rocksburg's finest. Think you can remember which door you used the last time you were here?"

Go fuck yourself, Carlucci thought, and you would have to because there isn't anybody on this planet that would want to, but he kept that thought to himself, doing his best, given the state of his face, to smile.

He knocked on the door to Valcanas's office, heard what he thought was an invitation to come in, and went in to find Valcanas near a stack of long-playing record albums in his T-shirt, boxer shorts, ankle-high black socks, and sandals, fanning himself with one of the record covers.

"Come in, come in, Detective," Valcanas said while blowing dust off a record. "Don't mind me, my AC went kaput this morning and I can't find one damn repair shop to make an office call. If Muscotti ever turned his AC on, I'd happily conduct business there, but, he's old, he's stubborn, he's Tuscan—oh hell, that's enough about that."

Valcanas looked up from the records he was examining and started to say something about Carlucci, but stopped as soon as he saw Carlucci's face. "Ouu. Excuse my staring, but, uh, as I recall, the last time you were here it was just your upper lip. I'm sorry, uh, I can't help staring. I don't think I've ever seen anybody's nose and cheeks that particular color. Looks sort of like the sky right before a violent electrical storm."

"Yeah, well, that's sorta the way it feels too."

"Not your mother again, I hope."

Carlucci nodded, but said nothing because he heard somebody moving around in the bathroom at the far end of the room and heard the toilet flush. Then he heard coughing and water running. He thought it was Failan and was very surprised when the door opened and John Czarowicz came out, wadding up paper towels.

Czarowicz paused at the sight of Carlucci, then kept moving into the room, dropping the towels into a wastebasket near Valcanas's desk.

"Mister Czarowicz," Carlucci said. "Didn't expect to see you. Thought I was gonna be seein' Failan."

"Well, he's who recommended this meeting," Valcanas said. "And John is who requested it. And I'm just the facilitator, that's all. I'll lay out the ground rules, and there's really only one, and then you two can have the office, okay?"

Carlucci shrugged. "Okay with me."

"Okay. Have a seat. Want a record cover?"

"Huh?"

"To fan yourself with. It's about eighty-five degrees in here, it's only gonna get hotter. Take one, it's the best I can do."

Carlucci took a record cover from Valcanas's pile. There was a photograph of a very large, very round black man playing the piano. The words read simply, *The Oscar Peterson Trio*. Carlucci fanned himself for a moment, then shrugged and put the cover back.

"We've been discussing—we being John here, Howard Failan, and myself—at length, in private, and off the record, the facts of life in John's future. Which future, as I've pointed out to John in great detail, looks to me exceedingly bleak. John, from where he sits, doesn't much care how bleak it looks. He says it isn't any bleaker than his past, and his past, especially since 1985, has been pretty damn bleak by anybody's standards. For some reason, John wants to get something straight with you, Detective. It's very important to him, that's all I know. I've argued against him saying anything to anybody, and I believe that you were the first to advise him to do exactly that and also to hire me.

"So the rules which I've worked out with Howard are these, which, essentially, is one rule: everything said here today between John and you stays in this office. You will not be required either by Howard or by me to testify about what's said here today in any judicial proceeding of the Court of Common Pleas of Conemaugh County. Beyond that, all deals, promises, validations, affirmations, confirmations, whatever they might be called now or in the future, are off. For example, if, at some future date, you are subpoenaed by any officer of the U.S. Court of the Western District of Pennsylvania, you're on your own. If you wanna call Howard to confirm what I've just said, his home phone's number one on my speed dialer, help yourself."

"He's at home now?" Carlucci said, reaching across the desk to pick up Valcanas's phone. He picked it up, pushed the top speed-dialer button, and waited for the message beep to sound so he could identify himself. As soon as he did, Failan picked up. Carlucci repeated everything Valcanas said and asked Failan to confirm it. Failan did.

"What's goin' on, Mister Failan?"

"Mo'll explain," was all Failan said and hung up.

Carlucci hung up and said, "What's goin' on, Mister Valcanas?"

Valcanas coughed and cleared his throat. He looked at Czarowicz, Czarowicz nodded, and Valcanas slowed his fanning.

"What's goin' on," Valcanas said, "is Howard's been gettin' some phone calls. Got one two days ago and another one yesterday afternoon in his office, and another one last night at home. The caller has identified himself to Howard in such a way that Howard knows the calls are genuine. And he's made it very clear that John is a, uh, well, no other way to say this, he's, uh, looking at a very short future. Uh, the fact is, Howard's been told, John can't be protected."

"Don't wanna be protected," Czarowicz said. "Nobody protected me since '85, why the hell should it be any different now?"

"That's accepted, John, you've made your thinking very clear to us, Howard and me. I accept it, Howard accepts it—"

"Yeah, I know, just had to say that, that's all."

"What, somebody tellin' Failan this guy's gonna get whacked?"

Valcanas nodded to Carlucci's question.

"And Failan knows the caller?"

Another nod.

"He knows? He knows the caller? What the fuck—he knows the caller and that's it? He's not gonna do anything?"

Valcanas cleared his throat again, licked his lips, and chewed his lower lip before responding. "Detective, I know you learned a lot of things about this town when your old boss was involved with the, uh, the former councilwoman who had the audacity to suggest that the firemen here should pull their own weight, am I correct? You remember the work you did regarding the Rocksburg Foundation and all its progeny?"

"Yeah. So what? You mean somebody from that level is puttin' out a contract?"

"No no no, just listen, I'm not suggesting for a second that anybody from around here's involved. I'm guessing these calls are coming either from New York or Washington. You've had your own problems over the past few days, as anyone can readily see just by lookin' at you, so I'm sure you're not aware of the tremendous pressure that's being brought on Howard to reach a resolution here, for want of a better phrase. And with all that pressure, which I assure you, nobody around here's ever felt before, I mean all those people with cameras and microphones and tape recorders, hell, you can't move in the courthouse, they're camped all over Howard's front yard, it was inevitable that some money was gonna get offered around, and, uh, people are only people, Detective, I don't have to tell you that."

"So?"

"Well, obviously, word got out that Howard had a primary, and the primary had made a taped confession, and Howard had that tape. And now it's gone—"

"Gone? What, outta his office? You shittin' me?"

"Wish I were, but I'm not—and you can imagine, I think, Howard's predicament, I mean, the national media has turned him into sort of a joke—and if this gets out that the tape's gone—"

"Wait wait wait," Carlucci said, scooching forward to the edge of his chair, "somebody stole the tape outta the DA's office and Failan's gettin' calls from some fucking what, the phantom of New York or some shit? And the papers and TV's makin' a joke outta him and so fucking what? What's this have to do with this guy here gettin' whacked?" Carlucci hung his head. "Oh I get it, Failan can't make a fucking case, so he sold this fucker's ass out, didn't he, huh?"

"Take it easy," Valcanas said. "That's not it at all, c'mon."

"Oh take it easy, right, this is fucking perfect. Just fucking perfect."

"Look, all anybody knows is the tape's gone—"

"So what? So the tape's gone? What's that mean?"

"It means what it means, Detective, just stop ranting for a moment and think about it. Very soon you're going to be hearing it over every national news show on TV and radio and reading about it in every newspaper with a wire service—that's across the world, Detective. This isn't a local story. And there are two voices on that tape, son. You're goin' to be ridiculed and vilified in more languages than I can count—"

"'Cause I didn't Mirandize him? So what? Who cares? You think I do? That's easy, that's not my problem, that's Milliron's. He was the first cop to start talkin' to a suspect, not me, I don't give a fuck who tries to bust my balls about that. If they do it it's 'cause they're stupid. But that ain't the issue here, Mister Valcanas. The issue plain and simple is the guy who's supposed to enforce the laws in this county, he's fuckin' thrown up his hands. He's sayin' this guy's gonna get whacked and he can't do nothin' about it, what the fuck? If he can't who the fuck can? And I'm supposed to worry what the fuckin' papers do to me? Piss on that! Piss on them, who cares?"

Carlucci hung his head and covered his eyes. When he picked his head up and looked at Czarowicz, his vision was cloudy with tears. He couldn't speak.

"John wants to talk to you alone," Valcanas said, standing and slip-ping out of his sandals so he could put his trousers on. Then he fin-ished dressing and said, "I'm gonna go talk to my secretary for a while. You let me know when you're done, okay?"

Carlucci nodded and tried to get control of himself as Valcanas left and closed the door behind him.

Czarowicz dragged his chair across the floor until his knees were only inches from Carlucci's.

"I'm sorry, Mister Czarowicz, honest to God I am—"

"Forget about that," Czarowicz said. "I just wanna know one thing, okay? I mean, all them other pricks, I know they'd do me any fuckin' which way. But I thought you was, you know, you was just like me. You been in deep shit, I can tell that. I knew it soon as you started talkin' to me."

"Don't, Mister Czarowicz, please. I feel shitty enough."

"I ain't tryin' to make you feel shitty, Detective. I'm just tryin' to understand ya, that's all. I understand the pricks. They do whatever they have to, they don't give a shit, never did, never goin' to. Only time they understand anything is when it happens to them, then all of a sudden, you know, it's hey! Hey, anybody gonna do anything about this? You know, just runnin' around like chickens with their fuckin' heads off when the shit happens to hit their fan. Shit hits my fan or it hits your fan, it's fuck us, kiss their ass, they don't understand, they don't wanna understand, they don't want anybody tryin' to make 'em understand.

"It's like this, lemme tell you somethin'. I never knew what a nig-ger feels like, never had no idea, till them fuckers down the Medic-aid office told me I made too much money to qualify and that cocksucker doctor, he sicced the collection agency on me. I mean there I was. I did everything I knew how to do to be right, you know? To get right with the whole system? And those fuckers talked to me and my wife like we were niggers. I seen the way some of them clerks talked to 'em, you know, the niggers in the welfare office? Next thing I know, they're talkin' to me same way, and the only thing I did wrong was make too much money to fit in their little rows of numbers on all their goddamn papers there. One dollar over the limit's good as ten thousand, don't matter to them. If you don't qualify, all of a sudden, you ain't human. You're just somebody they can talk to any goddamn way they want."

"Mister Czarowicz, I'm sorry, honest to God I am, if there's anything I can do for you—"

"Just hold it a second, okay? All I want you to do is just tell me somethin', that's all. I want you to tell me, I want you to swear to me, that that sonofabitch had cancer. Failan told me, and Mister Valcanas told me, but I wanna hear it from you again. Did he have it, yes or no, huh? Bad enough to kill him?"

"Yes," Carlucci said, his voice cracking, tears welling up in his eyes.

"Then here's what I'm tryin' to understand, okay? Why'd you tell me that, huh? Why did *you* tell me that?"

Carlucci looked at his shoes. "'Cause, Mister Czarowicz, I mean it was the only way . . . only way I knew how to . . . how to get you."

"To get me. That's why you told me? Just to get me?"

"Yes sir. I knew what kinda man you were—are. I knew what it woulda done to me, uh, you know, if we were sittin' in opposite chairs. And somebody told me, you know. What I told you."

"Well . . . then I guess you got me."

"Yes sir. I did."

"You know I wasn't tryin' to kill him, I told ya that. You 'member I told you that?"

Carlucci nodded.

"Well I wasn't lyin'. I wasn't. The sonofabitch moved. Goddamn instant I fired, he moved, he just bent back and down just that little bit so instead a catchin' him in the spine, instead a paralyzin' that prick . . . shit. Got so goddamn flustered, I went runnin' up to him, left my goddamn empty in the grass back there, and after I seen he was gone I went back and I couldn't find the goddamn thing. Then you hada tell me that, ah shit, I don't know. 'Bout me doin' him this . . . this favor . . . this act of mercy . . ."

Czarowicz blew out a long sigh. "You gotta do me one now."

"Huh? Excuse me? Do you one what?"

"A favor. Act of mercy." Czarowicz put his hand on Carlucci's wrist.

Something in those words, something in that touch, something in Czarowicz's eyes sent something cold shivering up Carlucci's spine and he stiffened and pulled back. "What're you sayin'? Huh? You sayin' what I think you're sayin'?"

"You heard what Mister Valcanas said. 'Bout what the DA said, huh? They're gonna do me one way or another, you know that sure as we're both sittin' here, I mean you do know that, right?"

Carlucci tried to speak but he couldn't.

"You don't have to say it, I know you know it. Thing is, see, I don't want the last thing I see to be one of them pricks, one of them cocksuckers doin' it just for money, you know—"

"Aw no. Aw no you don't, Mister Czarowicz," Carlucci said, pulling his wrist back from Czarowicz's hand. "I know where you're goin' now, and you can't ask me this, this ain't right—"

"Can't do it myself, Detective. Rugs? That's your nickname, right? That's what they call you, huh? Rugs? Rugs, listen to me, I can't do it, I tried, you hear? Soon as I seen he was dead, I knew I fucked up, right away I knew that, and I put the barrel in my mouth but I couldn't do it, man. I couldn't touch that trigger—"

"Hey, wait wait wait, that was your choice. Everything you did, those were your choices. I understand why you did 'em, and if I was you, if I'd gotten as fucked over as you did, I'm not sayin' I wouldn't've done what you did, but I understand why you did it, believe me. But you don't know what you're askin' me, man, I'm not gonna do this, don't ask me again, please, I feel bad enough—"

"C'mon, you had to do what was right, that's why you told me, that was your job, I understand that now. I'm satisfied now, I know why you did it. You didn't have nothin' else to get me with, but you had to do your job, you saw what needed to be done, and you did it. But now they got the tape, the rich pricks, you know? And you know who I'm talkin' about. That was your tape, and you heard what Mister Valcanas said they was gonna do to you, and you wasn't the one that fucked up, it was that state trooper, you know that and I know that, but it's you on that tape with me—"

"Aw no sir, you're not gonna lay this on me that way, 'cause it's my tape, bullshit, you ain't doin' this to me, no sir," Carlucci said, shoving his chair back and standing up. "I'm sorry I had to be the one to get you, honest to God I am, 'cause I know you been fucked over and fucked over bad, but you can't—no sir, you can't ask me to do what you're askin' me to do—"

"Listen. We're soldiers, you and me. Marines, army, don't make no difference, you know what I'm gonna say. I had buddies, they were dead but their head was still alive, they were talkin', they were so fucked up it was only a matter of time. And when they asked me, I did it for them, that's all I'm askin' you now. You can't tell me you didn't do the same for your buddies when you were over there in the deep shit, I know you did—"

"No you don't. you don't know anything about me. Nobody ever asked me that. Maybe I was luckier than you, I don't know. But I didn't do that then and I'm not gonna do that now. You think that tape's gonna give me trouble? Man, you haven't thought what kinda trouble I'd get doin' what you're askin'. No fuckin' way, Mister Czarowicz, don't ask me again. I'm leavin'."

"Whoa, whoa, listen. You don't, then it's gonna be some cocksucker without no name is gonna do it, you know that, some fucker just doin' it for money, you know that, you know how they work."

Carlucci hurried to the door, saying, "Can't help that, sir, and I can't help you," and then he was out of the office, running down the hall to the front door and out onto the sidewalk where he nearly collided with Valcanas, who tried to say something to him, but Carlucci didn't stop running until he was in the courthouse garage. "Jesus Christ," he gasped, his face throbbing, his heart pounding, pulses in his neck and face hammering, his mouth coppery and cottony and sour. "Jesus Christ, the fuck's with me?" he said, trying to suck in air slowly and let it out even more slowly. "Flippin' out here. Jesus Christ, I'm flippin' the fuck out . . ."

arlucci got himself together enough to drive home to his mother's house. The first thing he did was unplug the phone and then he decided he wouldn't turn on any lights, so for the next couple of days he prowled from room to room, but only when there was sunlight to light it. As soon as the sun set, he got into bed and stayed there until it came up again, except when he had to eliminate his wastes or to drink water or eat what was left of the soup he'd made. The first day the only reason he left was to check on Mrs. Comito, and the second day he only left to get bread from Mrs. Oriolo's confectionery.

Sometime late in the morning of the third day, it finally sank in that he couldn't skulk around in all that emptiness any longer or he'd lose what little grip he had left on reality. He was as close to the edge as he'd ever been and being that close was scaring him badly. All he was doing was thinking about his mother and Mrs. Comito and Fischetti, or about Valcanas and Failan and whoever was calling Failan, or about John Czarowicz, and he couldn't stand thinking about any of them anymore, especially Czarowicz because every ten minutes or so there was Czarowicz's face, asking him that impossible question. Once, in his mother's bedroom, he became so hung up thinking about Czarowicz he wished he could take his mind out of his head and beat the hell out of it so it would stop thinking. Another time, when he was in the kitchen on the second day, he thought his mind had assumed a human form and he had it by the throat and was trying to strangle it.

Carlucci kept seeing Czarowicz, kept seeing those eyes whose color he couldn't remember now, and hearing him, always asking that same question. So Carlucci forced himself to shower and dress and drive to the ER to have the stitches taken out of his upper lip. He arrived there a few minutes before noon, and there was nobody ahead of him, so a clerk processed him quickly and sent him to a doctor he'd never seen before who took the stitches out in less than a minute. For that short time at least, he was able to stop thinking about anybody but himself.

On his way out of the ER, he bumped into Dr. Marino, who said as long as Carlucci was there it was as good a time as any to examine his nose, and after Marino had done that he said the swelling was down enough for Carlucci to see the plastic surgeon. Carlucci said he would except he'd misplaced the card Marino had given him with the surgeon's name and address on it.

As Marino was writing the name, address, and phone number of the surgeon on the back of his own business card, he reminded Carlucci about taking photos with him, full front and profile so the surgeon would know what Carlucci looked like before. Then Marino lowered his voice and said hesitantly, "Uh, don't want to put you on the spot here, Detective, and I'll understand if you can't talk about it, but, uh, lotta rumors flying around, you know, about the fellow who shot himself? Was he the one, huh?"

"I don't know what you're talkin' about. One what?"

"The one who shot—oh wait, you're probably not working, are you? You're on sick leave, aren't you? Probably don't know any more than any of us do."

"I'm not workin' that's for sure. Haven't been outta the house in two, three days—except to come up here. What're you talkin' about?"

"Don't you watch the news? Or read the papers?"

"Nah. Just watch the cookin' shows, that's all, never watch the news. Don't read the papers either, 'less I have to for some reason. Why don't you just tell me what you're talkin' about?"

"Well I don't know if that's even what it is, but Grimes just finished the PM a little while ago—on somebody. Least that's what I heard. Just hear these rumors, you know, rumors being rumors and all that, but I thought it wouldn't hurt to ask, maybe you might know—"

"Told ya, only been outta the house couple times—what rumors?"

"Well the big one of course is that he's the one that shot Lyon. And that union guy. What was his name? Krall or something?"

"Krull."

"Yeah, that's it, Krull."

"Didn't have any trouble rememberin' Lyon's name, did ya?" Carlucci said, walking quickly away, his stomach suddenly queasy.

"Excuse me? I say something wrong? Uh, don't put off seeing the surgeon—"

"I won't," Carlucci said over his shoulder, hurrying out of the ER and down the corridor past the pathology labs to Grimes's office.

Grimes was sitting at his desk talking into a tape recorder. Carlucci stopped in the doorway until Grimes noticed him and waved him in. Grimes turned the recorder off and said, "Detective Carlucci, what's on your mind?"

"You just do a post on a suicide?"

"Well I haven't ruled yet, but, yes, I'm just summarizing my observations on what was, uh, certainly made to appear to be one."

"Been ID'd? What's that mean, made to appear to be one?" A cold jolt went through Carlucci's queasiness.

"Yes. Czarowicz, John Joseph."

Carlucci fought down a sourish gag. "Uh, can I see the, uh, particulars? Anybody here—uh, I mean, who was here?"

"Who observed? Oh, there was quite a crowd. A Corporal Mickler or Meckler, I'm not sure which, from Troop A CID, and Trooper Milliron, same unit, and also, Howard Failan himself, along with several of his detectives. Can't recall a crowd like that before."

"Failan was here? No shit?"

"Surprises you, eh? Surprised me too. Uh, you want the particulars, they're there." Grimes pointed at an aluminum clipboard on the corner of his desk. "Want to see him?"

Carlucci shook his head quickly. "Uh-uh, no thanks." He grabbed the clipboard and started reading aloud. "Uh, found 6 A.M. by Charles Jurista, on his farm off Route 130 blah, blah, blah, twelve-gauge shotgun, single-shot, found right side of body, entry wound midchest? Found on his back? On his fucking back?

"Take a twelve-gauge in midchest and you wind up on your back? What'd his heart look like—he take it in the heart?"

"Want to see it? Not much left—"

"And found on his back? And you're sayin' suicide?"

"Told you, Detective, I haven't ruled yet, so put that look away, and that tone too, if you don't mind, and come here, I'll show you something." Grimes motioned for Carlucci to follow him into his examining room where a body lay under a sheet on the autopsy table. Grimes lifted one side of the sheet and touched the left wrist.

"See this? If you look at his other wrist, you'll see the same discoloration. Corporal Mickler or Meckler or whatever his name is suggested that it happened when the EMTs picked him up to put him on their gurney. I said no, not possible, this was ante, not post. This seemed to upset the corporal, uh, didn't please him at all. And I must say, didn't please Howard much either. Uh, you alright? I mean I'm jumping to conclusions here, but are you feeling the effects of whatever happened to your nose, or are you otherwise ill, or is it something else?"

Carlucci shook his head. "Uh-uh. No. I'm just, uh, you know, got a buncha things whizzin' around my head, and none of 'em feels very good." He made himself pull back the sheet to look at Czarowicz's face, but it was not recognizable, distorted as it was by the procedure Grimes had just done but not completed. Czarowicz's face lay like a rubber Halloween mask over his skull.

"Aw fucking Christ. I'm sorry, man."

"Excuse me?"

"Talkin' to him."

"Oh. You knew him? I thought he was just a suspect, you didn't say anything, I hope I didn't say anything disrespectful—"

"No no, you didn't say anything, no. But he was, uh, he wasn't just a suspect—hey I gotta go."

Carlucci dropped the aluminum clipboard on Grimes's desk on his way out. He tried to walk normally, tried to do the same with his breathing, but his legs and his lungs were jumping with electricity; it was like he'd stepped on a hot wire and it had stuck to his shoes and nothing he could do could shake it off. By the time he got, out to his Chevy, he was gasping, breathing way too fast; and his vision, especially in his left eye, was shimmery, as though there was a waterfall going from the top lid to the bottom. His hands were suddenly cold and now the electricity was passing from his lungs to his left arm.

He put his left arm on the roof of the Chevy and leaned his forehead against it and whispered to himself, "Slow down, man, slow it down, breathe slow, count to eight on the exhale, hold it for four, count to eight on the inhale, hold it for four, c'mon, count to eight on the exhale, hold it for four, c'mon, you know how to do this . . ."

It took him ten minutes to get his breathing and pulse back to near normal. His shirt was soaked with sweat when he slumped behind the wheel, and despite the heat of the car's interior, he was shivering and trembling as he put the key in the ignition and turned it.

He drove south out of the parking lot to a self-serve gas station three blocks away where he pulled in near the pay phone, and after he got out and dropped a quarter in the phone, he pushed the buttons for Franny Perfetti's home phone. Her mother answered on the second ring.

"Missus Perfetti, this is Ruggiero Carlucci, I have to talk to your daughter, it's very important, would you get her for me, please?"

He couldn't stand still. Every time he shifted his weight, the other heel came up and started bouncing, and his free fingers drummed the top of the cowling around the phone.

"Oh, I'm sorry," Mrs. Perfetti said, "she's not here right now, she went to get her hair cut, but she should be back real soon. Can I tell her something, huh? For you?"

"Uh, no ma'am, thank you—oh wait, where's she go to get her hair cut, you know?"

"No, I don't know anymore, she just changed, she didn't like the way they did it at the other place, so I don't know, but if you have to see her why don't you come here, she's gonna be back anytime now, I know she is, and anyway I would like to meet you, you know? She talks about you all the time, she says what a nice boy you are."

Boy? Nice boy? God, lady, if you only knew. "She talks about me? Really? To you?" Well who else, dummy?

"Sure to me. I'm her mother. She meets a nice boy, who else she gonna talk to, huh? She don't tell me about the bad ones she meets.

You know, I hope you don't mind my sayin' so, but you, uh, you sound like, uh, I don't know, maybe you don't feel so good? You upset about something maybe?"

"Yes ma'am, uh, I am I guess, yeah. A lot."

"Well come on here then, why don't you? I make you cupa nice tea, put little lemon in it, little honey, little wine maybe, you know, make you feel better right away, come on. You want it cold, we put ice cubes in it. Come on, I wanna meet you. My Frances, she talks about you alla time, we gotta meet sooner or later, don't you think?"

Carlucci couldn't answer for a long time because he was crying, and he didn't know why, but he was afraid that if he tried to talk he was going to lose it, and that was the last thing he wanted this sweet woman to hear. Finally he blurted out, "Sorry, gotta go, I'll call back later," and he hung up before she could say anything else.

He drove around town for ten minutes, then he stopped at another pay phone and called Troop A Barracks to ask where Charles Jurista's farm was. He made up some lame excuse about just getting back from a hearing in Pittsburgh. The dispatcher bounced him to CID and he talked to a sergeant who recognized his name, asked him a couple of questions to confirm his identity, and then gave him directions to Jurista's farm in Westfield Township. It turned out the farm was very near town, only a couple of miles east on Route 130.

Even before he turned off 130 onto the access road to the farm, he saw all the TV trucks and crews, every one of Pittsburgh's three channels and one from Johnstown, parked around three buildings less than seventy-five yards off the access road. There were dozens of other cars around, and reporters and TV crews were milling everywhere around the house, a small bungalow with yellow aluminum siding and a pale green shingle roof. There were two other buildings set apart from the house by thirty or forty yards, each building twice the size of the house, with more people around them, peering in windows and trying the doors.

Amazing, Carlucci thought. Never entered my mind they'd be here. I must be the biggest fucking rube in America. Where else would they be, asshole? There's blood in the water, and rumors in the air. The man who shot J. D. Lyon shot himself, and even if he didn't let's say he did, who's gonna check, not that fuckin' rube Carlucci. He can't even get out of the way when his mother's swingin' cast iron. And who's gonna care anyway? They don't even care they left marks on his wrists.

The man practically begs me to do it 'cause he didn't want some nameless cocksucker doin' it for money and that's just who did it, bet your ass. Three of 'em. At least. Three nameless cocksuckers. Held him up, the pricks, held him up, stuck it against his chest, and blew a hole in his heart for fucking money. Only fucking mystery here is there was anything left of his heart to blow a hole in. . . .

Carlucci's mind was getting staggery again and he knew it, but he had enough sense to stop, put the Chevy in reverse, and back out onto Route 130, where he headed back into town. Then, just as he turned onto North Main Street, he had a flashback, as clear as if it were playing on a movie screen on the inside of his windshield: he was slogging down a dusty road, bringing up the rear of his platoon, a column on either side of the road through two rice paddies. It was so hot everything was shimmering, and then the mortar shells started marching toward them right down the road, one, two, three, and he didn't see the third land, just heard it, because he was face-first in the paddy, but he could feel the rest of them still coming, working their way toward him because the first three were fired just to get them off the road into the muck where they couldn't move as fast. This was NVA Regulars at work, this wasn't any Viet Cong amateur mother-fuckers, this was pros on those mortar tubes . . . incoming, incoming, incoming, everything in threes, one more time, one more time, one more time, you cheat death, you cheat death, you cheat death, each one that goes wide, goes short, goes long, you cheat death, everything in threes, USA, NVA, exploding water, mud, and muck, hair, blood, and eyeballs. . . .

And here he was, driving south on North Main, in the brilliant light of midafternoon summer 1998 in Rocksburg and he was grabbing frantically at his belt because his Beretta wasn't there on his hip where it normally was, and then he was reaching for the .22 in his ankle holster but that wasn't there either, he'd left them both back in his hooch, then he was jamming his right palm into the horn and shouting, "Incoming!" And then he was looking around to see where he was and if anyone was eating mud right along with him or if they were just watching, or just walking, or driving, minding their own civilian business.

He was still on North Main Street. And nobody was watching, at least nobody he could see. And his was just another horn, and he was just another happy driver shouting about the traffic or the weather or rapping along with his stereo. Or maybe not. He wasn't sure for nearly ten seconds that he was stopped at a red light until there was a horn behind him. Just a timid little toot, to bring him back, nothing angry.

And back he came from Vietnam, back to Rocksburg, but he was not just another happy driver. He was panting like a dog, sweating, and the waterfall in his left eye was back again and he couldn't make it stop, and because he didn't know what else to do he drove to Franny Perfetti's house and banged into the curb and sat there with the right front tire half up on the curb.

Then a car parked in front of him, and Franny got out and came back, smiling at first and hurrying, but the closer she came the more uncertain her smile became and then she was peering in at him, very puzzled.

"Rugs, you alright? God, you look—you okay?"

"No. Don't know how I look . . . guaranteed I feel worse."

"What's wrong, what happened? I haven't heard from you since, Jeez, almost a week now. I thought—I don't know—did I say something wrong? I thought maybe I said something—"

"No no no, this isn't about you, this isn't about . . . not about that, no, this is, uh, this man. He, uh, he asked me to do somethin', to do him, uh, you know, he tried to make it like an act of mercy and I couldn't. . . . I couldn't do it, not even for that, you know? Fact, I got real pissed off at him. I mean, really furious, you know? And you think I'm this great guy, you even got your mother thinkin' it, you know? Thinkin' I'm all fulla duty and honor and obligation and re-

sponsibility and all that other good shit, thinkin' I'm *nice* for shit
sake . . . but when a man asks me to do him an act of mercy . . . I
just told him no fucking way . . ."

"Rugs, I don't understand, I mean I'm sure you know what you're
sayin', but I'm not followin' you, 'cause you're not really makin'
sense—come inside, okay? C'mon in, why don't you?"

"Your mother's in there, I already talked to her."

"She's always in there, Rugs, that's where she lives—except when I
take her someplace. And if you already talked to her, I know she invited you in, she wouldn't let you sit out here—"

"No I mean I talked to her on the phone."

"Oh. Well that's alright. Still, she's been asking me, you know, for
a while now when was she gonna meet you—c'mon, Rugs, you can't
sit out here, you look awful, I've never seen you look like this—"

"Just my nose, that's all. Got the stitches out, look." He pulled back
his upper lip to show her.

"Yeah, I see, but I'm not talking about how you look, I'm talkin'
about how you're lookin' at me. You're, uh, you're scarin' me. A little
bit. You know? Just a little, not a lot."

"Aw, Jesus no, that's the last thing I wanna do, scare you, uh-uh . . .
I'm just, you know, I'm just scared, that's what it is, it's me. Not you.
I'm scared."

"Of what?"

"I don't know. All this shit . . . all this shit that's bigger than me. It's
everywhere."

"Uh-ha. Okay. But why don't you come inside and tell me, okay?
C'mon, you can talk in front of my mother, she's sweet, she really is,
I'm not just sayin' that 'cause she's my mother, c'mon, you'll see."

"I don't want her to see me like this, okay? Really, please?"

"Rugs, I promise you, she won't ask you anything you don't want
her to ask, honest, she'll just be nice to you, c'mon. C'mon, those
jagoffs across the street are already startin' to look at us. C'mon, back
up, back off the curb and c'mon inside, honest, Rugs, don't sit out
here and, uh, you know, don't—just come in. You'll see. It'll be alright. Please. You can tell me everything—or you can tell me nothin',

I don't care. And she won't care either, my mother. C'mon, Rugs, God, you need somebody, you do."

He hung his head and the tears poured out.

She opened the door, reached in with both hands, and began to tug on him, gently, to get him out and into her house. He came out, sobbing, and wiping his nose on the back of his hands, then held her out at arm's length and said, "I'm a fucking coward—"

"Oh you are not, what're you talkin' about?"

"Listen to me! Listen! I am! I shoulda done it—"

"Should've done what? You are not a coward, stop saying that!"

"Listen! A man, a good man, you hear? He asked me to do him an act of mercy . . . and I couldn't do it. I knew what was gonna happen to him, he said it was gonna happen to him, and I know it happened the way he said, and it shouldn't've happened that way . . . it was chickenshit what they did to him, those pricks, and I coulda done it the right way . . . the way he wanted. But I couldn't . . . I couldn't do that. Honest to God, when he asked me, I mean, I just . . . I just couldn't. I just fucking could not do that. 'Cause I knew, you know? What would happen to me? He thought I'd been in deep shit, but he didn't know what kinda deep shit he was tryin' to put me into, you know?"

She reached into her purse, pulled out a wad of tissues, and wiped his eyes for him. Then she turned around and shouted, "What the hell you gawkin' at? Get inside where you belong, you jagoffs!"

Then she took his arm and pulled him around. "You listen to me, Carlucci, you are not any goddamn coward I don't care what you say. I don't know what happened today, but I'm not gonna let you talk to yourself like that. You're comin' inside with me, and I'm not askin' anymore, I'm tellin' you, so just keep quiet and come on in, you hear me? If you wanna tell me what happened, I'll listen, and if you don't, if you wanna talk about something else, I'll listen to that too, and if you don't wanna talk about anything, that's okay too, you can just sit there and listen to my mother and me. We'll talk about you, we're gettin' real good at that. So okay now, you comin' in or not, huh?"

He couldn't talk. He was struggling to stop his tears. All he could do was nod. But then he started walking and he kept up with her, up the steps, across the porch, through the front door, down a short hall, and into Mrs. Perfetti's kitchen, where she was pouring hot tea into three tall glasses filled with ice.

"Besides," Franny whispered to him after she introduced him to her mother, "I wanna know how come you haven't called me."

"Huh?"

"You know. *Called* me?" She held up her hand as though she was holding a phone. "I've been waiting. Every night."

"That's another thing," he croaked. " 'Nother thing I'm a coward about—"

"Stop it! I mean it, stop talkin' like that! About yourself."

"Stop what?" Mrs. Perfetti said, putting a glass of tea in front of Carlucci and telling him, "Sit, sit."

"Nothin', Ma," Franny said.

Yeah, right, Carlucci thought. Some nothin'.

"Oh my God," Mrs. Perfetti said. "You hurt your nose? That's why you cryin', huh? What happened, huh? Here, sit, sit."

"I think maybe he doesn't wanna talk about it, Ma, okay?"

"Oh, sure sure, that's okay, I understand, don't wanna talk, fine. Frances, get him some Kleenex, huh? Here, Detective—oh my God, first time I ever have a detective in my house, better watch what I say, huh?" She gave him a gentle poke in the shoulder with her elbow, and then she smiled.

"Boy," he said to Franny but nodding toward her mother and struggling to control his voice. "I see where you get it."

"What?"

"That smile. Lights up the whole room. Just like you."

"Oh my," Mrs. Perfetti said to Franny. "I see everything now, huh? Hey, drink, drink, I'm gonna get some cookies I made yesterday, anise, you know? Go real nice with tea, you're gonna like 'em. Tell him, Frances, how good they are. She loves 'em, Frances."

"Won't have to tell him," Franny said, reaching for a box of tissues on top of the fridge and putting it by his elbow. "Soon as he eats one, he'll know."

"See how my Frances is?" Mrs. Perfetti said, easing into a chair across from him and taking his left hand in both of hers. "See how nice she talks to me? You're a lucky boy." She patted his hand with each word. Her hand was very soft.

He couldn't speak. All he could do was nod and smile. He was afraid if he tried to speak he would lose it, and then he'd have to explain and that was the last thing he wanted to do. So he just ate the anise cookies and drank the lemony tea and only spilled a little on himself and listened to them talk about the most ordinary things, haircuts and cookies and how little wine you needed to flavor iced tea to give you that nice little afternoon pick-me-up.

"It's nice to have a little something in the middle of the afternoon," Mrs. Perfetti said. "Don't you think? Nice drink, nice cookies, nice talk with your friends, huh?"

"God, is it ever," he said, thinking for the first time since he'd come in the door that he wasn't going to lose it when he opened his mouth to speak. If only it could be like this, he thought. Just once in a while, you know? Was that too much to ask?

"This is all Czarowicz wanted, you know? Just this. He didn't want anything more than this."

"Who?"

"Oh God. A guy I know. Knew. Just a guy, you know? But he would've given anything for this. What I got right here, right now, this minute."

"Oh see? Huh? How nice, you think about somebody else," Mrs. Perfetti said. "My Frances is right, you're a sweet boy."

"He's a man, Ma."

"I know he is, I'm just talkin', that's all. I know he's a man, anybody can see that—my God, he's a detective, huh?"

He made himself say, "Thank you," because he knew it was expected. But it was an effort because suddenly he was in another kitchen, not very far from this one, and the voice he was hearing was not Mrs. Perfetti's but his mother's and she was thrashing wildly and swinging a pan and screeching that he was not hers and had never been hers.

He reached down to his knee and pinched the skin hard to bring himself back to this kitchen. He looked at Mrs. Perfetti and then at Franny, and he forced himself to smile and to say "thank you" again. This time, it was less of an effort, but it still wasn't easy. He wondered if it ever would be. Then he wondered if even that was too much to ask. But the next thing he knew Mrs. Perfetti had her hands around his left hand again and was patting it and saying, "You're welcome, Ruggiero—what a nice, strong name, Ruggiero," and he found himself thinking, maybe it isn't too much to ask.

"Really? Think that's a good name? No kiddin'?"

"Oh listen to him," Mrs. Perfetti said. "You're gonna have to watch what you say to him, Frances. I think maybe he's always gonna be a little bit suspicious, this detective, huh?"

"Oh no, uh-uh, really. Anything you say now, I'll believe it. Believe me I'll believe it." Those words came out so easily, so effortlessly, he almost believed them himself.